Praise for *Other Parents*

'Deft, wry and perceptive, this drama targets
class and modern parenting.'
Daily Mail

'Stovell's novel is a smart, wry and witty look at
some of the pit-falls of modern life.'
The Sun

'PTA politics, school gate tensions, the perils of living in
a small town where everyone knows your business – both
funny and engaging while tackling some serious stuff.'
Jane Fallon

'A well-told (and latterly suspenseful) story that
examines some tricky contemporary issues.'
Daily Express

'I only put it down when I finished it! Cringe-inducing,
agonising, truthful, heartbreaking and hilarious.'
Janice Hallett, author of *The Appeal*

'Known for the crime thriller *Exquisite*, Sarah Stovell follows
up with this equally tense novel … an equally hilarious and
gripping read that's sure to linger long after you've finished.'
OK!

'Funny, moving, insightful and so sharp on the politics of
the school gate and beyond. Couldn't put it down.'
Laura Marshall, author of *Friend Request*

'A gripping, thought-provoking read with the pace and tension
of a thriller. This will have book clubs debating for hours and
is set to be one of the most talked-about books of 2022.'
HELLO!

'Examines some tricky contemporary issues, exploring how our
society has become polarised and why more and more people
hold such rigid and strident views. It's also very funny.'
Daily Mirror

'Clever, thought-provoking and darkly funny.
Tackles big issues with a light hand.'
Tina Baker, author of *Call Me Mummy*

Sarah Stovell was born in Kent in 1977 and now lives in Northumberland with her partner and two children. She has an MA and a PhD in creative writing and is a lecturer in creative writing at Lincoln University. She is the author of four previous novels, *Mothernight*, *The Night Flower*, *Exquisite* and *The Home*.

Also by Sarah Stovell

Mothernight
The Night Flower
Exquisite
The Home

Other Parents

sarah stovell

ONE PLACE. MANY STORIES

HQ
An imprint of HarperCollins*Publishers* Ltd
1 London Bridge Street
London SE1 9GF

www.harpercollins.co.uk

HarperCollins*Publishers*
1st Floor, Watermarque Building, Ringsend Road
Dublin 4, Ireland

This edition 2022

1
First published in Great Britain by
HQ, an imprint of HarperCollins*Publishers* Ltd 2022

ISBN: 9780008538293

MIX
Paper from
responsible sources
FSC™ C007454

This book is produced from independently certified FSC™ paper
to ensure responsible forest management.

For more information visit: www.harpercollins.co.uk/green

This book is set in 10.7/15.5 pt. Sabon by Type-it AS, Norway

Printed and Bound in the UK using 100% Renewable Electricity at
CPI Group (UK) Ltd, Croydon, CR0 4YY

For the teachers, parents and children at
the Sele First School, Hexham.

And in memory of Emily Herold, whose smile
in the school yard is greatly missed.

She'd only ever known what it looked like from the outside. When they were finally given a date for the trial, they'd come here and walked along the quays, so they could examine the sandstone building and the huge silver lettering above its doors. Everyone told her it would help if she knew what to expect.

The Law Courts.

'There. It's not too bad. It's fine, isn't it? No worse than a school.'

She'd been expecting something like the Old Bailey, something ancient and imposing with turrets and stone columns. But it was just a building like any other. She looked at it and shrugged. 'It looks all right,' she said. 'I think I'll be OK.'

Inside, though, everything was different. The judge, inhuman in his white wig and black robe, peered at her from his platform. He towered above her, like God. She felt herself shaking, and wished she could run far away from here.

She'd never been in a court before. She'd barely even been in trouble before.

She looked towards the public gallery. Both families were

up there, as far away from each other as possible. All of them stared straight ahead, towards the witness box and the judge.

The judge cleared his throat and called the defendant to the stand. From the notes on his bench, he read out the details of the crime in a voice that did no justice to its horror.

'How do you plead?' he asked. 'Guilty, or not guilty?'

The court held its breath.

I

Jo

When she eventually came to write her memoirs, *The Unexpected High Dramas of a Northumberland Headteacher,* Jo thought she'd probably start them during the PTA meeting at the end of her first half-term at West Burntridge First School. Until then, everything about her new post had gone well. The teachers had responded to her leadership without too much resistance; the children liked her; and the parents, on the whole, welcomed her, despite the initial rumblings that if she didn't live up to her retired predecessor, house prices in this part of town would begin to slump. People moved from all over the Tyne Valley to get their children into West Burntridge. It had the academic standards of a private prep, but was funded by the state and enhanced by a few generous parents and a zealous PTA.

Jo allowed herself to experience the first stirrings of relief as she cleared her office that Friday afternoon. She'd decided long ago that this was to be her last job before retirement and she would end her career among the happy, high-achieving children of the clean-living middle classes. Jo had done her time in the inner cities, transforming failing schools. In the end, it ground her down. She was fifty-three years old and on bad days reckoned she already looked at least sixty-five. She'd tried investing in a good moisturiser, but it was delusional to think any overpriced cream flogged to her by a teenager – everyone looked like a teenager now – could undo years on the frontline of poverty and everything that went with it.

But still, she was here now, and she'd done it. She had half a term under her belt, the school was still officially outstanding and the empire ruled over for twenty-five years by the formidable Mrs Pearson had not fallen. In fact, word had reached Jo that there were murmurs about her having made things even better: there was now more music, more outdoor learning, more pastoral care.

Things were good, she acknowledged, slinging her bag over her shoulder, then locking her office and heading down the corridor to the staffroom for the PTA meeting. She did wish they hadn't chosen this – the last day of the autumn half term – as a time to meet, but the treasurer apparently couldn't make it on any other day and nothing was allowed to happen without the treasurer present. They were a force at this school, the PTA. They saw themselves as an integral cog in the managerial wheel.

Jo had never known this in any of her previous schools. There either hadn't been a PTA at all, or the one they had was so small she'd only really spoken to them once a year when they told her they'd raised three hundred pounds at the summer fete. A pound for each child. Jo had seen the accounts and knew that at West Burntridge, last year's summer fete alone had brought in over £6,000. She realised quickly that these fundraising mothers were not to be offended.

The trouble was, they were all really bloody annoying. In

every meeting, they talked in painstaking detail about their fundraising ideas for the month ahead: the usual weekly cake stall; a craft fair; an art competition; perhaps a Christmas ball so their husbands could finally all meet each other. Sometimes, Jo found these plans so dull she had to control the urge to suggest something radical and shake them all up a bit. It wouldn't take much. As a group, they were devastatingly shockable. *Drugs*, she wanted to say. *A sponsored experiment to see if any of you become more interesting coked off your tits.*

Instead, she nodded and thanked them for all their hard work raising the valuable funds the school couldn't manage without. Then she'd move to leave, and that was when the trouble would start.

'Ms Fairburn, could I just have a quick word?'

That was it, the line they always opened with. Everyone knew it was never going to be a quick word. It was going to be a lengthy forty thousand words, possibly stretched over several meetings for the next six months. But still, 'a quick word' was what they called it, in recognition of the fact that they understood Jo was a busy woman and didn't want to take up her time; it was just this *one thing* they were worried about and they needed their minds putting at rest.

There were three women today, wanting a quick word, although two of them came together, as a package of joint concern. 'We just wanted to talk to you about the changes you're making to Toy Day this term,' one of them said. Kate Monro, the all-powerful treasurer.

Toy Day was a cherished ritual at West Burntridge, a legacy Jo had inherited from Mrs Pearson but which she herself would rather do without. On the last day of every half term, children were allowed to bring a toy from home to play with during that final, golden hour before freedom. Jo had decided not to do away with it entirely, on the grounds that it was a small issue and she didn't want to upset everyone so early on, but she had made it clear there were to be no electronic devices. This, no doubt, would be Kate Monro's point of irritation. Her daughter was in year one and obsessed with screens and everything in them. Already, she had her own deeply obnoxious YouTube channel in which she starred alongside her mother, the two of them dressed in sparkles and tiaras, performing godawful karaoke. *The Monro Girls*. It made Jo want to vomit. She had little patience for a woman in her forties calling herself *girl*, and even less for anyone who encouraged their child to dress and behave as a sex symbol.

Jo smiled professionally. 'OK. I'm all ears.'

'Well, we don't think it's completely fair that those children, like my daughter Kendra, who love making videos with their friends, are no longer allowed to bring iPads.'

'iPads aren't sensible things to have in school, Mrs Monro. They're expensive items and we just can't run the risk of them being broken.'

Kate looked unconvinced by this and in truth, it was only part of the argument, but Jo wasn't about to share the other part, which was that she needed to poverty-proof this place. She couldn't allow the affluent eighty per cent of children to bring iPads and handheld Nintendos while the poorer twenty per cent played with bouncy balls and string.

She wondered if Kate was going to argue further. She looked as if she might, then clearly thought better of it.

Jo turned to the next woman in front of her. Laura Spence,

PTA secretary, single mother of Max in year one. Jo imagined she probably didn't get out much. The PTA was her social life, her connection to the world. She took it seriously. If she slacked, the rest of them would boot her out and there she'd be: night after night spent in loneliness on the sofa, eating too many KitKats and watching iconic episodes of *Friends* on repeat, wondering what had happened to all the spark and promise she'd had in her youth. (She'd exhausted it on the wrong kind of men, of course – the ill fate of so many otherwise sensible and intelligent women.)

Laura glanced furtively around the staffroom at the other members of the PTA who were failing to leave, and lowered her voice. 'I'm just a bit concerned,' she said, 'about this new idea that children have to be taught about the issues of LBG ... LTP ...'

'LGBTQ.'

'Yes, that. All that. I wondered what your view on it was, and whether you intend to bring it into this school?'

'My view,' Jo said, smiling politely and pleasantly, 'is that I am obliged to run a school that delivers the current curriculum and I am fully supportive of promoting inclusion, acceptance and equality in all areas of life.'

Laura looked crestfallen, and anxious. 'But homosexuality? For *children*?'

It was as though the woman thought they'd be showing gay pornography in the classroom. Jo went on smiling. 'It will all be age-appropriate, Miss Spence,' she said. 'When we talk about families, we will talk about families with same-sex parents, in the same way we talk about families with one parent, or step-parents, or your bog-standard married mum and dad.'

7

'But my son came home the other day and told me a teaching assistant had said it's OK for men to marry men. I just don't want—'

The smile was beginning to ache. 'The thing is, Miss Spence – and I say this with the utmost respect for your beliefs – it *is* OK. It's part of UK law now that men can marry men and women can marry women. As a school, we have a duty to impart the values of—'

'I'm very unhappy about it.'

'I'm sorry to hear that.'

'I don't know why it's necessary ...'

'It's necessary because there are children in this school and in other schools in the country being raised by single-sex parents who have a right not to feel ostracised from their peers because of that.'

'Well, of course. It's not the children's fault, is it? Poor things,' Laura said, though not without first registering shock at the idea that such grubbiness had forced its way through the gates of West Burntridge First School.

'Have a good half term, Miss Spence,' Jo said, by way of ending the conversation.

Laura nodded and strode purposefully away from Jo, towards the other mothers. She was angry. Fuming. The whole group of them left quickly after that, the indignant murmuring beginning before they'd even closed the door.

2

Erin

Even now, a pond-grey afternoon in late October, the park was heaving with its usual after-school crowd. Red-uniformed children dangled upside-down from the climbing frame, or hurled themselves down slides, or ran in dizzying circles as they spun their friends on the roundabout that had been whirling in defiance of health and safety laws for the last twenty years.

Erin was new to all this. She stood at the edge of the playground, trying not to look self-conscious and resisting the urge to scroll through her phone so everyone would know she wasn't alone in the world. All around her, groups of women stood chatting to each other, cemented to one another by bonds of friendship that had been forged years ago, when they'd all plunged into the tumultuous waters of motherhood. Together, they'd spent years barely keeping afloat amidst the sleeplessness and the mind-wrecking boredom of baby groups, while the women they used to be drifted further and further out to sea, never to return.

It was a world Erin was still navigating her way through: sudden parenthood and everything that came with it – the schoolyard, the PTA, the groups of women and where she fitted among them.

She watched Tess playing football with a group of boys from her class and wondered when would be a good moment to break it to her that they'd need to leave soon and meet Maia from the high school. Tess's moods were difficult to read. It felt sometimes that Erin was making progress with her and they were getting along the way she'd always hoped they would, and then Tess would suddenly remember who Erin was. She'd back off and say something angry and rude, unwavering in the determination to hate her.

She noticed another woman standing alone a few feet away and smiled at her. She thought she might as well. The woman didn't smile back. Then suddenly – so suddenly Erin couldn't work out how it had happened – a boy lurched himself to the ground at the woman's feet and began howling, waving his limbs in all directions.

Erin shot a glance around the park. No one else seemed to be taking any notice.

The woman kneeled beside him and bent her head low so her hair shielded her face from Erin's view. The child went on kicking.

Erin watched with mounting horror as the boy's fist flailed and struck his mother in the face, forcing her to stand up and step back.

Erin had never seen anything like this. The woman looked mortified and close to tears. Why was no one helping her?

Erin couldn't stand it. She headed over. 'Are you OK?' she asked. 'Can I help you?'

The woman was silent for a minute, her face registering shock, then she smiled appreciatively. 'Thank you,' she said. 'He gets like this sometimes. It's hard.'

Erin didn't know what to say, so she just said, 'It looks it.'

Beside them, the boy's howls continued.

'There isn't much I can do, except weather it out. I've got better now at spotting the signs and I can usually get him home before he starts, but I missed it today. I was at a PTA meeting. He went to the after-school club for half an hour and that seems to have done it.'

She sounded apologetic.

Erin looked from the mother to the child and back to the mother again. She was young. Erin wouldn't put her much over twenty-five. She had an image of herself at that age – sharing a damp flat with her best friend in Lewisham, drinking most evenings, occasionally taking Class A drugs at weekends, shirking responsibility. There was no way she'd have had what it took to devote herself to a child. She felt a mixture of pity and awe for this woman.

Beside them, the boy's howls grew slowly quieter.

The woman sighed deeply and said, 'He'll be exhausted now. I have to get him home …'

She looked desperate. Afraid.

Erin glanced at the abbey clock, visible between the gaps in the trees. She needed to be back at the car in ten minutes. Maia would be leaving the high school by now, walking expectantly towards her waiting chauffeur service. She'd be angry if Erin was late, and Erin hated the thought of giving her any more reason to hate her.

She said, 'Can I get you anything? I could run over to Costa and pick you up a coffee or something?'

The woman flushed, embarrassed. She shook her head. 'It's OK. We'll be fine. It's not far.'

The sobbing stopped, but the child didn't move.

Erin nodded. 'OK. I'm going to have to go. I've got a high-schooler to meet. I'm Erin, by the way.'

She offered her hand and the woman shook it. 'Laura. Thank you,' she said. 'Thanks for speaking to me. People don't like to …' She let her voice trail off.

Erin looked towards the football game and shouted for Tess.

Laura stared at her quizzically, as if piecing a puzzle together. 'Tess is … Are you …?'

Erin nodded. 'Yes, I am. Tess!' she called again. She knew what Laura had wanted to ask. *Are you the woman Rachel Saunders left her husband for?*

Tess bounded over, red-faced and streaked with dirt. Erin reached into her bag and handed her a treatsize Crunchie, which Tess took without thanks.

Erin turned again to Laura. 'I hope it goes OK,' she said. 'See you again.'

'Bye.'

Erin checked that Tess was with her, and together they left the park. Out of loyalty to her father, Tess had a strict policy of not holding Erin's hand and walked behind her as they headed down the path and past the school, where the children from the after-school club still charged about the yard. Erin marvelled at this place – a Victorian grey stone school, set in the heart of a huge park, as if whoever designed this town had done so with the happiness of its child population in mind. The high school was just as impressive, with acres of playing field and professionally equipped music rooms, and an ancient clock tower that soared into the sky and could be seen from all over town. Erin's own secondary school had been a 1970s concrete block, with views over a motorway and the scent of chips and stale beer from the pub next door. She was disappointed now to find in herself a deep, puritan conviction that no one could consider themselves properly educated unless they'd spent every lunchtime smoking B&H behind the pub, being regularly flashed at by old men who'd gone out for a wazz and decided to try their luck on young girls.

She shouldn't think like that. Really, it was charming that Tess went to an outstanding school in a park and Maia played the flute in the high school orchestra, and of course it was long-overdue progress that flashers were no longer accepted as just another tiresome thing a girl had to put up with, like monthly cramps and the glass ceiling.

'Is Mummy at home?' Tess asked, and Erin could see the residual anger over the fact that it had been Erin who'd picked her up from school today and not her mother.

'She'll be back a bit later,' Erin said breezily, as if she hadn't noticed the war this child had been raging against her for the last six months.

'Do we need to get Maia?'

'Yes.'

The high school was on the other side of Burntridge. Maia finished later than Tess, and because no fifteen-year-old could respectably be collected from the school gates by an adult, a great deal of Erin's time seemed to be spent sitting in the car, waiting while Maia made her way across town in the style of someone entirely lacking any sense of urgency. Erin supposed there was nothing to be urgent for. She was, after all, a child. Her day had finished, and why shouldn't she stroll through town, peering into the windows of charity shops for some incredible vintage outfit, the component parts of which she could throw recklessly around her bedroom and then three days later claim someone had stolen?

It was all part of her new life. She'd signed up to it when she moved in with their mother. She'd never had her own children – a deliberate choice, which she only occasionally regretted – but in her mind she'd created a world where she would become the stepmother everyone dreamed of. She'd thought she knew how to do it. She wasn't going to bulldoze her way in, or change anything, or take on a parental role. She was going to be a friend to them, someone they could talk to and confide in easily because she wasn't their mother and wasn't going to shout at them if they'd lost their blazers or if Maia wanted to go on the pill or Reuben had skipped a lesson at school. Tess was going see her as somebody fun, someone who'd pick her up from school and take her swimming or play games with her.

It was naive and foolishly hopeful. None of it worked in the face of stark reality: three children who were missing their old family life, who saw their father as having been deeply wronged, and whose mother and her lesbian lover were an excruciating public embarrassment.

Still, she would keep working at it. She'd keep muscling on, keep being kind in the face of resentment, keep on hoping that one day they would become a family and this early strife would be remembered for what it was – nothing more than a period of adjustment after a major life-shift. And at least none of the children were like the boy in the park. That image of him, curled on the ground like that, was haunting her, like a low-grade trauma.

'Do you want to see my drawing?' Tess said, once they were seated in the car, waiting for the eventual appearance of Maia.

'I'd love to,' Erin said.

She could hear Tess shuffling pieces of paper in her book bag, then an arm came between the seats and a piece of paper was thrust towards her.

She looked at it. There were some coloured swirls, a splodge of grey and an attempt at labelling. *Fevver*, it said.

'What's this word?' Erin asked.

'Fevver,' Tess said.

'Does that mean anything, or is it a made-up word?' Erin was all in favour of children discovering the inventiveness of language.

Tess frowned. 'Fevver. Like on a bird.'

'Oh, right. *Feather*. I see.' Her momentary enthusiasm for linguistic invention disappeared.

No wonder the children hated her.

They sat in silence for a while, then she noticed Maia in the near distance, ambling along with her backpack, her flute and a group of boys. She was, quite clearly, the comfortable centre of their attention – the sort of clever, attractive girl that boys were in awe of, and had no idea how to get close to. She chatted animatedly to them as she walked and called goodbye cheerily enough, but started scowling the minute she opened the car door and flung her stuff on the back seat. 'Tess,' she said. 'Will you move your crap? For God's sake. I can't get anything in. And where's Mum, anyway? I thought she was picking us up today.'

Erin waited until Maia had arranged her precious things to her satisfaction, slammed the back door, and then arranged herself in the front passenger seat. 'Mum's still at work. A crisis of some kind.'

Maia grunted.

For a while, Erin's attention was taken up with turning on the ignition, putting the car into gear and easing out of the parking space, so she was able not to feel too deeply the atmosphere Maia had just created. Once all that was done, though, there was no mistaking it. Maia was pissed off. Clearly, mightily pissed off. Erin suspected it had something to do with her own presence, or more likely, the annoying fact of her mere existence, so decided the best tactic would be to say nothing.

From her place in the back seat, Tess said, 'Why are you in such a bad mood, Maia?'

'Oh, I just am. Leave me alone.'

'Maia,' Erin remonstrated, lightly but unmistakably.

Maia carried on staring out of the window. 'Fuck off,' she said. 'You're not my real dad.'

Erin retreated to her silence, and drove her new family home.

3

Laura

Laura realised she was marching, not walking, dragging Max along the pavement like a poor exhausted puppy, but she couldn't help it. She'd never been so desperate to get away. That scene in the park ... It made her heart race and her cheeks flame to recall it. Max, hurling himself to the ground like that for no reason anyone could see, and all those probing eyes pretending not to be on her, pretending to look away, pretending they weren't smugly congratulating themselves for not having produced children like hers.

That, she knew, was what they were all thinking. Laura was his mother, and so it was because of her – some fundamental flaw in her parenting – that the school had to tolerate this wild, uncontrollable boy.

All she could do was kneel on the ground beside her son, let her hair hide her face and try to make herself invisible.

Then that lovely, well-meaning woman had taken pity on her, which was almost as bad as the groups of judgemental mothers and put Laura at risk of crying in public. She'd been torn between saying, *Go away. Leave me alone,* and blurting out, *Please help me. Please. I am at the end of my tether.*

Instead, she'd forced herself to be polite and grateful, and nothing like as desperate as she felt.

On top of all that, she was still angry with Ms Fairburn. (Of course she called herself *Ms*, of course she did; she was obviously one of those feminists who thought having a husband and a stable family was something to be ashamed of. How dare she imply Laura was some kind of bigot for questioning whether five-and-six-year-olds should be taught about gays? Five-year-olds, for God's sake. Five! It was theft of innocence. It was … It was … It was just awful.

'You're hurting my hand,' Max said.

She loosened her grip and tried to slow her pace. If she walked any faster, his feet would leave the ground and he'd end up flying behind her, waving about like a three-stone streamer.

'Sorry, love,' she said, trying to focus on her breathing, the way the books said you should when you were angry. Something about concentrating on slowing your breath down was meant to calm you and root you inside your body, restoring your inner peace instead of letting you flail about like a mad thing for all the world to see.

Laura would have loved to be less angry. Sometimes, she imagined being like those confident, competent mothers in the schoolyard, the ones who always flew in ten minutes late, sharply dressed in their work clothes, hair blown sexily awry in the rush. 'So sorry,' they'd laugh breezily to the teachers. And the teachers would smile kindly because they understood the lives of these important women who were successfully juggling careers and children, managing the domestic drudge while keeping the world turning, all of them frantically busy yet radiating such a deep sense of fulfilment, you knew any outburst from them would be over in a flash. Anger wasn't the fuel their hearts pumped round their bodies, that powered them up the road and went into every meal they cooked.

She smiled at her son. 'What was the school dinner today?'

He was silent for a while as he tried to remember. 'Jacket potato,' he said, 'with tuna.'

'And did you manage to eat any of it?' She kept her voice light as she posed the question. Her son was a fussy eater, but there was more to it than that. Certain textures made him retch: the slimy ripeness of a mango, the wet flesh of an open apple, the stringy white mass beneath the skins of satsumas … The list went on and on. It used to be simply that he couldn't bear the sensations against his tongue, but it had become worse than that in recent months. Now, his mouth revolted early. One sight of the prickly hairs growing out of raspberries and he vomited.

'I ate some,' he said.

She left it at that and they walked up the hill towards the flats while she wondered silently whether she ought to switch him over to packed lunches. At least then, she'd have some idea of what he ate. But school dinners were free. If she made his lunch herself, it would be an extra twenty pounds on her shopping bill each week and she just couldn't …

They turned left off the main street that ran through Burntridge and began the long slog up the hill to the flats at the top. The council had done away with half the allotments when the builders applied for permission to build these flats and Laura knew that the residents' protests about it had been long and intense. The builders had won in the end, as they always did, but things settled down in time for Laura and Max to move in without feeling the neighbours' residual anger about the slain beetroot plants, the destruction of insect life and their own ruined views. Still, she hoped Frank wasn't going to be there this afternoon, hanging round the pigeon huts opposite, slurping filmy tea from his camping mug and talking with a no-offence-meant nostalgia about the days before the flats came, when his old friend Pat (God rest his soul) had grown prize-winning cucumbers under the very spot where Laura and Max now had their kitchen. 'The very spot,' he'd say, slowly shaking his head as if he still couldn't believe it, or understand it.

'Maybe you could grow some prize-winning cucumbers in his memory,' Laura had suggested brightly, the last time she'd been caught up in his lament.

The idea seemed to cheer him. 'Maybe I will,' he said. 'Aye, food for thought ye've just given me there, lass. There's food for thought in that.'

It was odd, Laura thought, how life worked out. Not all that long ago really, she'd imagined herself in New York City, living in one of those apartments that formed the Manhattan skyline, walking a small dog in Central Park while sipping a Starbucks takeout, and meeting a distinguished, passionate male who would love her for all the sharp edges that put other men off.

And now, here she was. A single mother living in a shoebox flat in a rural town where men kept pigeons and dreamed of growing prize-winning cucumbers. She reminded herself often that it was better than where they'd lived before. Far better. Her last flat had been in a Newcastle tower block, where the lift always stank of urine and the stairs were a health and safety risk. As well as that, the only school in walking distance was a failing one and Laura wasn't stupid. She understood the importance of a good school. After she had Max, she was determined he wouldn't have to struggle through life the way she did. She couldn't provide for him as well as other parents did, but she would do whatever she could. She'd heard that children performed better at school when their parents were involved, so she joined the PTA. A year on, she wasn't convinced it was helping Max at all, but at least it gave her something to do, and people to see.

'Here we are,' she said to Max, as they rounded the bend in the road and the flats came into view, together with the small patch of green that separated them from the pigeon huts and the last remaining allotments.

Frank was there at the huts. She saw the curve of his backside first as he bent over a large cardboard box into which he was piling his pigeons. He stood up at the sound of her voice and dragged a hand over his face, leaving a tiny, downy feather on his forehead.

'Alreet, Laura,' he said. 'And Max. How's it gan, lad?'

Max looked at Frank and said nothing. The old glazed look came down over his eyes.

'Say hello, Max.'

He stayed silent.

'Sorry,' Laura said. 'It's Friday. He's tired.'

Frank gave a salute to show he understood and Laura shepherded Max inside.

In the kitchen (beneath which, she imagined, lay the graves of the prize-winning cucumbers), she made herself a cup of tea and poured a glass of orange squash for Max, while he fumbled with his jacket and book bag, slumping them half-heartedly over the peg she'd fixed at his eye level. Whenever she saw that peg, she was reminded of the morning she'd woken up in a state of pure rage (it must have been building up overnight as she'd slept) and could no longer bear the mess that came with a tiny home and a five-year-old boy. One coat, one book bag on the floor and that was enough to make the whole place shambolic. 'From now on,' she told Max, holding his head right up to the peg and the cracked plaster from where she'd hammered the nail too hard into the wall, 'you will hang your things here the *second* you walk through the door, do you understand me?'

He'd looked at her with his meek brown eyes and nodded, and she'd felt immediately guilty. It wasn't his fault. None of this was his fault. He hadn't asked to be born to a mother who didn't know where to start and a father who'd left them after two weeks. 'I wasn't cut out for this,' he told her, as if anyone was, as if anyone had a clue what they were letting themselves in for when they came home with a person the size of a cat and were hit with the force of being alone and having to look after it forever.

Laura set their drinks down on the table, along with a small plate of malted milks.

'Max,' she said gently, ignoring the coat that was moments away from falling off the peg and on to the floor, 'there's a snack ready for you.'

She tried to do this in the afternoons – sit down with him for ten minutes when he came home from school and talk about whatever he felt like talking about. It was important, she reminded herself, to make space in every day, space where she wasn't cooking his tea or running his bath or cleaning the flat, and just be his calm, interested and loving mother. Because she was those things. She loved her son so much that every night she went to bed and thoughts of everything she'd done wrong during the day wrung tears from her eyes. And every night she vowed she would do it better tomorrow. She'd shout less and play with him more. That was it. Those were the two simple things she knew she needed to do, and they shouldn't be that hard. But they were that hard and every single day she failed at it.

They sat together at the table. It was a tiny two-seater and took up most of the room. It folded down when they weren't using it because, really, it was designed for gardens. Silently and without looking at her, Max nibbled the edge of a biscuit.

'So,' Laura said, 'half term. What would you like to do?'

He looked up at her hopefully. 'What is there?' he asked.

'Well,' she forced herself to sound upbeat so he wouldn't see how that sad, expecting-of-nothing expression had just devastated her, 'let's see. We can take your skateboard to the park one day, we could do some baking, you could have a friend to play ...'

'Tess,' he said.

'Tess?'

'She sits next to me now. She's really nice.'

'Right. I'll have to think about it. What about Robbie?'

'I like Tess.'

Tess. The daughter of Rachel Saunders and Will Kernick, the sort of child who always had the main speaking roles in class assemblies, and who took the job of narrator in every nativity because she was able to read, recite and speak clearly. She was the sort of child the teacher would put next to Max because she was so clever and well-behaved and faced none of the struggles her son faced, day in, day out. She'd be a good influence.

Rachel was hardly ever in the schoolyard, but everyone knew who she was: the high-flying medical researcher, always presenting her findings to the government, often being quoted in newspapers for something she'd found that outraged her. Recently, she had been on the front page of the *Guardian*: Health Inequality in Britain at All-time High, with five entire columns devoted to Rachel's findings and her declaration that *This is wrong*. Apparently, if you lived in Sunderland (where Laura grew up), you could expect a life thirty years shorter than if you lived in Kensington, and were ten times more likely to suffer from post-natal depression. The way Rachel went on about it, you'd think she lived in bloody Sunderland, or had some idea of what it was like to live in bloody Sunderland, but she didn't. Laura had never been to Rachel's but everyone knew where she lived: a massive house where each room was probably the size of Laura's flat, and where there was a swimming pool in the basement and a grand piano in the dining room. And as for Rachel herself, whenever she spoke she sounded like the Queen. Or she would, if every second word wasn't *fuck*.

Now, Rachel was at the heart of a local scandal. She'd kicked out her husband and there'd been rumours that she had a lesbian lover. Laura had realised this afternoon that it was Erin, the woman from the park, and everything suddenly made sense. It was so typical of Rachel Saunders to have picked a do-gooder. She would never have gone for anyone else.

Laura wasn't sure who she felt most sorry for – the children or Will. She knew Will because he'd come to see her at work a few weeks ago and he'd told her he was still devastated. He didn't mention the lesbian, but he was beside himself about this violent ripping apart of his family. Laura didn't blame him. She used to see him when he picked Tess up from school, always so loving and attentive, always taking her to play football in the park, always bringing a bag full of treats. Laura would have cut her eyes out if it meant she could give Max a father like Will and yet here was Rachel, robbing her own children of this most precious gift, just so she could act out some disgusting homosexual fantasy because she was, of course, far too cool to simply enjoy being ordinary like everyone else.

Laura sighed. All she'd ever wanted was to be ordinary, and yet it seemed so out of her grasp.

4

Rachel

Rachel hadn't meant to be this late home from work. She'd been caught up in an interview with a distressed new mother and couldn't leave until the woman was calm again. It was nearly half-past seven when she walked through the front door to be greeted by a family mostly full of resentment.

'Mum, you said you were going to take me to Tom's for band practice. I'm meant to be there in five minutes.'

'Mum, why are you always so late? Tess has been crying for ages. You need come up and see her.'

Rachel rummaged in her bag for her purse and handed Reuben ten pounds. 'Sorry, love,' she said. 'I was held up. Get a taxi.' He took the money with a noise that she allowed herself to believe meant *thank you.*

She glanced upwards, to where Maia was leaning over the bannister. 'She needs to see you, Mum.'

'All right, all right. Just give me one minute to get my coat off.'

She slung her coat over the stand in the corner, but instead of heading upstairs went through to the kitchen. Erin was standing at the island, alternately chopping onions and sipping from a large glass of white wine. The sight of her still went straight to Rachel's chest – that fleshy bloom of love, like a rose or a wound.

She leaned towards her and kissed her.

Maia burst into the room. 'Mum, will you please come and see Tess? She's been upset for ages.'

Rachel sighed. 'OK, I'm coming.'

God forbid that she should grab a kiss from her almost-wife before facing the emotional drain that was her six-year-old.

She went upstairs. Tess was tucked up in bed, fighting sleep. Rachel sat beside her and pressed her lips to her forehead. 'Hello, sweetheart,' she said. 'Sorry I was so late.'

'I wanted to show you this picture,' Tess said. She sat up and reached for the sheet of paper on her bedside table.

Rachel looked at the mass of paint swirls, the colours all falling over each other so that they met in the middle of the page in the form of something like a cow pat. 'Wow,' she said. 'This is beautiful. I love the colours you chose.'

Tess smiled contentedly and lay back down.

'How was school today?'

'Boring. I thought you were going to pick me up.'

'I couldn't today, but I will make sure I do next time, when you go back after half term.'

'I don't like it when Erin picks me up.'

'I know you don't.'

'Am I going to Daddy's tomorrow?'

'Yes. It's time to go to sleep now, Tess. And I need to have my dinner. I'll come and check on you when I've finished.' She leaned over and kissed her again, then moved towards the door.

'Mummy …'

She stopped. 'Yes?'

'Can I tell you something?'

'Anything.'

'I don't like Erin.'

'I know you don't.'

'I wish she didn't live with us.'

Rachel went back to the edge of the bed and repeated the talk she'd delivered daily for the last six months. The need for it was showing no sign of abating. She told Tess that Erin was going to keep living here, that they both loved her, that Erin wanted to be a friend to her, that Daddy loved her, that … Oh Jesus Christ. Why was it all so hard?

Tess sighed, deeply unsatisfied as usual. Then she rolled over and said goodnight.

It wasn't supposed to be like this. A year ago, Rachel had worked it all out. She and Will would amicably separate; he'd move to a house close by so the children could see him any time they liked; then she'd bring Erin into their lives slowly, step by step, introducing her as a family friend until she was sure they all liked her. Only once they'd all got to know each other by bonding over evenings in front of *Strictly* and weekends in Amsterdam, would she let them know that Erin was more than a friend and that she was coming to live with them and – oh, a surprise! – share Rachel's bed. In her head, the transition from nuclear family to same-sex stepfamily was going to be seamless, and even included a puppy. Rachel had professional expertise in maximising other people's well-being. She knew how to do this. The children were meant to be unharmed. Erin was meant to feel loved. Everyone was meant to be happy.

Of course, it hadn't worked according to plan. It all seemed so obvious and inevitable now, with hindsight, she could hardly believe she'd been deluded enough to think it would be easy. The separation from Will turned out to be devastating. He knew as well as she did that their marriage was over but he hadn't expected either of them to do anything about it. His own plan was that they'd just muscle on through it, side by side in silent misery, until the children had grown up and gone.

'I don't want to lose them,' he said wretchedly, and she said, 'You won't lose them,' and he said, 'I won't live in the same house as them. I won't be able to get Tess up in the morning, or help Maia with her music practice, or Reuben with his UCAS form. What's that if it's not losing them?' And she hadn't known what to say. The day he moved out was the worst day of her life. The children had all gone to friends' houses so Will and Rachel could thrash out ownership of the last, unimportant, possessions in private. Neither of them cared who kept what by that stage. They just wanted it all to be over, but the image of Will carrying the last of his boxes out the front door, his face rigid with the grief he was holding in check, continued to haunt Rachel and probably would till the day she died. *I'm sorry*, she wanted to say. *You're a good man and I've ruined your life.* But what difference would some feeble apology make? None at all.

Introducing Erin slowly hadn't worked, either. She'd come for lunch one Saturday a couple of months after Will left. 'This is Erin,' Rachel had told the kids. 'She's a friend from work.' Maia looked her up and down and was then perfectly civil but ice-cold for the whole afternoon; Reuben barely managed to look up from his iPad; while Tess, who seemed to have an instinct for detecting interlopers to her family, simply eyed the newcomer with suspicion and asked when she was going home.

As soon as Erin left, Maia asked, 'So is that it, then? Is she your girlfriend? Are you one of those middle-aged lesbians?'

What could she do but be honest?

'Yes,' she told her fifteen-year-old daughter. 'Yes, Erin is my girlfriend and I am one of those middle-aged lesbians.'

Maia smirked, then shrugged, then said, 'OK. Cool.'

'Really?'

'Yeah, why not? I'd rather you brought a woman home than a bloke.'

Rachel smiled. 'Thanks, love.'

'Does Dad know?'

'No. Please don't tell him yet. I'd also prefer it if you could let me tell Reuben and Tess. I wasn't planning for it to be this sudden. I wanted it to be gradual …'

'OK.'

'You seem to be taking this very well.'

'That's because you've always been literally the most boring mother ever. Now, I can tell everyone my mother's gone full gay. We should go to Pride next year. Reuben and I can make a banner that says *We love our lezzer mother* and march past Mrs Robinson's house and watch her get all uptight about it.'

It didn't take long for Maia's enthusiasm over her mother's new sexual identity to dwindle, however. Once Erin demonstrated that she had no exotic features other than being gay, Maia made it clear that she didn't really like her but was simply tolerating her because she had to.

Reuben, who was seventeen and had always been the only laid-back person in the family, seemed fine with the arrangement and liked Erin, which was a blessed relief for everyone and gave Rachel hope that the girls might come round, too.

Now, she sat at the table opposite Erin, reached for her wine glass and said, 'I'm sorry my kids are so fucking awful.'

Erin smiled at her, 'They're just normal. It's a lot to ask of them and really, if they were making this easy, our life would be so perfect everyone would absolutely have the right to hate us.'

'I suppose so.'

'They'll come round.'

Rachel was silent for a while, then gave voice to the idea she'd been thinking over for a while. 'Maybe,' she said, 'maybe we should move.'

Erin paused with her fork in mid-air. 'Are you serious?'

'I don't know. Maybe not. I just always assumed the best thing for them was to stay in their home, keep them as settled as possible, but now I wonder if there are just too many memories here. Will is everywhere they look – he made their breakfast every day in this kitchen, he watched films with them on that sofa, he went in the pool with them every Saturday morning. Maybe that's partly why they find it so hard to accept that he's gone and you're here instead. We could start again, in a new house.'

'You know that isn't going to change how they feel, Rachel. If they're determined to hate me, they will. You might have a point about the house, but overall, it's a minor detail. They've had enough disruption. We need to stay put and just weather whatever storm they throw at us. It will pass. Things always do.'

'OK,' Rachel said. 'Thanks.'

There were so many reasons to love this woman. A while

ago, Maia had said, 'I don't really get what's so special. I mean, what is it you love about her so much?' and Rachel had forced herself to say only, 'I just do, Maia. These things can't always be held up to reason.' It wasn't true, though. She could make a list of reasons why she loved Erin and it would go on for miles, pages and pages wrapped around the Earth. But she wasn't about to share them with her daughter.

Erin said, 'There was a horrible scene in the park today.'

'What sort of scene?' Rachel asked. Scenes in Burntridge weren't like the scenes in other towns. They lacked the drama. The only scenes she'd ever witnessed took place on the school Facebook page, when parents wound each other up about the lack of vegetables on offer in school dinners, or became outraged about the poor casting choices for the class assembly.

'A boy just seemed to lose it. I mean, completely lose it. Just laid down on the floor and howled. It wasn't like a tantrum. It was more than that. He kicked and punched and he hurt his mother. She was so embarrassed. I felt awful for her.'

Rachel knew this child. He was in Tess's class. 'That'll be Max,' she said. 'There's stuff going on there, but no one really knows what.'

'His mother looked like she was going to cry.'

'Laura. She's an odd one. Prickly. I don't know her very well. She's on the PTA, so she knows Kate Monro, who I can't stand. Apparently, the two of them are about to wage a campaign against discussions of homosexuality in the classroom.'

Erin's expression changed. 'Are you serious?'

'Completely serious.'

'I regret being so nice to her now.'

Rachel shrugged. 'She's all right, I think. Harmless apart

32

from her prejudices. But there's definitely something going on with Max that she's trying to hide. I'd put money on that.'

'What sort of thing?'

'I don't know exactly,' Rachel said. 'But he always seems so unhappy. I'd just give her a wide berth. You don't want to get sucked into whatever it is.'

Rachel knew what she sounded like: a self-appointed expert, slightly patronising, speculating without evidence. But this was her field of work. She knew desperate parents and suffering children when she saw them, and the worst thing any outsider could do was allow themselves to become bogged down in the endless, futile pain of trying to help. Rachel knew this as surely as she knew night from day: compassion needed to be held in tough edges, or it could unleash a drama that destroyed everyone.

5

Maia

Maia sat cross-legged in front of the full-length mirror in the corner of her room, using a tiny brush to paint her eyelids turquoise. When she'd finished, she stood up and examined the effect. Striking, she thought. They matched her cardigan, which was a crocheted vintage thing she'd picked up in Totnes last summer and cost a lot more than she'd admitted to her mum. Not that her mum really gave a shit anymore about what Maia spent her money on or even, as far as Maia could tell, what she did with her life; she was only interested in Erin and their disgusting, menopausal romance. Maia could probably run away, right now, and her mother wouldn't even notice she'd gone.

There'd been an article in *Cosmo* last week about women like her mother. The journalist said they were called LOLs, a recognised term which stood for Late-onset Lesbians.

'Look, Mum,' Maia said, pushing the magazine into her mother's hands. 'You have a proper condition, with a name. Late-onset Lesbianism.'

Her mother skimmed the article, looked slightly angry for a moment, then laughed as if she didn't care. 'Oh, of course,' she said. 'Of course I do. A real illness. Late-onset Lesbianism, early-onset Alzheimer's … They're all medical conditions.'

'It's probably the menopause,' Maia said, darkly.

'I'm forty-six, Maia.'

'So? That's when it all kicks off. That's when you start going mental.'

'Then you mean the peri-menopause, not the menopause, which is still a while away. Besides which, some things in a woman's life are actually real, Maia,' she said. 'Sometimes, women make big decisions that are entirely uninfluenced by their hormones. Sometimes, we get angry, not because we have PMT, but because we are perfectly reasonable beings and some bastard has pissed us off. Sometimes, we …'

Maia tuned her out. She was always like this, her mother, always banging on about things that were completely normal and giving them her own weird twist. And she always, *always*, did stuff like that menopause/peri-menopause thing she'd just done. No one else bothered to make distinctions between the two. Everyone knew what you meant when you said, 'My mother's menopausal and gone mental.' She wasn't sure why her own mother had to be so precise all the time. Well, she did know. It was because her mother was trained as a doctor and therefore used only the most accurate terms for body parts and bodily processes. Maia was pretty sure she was still the only girl in her school who knew there was a difference between the vulva and the vagina, and was able to say the words out loud because of her mother's habit of bandying them about throughout her childhood, as if they were no more weird to say than, 'You need to practice your flute, Maia.'

It made her a bit odd at school, but Maia didn't care. She stood out. She was used to that.

She turned away from the mirror and flopped down on her bed. It was Friday night and she was nearly sixteen. She ought to be out at a party or something, drinking vodka and snogging boys. That was what she always thought she'd be doing at sixteen, but instead she was here in her room on her own. She wondered what everyone else in her year was doing. Probably the same as her. Burntridge was a shit place to be young. Nothing ever happened, all the pubs were really strict about ID, and her mother wouldn't let her hang around the park in the evenings because she said it was 'purposeless'. Jesus. Why did everything have to have a bloody purpose?

She shot a text to Clara. **What you doing?**

Babysitting. Eating crisps. Watching crap TV. What you doing?

Fuck all.

She tossed the phone aside. She couldn't go on WhatsApp because her mother had made sure the WiFi didn't stretch upstairs so no one could have access to the internet in their bedrooms. 'It's so you can't watch porn, Reuben,' Maia had said, when they'd argued with their parents about it.

'It is not,' their mother told them, as if she knew she had no need to prevent her son from watching porn because she'd spent the last seventeen years instilling in all of them the exploitative evils of the porn industry, and of course her precious son would have listened to her. 'It's because everyone needs a space in their lives that is their own, where no one else can get them.'

A sanctuary. An internet-free sanctuary, that's what her room was meant to be. Really, it was just boring. It was so boring, it made Maia want to stick pins in her eyes. In the olden days, before her mum had had a lesbian affair and kicked her dad out, she would have gone downstairs and happily chatted to them, or played the piano for them, or helped herself to a massive bag of crisps and watched *Gogglebox* on the sofa with them. Those days were over now. Maia hated going downstairs in the evenings, especially Friday evenings, when her mum and Erin would drink a bottle of wine and forget there were other people in the house. They were always snogging and there was one time when Maia had gone into the living room and both their bras had been cast off onto the floor. They were still fully clothed and everything, and Maia did know that the first thing her mother had always done when she sat down in the evening was take her bra off and fling it wherever it landed, but still … The sight of two bras, side by side on the floor like that, was disgusting.

So she couldn't go downstairs. And Reuben was out and Tess was asleep. If she had a boyfriend, she thought, it wouldn't be like this. She'd have someone to go to the cinema with because even Burntridge wasn't shit enough not to even have a cinema, or she'd be able to just hang around his house with him, curled up on the sofa like her mother always was with Erin. And maybe they'd even have sex eventually because Maia would be sixteen soon and sex definitely needed to get on her horizon. Some of the girls at school were already on the pill, and one even had that weird-looking implant in her arm. Not that Maia especially wanted to be one of those girls. Privately, she thought they were idiots, waving their pill packets around as if there was some reason to bring them to school other than to let everyone know they were shagging their boyfriends. But still, she didn't want to be the last.

She reached for her phone again and scrolled back through recent messages from James. He was in year thirteen, same as Reuben, although the two of them weren't really friends. Maia knew him from orchestra. He played the saxophone and had recently been to London to audition for a place at a posh conservatoire once he'd finished his A levels. Reuben, Maia knew, thought of him as square but he wasn't when you got to know him. He was talented and clever and quite shy, which Maia found endearing.

You are fantastically attractive, one of his messages said. He'd sent it late one evening, after they'd spent the day together practising for the school Christmas concert. It still made Maia's cheeks flame to read it, even though she realised he'd probably been drunk when he sent it. The following Monday, when she saw him at school, he could barely look at her. 'Sorry about that message,' he mumbled eventually, and she'd been disappointed. She liked the idea of being fantastically attractive.

She wondered what he was doing tonight, wondered if he was lying on his bed, bored, while his mother snogged her new lover downstairs on the sofa. Probably not. He was eighteen, he could drink, he drove a car. He could be anywhere.

Her mind drifted to Luke Fairburn. He'd moved to London a couple of months ago, after being back at his mum's all summer. Maia liked him, even though she knew he was way out of her league: older, good-looking, a graduate and now a cool young professional as well. She tried to imagine what his life was like and pictured him swaggering into Soho bars, surrounded by pretty and intelligent women who fawned over him. Girls had always liked Luke. Maia hadn't even bothered trying to get his attention over the summer, when she saw him with a new girl nearly every week. She was fifteen. He barely even noticed her. She didn't stand a chance.

There was a knock at her bedroom door and her mum poked her head in. 'We're going to bed now, love,' she said. 'Goodnight.'.

Maia didn't look up. *We're going to bed.* Her mother had pretended she wanted to say goodnight, but what she was really doing – it was so obvious – was checking to see whether Maia had gone to sleep yet, so she could have noisy sex with her girlfriend. They seemed to think Maia had no idea but every night she heard them, moaning and groaning like pigs being slaughtered.

'Night,' she muttered.

Her mother blew her a kiss.

Maia picked up her phone and texted James. **What are you doing tomorrow?**

6

Jo

People had warned her about living in the community where she worked. You became a focus of local interest – you wouldn't be able to walk down the high street without people stopping you; couldn't do a food shop without attracting commentary on which supermarket you favoured; could barely stand in line at the pharmacy without rumours flying round the schoolyard that you probably had chronic thrush.

But Jo had lived here for twenty-five years in the village of Maltley, three miles outside Burntridge. There were thirty houses, mostly arranged around the village green, plus a tiny church and village hall. Maltley was a relic of a bygone era, and people embraced it, preserving its quaint Victoriana so enthusiastically that Jo occasionally feared Jacob Rees-Mogg might move in and make himself mayor. They held an annual fete and a monthly tea dance, and every year the whole village gathered at 7pm on the first of December for hot chocolate, mulled wine and the switching-on of the Christmas tree lights.

Of course, Jo knew it was all a load of rural middle-class bullshit, but it was a rare and beautiful sort of bullshit they'd all loved when the children were growing up and which she was never, ever going to move away from. Her last job had been in Newcastle and involved a half-hour commute along the A69. It was a commute which Jo appreciated – that sense of travelling away from the wreckage of the city, leaving it all behind for the simple sanctuary of Maltley.

Now that she worked at West Burntridge, things were different. Three of the families from school lived in Maltley, on the opposite side of the green to Jo, and she'd known them years before becoming their headteacher. Rachel Saunders was one of her best friends and her husband – ex-husband now – had been one of Dave's great hiking mates, but when Jo and Dave reached an inevitable parting of the ways after the kids had grown up and gone, Will had kept his distance. It always happened that way, however hard you tried. Judgements were made, sides taken, friendships broken. Rachel had stayed loyal, though, because Rachel didn't know any other way to be. 'Bollocks to the men,' she said. 'Let them carry on. You're my mate.' It became even easier once Rachel's marriage failed as well. It meant they could call in on each other for coffee or dinner, without the awkward distance of their awkward men.

The two other school families in the village went as far as smiling if they saw her getting into her car or tidying up the hedge, but mostly they just ignored her. This was the difference, Jo realised, between being a classroom teacher and being a headteacher. The class teachers were approachable. Parents happily accosted them in the park at weekends, or in any of the town's several cafés, but no one ever came near her. She was, by virtue of her job, someone people wanted to steer clear of. They didn't stop and say hello if they saw her in Waitrose. The more audacious of them would sneak a glance at her trolley and she'd see them mentally noting the bottles of Pinot Grigio, as if trying to decide whether she was a high-functioning alcoholic or just a normal woman who liked a drink after dealing with their children all day.

On the whole, Jo didn't worry anymore about venturing into Burntridge. It had bothered her in September when she'd first started, so much so that she had her food shopping delivered for the first few weeks and didn't even venture near the cinema or abbey but everything had settled down now and she felt easy wandering luxuriously round the supermarkets on a Wednesday afternoon, picking out meals and thanking God for half terms.

It was two years since Dave had moved out, but Jo still hadn't quite shaken his habit of splitting the weekly shop between Waitrose and Aldi. They could only afford food at Waitrose, he claimed, if they bought the washing powder, cleaning products and booze at Aldi. He'd used this argument for the whole thirty years they were together, despite the fact that their joint income over that time had more than quadrupled. But once the 5p carrier bag charge had been introduced, towards the end of their marriage, one of the biggest joys of Jo's life was to occasionally sweep through Waitrose, piling her trolley high with red wine and fabric softener, then packing everything into plain brown hessian bags, happy in her quiet knowledge that he could never, ever find out about her transgression. She loved these small triumphs over his miserliness. They made her feel she was continuing her bit for female emancipation.

Still, here she was, pushing her trolley round Aldi, semi-carefully choosing wine for the weekend. Aldi was a miserable place, full of irritable parents and their irritable children. She kept her eyes on the white wine shelf and tried not to listen to a familiar voice laying into a silent child. 'For God's sake, Max. Why do you always do this? Can't you just stand to the side of the trolley, instead of in front of it where I'm going trip over you?'

Laura Spence.

Jo couldn't help it. She looked up and caught her eye.

Laura flushed. 'Oh, Ms Fairburn,' she said. 'Hi. How's your half term going?'

Laura, being a crucial member of the PTA, wasn't afraid to speak to her outside school.

Jo smiled lightly, 'Lovely, thank you. Yours?'

'Oh, you know …' She looked harassed.

'I know,' Jo said, and flashed an understanding smile. She turned to Max, 'And how are you, Max? Are you having a good week off?'

He nodded. Jo noticed a small purple bruise on his cheek. She resisted the urge to reach out and touch it.

Laura saw her looking. 'He fell off a chair when he was helping me with dinner,' she explained.

'Easily done,' Jo said.

It was true. It was easily done. Jo had brought up two children of her own and knew how accidents happened, even when you were right there next to them. But she had an uneasy feeling, looking at Max now, cowed and silent beside his highly-stressed mother. Holidays, she knew, were a prime time for violence against children. Money was tighter, parents were more anxious, children were bored and short-tempered. Families like Max's were particularly vulnerable. Laura was on her own without money and without respite. The social

43

outlet of the PTA had shut down for the week. And Max was a boy with problems. He struggled at school. He was a loner, quiet with occasional bursts of sudden, uncontrollable fury. His teacher had him flagged as needing intervention.

She watched Laura as she walked away. If ever she'd mentioned concerns like this to Dave he'd tut and accuse her of sounding like a *Daily Mail* reader. 'Just because she's single and hasn't got a lot of money doesn't mean she beats her kid.' No, it didn't. Of course it didn't. But it made her more vulnerable to losing control than someone without financial stress and another parent to share the load with. Jo had seen it in her previous schools lots of times, and whenever she'd had this feeling before – a deep sense of unease and the urge to reach out and do something – she had never once been wrong.

She thought about Max as she drove home to Maltley. Already, she'd spent the first two days of half term on school work. Today was meant to be her day off, but she'd just log herself into the network and check his file, get a quick reminder of his circumstances.

She saw Rachel in her front garden as she pulled into the drive and waved as she climbed out of the car. Rachel smiled and waved back, then put her shears down and crossed the green towards her, brushing the hair out of her face as she walked. She was an attractive woman, Jo thought. Not glamorous – just one of those decent, lovely people whose decent loveliness somehow showed on their faces and made them easy on the eye.

Jo greeted her warmly. 'I haven't seen you for ages, which is ridiculous. We're neighbours.'

Rachel dusted her hands off on her jeans. 'You know how it is,' she said. 'Fucking work, fucking kids.'

'Divorces.'

'Those, too.'

'It's not often we see you at home at this time of day.'

'I booked half term off work to be with the kids. They've gone to Will's, though, so now I'm just pretending I know what to do with a garden. I haven't a clue. I'm just taking the shears to whatever's in my way.'

She seemed unconcerned by her cluelessness. Proud of it, even. Rachel, everyone knew, was concerned with higher things. She'd have a view on Max Spence if Jo were to tell her what she'd just seen.

'Still,' Jo said, 'it's nice to have the break, isn't it? Step off the treadmill for a day or two.'

A shadow passed over Rachel's face and for an awful moment, Jo thought she might cry. 'Everything OK?' she asked tentatively. Jo knew that people at their stages of life were adept at hiding problems. For years, Rachel and Will had been regulars in Jo's home – coming over for takeaways at weekends, parties at Christmas, heading out to the hills for walks. They'd even holidayed together a few times. Never, in all that time, had Will or Rachel presented themselves as anything other than a happily married couple, devoted to their family life and each other. But then, she supposed, neither had she or Dave, and yet here they all were: divorced after what must have been years of misery, and now Rachel was living with another woman. No one had seen that coming, although presumably Rachel had always been aware of it as she'd pushed on with her front of heteronormativity until she could (Jo assumed) bear it no longer.

45

These middle-aged friendships were so important, and yet so fundamentally dishonest at their core.

'Everything's fine,' Rachel told her. 'Though the kids are having a hard time adapting to it all.' She shrugged and looked momentarily helpless.

'All of them?' Jo asked. She was sympathetic to this problem. It was why she and Dave had stuck it out for so long; she wasn't sure she could deal with the guilt of making her children miserable, although even at 24 and 22 they hadn't taken news of the separation well. They blamed her for it. Luke, she knew, thought the whole shambles of their broken family was because of nothing more than his mother's selfish determination to be discontented with her perfectly acceptable life.

'Tess, mainly. Although Maia is suffering in her own way and it's coming out as contempt. For me, of course. Reuben's fine, but it would take a nuclear fallout to disturb him. As long as he has his guitar and his mates, he seems to be OK.'

'I'm sorry, Rachel. They'll adapt. It just takes time, unfortunately.'

She was aware of herself speaking in the tone of a sage about something she had no real experience of. But it was true, wasn't it? Time was the key to everything. It all passed. It was why you had to grab any happiness while it lasted.

'I know,' Rachel said. 'Thanks. Stupid of me really, but I just didn't think it was going to be like this. I had a plan …'

'Oh, we all have those. Other people tend to screw them up.'

Rachel smiled again. 'I'd better get back to the hedge. But we need to catch up properly. I'll check when the kids will next be at Will's and we'll sort a date out for you to come over.'

'I'd love that,' Jo said.

Rachel set off across the green and Jo took the shopping bags from the car and let herself into her own, smaller house. Empty. It was always empty. She didn't mind. She was too busy for loneliness, but while she used to crave the silence of an empty house, there were times now when all this silence felt a little dangerous. She was fifty-three, her family had grown up and gone and if she wasn't careful, all that lay ahead of her would be more of the same – the retreating of people and an ever-expanding silence. She needed to shoot a rocket into her life before age crept up on her, in the way age had a habit of doing.

A line from a film she'd seen recently came back to her. *Sort your shit out, girls, because it's later than you think.*

She draped her coat over the bannister and walked through to the kitchen to unload the shopping. She felt like eating, but everything was boring. KitKats, breadsticks, hummus, broccoli, chicken, salmon, pasta, potatoes, bananas … She'd eaten it all, all her life, and she was fed up with it. Dear God, was there nothing new in the world? Maybe she should go to Japan and try some outlandish delicacy like *shirako*, which her daughter, Rebecca, told her was a fish's sperm sack and you ate it either deep-fried or steamed. Jo recalled how her response to that had been the final nail in the coffin of her sex life.

She grabbed a handful of breadsticks, which she ate while firing up the laptop, then logged into the school's network, went to the pupils' files and typed in *Max Spence*. She checked his address. *Flat 2b, Windsor Road*. The wrong side of the tracks. Most children at West Burntridge were from the affluent end of town, where a private music tutor lived on every street, and even the litter was nothing more harmful than the occasional discarded bruschetta or a couple of cherry tomatoes. Litter on Windsor Road was far more sinister: syringes, condoms, empty cans of Special Brew.

She clicked on through his file. There were no emergency contact details for his father, only for Laura. He'd barely passed his phonics test at the end of his reception year, his level of numeracy was low and he had trouble managing his anger. *Like his mother,* Jo thought. Laura Spence was seething, all the time. She latched on to anything as an outlet for it. Sometimes it was her idea of the over-liberal curriculum (if only she knew how rigid and awful it was, how it did children like Max no favours at all), sometimes it was other parents, and sometimes, Jo suspected, it was her small, troubled young son.

7

Erin

For once, all three children were at their dad's at the same time and Erin was trying hard not to admit the relief she was feeling. The atmosphere in the house had suddenly become relaxed and peaceful. She and Rachel could talk together, eat together, simply just be together without someone trying to make them feel they were guilty of a terrible crime. She understood the resentment, of course she did. Her own parents had separated when she was a similar age to Tess and she'd been miserable about it for years, always hoping her mother's new man would disappear, her dad would move back in and they'd carry on as if nothing had ever happened. 'Don't you want me to be happy?' she remembered her mother asking tearfully, after five years had gone by, every day of them filled with Erin's relentless hatred of her stepfather. Erin had stared at her blankly, not really understanding the question. It was foolish for any parent to think their child cared about their happiness. All they wanted was for their family to be together.

But for now, the children were away and it was the anniversary of the day Erin and Rachel had finally acknowledged and then given in to the crazy fact that they'd fallen in love.

Never before had Erin marked a romantic anniversary. It was something she'd always found tedious in other people – the constant need to prove the perfection of their relationships, as if love might come tumbling down if it weren't bolstered by ritualistic remembrances of the first meeting, the first shag, the engagement, the wedding. There was a silent competitiveness in the photos rolled out all over Facebook and Instagram. *You think you're happy? We're happier than you! We're the happiest!*

This time, though, she found she wanted to celebrate everything and so did Rachel. They'd decided not to go out. They wanted to be able to touch each other during a meal without surreptitious glances from uninvited visitors to the Theatre of Middle-Aged Lesbians. They also wanted to be able to abandon dessert in favour of immediate, I-can't-keep-my-hands-off-you-let's-do-it-on-the-kitchen-floor sex if they felt like it. And Erin suspected they probably would feel like it.

Erin was doing the cooking. Sea bass with wild mushrooms and crushed new potatoes. Rachel sat at the other side of the island, making herself useful by refilling Erin's champagne glass so often Erin couldn't keep track of how much she'd drunk. She had to maintain strict control these days. Three glasses were OK, but if she let herself slip recklessly into the fourth, she'd spend the next day cowering under the duvet, crippled with existential dread. Her alcohol-induced depression held a new level of bleakness now she woke up in a home where eighty percent of its members wanted her to die. ('They don't want you to die,' Rachel told her, but Erin wasn't so sure. Tess's face could be as fearsome as Myra Hindley's if she tried hard enough.)

Everything was in the oven at last: the exotic-looking mix of garlicky wild mushrooms pressed into the potatoes and the slashed, thyme-filled seabass roasting on top. Erin loved Rachel's kitchen – she still thought of it as Rachel's kitchen – with its breakfast pantry, its giant slabs of worktop space, and its vast, built-in wine rack. Her flat in Primrose Hill hadn't been much bigger than this kitchen. But then again, she'd had London on the doorstep instead of … Northumberland. A wild, empty space. Sandy beaches. Castles. An ancient wall she couldn't quite bring herself to give a shit about. But still. Here she was.

And Rachel was with her.

And the children weren't here.

It was just her and Rachel, alone, like it used to be when they snatched nights together in London if Rachel came to give one of her intimidatingly impressive presentations at medical schools, or for meetings with features writers and government lobbyists so she could bring attention to all those things she was passionately researching: food poverty, health inequality, their impacts on maternal mental health.

It was how they'd met. Erin's editor had sent her out to interview this woman who'd just released her second book, after the first became an unexpected bestseller. Erin had been expecting someone lofty and arrogant, and probably quite difficult, too. Writers like that usually were. They enjoyed the fact that their expertise elevated them and shut people out; they liked to smirk at questions that were too simple, that didn't allow for the many nuances of the subject matter; they flared up at any hint of disagreement from someone too stupid to grasp their arguments. On the whole, they were arseholes.

Rachel wasn't like that. She wasn't like that at all. They met in a café near Doughty Street, where Erin fired questions at her and Rachel gave easy answers, punctured with wit and friendliness. Erin came away feeling that this woman was the cleverest, most interesting and yet most refreshingly ordinary person she'd ever met.

They stayed in touch by email, at first just so Erin could ask any follow-up questions before the interview went to print, but then slowly their chat strayed away from the professional until a few months later, they were arranging to meet the next time Rachel was in London and Erin found herself anticipating it with the nervous excitement she hadn't experienced since youth.

It took a long time for them to admit that the chemistry was love. They skated round it until the thrilling weight of it burst through the boundaries and there it was between them, like liquid gold.

Now, every morning, Erin woke up beside this woman and still couldn't believe her luck.

She set the timer on the oven. 'Twenty minutes.'

Rachel smiled at her. She was always smiling, always looking at her, unable to conceal the happiness she felt when they were together. It overwhelmed Erin sometimes. She had to fight the urge to push it away, to screw it all up in some crazy pre-emptive strike because surely, no one really deserved to be loved this much. She worried sometimes that Rachel had somehow got the wrong end of the stick, that Erin wasn't all she thought she was. Sooner or later, Rachel was going to find out she was just an ordinary woman after all, and everything would come crashing down.

In other, saner moments, it simply sent a shot of desire straight through her so strong she wondered why she was still dressed. It never felt quite right to be clothed around Rachel, but on the other hand, there needed to be some conversation, some civilised attempt at sea bass and wild mushrooms or they'd collapse into the purely animal.

Rachel refilled her glass again. 'I saw Jo Fairburn today,' she told her. 'Tess's headteacher. We've been friends for years. I said she should come over soon. You'll love her.'

'Cool.'

'Apparently – I didn't hear this from her, but from someone else – she's meeting resistance from the women on the PTA about all sorts of stuff. There's Laura Spence and her anti-LGBTQ shit, and now Kate Monro doesn't like her new attempts to poverty-proof the school.'

'Poverty-proof?'

'Attempts to not make the poor kids stand out. No need for the expensive jumpers with the school logo on – a plain red one from Asda will do the job. But the thing that's really got up Kate's nose is that on Toy Day there are to be no electronic devices, which means her obnoxious daughter can't go round shooting videos of herself dressed in leopard print and singing about longing for a man in her bed.'

'The PTA can't stop her, can they? She's the head. Their job is just to raise funds.'

Rachel laughed. 'That's not how they see themselves. They want a say in how the school is run.' She stopped talking for a moment, then looked at Erin and said, 'Why am I doing this?'

'Doing what?'

'Talking about all this crap when the house is empty and you're sitting opposite me, and …'

She reached for Erin and pressed her lips to hers.

Oh, God. The dinner was going to burn. It was going to burn. The dial on the oven was just above her head. She could reach up and turn it down if …

No, she couldn't.

This was what they'd been missing. The passion, the rawness. It didn't matter what they did or where they did it, because the children were away and they were unleashing it all, right here. They were breathless, mad for each other. It was making them sweat, making them shout.

It was fucking bliss.

And then, suddenly, it was over. It had stopped.

Rachel sat up. Erin sat up.

Maia stood before them, a look of absolute disgust on her face.

Rachel grabbed a tea towel from where it hung over the oven door and attempted to cover herself with it. Erin shamefully noted that her left breast, the nipple still hard and wet with Erin's saliva, was exposed because the tea towel was too small. It was too small and she herself was just sitting there, crouched into a ball, her legs curled around each other and …

Everything was awful.

There would be no funny side to this. Not ever. Not even when Maia was forty would she be saying, 'Hey Mum, remember that time I walked in on you and Erin having sex in the kitchen? It was awful at the time, but isn't it funny now? You tried to hide behind a tea towel with sheep on it and your tit was hanging out and everything.'

'Maia …' Rachel began.

Maia was speechless. For a while, she stood staring at them, as if she couldn't bring herself to walk past.

'Maia, I …'

Maia turned and left the house.

8

Laura

Soft play. A child's birthday party. Plastic balls flying into plastic cups of orange squash. The squeak of feet against a plastic slide. Screaming. Sausages on the floor. Wee in the ball pool. A smear of snot on the trampoline. Katie Price and Peter Andre singing 'A Whole New World'. The frequent waft of a soiled nappy.

This was life. This was the life all these parents had chosen. Or rather, it was the by-product of a life they'd thought they were choosing that day they decided the time had come to throw contraception to the wind and produce a precious, smiling baby who would grow into a wonderful, creative and gifted child. Laura looked at the women around her sipping their metallic-tasting coffees, and wondered what had happened to those dreams. They were probably lying dead in a corner, along with all their other plans to be More Than This. She wondered how many of these women were wondering, right now, right this second, if they could go home and talk their partners into getting the snip.

The woman opposite seemed to read her thoughts. 'God, why do we do this to ourselves?'

Laura shrugged. Why did they?

Someone else said, 'I think it's because we love them. But seriously, if anyone else in the world demanded I put myself through this sort of hell for them, I would just … stop loving the bastard.' She paused, then added, 'I think I'm getting close to that point with my kids, to be honest.'

Everyone laughed. Oh, to be one of those women, Laura thought. To be able to amuse with this pretence at misery when it was so clear that, no matter what they all said about the graft and the exhaustion, none of them would be anywhere other than here, tossed about on this bizarre sea of parenting, hearing themselves saying things they never thought they'd say, doing things they never thought they'd do, and loving with a fierceness that devoured them until there was nothing left. They cast themselves aside, and let their children replace them.

She noticed Kate, her friend from the PTA, moving about the tables with a clipboard and some pieces of paper. The petition. Kate must have done it already. Last night, she'd come over when Max was in bed and they'd agreed to put it together in time for Monday morning, but Kate had obviously gone home riled and ready to fight. It was that woman on Twitter who'd been the final straw. For both of them.

As soon as Kate had taken a seat in Laura's tiny living room, a glass of white wine in her hand, she'd asked, 'So what do you think of Jo Fairburn?'

Laura reached for a handful of crisps from the bowl on the coffee table. 'I liked her until she said she was going to deliver the gay stuff.'

'I know. I've been looking into it, actually. There's a whole campaign group on Twitter. A woman thinks they're actually *indoctrinating* children to become homosexual. Hold on while I find it.'

She pulled her phone out of her bag and did some scrolling. Then she handed it to Laura. The page was full of brief snippets of information, with links to articles from education authorities or newspapers about the new sex education curriculum.

By promoting homosexuality as a positive choice, we are encouraging it in our children.

There is an LGBT agenda and it is being forced on our children. Gay teachers are encouraging children to develop an attraction to the same sex and lead a double life their parents know nothing about.

Stop gays from infiltrating our schools and telling our children it is normal for people to marry from the same sex. It is not normal!

Laura handed the phone back in silence.

'What do you think?' Kate asked.

'I think she's right. Of course she's right. Children are vulnerable and impressionable. The world has gone too far with all this.'

'Do you think it's really an agenda, like this woman says? A conspiracy to turn children gay?'

Laura shrugged. 'I don't know. That might be a bit extreme. But it's not stopping them, is it? Whether people like it or not, being gay is not normal. They need to know the pain it causes. Imagine being the parent of a gay child. No weddings, no grandchildren …'

'And,' Kate said, sipping her wine, 'look at what it's done to Will Kernick to have his wife run off with a lesbian.'

'That's even worse. Those poor children. I can't imagine what they're going through. Max has become friendly with Tess recently. He wanted to invite her over. I had to say no. I feel bad about it, but what can I do? If she comes here for tea, then he'll end up being invited over there in return, and I just can't have him exposed to that. He has enough problems without confusion about what's normal added to them.'

'But he's going to get that anyway, if they start teaching it at school.'

'Which they will. Jo Fairburn made that clear when I spoke to her about it. It's a real worry.'

'I was wondering whether we should start a petition. Some parents don't know what's going on, so I can send them a letter from my PTA email address to tell everyone and raise our concerns. I can do that tomorrow. Then we can take the petition in from Monday onwards.'

Laura had been relieved. It was never easy, in these days of Political Correctness, to express your views without being accused of bigotry. She didn't often put her head above the parapet, but considered this too important. Her son was already disadvantaged by not having a father. She was relying on the world to act as his role model and show him what families ought to be, what he should be striving for: one woman, one man, their children. She wanted to set Max on a path that would see him grow into a good, decent family man with all the values his father hadn't had when he deserted them. To suggest that anything else was acceptable would undermine her work and also, it was simply wrong. Men were not made to have sex with each other. That was just the way things were. It was biology.

Now, as she watched Kate approaching other parents, explaining the purpose of the petition and asking them to sign it, she noticed many people politely refusing. At the table next to hers, Will Kernick sat talking to a couple of mums and the only other dad here. Was Kate going to be bold enough to ask for his signature, Laura wondered? Probably. She wasn't a woman to hold back and besides, she fancied the man Will was talking to. His wife had died last year and now he was the single father of a small boy. Single fathers, Laura realised long ago, held an allure that single mothers could only dream of. Single fathers were rare wonders, heroically taking on the tough yet tender task of raising their children without the nurturing guidance of a good woman by their side. At school, Laura had seen mothers flock to this man. They were all married, but still they fantasised about the chance to heal his wounds, take on his child, cook him a nourishing meal and show him that there was another chance at love, that he didn't need to masturbate in the cold darkness of empty sheets every night, sobbing for his lost wife at the moment of lonely climax. (Because this, surely, was all he could be doing.)

Single mothers, on other hand, were to be avoided. No one wanted an abandoned woman with all that grimy baggage.

'That kid in the baby area looks old enough to drive,' someone at Laura's table said. 'He's a menace. Does anyone want to share these chips? I bought them to ease the pain of soft play – I love chips – but they're kind of flabby and I'm not sure they're worth the calories. They gave me a bottle of watery ketchup as well if you want it.'

A few people reached over for chips, then complained about them. Laura resisted, but her mouth watered. She was hungry, and if she took just one of those chips, no matter how flabby and disgusting they might be, she knew she wouldn't be able to stop. She'd gobble them all, and then people would talk about her. Laura Spence, the scavenging chav.

Instead, she kept her eyes on Kate as she moved closer to Will and his mate, brandishing the petition. 'Hi there,' she said brightly and pulled up a seat. 'I don't know whether you'll have seen my email yet. I only zipped it out late last night. But some of us are concerned about the new headteacher and her plans to go ahead with the curriculum that includes teaching children as young as five about homosexuality.'

Everyone at the table looked at her.

She went on. 'So we've decided to let our voices be heard and protest with a petition. I'm collecting signatures today and I'll be in the yard all next week if you want to have a think about it. I've also got some addresses of websites here, with details about what our kids will be learning. It's quite eye-opening to have a look at these.'

There was a pause while people took this in. Then the single dad that Kate fancied said, 'No, thank you. I won't be signing.'

'I won't, either. It's right that children should know about this. My best friend is gay.'

Oh, that old line.

Will looked as though he was trying to keep quiet, but couldn't. Then, very calmly, he said, 'I find this incredibly divisive. All you will achieve is the passing-on of your own prejudice. You will also be singling out children growing up

61

with same-sex parents. It's no good saying they're just a tiny minority. They exist. They go to West Burntridge.'

A few people looked uncomfortable. Kate, however, was clearly enjoying herself. 'But really, do you want homosexuality encouraged in schools?'

Will stared at her as if he couldn't quite believe how stupid she was. Oh, it was alright for him, with his lengthy education and all his titles, Professor of This, Doctor of That, so aroused by equality he refused to send his children to private schools, even though everyone knew he could afford it. Laura felt sorry for him, but that didn't mean he wasn't as nauseating as his ex-wife.

He said, 'You cannot encourage homosexuality. Either some-one is, or they aren't. It needs to be talked about. It needs to be made normal so children don't feel ashamed of who they are.'

Laura raised her eyebrows. How right-on he was. How accepting of his ex-wife's decision to throw him out of the marital bed and welcome a woman instead. He had no idea, sitting here in this child's world of soft play and birthday cake, who she was, and how she was the one he'd opened his heart to, how he'd told her about the torment he suffered to think of the secrets Rachel must have kept from him through years of marriage, and the chaos people caused when they decided to follow their hearts.

9

Rachel

No one had ever seen Rachel cry. She could go years and years without shedding a single tear. Now and then, the question came up in Facebook quizzes posted on her timeline by friends who knew she never watched TV but that social media was her weakness. Not even Dr Rachel Saunders was too highbrow for the occasional meaningless quiz. *What was the last film you watched? When did you last read a book? When is the last time you cried?* She'd had to really think about her answer. She couldn't remember. Her mother's funeral last year had passed in a state of stoic numbness on Rachel's part. She'd stood at the front of the chapel and read a poem about gratitude without a waver to her voice, then hosted the wake with lightness and dignity. Sometimes, she knew, people suspected her of being inhuman. She wasn't inhuman. It just took an awful lot to make her cry.

Now, as she stood in the park after school, waiting while Tess played football with her friends, she saw one of the mothers openly weeping. A small clutch of caring friends was gathered by her side. One of them had her arm soothingly about the crying woman's shoulders and everyone listened as she sobbed the reason for her grief.

Rachel watched discreetly and felt an unexpected lurch of envy. *I wish I could be like that,* she thought. *I wish I could break down in the park with reckless abandon, and know I would be comforted by someone who would listen.*

'Tess!' she called. 'Two more minutes!'

She couldn't break down, though. She was Rachel Saunders and her identity was carved in stone. Strong, successful, acerbic. Especially acerbic. To cry would be like stripping her skin off and giving people free rein to peer at her insides.

'Tess!' she called again. 'Time to go now!'

Her daughter abandoned the friends who were trying to kick a football between two filthy red jumpers on the ground and came over willingly. Her hair had mostly fallen loose from its ponytail and now hung in tangled chaos around her face, and whatever had been her school dinner was still smeared above her top lip. To anyone else, she would look like just another slightly unattractive and possibly revolting child. To Rachel, she looked feisty and adorable. She kissed the top of her head and said, 'Shall we go for a hot chocolate before we go home?'

Tess beamed and took her hand. Rachel smiled down at her. This was the way things used to be, the way they were meant to be. She wondered how long they could make it last.

They sat opposite each other in Costa. Tess nibbled a Halloween spider biscuit and took semi-frequent sips of hot chocolate with whipped cream. Rachel was drinking a flat white because she wanted to work out whether it really was superior to her usual latte. As far as she could see, the main difference was that the flat white was both smaller and more expensive, and also: when did people start thinking £3.00 was an acceptable price to pay for a cup of coffee? She'd just spent nearly a tenner on all this, which was no doubt more than the woman behind the counter was paid for every tedious hour she spent grinding beans and frothing milk and bashing that metal arm from the coffee machine against the work surface only so she could start the whole process again.

But this was what she had to do because this was the world she lived in, and because her six-year-old loved it. She forced herself to concentrate on Tess and her litany of after-school woes. 'Do you think this is fair?' Tess would say every few minutes, and then she'd present Rachel with a report about procedures in the dining room or the playground or this morning's maths lesson, all of which struck Rachel as being very fair indeed, but which had injured her daughter's strongly-developed sense of what was acceptable to expect from a six-year-old. 'We even had to know all our number bonds to ten,' she said, looking at Rachel expectantly, longing to rouse maternal outrage and, Rachel suspected, a promise to rampage through the school and put an end to all this nasty education.

'And did you manage it?'

Tess skimmed the rest of the cream off the top of her hot chocolate with a long teaspoon. 'Yes,' she said.

'Well, then.'

'And now we have all these spellings. I'm in red group and we have twenty. All the other groups only have ten.'

'So what does that tell you about red group?' Rachel asked. She wasn't after an obnoxious answer like *We're cleverer than everyone else*, merely some acknowledgement from her child that none of this was unfair and she was, in fact, one of the lucky ones. A futile aim, of course. She was six years old.

'That red group's boring,' she said, in a tone that was definite and not to be argued with.

Rachel heard the beep of a text message arriving on her phone. She forced herself to ignore it. She was here to focus on Tess, to give her time without distraction. Besides, it wasn't going to be Maia. For now, and possibly for a long time to come, she'd lost her.

Rachel wasn't sure she'd ever be able to bear the memory of that night. The world would need a whole new language if there were to be words strong enough to describe how she felt whenever the scene replayed itself in her head. *Mortified* didn't come close, and neither did *shame*. All she'd wanted at the time was to hide away and never be seen again.

She hadn't done that, though. She'd left it till the next morning, then phoned Maia's mobile. It rang twice and went to voicemail when her daughter declined her call. Rachel sent a text message. **I'm so sorry**.

Maia didn't reply. Rachel knew not to harass her. She needed to step back and let her come to her when she was ready, but she also needed to make it clear that she wanted Maia to come home and sort this terrible mess out. There was a balance to be struck here between giving her daughter space and allowing her to think she didn't care, that it was fine with her that her fifteen-year-old had walked in on her having sex on the kitchen floor (with a woman, let's not pretend that didn't count) and then left home.

It should never have happened.

That was the conclusion she always came back to. They should never have been so reckless. No teenager wanted to face the excruciating reality of their parents' relationships. It

66

was bad enough when it was just their mum and dad, without it being their mum and the lesbian she'd broken up their home for.

'*Mummy*,' Tess was saying. 'You're not *listening*.'

'Sorry, sweetheart.'

'Can we go to the bookshop after this?'

'Yes, of course.'

Rachel had done this with all her children. She refused every material request they ever made unless it was for a book, which she would always buy them. Reuben and Maia had always tried their luck, although she'd never understood why because she never backed down. But they tried it, anyway. 'Mum, can you buy me a Spiderman toy/a remote-controlled car/a pair of shoes/some earrings?' moving through a long list of consumerist desires until eventually they gave in and said something along the lines of, 'The new Philip Pullman book?'

Tess had seen the light much earlier than her other two. She didn't waste time, just shot straight to the request that was guaranteed a *yes*. 'Please can I have another one of those *Daisy* books?' she said. 'And will you read it to me when we get home?'

'I would love to,' Rachel said and for once, this wasn't a kind, nurturing lie. Some of the happiest times of her life had been spent reading to her children. Maia had only put a stop to it when she hit year ten.

'Ah, Rachel. Hello.'

Rachel looked up. Kate fucking Monro, PTA heavyweight and professional mother of one. For the last two years Rachel had tried hard, if not to like her, then at least to support her fundraising efforts. She could see that the woman was a force of nature. Every December, she blazed a trail of polite aggression through Burntridge, persuading shop owners, restaurateurs, hoteliers, managers of tourist attractions and pretty much anyone she bumped into, to hand over something of significant value for the Christmas raffle. There were no rose-scented hand creams or lavender bath salts at West Burntridge First School. It was all weekends at castles, dinners at Michelin-starred restaurants, theatre tickets and magnums of champagne. Last year, one woman had been known to formally complain when all her ticket won her was a free swim at a private pool.

'Hello, Kate,' she said. 'I haven't seen you for a while. Still doing great works for the school, no doubt?'

'Oh, you know,' Kate said, with a modest flick of her hair, 'I do my best.'

Oh, go fuck yourself, Rachel thought. She didn't even rebuke herself for being so harsh. It had been her default response to anything Kate said ever since the day she'd cornered Rachel in the yard and asked her to bake something for the Friday cake stall. She'd actually run her eyes down a list and said, 'I'm not sure we've ever had a cake stall contribution from you, Dr Saunders.'

Rachel had almost choked. 'You keep a list of this stuff, Kate? Really?'

Kate spoke slowly and calmly, like a woman trying to control her temper. 'You'll understand it's very important that we keep things fair. If we don't ask for something from everyone, then it's always the same five or six people who end up doing everything, while others do nothing but still expect the same advantages for their children.'

'Listen mate, I'll do a deal with you. I'll give you a hundred quid every September, if you excuse me from baking duties for the rest of the year. How does that sound?'

'You know that's not really the spirit we want to embrace in the school community.'

'I'm sure it's not, but a hundred quid in exchange for my personal lack of effort is my final offer.'

Kate reluctantly accepted, then went away and spent the next fortnight slagging Rachel off for 'thinking she was too important to involve herself in the school'. In reality, Kate had no idea what Rachel did behind the scenes, in private, and without needing credit for it. She was the one who financed the food at breakfast club for those children who came to school on empty stomachs; she was the one who ensured every child had music tuition, regardless of parental income; she was the money behind the fund that enabled all children in year four to go on the residential trip to the Lake District. And although she wanted to keep this strictly confidential, known only to herself and the head, she didn't necessarily relish Kate fucking Monro spreading word through town that Rachel Saunders considered herself too good for West Burntridge First School.

Now Kate waved a bright red clipboard in front of her and said, 'You might not be aware of the new plans to introduce teaching children as young as five about homosexual relationships ...'

'I am aware of that and fully supportive of it, as I'm sure you well know.'

Kate widened her eyes with pretend innocence. 'I didn't know. Of course not.'

'Please, Kate. You know as well as everyone else in this town – and probably for six hundred miles around – that

I am in a relationship with a woman, so I'm not sure why you brought me this petition other than to try and shame me, which you are failing to do. So please take your bright red clipboard and shove it up your vagina.'

She'd meant to say *arse*. She really had.

Kate was staring at her, open-mouthed with shock.

Rachel said, 'My daughter and I are having a drink together. Please fuck off.'

Kate left. Rachel sat and shook for a moment or two, partly with rage and partly because she knew she was going to be talked about, yet again. She'd confessed about her lesbian relationship, that would be the first outrage. (Did she have no shame?) The second outrage would be that she'd told Kate where to shove her petition. The final outrage, cementing her reputation as a Burntridge degenerate, was that she'd sworn in front of her child.

'Just wait,' she'd say, when she repeated the story to Erin this evening, 'by next week, they'll have deemed me an unfit mother.'

10

Maia

Maia spooned milkshake into her mouth. Her mother had drummed it into them that plastic straws were an unnecessary environmental disaster, so Maia never used them, although it dawned on her suddenly that she could now. There was no reason at all to take notice of anything her mother said and besides that, Maia didn't even live with her any more, so what could she do? Nothing.

Opposite her, James sipped coffee. He'd asked what she wanted before he placed his own order, and she'd said a vanilla thick shake with honeycomb pieces because that was what she loved. James smiled as if this amused him, then ordered the thick shake and a cappuccino with almond biscotti for himself. It made Maia feel as though he believed he was on a date – was it a date? – with someone who could barely even pretend to be grown-up. None of her friends would meet a bloke in a café and then order a milkshake like some bloody ten-year-old, but Maia's mother (she must stop thinking about her mother) had always said that the mature thing was simply to be yourself and fuck what anyone else thought. Therefore, she would eat-drink as many vanilla milkshakes with honeycomb pieces as she wanted, and if that turned out not to be sophisticated enough for whoever was with her, then they could get on the next flight to Rome and find a woman who richly roasted her own espresso beans. Maia didn't give a shit.

This was the first time she'd met up with him outside school. Recently, they'd started hanging round the hall together during concert practice when there were long gaps between their individual performances, then at lunchtime today he'd asked if she wanted to meet at Maddison's after school. It was the only café in town for students from the high school. Everywhere else was always full of parents and children, or old people squelching cheese scones between their teeth. They made Maia wonder whether teeth lost some of their sharpness with age, or whether old people were too tired from life to chew any more, or if everyone just reached a certain age and thought, 'Fuck it. These public manners are a nuisance' and threw decorum out the window. Whatever it was, it always turned Maia's stomach a little when she witnessed the noisy non-chewing of cheese scones by the elderly.

Casually, James rested his hand right in the middle of the table so that it hovered very close to hers. Maia cast her eyes downward. She wasn't used to this and felt uncertain how to respond. She'd snogged boys before, of course she had, at old middle school discos and Valentine's parties and in the park a few times, but she'd never actually met up with a boy because he liked her. She'd never had to make conversation with a boy or navigate her way through a blossoming romance. She wasn't even sure she wanted a boyfriend. From what she'd seen so far, they just caused drama and tears.

'So, what are you doing after this?' he asked.

She shrugged. 'I'll just go back to my dad's. I haven't really got any plans. Just homework, really. Coursework and stuff.'

He nodded understandingly. 'Sure,' he said. 'If you get enough done before eight, maybe we could go to the cinema later. I'm not sure what's on. What sort of films do you like?'

'I like lots of things,' she said. 'Dramas, mostly. Comedies never make me laugh, though.' She worried then that she'd made herself sound miserable, so added, 'Just because they're usually stupid and lack any real wit. Not because I'm a depressive.'

She didn't want to say what she was really thinking: *It's only Wednesday. I'm not allowed out after eight on a school night*. But then she realised; she'd left home. Her mother no longer had a say in what she did, and their dad had always been more relaxed about how she and Reuben spent their free time. As long as homework was done, it didn't really matter to him if they went out on a Wednesday.

She said, 'I'll watch anything else, though.'

He said, 'I'll check out what's on and text you later. I can always drive you home.'

'Oh, it's OK. I live with my dad now. His house is in Burntridge.'

She could see she'd kindled his interest in her home life. He raised his eyebrows. 'I thought you lived in Maltley with your mum and her …'

'I did,' she said, shrugging coolly. 'It went to shit.'

'Yeah?'

Now, he did take her hand in his, letting his fingers entwine with hers. She didn't stop him.

He looked at her with an intense sort of concern that she'd never seen on the faces of boys her own age. 'Do you want to tell me what happened?'

'Well …' she started. She'd never planned to share the details of that night with anyone. It was mortifying. Shameful. It had left her feeling appalled and angry. Never in her life would she be able to get that image out of her head: the sight of her naked mother's head between Erin's legs, and Erin moaning in what Maia supposed must have been ecstasy but sounded a lot like pain to her.

She couldn't bear to even think about it, let alone talk about it with anyone else. And yet …

And yet …

She told him.

She hadn't meant to, but she ended up telling him about how angry she was that her mother had met this woman and had an affair with her. 'She said she didn't mean to. She said it just happened. But it can't have *just happened*, can it? I mean, she used to travel all the way to fucking London to stay with her every week. That takes effort. It's a deliberate affair. It's not one that just happens. And I'm not homophobic, I'm really not. The fact that Erin is a woman is … Well, it's not that much of a big deal, except that it must make my dad feel like shit … But I know I'd feel like this if it was a bloke my mum had gone off with. It's just that I walked in on them one time … I was at my dad's and I left my flute at home so I went back to get it and there they were on the kitchen floor …'

Her voice trailed off and she shook her head, unable to finish.

James sat in silence for a while. Maia was aware of him

filling in the gaps in her story and gazing at her with sympathy and something that looked like … respect? She wondered if he still thought she was fantastically attractive, even when she spoke so angrily. She'd been aware of it while she was talking – the unmistakable fury in her voice that made her sound possibly a little bit crazy.

'You've been through a lot,' he said.

Maia said, 'I suppose so. Anyway, after that, I knew I could never look at them again, so I moved in with my dad. It's better now. Calmer. I miss my little sister sometimes, but there's no drama. I hate drama. And I hate my mum. She's so obsessed with that woman. Completely obsessed. I mean, Erin's OK and everything, but really, she's not all that. I'm so angry with my mum for wrecking everything for the sake of this … this *nothing woman*.'

'I don't blame you.'

She looked up and met his gaze. 'Really?'

'It's terrible, what she's done to her family. If my mum did that, I'd …' He broke off, as if he couldn't even imagine what he'd do.

Maia smiled gratefully. Sometimes, she'd been made to wonder whether she was wrong to be so angry. Her dad told her she'd have broken her mother's heart because for some reason, he still saw fit to stand up for his ex-wife. Habit, Maia supposed. All her life, her mum and dad had presented a united front when dealing with their kids, and her dad wasn't going to stop now. Whenever Maia's phone beeped with a message from her mum, or *Mum* flashed up on the screen when it rang, her dad would say, 'You ought to answer that, Maia. She's trying to sort this out.'

But Maia was too angry. She didn't want to see her mother again, and she couldn't believe her mother had so little shame that she would actually try and contact her. She ought to be burying herself in the ground after what Maia had seen.

'Try to be understanding, Maia,' her dad said. 'Your mum will be feeling terrible about what happened. And none of this will have been easy for her. We don't know how long she'd been feeling this way about women, but I suspect a long time. For years she tried to keep everything normal for the sake of you three but now she's met someone she loves and she can't do it any longer. Try not to be too hard on her.'

God, he was just so reasonable. He still loved her, that was why. It made Maia even more angry to think how her mother had sacrificed everyone else's happiness for her own. Her dad didn't deserve this and besides, Maia knew it was all bullshit. He pretended to be cool and strong, but she could see he was miserable. It was there in his face, and the way he couldn't help sighing his way through the evenings while they watched box sets on Netflix. He didn't even seem to realise he was doing it. Sometimes, when Maia looked at him for too long and saw all the sadness he was trying to keep from her, she felt an ache in her chest so deep and so painful, she couldn't bear to linger on it. It was easier to feel it as anger.

'I like having you here,' her dad had said last night, dropping a kiss on her forehead as he stood up to go to bed. Maia could see his grief as clearly as if he were sobbing. She wondered how he could still bear to stand up for her mother, after all she'd done. Also, she wished he would just be on her side.

So it was a relief, now, to have someone sitting opposite her, someone who understood and didn't make her feel she was unreasonable for being so pissed off, someone who was even saying, right now, that he admired her for being so strong. He seemed to mean it, too.

'Thanks,' she said, and smiled.

They finished their drinks. James pushed back his chair, stood up and put his coat on. 'I'll walk you home,' he said.

Maia tipped her head back and drained the very last of her milkshake. 'Sorry,' she said. 'I'm such a child. But I love this stuff.'

He grinned. 'You drink whatever you like.' Then he looked at her intensely for a long moment and said, 'But you're not a child, Maia. Not at all.'

He took her hand and they left together. When they reached Maia's front door, he paused for a while and said, 'I really like you, Maia.'

She didn't know what to say, and cast her eyes downward again. He placed two fingers under her chin, lifted her face to his, and slowly kissed her.

Jo

Oh, what fresh hell was this?

There they both were, Laura Spence and Kate Monro, sitting opposite her in the office while her stack of paperwork grew higher and her inbox overflowed, presenting her with sixty-four signatures from parents protesting LGBTQ awareness in their children. Sixty-four parents of 400 children in the school. Jo suspected she could probably shave off at least twenty, on the grounds that in those families with particularly strong feelings on the matter, mum and dad would both have signed it, not just whichever of them had happened to be on the yard the day Kate Monro accosted them.

Jo said, 'Thank you for bringing this to my attention. I think the best action I can take now is to send out a letter to all parents, in which we detail the information we will be giving to the children. As I've said before, it will all be age-appropriate and will be addressed purely in the context of discussions about families and love. I'm sure I will be able to reassure those people who have any concerns.'

'But we don't want this sort of thing normalised, Ms Fairburn.'

'It is part of the world we live in, Miss Spence. As a school, we have a duty to educate the younger generation and in doing so, help wipe out prejudice. It is part of this school's values ...'

'Can I take my son out of these classes?'

Jo wanted to bang her head against the wall. She ought really to have got her deputy to deal with this, but because Kate and Laura were such prominent fundraising forces, she felt she owed it to them to give them her time.

'We aren't running classes on homosexual sex education. We are simply being open and honest with children as part of daily life in the school. Sometimes, we have lessons on human rights where we look at the right to love without fear in those classes.'

'Then I want to remove my son from those classes.'

Wow. She wanted to withdraw her son from human rights lessons. What a woman.

Jo looked her square in the face. 'I'm afraid we don't allow the removal of children from particular lessons, Miss Spence.'

'Then what can I do?'

'That is entirely your decision. But the curriculum will continue to stand and you will find the same curriculum at all other schools in the country.'

The two women sat in appalled silence for a moment. Then Kate said, 'I would also like to make a formal complaint about another parent I had to deal with when I set up this petition.'

Jo got herself ready to fight. It was going to be Rachel. Of course it was.

'Rachel Saunders,' Kate continued.

Jo nodded. 'OK. Would you like to tell me what happened?'

'Well, she was in Costa with her daughter. Tess. She's here in year one.'

'I know Tess.'

'And so I went up to her and explained the petition. She accused me of trying to shame her because of her relationship – which I knew *nothing* about …'

Bullshit.

'… and then she swore at me. The most vulgar and offensive of all swear words. In front of her child. In front of Tess, who is only six years old. And she also told me where to put the petition. If you get my drift.'

Jo felt her lips twitch. Good old Rachel.

She said, 'Rachel Saunders will have been understandably offended by your petition. I won't defend her language, but what I can tell you unequivocally is that Rachel is a huge supporter of this school. It's possible that she isn't always the finest example of what to say in public—'

'That's an understatement.'

'… but as this fracas happened off school grounds, I don't really see it as being a school matter.'

'But—'

'Is there anything else you want to discuss?'

Both of them looked as though they were about to burst with rage.

Laura said, 'Can I have my son moved to another class?'

Jo sighed. She couldn't help it. She was tired. 'While we do have some flexibility with classes when a child first joins the school, Max will be settled in his class now. He was there all through nursery and reception and now he's in year one. It would be very disruptive to move him at this stage.'

'Right,' Laura said. 'So I have to sit back and put up with the fact that my son is in a class with a child who swears …'

'Her mother swears. We haven't ever heard Tess swear in school.'

'But it's only a matter of time, isn't it? When she's exposed to that sort of language so openly—'

'I can only deal with what I see in school, Miss Spence. So far, there have been no concerns about Tess at all. It isn't the school's place to dictate the language parents use in the privacy of their own homes.'

'But this wasn't the privacy of her own home ...' Kate interrupted.

Jo held up her hand to show she was reaching the end of this conversation. 'It was out of school hours, and away from school property. If a fight had broken out between you and Rachel Saunders on the schoolyard – and I'm sure that would never happen, with you both being adults – then I might have something to say about it. But as it stands, it isn't for me to become involved in a disagreement between two parents.'

'So let me make sure I've got this absolutely right. We have brought you a petition with signatures from more than sixty very concerned parents who want their children protected from learning about homosexuality, and you tell us you're not going to do anything about it. Laura would like her son removed from these classes, but you're not going to allow that either. She then suggested that her son move to another class so he doesn't have to mix with a child who has homosexual parents and who swears, and you say that is impossible. And you don't believe the fact that I was verbally attacked by another parent from this school has anything to do with you?'

Jo nodded sedately. 'I will send a letter to all parents about our LGBTQ curriculum to put everyone's minds at rest.'

Both women pushed back their chairs in silent anger. Jo wondered how the previous head would have dealt with this. Better than Jo, she suspected. But she had no time for this. It was prejudice, plain and simple, and there was no room for it in her school.

'Thank you for bringing your concerns to me,' she said.

She thought about going straight over to Rachel's as soon as she finished work. The trouble with Rachel was that you never knew when she'd be home and Jo also felt slightly uncomfortable at the thought of just dropping round after Rachel's confession that unhappiness was stirring at the big house.

As it turned out, Rachel had been waiting for her. She rang the doorbell so quickly after Jo had stepped inside, Jo felt sure she must have been standing at her living room window, waiting for her.

'That fucking woman,' Rachel stormed, once the initial niceties were out of the way. It was one of the things that most amused Jo about her friend – the discrepancy between her Woman's Hour accent and the trash that came out of her mouth.

'Oh, I know,' Jo said. 'She's completely obnoxious. But don't worry. I have no intention of listening to her.'

Rachel pulled a chair back from the kitchen table and accepted Jo's offer of a glass of wine. 'Does she know that?' she asked, taking a drag on her e-cigarette and blowing berry-scented clouds into the air.

'I met with her after school today. Her and Laura Spence. They're on the rampage. I seemed to do nothing to cool their flames, unfortunately.'

'You know they'll end up on PTA strike if you don't do what they say.'

'That's fine.'

'Did Kate Monro tell you what I said to her?'

'Of course she did.'

'Did you tell her I'm your mate?'

'I think that would be a tactical disaster. But I did defend you.'

Rachel looked thoughtful for a moment, then bleak. 'You know they're not going to leave it at this, don't you?'

'It was certainly the feeling they gave me, I must admit.'

'Do you think they'll arrange a day to go on the rampage through Burntridge and bash all the gays?'

'They might try, but I think you'd have them in a fight. Most people didn't sign the petition, Rachel. The ones who signed are a minority. A large minority, but a minority nonetheless.'

'Did my daughter sign it?'

Jo smiled. 'I didn't see her name.' She paused for a while, then said carefully, 'How are the girls now?'

'Well, let me see … One is still absolutely determined to despise the love of my life forever. She really works hard at it. You can see her just beginning to thaw after Erin has devoted a whole afternoon to playing snakes and ladders without losing the will to fucking live, and then she'll stop herself. It's like she suddenly realises she's been having fun with her and has to revert to rudeness and hatred. The other one … Well, she seems to have moved out.'

'Oh, Rachel. I'm sorry.'

Rachel shrugged. 'It's my own fault. I've pursued my own happiness at my children's expense and now I have to live with the consequences.'

'Don't be so hard on yourself. You aren't the first person in the world to reach a point in your marriage where you can bear it no longer. This stuff happens. The kids will adapt. Has Maia gone to her dad's?'

'Yes. And apparently, he's miserable so she can witness his misery and hate me even more.'

'And Erin? How's she?'

She could actually see Rachel's eyes light up, purely at the mention of the name.

'She's amazing,' Rachel said. 'So patient and supportive, although I wonder what goes on in her head, what she doesn't tell me. She's never going say, *I can't bear your kids. I can't go on living in a house where I am so loathed.* But she must be thinking that, mustn't she? I mean, who wouldn't?'

'She loves you. She'll see it through.'

'Yes, I know. I know she will. It's just that I feel like this thing that was supposed to be good has been bad for everyone. Will, the girls, Erin … None of them are happy, and how can I be happy, knowing I'm the one that caused it?'

'It takes two to break a marriage, Rachel. You know that as well as I do.'

'Yes, and I can tell you, that makes me fucking mad. Will gets to avoid any responsibility for it ending because I'm the one who met someone else. He can just tell everyone it's over because I had an affair and instantly, he's the injured party and none of it had anything to with him.'

'I know. That's how it goes.' She thought of Luke again. The angry son, determined to take his life away from her, to shut her out because she'd broken his home.

'I hope word doesn't get out to the two homophobic witches

84

that my entire family is now falling apart. They'll probably use it as ammunition.'

Jo stayed silent. The thought had crossed her mind as well. She'd seen Kate Monro's type before. Once they took on a cause, they were like a dog with a bone. She suspected Kate would stop at nothing, fuelled by Laura's background rage. Kate struck Jo as being that dangerous combination of a little bit stupid, hugely opinionated and completely lacking in emotional intelligence. She could do a lot of harm, if she really wanted to.

She thought about Laura Spence's troubled son and the bruise on his face. 'Don't worry too much,' she said. 'I've got my eye on those two.'

12

Laura

Her office – she liked to call it that – was just outside Burntridge, in a small building on an industrial estate. Next door to the left was Tommy's Tiles and to the right was Screwfix, while opposite stood Graham White PhD (Plumbing, Heating and Drainage). On Mondays and Wednesdays, a fast food van called *Burger, She Wrote* spent the day parked on the grass verge by the turning from the main road. People here had a sense of humour, at least, although Laura had no idea what writing had to do with burgers. Probably nothing.

Like most mothers at West Burntridge First School, Laura worked part-time. Three afternoons a week, while Max went to after-school club. She told her boss she wanted regular hours and he'd obliged, which surprised her. She'd imagined it would be the sort of work where he'd just phone her if she was needed, but it turned out that the hours between one and five were busy. They were the prime hours for businessmen after lunch meetings, or on their way home to the chaos of their young children and the marriages that had slipped into celibacy because their wives were too damn knackered and too covered in sick and because they'd spent too much time in village halls singing 'The Wheels on the Bus' to feel sexy any more. Also, they wanted their bodies back. All day, they had infants attached to their nipples and toddlers climbing recklessly on to their laps. The last thing they wanted was to climb into bed, roll over and then be poked in the back by a giant, hopeful cock.

Laura stepped off the bus and walked the short distance to the office, which was discreetly situated in the basement of a building that housed above it the head offices of an upmarket soft drinks company and a firm that hired out industrial carpet cleaners. There weren't many visitors to those places, not like Tommy's Tiles and Screwfix which, while not busy exactly, could still rely on several customers passing through each day.

'Afternoon, Evie,' her boss greeted her as she walked into reception. He always called her that.

'Hi,' she said.

He checked a spreadsheet on the computer in front of him. 'Room three today, sweetheart. You've got a couple of bookings so far. First one in fifteen minutes. I expect there'll be more.'

She nodded, reached for the keys from the hook behind his desk, and headed down the corridor to room three. Inside, it was furnished with a double bed, a single wardrobe, a dressing table and a vanity unit with sink. It looked like any couple's bedroom.

She started preparing for her first client: a quick change from her usual mumwear of jeans and a sweater into a tight blue dress over white lace underwear; a long black wig; and slut-red lipstick. She liked that description, *slut-red*. There was defiance to it.

She looked at herself in the mirror. Unrecognisable, but not really any different to anyone else in the world. It was a fact of life. People had to do awful, soul-destroying things for money.

He came in just after five, dressed in his work suit without a tie. He wasn't a bastard, or a dirty old man. He was Will Kernick, heartbroken family man in need of comfort, with nowhere else to go.

For the purpose of business, he called himself Nick.

The trouble was, he was so sweet, he couldn't bring himself to go ahead with it. All he'd done last time was pay for a session, then sit awkwardly in the room with her, unable to reduce himself to becoming a man who paid for sex.

Instead, after she'd tried her best to give him what he'd come here for and taken his shameful refusal on the chin, he'd delivered a fumbled apology and sat for a while with his head in his hands before saying, 'I don't know why I'm here. I'm sorry for wasting your time.'

She didn't care. She had the money. If he wanted to let her rest for an hour instead of work, then that was a welcome relief.

She'd said, 'Would you like me to make you a cup of tea instead?'

He looked at her as though she'd just handed him the world and everything on it. 'Thanks,' he said. 'That would be great.'

She made the tea and brought it to him. 'So,' she said. 'What happened?'

He shook his head. 'I'm not …' he trailed off.

'You're not a man who pays for sex,' Laura said, matter-of-factly.

'No.'

'You're just lonely.'

'I ... I'm shocked and bewildered,' he'd told her, and unleashed the story that had been sitting inside him, desperate to come out and relieve him of its weight.

It looked like he'd come here today for exactly the same reason. She wondered why he didn't see a therapist instead.

'My wife made the money,' he said. 'She wrote a couple of bestselling books.'

Laura didn't know that. She'd assumed Rachel was just paid handsomely for all her research work. 'Really?' she said, with genuine interest. 'Books about what?'

'Non-fiction. Accessible stuff about social issues.'

Oh, of course. Write a book about the hardships of living in chavdom, make a million, drink Dom Perignon for breakfast. Of course that was how it worked.

'How are you managing now?'

'Financially, it's fine,' he told her. 'She's very fair. We split everything fifty-fifty, the way you're supposed to. But it's hard. It's harder than I thought, and I'm angry. I'm angry that she's so happy. How dare she be happy when she's done this to me?'

'Mmm,' Laura murmured, hoping she sounded sufficiently sympathetic.

'I was on Facebook the other day,' he continued. 'Someone was selling bookshelves on a vintage furniture page, and she'd asked how much they were. I thought, 'Why are you doing this?' How can she be thinking about bookshelves while I'm alone in my house, missing her, missing my kids? I couldn't believe she could even speak.'

He wanted her inarticulate with guilt. Laura understood. She'd felt the same way when Max's father walked out. The thing about these people, though, was that they felt no guilt.

They were selfish, selfish arseholes, abandoning their families, leaving a trail of devastation in their wake, then barely glancing back over their shoulders at the mess. They didn't care.

'And how are your children coping?' she asked.

'Badly. I have three. My son's OK, but my daughters aren't. My eldest has just moved in with me, actually.' His face brightened as he spoke, as if he'd only just remembered.

'That's nice.'

'Well, it is nice. I like having her around. She's great. But she left her mother's house because she was unhappy. She was furious. And I don't like her feeling this way. I don't like seeing her so angry. She's a lovely girl. Clever, kind, hard-working. I hate what she's becoming. And my youngest daughter – she's only six – doesn't like the new arrangement at all. She doesn't like my wife's new partner, and now her sister has moved out I think she must be even more unhappy. I suppose she'll adapt in time. I mean, they do, don't they? Everyone says kids are good at adapting.'

'Maybe.'

'Have you got kids?'

Laura shook her head. It was the first rule of work. Never give away personal details.

There was something endearing about the way Will Kernick just prattled on, so unselfconsciously, as if it hadn't even occurred to him to consider who she might be beneath the wig and the make-up, as if calling himself Nick was enough.

He glanced up at the clock. 'I'd better get going,' he said, even though he hadn't used anything like his full hour. 'Thank you,' he added gently. 'I'll see you soon.'

He wasn't her usual sort of client, although there were many like Will who wanted some pretence at loving intimacy as much as they wanted sex. Others were bolder. They came here to act out what they'd seen on screen. Laura could always spot the pornography addicts. When she'd first started this work, when Max was a baby and she was depressed and surrendered her attempts to breastfeed and when she'd spent three days feeding him cold boiled water because there was no money for expensive formula, the porn addicts were quite rare. Now, there were more and more of them – young men usually, who couldn't persuade their near-virginal girlfriends to indulge their fantasies and so paid someone else to do whatever they wanted. They were dangerous fantasies sometimes, and Laura was able to command a lot of money to allow one lad, a returning client, she hadn't seen for months now – to hold his hands to her throat and squeeze and squeeze until she could hardly breathe.

At those times, Laura would close her eyes and feel herself leaving her body, allowing it all to happen to someone who wasn't really her. She'd float above herself, watching and waiting for it all to end. And then she'd go home, and put food on the table for her son.

13

Maia

Maia had been given her school report today. It was good. She'd always had good school reports, all her life. She was clever and she worked hard, and that was all it took to shine. When word reached her teachers that Maia Kernick's parents had separated and now Maia had moved out of the family home because of conflict with her mother, there'd been concern that she might go crazy – start misbehaving in class like troubled kids did, or stop working hard in favour of taking drugs or drinking. Staff made a real movement to support her. The music teacher had asked her to stay behind after class and said she'd always been his shining star and he wanted to help her. He didn't want problems at home to affect her practice or performance. 'Stay strong,' he said. 'We all have high hopes for you, Maia.'

Her English teacher had done the same. 'We want you to take this subject at A level,' she said, 'and possibly beyond. I know you're having some difficulties, but don't let it affect your schoolwork. Just let us know if we can help in any way.'

Maia nodded, but really, what did these idiots think they could do to help? *You can start by making my mother stop being a lesbian.* That was the only way to solve Maia's problems.

None of the other teachers said anything to her directly, but Maia was aware of them watching her sometimes, no doubt thinking, *That's the girl whose mother suddenly became gay at the age of forty-six. She's bound to go off the rails now, like all the other loser kids with loser parents.*

Maia, however, was not going to go off the rails. She'd always liked her status among the handful of the brightest kids in school. She liked it when Mr Holliday asked her to play flute solos in concerts because she was the finest player they had. She liked the fact that she was cleverer than some of her teachers (because she was, and they knew it and so did she). And she realised now that if she could come through her parents' separation and her own dramatic move away from home without even the slightest drop in the standard of her work, everyone would leave her alone. She could keep seeing James or any other boy she felt like and no one would say anything about it because Maia was that wonderful thing that everyone loved: *mature*.

That was the most frequently occurring word in her report. On the first page, her form tutor had written, *Maia remains an intelligent, lively and mature member of the school. If she maintains her current standard of work, she should have no problems achieving the very best results in her exams next summer. As usual, we predict great things for her!*

Mr Holliday said she played with 'depth and maturity'. Her history teacher said the level of insight in her essays showed she was 'mature and very able'. Her English teacher said she showed 'exceptional maturity in her writing.'

She tossed the report on the kitchen table for her dad to find when he came home. She wanted him to see it, of course, but wasn't about to push it into his hands like a little girl desperate to please her parents. No way.

He saw it as soon as he came in, and read it there and then. Maia couldn't mistake the glow of pride on his face. 'This is brilliant,' he said. 'Well done.'

She shrugged. 'It's OK. No one's called me a genius yet, though.'

Her dad smiled at her. 'I think it's implied.' He paused for a moment, then said, 'Are you going to show this to your mum? She'll want to see it.'

'I think she's less bothered about my life than you realise, Dad.'

He spoke sharply, in that old no-nonsense tone he'd always used if one of them said something stupid. 'That's rubbish and you know it.'

'It's not rubbish. It's true. She doesn't care about anything except her revolting lesbian romance. Seriously, Dad. I've never seen anyone so *obsessed*.'

He sighed. 'It's hard, I know, when someone who has always placed you at the centre of their lives suddenly has a new ...'

Maia shot him a look of disdain. 'What, you mean you actually think I'm offended that I'm no longer the centre of attention? You are so off the mark with that one. I can't believe you're ... For God's sake, Dad ...'

He backed down. 'OK. I'm sorry. It's true. She's immersed in a revolting romance and it's making everyone sick. I know.' He smiled, to show he was joking. 'I know you feel like I'm not on your side, Maia, but I am absolutely on your side. It's just that being on someone's side doesn't always involve agreeing with everything they do. I don't want you to cut your mother out of your life because whether you believe it or not at this moment in time, you love her ...'

'I hate her.'

'Same thing.'

'It is not.'

'Look, I understand why you're angry with her. I really do. But you're hurting yourself by cutting her out. Next time she calls, why don't you just answer your phone and ask her if she'd like to see your school report? It puts you in a very strong position. She will only be able to heap praise on you. She'll have nothing at all to be angry with you about because look at you ... You've been through a crisis and you're still brilliant in every way. She'll be proud, and probably humbled.'

'Humbled,' Maia repeated, and laughed. 'I don't think so. Anyway, I'm going over to James's. Is that OK?'

'Sure.' Her dad looked at her for a while, as if wondering whether he should say what was on his mind. Maia braced herself for him to skirt round the issue of sex. *Be good,* he'd probably say, *and if you can't be good, be careful.* And Maia would cringe and blush and they'd both decide he should never mention it again.

Her mum would have been all over the issue. She'd have insisted on lots of long, serious talks, then hauled Maia to the GP for the pill, pretending to be cool about it and yet secretly not being at all cool. She'd give it a few weeks and then from nowhere, she'd find some completely trivial, unrelated thing to have a go at Maia about and they'd both know it was nothing at all to do with the fact that Maia hadn't put her dirty washing in the laundry basket, but because she was having sex. That was the way her mum rolled.

But her dad didn't mention sex, or even hint at it. He just said, 'When do I get to meet this James?'

'You've met him, Dad.'

'I've seen him briefly once when he dropped you off. I'd like to meet him properly.'

'OK. Soon.'

Maia grabbed her coat from where it hung on the back of a chair and headed out.

She'd not actually had sex with James yet, although they'd talked about it. He was worried about her being underage, but she'd be sixteen soon. She thought she'd like to do it on her sixteenth birthday. It could be a coming of age ritual, like an up-to-date bat mitzvah for heathens.

The only trouble was that recently, James had started getting all intense. He kept gazing at her, and when they lay on his bed after they'd been kissing and kissing for ages, he would turn on his side, stroke her face and whisper things she wasn't ready to hear. She didn't want him to be like this.

She liked him, though. She did like him. But she hadn't escaped from her mother's revolting romance just so she could start one of her own, nor had she freed herself from her mother's oppressive regimes only to be tied down by an over-intense boy. Mostly, she just wanted to spend some time with somebody who was on her side about her shambolic family, and to find out what sex was like. She didn't want anyone declaring that they were falling in love with her.

His parents were out. They wouldn't let her stay over, but she was allowed in his room. Maia really liked his mum. Her name was Sasha. James said she was of Lebanese heritage but had a Russian name for no reason that he knew of. Anyway, her family had been in England for three generations now, so what did it matter? Sasha was a Lebanese-English-Russian fusion woman. Mostly English, Maia noted with disappointment. There was nothing cosmopolitan about Burntridge and Maia was longing to meet someone from another culture. She wished she could learn a non-European language so she could spend time abroad in some far-flung place like Tibet or Mongolia, but the only languages on offer at her tedious high school were French and German.

Sasha did, however, cook amazing Middle Eastern food whenever Maia went over. Now, when she wasn't even at home, she'd left brightly patterned bowls all over the kitchen table, full of baba ganoush, tabbouleh, hummus, halloumi, pomegranate seeds and a plate full of lavash to pile everything on to.

'Your mum's amazing,' Maia said, reaching for a plate and loading it with tabbouleh.

James smiled. 'She likes you. She wants to feed you.'

'Really? Cool,' Maia said, taking from this comment that Sasha didn't think she was overweight.

'I think she sees herself as your adopted mum, considering ...'

'Fuck that,' Maia said, through a mouthful of food. 'One's enough. I don't mind her cooking for me, but she'd better not get ideas about nurturing me.'

'I think she'll leave that to me,' James said. He put his arm around her and nuzzled his face into her neck.

Maia pushed him away from her, then leaned forwards and kissed him suggestively on the lips. 'I don't want you to nurture me,' she said.

14

Erin

It kept surprising Erin how frequently she thought of London. Not with longing exactly, but with some kind of undeniable wistfulness for the vast world that used to be outside her door, even though she'd been more than ready to leave it by the time she met Rachel. She'd lived there for nearly twenty years, moving into a series of shabby rooms in shabby house-shares while she carved out a life for herself as a journalist and slowly climbed the ladder towards a decent reputation.

She'd had good friends and the sort of hectic social life people in their twenties somehow managed to combine with full-time work, rolling into the newsroom at 9am bleary-eyed and shaking from too many espressos, and getting straight to work, bashing out reports on last night's burglaries, or a local election campaign, or covering obscure stories from the zoo. Then she'd go home, sleep for a couple of hours, shower and start the evening crawling round Soho bars and finishing up in a kebab shop.

By the time she hit her thirties, the damp rental house-shares had morphed into a one-bedroom flat and a mortgage in Primrose Hill, she'd become a features writer and one by one, her friends were disappearing. The raucous nights dwindled. Even those who swore they were never going to succumb to convention started succumbing to convention, and Erin had to start dutifully dressing in her finest and going to weddings, where she witnessed the tragedy of women she respected throwing feminism to the wind and allowing themselves to be gifted from one man to another while they dressed in white and wore veils and thought this intrinsically sexist rite of passage was something for others to aspire to.

Erin was aware of being the only person who thought this way. She started to see weddings not as celebrations, but farewells: one last, lavish party before the happy couple shut their doors on the world. After that, Erin would hear from them mostly through Facebook – sharing photos of things they'd cooked, castles they'd visited and then, inevitably, the twelve-week foetus they'd created.

They'd been swallowed up, all of them, by the domestic machine. All that deliberate happiness. They would never understand if she tried to explain how frightening she found their world. Her own relationships were always short-lived. A flurry of passion, a brief infatuation and then all she wanted was her life back. She hated it when men stayed over and left their belongings in her flat, like excuses to return. The sight of a man's towel draped over her bathroom door carried the threat of someone trying to force their way in. At the very least, she needed them to take their shit home with them. She liked to know her relationships would be easy to dismantle.

But now here she was. Swallowed up by the domestic machine. Rachel's domestic machine. She'd given all her friends reason to believe they'd been absolutely right when they talked about her commitment phobia and said, 'Underneath, she's just longing to fall in love and have a hundred babies. She'll turn to mush in the end.'

There was no point trying to hold any of it to reason. Maybe she'd just been waiting for the right time. The right man. The right woman. In fact, maybe the reason men had made her nauseous all those years was because she simply hadn't realised …

How could she not have realised? She'd asked Rachel that the other day and Rachel said, 'Who knows? But you're here now, and that's all that matters.'

It was true. She was here, and it was all that mattered.

She sat at the kitchen table flicking through one of the women's magazines Maia had left behind when she moved out. Maia had actually left nearly everything behind when she'd moved out, which Rachel took as a sign that she might come home one day, but which Erin saw as the laziness of youth. She'd be back for her things if she ever needed them, and if she wasn't, then her mother would just tidy them away for her and keep them hopefully until such a time as Maia spoke to her again.

Reuben passed through the room on his way to the back door. 'See you later, Erin,' he said. 'I've got band practice. Tell mum Alfie's dad's giving me a lift back. I'll be home about eleven.'

Erin smiled at him. 'OK. Have fun.'

She watched him haul his guitar through the door. He gave her a funny sort of half-salute as he left, which made her grin. So far, he'd been the easiest of all Rachel's children. He didn't seem to harbour the resentment the girls both felt. She saw him as quite wonderfully sociable, welcoming anyone who would let him talk to them, which Erin did because she hadn't talked to a young person for years and found his enthusiasm for life refreshing. He told her the details of his history homework, about where his band would have their next gig, which places he planned to put down on his UCAS form and Erin remembered that excitement, the excitement of having the world at your feet and the absolute certainty that the future would be kind to you.

Maia was the most difficult one at the moment, though Erin couldn't blame her for that. God, it must have been awful to see what she'd seen. Awful.

The thought of it still made Erin's cheeks flame. Never before had she had such a profound longing for time travel. She'd love to just wind her way back through the weeks and stop it from ever happening, to keep Maia from walking in and stop Rachel's heart from breaking. Because it had broken, Erin knew that, despite Rachel's best attempts at bravado.

Still, Erin couldn't help but admire Maia's spark. She knew what she wanted – domestic peace, and safety from witnessing her mother's sexual practices – and she wasn't going to stick around in a home that didn't give it to her. She was more like Rachel than either Rachel or Maia would admit. Clever, confident, a ruthless taker of no shit.

Still, Erin thought, even Maia couldn't place herself beyond reach of these stupid magazines full of devastatingly bland ideas about what constituted a decent job and a good shag. On this one page alone, the instances of terrible journalism were rife. The model was described as *olive-skinned*. Erin wanted to find whoever had written this and interrogate them. 'Have you ever actually seen an olive?' she'd ask. 'No one has olive skin. Aren't you really just reiterating an unthinking racist shorthand for *the not-quite-white skin of someone from a place where olives grow*?'

But whoever had written this article would probably just stare at her and think she was a twat from the *Guardian*. Which she was. Or used to be. In the days before she gave it up and went freelance so she could be with the woman she loved.

She would never have done this for a man. Never.

Rachel was on her way home with a Friday night takeaway and some beers. Erin thought about heading through to the living room and telling Tess that Mummy was bringing her a chicken korma and some poppadoms, but thought better of it. The child was glued to some apparently endless episodes of a terrible cartoon and wouldn't welcome the intrusion from this most wicked of stepmothers. It wouldn't be too bad if she just ignored her, but Erin wasn't sure she could face another one of Tess's angry looks and the devastating, 'So?' which carried in all its scathing brutality the unspoken: *You're not my mum. Why are you talking to me? Why are you even looking at me? Go away. I hate you. And get your hands off my mother.*

Then again, maybe she should. To stride in there, hailing news of chicken korma and poppadoms just five minutes away, could only be a good thing. Perhaps Tess would do something wild, like smile. Still, that had been the plan with buying the puppy. Erin had presented it to Tess herself just after she'd moved in, and look what happened there. No one gave a shit about the dog and all Erin had done was lumber herself with something that needed walking twice a day and required her to carry poo in a plastic bag, in some grotesque mockery of an accessory.

She was overthinking it. Tess was a child, for goodness' sake. A grown woman of forty-three should not be afraid to walk into a room and tell a six-year-old that her mother was on her way home with a takeaway. This absolutely shouldn't be happening. A few years ago, Erin had walked the ganglands of Johannesburg with a notebook and camera so she could write a feature, and she hadn't felt as afraid as this.

Dear God, she thought, *what have I become?*

She decided to do it. She pushed the trashy magazine aside and stood up purposefully. It was an insanely long walk from one end of the kitchen to the other and by the time she'd reached the door to the living room, she was poised and steady.

'Tess,' she said, beginning another long walk, this time to the sofa, where Tess was sitting with her legs curled beside her, her hand resting against Potato's soft brown back. A stranger coming into the room right now would probably melt at this scene of a pyjama-clad small girl and her dog watching TV together, but the stranger had no idea of the resentment this child was capable of nurturing, the fear she could instil in a grown woman.

'Tess, some good news. Mummy's on her way home and she's bringing a takeaway!' Erin had never spoken in exclamation marks before. Now, she did it all the time. Look how exciting life is! Please like me! I'm trying really hard here!

Tess turned her head away from the screen and faced Erin. The promise of food got the better of her and she smiled. 'Really?' she squeaked. 'With poppadoms? Oh, yummy!'

Quickly, Erin decided she should make the most of this

moment before it slipped away. She sat down on the sofa, a safe distance from Tess, with the small body of Potato acting as a furry shield between them.

'Mind if I watch this with you?'

'If you like.'

'What's happening?'

Tess shrugged. Erin realised it probably wasn't complicated or suspenseful and there wasn't a great deal to summarise. Thank God. As far as she could see, the plot was hanging on a drive through the countryside, where the weather was doing crazily unpredictable things, and hark! There it was: a rainbow and a terrible song.

They sat together in a silence that wasn't completely awkward, and Erin felt a stirring of hope for the future.

The three of them ate dinner together and Tess managed to sustain her good mood. 'Mum,' she said, 'guess who I've got for the weekend?'

Rachel shot Erin a brief amused look, then said, 'Not Teacher Ted?'

'Yep.' Tess jumped up and ran out of the room, as she frequently did during mealtimes. She returned with a diary and a grubby, ancient-looking bear in formal academic dress dangling from her hand and passed them both to her mother.

Rachel opened the diary. Erin could see photos and various adult scrawls over the pages.

'Oh, for fuck's sake. Would you look at this?' She started reading out loud, 'We took Teacher Ted to our house in Windermere for the weekend. He enjoyed rowing on the lake with Daddy.' She flicked through a few more pages, 'Teacher

Ted played golf … Teacher Ted went to the spa … Jesus wept. Tess, go and find the Argos catalogue, would you? It's under the hall table.'

Tess ran off again. Rachel said, 'I refuse to join in with this. I refuse to get competitive over which family gave Teacher fucking Ted the best weekend. It drives me insane.'

'Here,' Tess said, hauling the catalogue on to the table.

Rachel sat the bear against a pint of Black Sheep. 'What do you think he should buy, Tess?' she asked. 'A bag to put his potatoes in?'

Tess thought about it. 'Maybe a bike?'

'Too expensive,' Erin said, finding herself unexpectedly swept up in this game.

Tess opened to the toy section. 'A plastic poo?'

'Perfect,' Rachel declared, and brought her phone out of her back pocket. 'Right, arrange the catalogue so we can see the poo. We need to get the beer in as well. Brilliant.' She snapped a couple of photos and showed them to Erin and Tess. 'Teacher Ted got off his face and pissed away all his money on plastic poo from Argos.'

Tess laughed, delighted. 'I'll be in so much trouble.'

Erin looked at Rachel. 'No wonder all the parents hate you,' she said.

But dammit, she loved this woman.

15

Rachel

Rachel's illusions had been shattered hard enough for her to know this couldn't last, but for the moment, Tess was happy again. They'd had a great evening last night, just the three of them; eating, having a laugh and then teaching Tess how to play Cluedo. Then, once Tess was asleep and there were still hours till Reuben was due home, she and Erin had gone to bed and they'd actually successfully made love for the first time since that last, disastrous encounter on the kitchen floor. Finally, Rachel had been able to close her eyes in pleasure without the image of her fifteen-year-old daughter bulldozing its way into her head and putting an end to everything.

She didn't like to admit it, and she would still cut her right hand off if it would bring her home, but Maia's absence had lightened the atmosphere in the house. At first, Rachel had worried and worried about Tess. She'd been afraid that her sister moving out would give Tess one more reason to be miserable, and possibly even that Tess would want to move in with her dad as well. The thought of it was unbearable and added to Rachel's guilt, giving her as it did a small glimpse into the way Will must be feeling all the time. But although Tess had responded badly to the change of Erin moving in, the change of Maia moving out barely seemed to have made it on to her radar. Unpredictable, that's what her daughter was. Unpredictable and wonderful.

Now, they were in Burntridge, shopping for new PE trainers. The puppy had eaten Tess's last pair, much to Rachel's annoyance and Tess's delight. Once they'd finished, they were going to have lunch at the cathedral café because it was usually full of old people instead of parents and their children, and Rachel wasn't in the mood for bumping into other parents today. That was the trouble with Burntridge. It was a small town. You bumped into people everywhere.

'I love these,' Tess declared, picking up a pair of white trainers with Buzz Lightyear on them. Rachel checked the price. Forty quid.

'No,' she said. 'Absolutely not.'

Tess's face fell, 'But Mum, look,' she said, turning them upside down and showing her the heel, 'you get a toy Buzz Lightyear in them.'

'Oh, that explains it,' Rachel said. 'I am not spending forty pounds on a pair of shoes with a toy in them. You need them for PE, Tess.'

'Everyone else has them.'

'I'm sure they do, darling. That's because everyone else is the offspring of at least one idiot.'

'Why can't I get them?'

'Because no one needs a pair of trainers with a toy in the heel. Seriously, Tess. No one. And you will lose it. Within five minutes of getting home, you will lose that piece of plastic and you know all about the problem of plastic pollution, don't you?'

'Well, yes. But—'

'Exactly. Very soon, probably by the end of today, that vile little Buzz Lightyear will be making its way to the Pacific Ocean, where it will be eaten by a dolphin and then the dolphin will be washed up on a beach and after an autopsy it will be declared on the front page of the *Guardian* – probably by Erin – that a completely unnecessary piece of plastic from a child's trainer was found in the body of a dead dolphin. I can't live with that, Tess. Can you?'

'Well …'

'No, you can't.' She turned to the shop assistant. 'Excuse me. Have you got any trainers without plastic Buzz Lightyears in them?'

'We have some with Woody, or Bonnie.'

'Yes, Mum! Woody!'

Oh dear God.

Suddenly, Tess said, 'Look! It's Max. Hi, Max. Are you getting shoes as well?'

Rachel glanced at Erin. They each heard the other silently saying, *Oh fuck.*

Laura, Max's mother, stood before them, her face visibly registering the sight of two loathsome lesbians attempting to buy trainers for a child that only belonged to one of them.

Don't do it, Rachel told herself. *Don't raise the issue. Don't cause a scene.*

She opened her mouth to say hello, politely but unmistakably coldly, as the situation deserved. 'Hi, Laura,' she said. 'How's your homophobic campaign coming along? I hear the petition didn't get as many signatures as you wanted.'

Bollocks. She knew without looking that beside her, Erin's

eyes would be closing in a moment of embarrassed resignation as she braced herself for a fight that could have been avoided if only Rachel had kept her mouth shut.

Laura, who had the courage to be confrontational only if she never actually had to confront the person she was confronting, squirmed. 'Well, we …' Her voice trailed off and she looked away for a moment, then grabbed her son's hood with her fist, ready to drag him away, kicking and screaming if it came to it. 'Max, I don't think they have what we're looking for in here.'

He stared at her in horror and dismay. 'But—'

Rachel smiled at him sweetly. 'What is it you're looking for, Max?'

'*Toy Story* trainers.'

'Ah, right. They have got them. We'd better head off before Tess starts World War Three. She's not allowed them.'

Laura smirked. Rachel didn't ask why.

'Come on, Tess,' she said. 'We'll go and have a look in the other place across the road.'

'But I want to stay with Max.'

'We'll invite Max over for tea one day soon. Oh, hang on …'

'*Rachel*,' Erin said, through gritted teeth.

'OK, let's go.' She took hold of Tess's hand and made a move towards the front of the shop. 'Nice to see you, Laura. Best of luck with your campaign.'

16

Jo

The day had started out badly and was getting worse. At eight o'clock this morning, Luke had texted to say he was coming home for a while. He didn't give reasons, or say exactly how long *a while* would be, but he'd be arriving this evening and Jo suspected he'd discovered that money didn't stretch as far as he thought it would in London, that he was probably completely skint and planned to hang around for as long as she'd have him.

She'd warned him about this, she noted, even as she reminded herself that she absolutely must not mention that small detail when he turned up. But she had warned him, lots of times. 'London is very expensive, Luke,' she'd said. 'How are you going to live?' He'd made some dismissive gesture, full of youth and optimism and arrogance, and told her London was where everything happened and that he couldn't be expected to fester in this northern backwater all his life, especially now his family had broken up and all its component pieces scattered.

He was good at that, so good at hurting her with his injuries, so good at blaming her for her failed marriage and his subsequent lack of a home. 'You've got a home, Luke,' she told him. 'You can stay here whenever you need to. Your dad will always have you, too. You know that.

Luke had merely grunted, and mumbled about it not being the same. *Of course it's not the same,* she wanted to say. *You're an adult. You and Rebecca have grown up and gone, and I need a life.*

But that, she knew, was the problem. It was exactly why Luke blamed her for the break-up of her marriage. He thought of Jo as the difficult one and, as far as she could tell, it was mainly because she dared to have a pulse. His father was so easy-going, no one could possibly blame him for anything. He didn't argue, didn't shout, made no demands, wanted nothing more than his home and his family. Why would any woman want to leave a man like that? She'd had plenty of reasons. *Because I feel like I'm already in my grave. Because he has no passion. Because he doesn't want to do anything except count money, look at funeral plans and prepare for death. I'm only fifty and he forces me to live as though I'm eighty.*

She hadn't been able to explain that to her son, though. Instead, she gave him some money for his first month's rent for a damp and poky room in a damp and poky house in Walthamstow, and told him he needed to get a job. Any job would do, she said, but she knew Luke well enough to know any job *wouldn't* do and that he'd retreat to this northern backwater within six months, cursing the television industry for its nepotism and failure to give him a job as Head of the BBC.

All this was still playing on her mind when one of the teaching assistants came to tell her that Max Spence had lost all control during maths. Now, her own son temporarily forgotten, Jo was crouched before Max in the quiet room, trying to soothe his anguish. The fury that boiled over so suddenly had given way now to a heavy sobbing that rendered him speechless. He sat on a soft chair while Jo placed a hand that was meant to be firm but comforting on his shoulder. Two hands, she thought, would be too much, too intimidating. It would feel to Max like restraint. One hand on one shoulder by a caring grown-up patiently waiting for the tears to stop was the right balance. Hopefully.

The crying slowed. She handed him a tissue. 'There. Dry your eyes, Max, and give your nose a wipe.'

He did as she asked, and smeared snot all over his face. She took another tissue and cleaned him up. He looked so sorrowful sitting there, his eyes red and swollen. The urge to hold him on her lap and wrap her arms around him was almost overwhelming, but physical affection wasn't advised any more. There was a risk it could open a floodgate in children who weren't held enough at home, make them want to do nothing but sit on teachers' laps with their thumbs in their mouths, like babies. It wouldn't be helpful to anyone.

'Now, Max,' she said gently. 'What brought all this on?'

He shook his head. She wondered if he could even remember. His teacher said it all kicked off when she'd asked him to swap places with another child because his mother had requested that he no longer sit with Tess Kernick. He didn't react well to even the slightest change. He built his secure, familiar world around himself. Pull one brick out and the whole thing came crashing down.

'Would you like a drink?'

He nodded, and she headed across the room to the water cooler in the corner. When she turned round again, he'd taken his jumper off. There were fresh-looking bruises on both his arms.

She handed him the cup of water. Lightly, she said, 'Those bruises look nasty. How did you get them?'

He shrugged and wouldn't look at her. 'Don't know.'

She couldn't ask him outright. She couldn't just say, 'Does your insanely angry mother beat you, Max?' She needed to pave the way for him to tell her himself, which was never easy. They worked on these things in school periodically. Class teachers played videos from the NSPCC, with songs about how adults shouldn't touch you beneath your pants, or beat you. There was advice on what to do if an adult ever did touch you beneath your pants, or beat you. It usually involved telling a teacher, who would tell the head, who would phone social services and all hell would let loose, usually right in the middle of preparing year six for their SATs, although now she was working in Northumberland, the only SATs she had to contend with were the softer ones in year two. The hardcore SATs were for the middle schools to deal with.

She could ask Max's teacher to show the video again, to children in small groups. Nothing too obvious, nothing too threatening. Just a group of four children in a room with a teaching assistant, watching a video about what to do if your mad mother was beating you up.

Carefully, Jo said, 'Will Mummy be picking you up from school today?'

He nodded, and gave nothing away.

She'd have loved the chance to speak to Rachel about this, find out what her thoughts were. This was right up Rachel's alley: a bit of poverty, an absent father, a mother permanently enraged, a bruised child. She would absolutely know what to do with this. But there was the problem of confidentiality and also, Rachel had her own prejudices now. Jo wouldn't ever suspect her of judging the situation with anything other than sound professionalism, but Rachel on the rampage was as bad as Laura Spence on the rampage. Rachel just rampaged with a touch more charm and a subtler, though far more savage, bite. Laura was likely about to realise this. She didn't stand a chance against Rachel Saunders.

Max said, 'I don't want to go home.'

'Why's that, Max?'

'I like it here.'

Jo understood that when he said *here* he didn't mean school, but this room overlooking the wildlife pond in the school garden, where it was quiet and everything was soft to the touch. There were beanbags and comfy chairs and books. Nothing more. It was meant to be a haven of tranquillity for children like Max, those who were prone to acting out their troubles with aggression instead of words.

She said, 'You can stay here until you feel calmer, Max, and you're ready to go back to your classroom.'

He shook his head. 'Don't want to go back,' he said.

She was no psychologist, but she wondered if she'd stumbled over the root of his problem. A deep longing for peace, and space from other people.

Laura Spence was a closed book.

'We had another incident with Max this morning,' Jo told her gently. 'His teacher said he erupted very suddenly and without provocation, for no reason that was clear to anybody.'

'What did he do, exactly?'

'He stood up and started shouting that he hated everyone, and he threw his chair – luckily not very far – and then hurled himself to the floor and kicked.'

'I'm sorry,' Laura said.

'As you know, we already have him in an intervention group to try and help with this sort of thing—'

'But it's not helping.'

'It doesn't seem to be.'

'So we need to think about what else we can do to help him.' Never in her career had Jo excluded a child from school, no matter how difficult. She would move heaven and earth before doing that.

'Like what?' Laura asked. She was unmistakably colder since Jo had refused to act on her petition.

'Our SEN coordinator, who has obviously been working with Max since he joined us in nursery and knows him far better than I do, has suggested we might ask the educational psychologist to do an assessment.'

Laura was silent for a while. Jo let her suggestion sink in.

'I don't think my son is ill, Ms Fairburn.'

'Oh, no. Not at all. But sometimes it can help get to the root of a child's behavioural problems. I think it might help.'

'My main concern is that he stops sitting next to Tess Kernick.'

'I'm not convinced that sitting next to Tess has been causing him any difficulties, Miss Spence. And we have moved him. We moved him today.'

Laura breathed an audible sigh of relief. 'Well, that's good. Tess has been talking to him, telling him how her mother lives with another woman she doesn't like, and it's been upsetting Max. I think he'll improve now.'

Jo bypassed that comment and went straight to her main concern. 'Does Max bruise easily, Miss Spence?' she asked.

'What do you mean?'

'We noticed some bruising on his arms today when he took his jumper off. We wondered how it happened.'

'Max hurts himself sometimes when he throws his temper tantrums.'

'Right. That would make sense.'

'I try and move him somewhere safe, where there's space for him to fling himself around without getting hurt, but my flat is small and he's getting heavier all the time.' She looked at Jo and added, 'I'm doing my best, Ms Fairburn.'

'I know.'

'I'm not a bad mother,' she added, dabbing at her eyes with her forefinger. 'I don't,' she said, looking at Jo squarely, 'I don't hurt my son.'

17

Laura

Suddenly, out of nowhere, the message Laura used to long for pinged into her life and knocked her sideways. It arrived on Messenger, complete with a thumbnail photo of the sender. *Drew Fuller.*

She saw the name and gasped. Then she shook for a while, but whether from fear, anger or excitement, she couldn't say.

Dear Laura, the message began. **I know you probably don't want to hear from me and you have every right to be angry.**

Here she raised her eyebrows and thought, *Yes, I bloody well do have every right to be angry, you bastard.*

He went on, **But believe me when I say that not a day has gone by over the last five years when I haven't thought about you and Max.**

She nearly spat at that. A day? What about an hour? How about *Not an hour has gone by when I haven't been tormented by what a prick I am?* But even that wasn't good enough. *Not a minute* would be better, or *not a second.* That was more like it. *Not a second has gone by when I haven't thought about drinking a bottle of vodka and hurling myself of a clifftop after what I did to you.*

His message was going badly.

Then he came to the point. **I would like to meet my son. I will understand if you don't want me to, but please think about it. I just want to visit him now and then. It is right that a child should know his father.**

She read it again, feeling the rapid burn of familiar rage. There was no mention of money, no acknowledgement of the fact that he'd contributed nothing to Max's life since the day he walked out on them five years ago. He just wanted to see him. Laura wondered what his idea of fatherhood had become now. Did he imagine hauling his son up in his arms and throwing him into the air, perhaps taking him to the beach in the summer, watching films on rainy Sunday afternoons? She would put money (if she had any) on the fact that he'd have given no thought to the daily realities of keeping him fed, clothed, educated, disciplined. No. He'd just dreamed up some idea of a small boy he could have fun with and then hand back to his mother so she could do the real stuff, the hard stuff, the soul-crushingly exhausting stuff.

She let her fingers hover over the keys for a while as she considered a reply. What she really wanted was to type out a response that was cold and brutal, something like, *Max and I are doing very well. We have no need to think about you because we spend all our time having picnics in the woods. Come and visit him if you like, but don't expect him to be pleased to see you. He has everything he needs and is very happy.*

But it wasn't true, and nothing she could say would ever make it true. A future began to unfurl before her, a future in which Max knew his dad and his behaviour improved, and his dad paid some maintenance, and she had a break, and someone to share this load with.

Dear Drew, she wrote …

Her boss had asked her to put in some extra hours to cover one of the girls who'd gone AWOL. She didn't mind. She needed the money after buying those trainers for Max. Forty quid. Forty quid for a pair of trainers, but the other children had them and he so desperately wanted to be like the other children, so she'd bought them for him. He was delighted. And now she was skint.

The trouble was, the hours her boss offered her were the night-time hours. Ten till two. The hours of drunks and depressives and bastards. But the money was better. She just had to bear it and she'd learnt ways of bearing it over the years. It was Max that was the problem now. There was no one she could ask to babysit at that time. She thought about messaging his dad. *Could you come and look after your son for the first time ever while I have sex for money because you left us with nothing?*

She couldn't do that, obviously, and the thought she'd been having too often since she received his message came to her again. What if, after meeting his son, he decided he wanted custody of him? What if he found out how she earned a living and had her declared an unfit mother?

She had to shake the thoughts away. She checked her watch. Nine-fifteen. She'd told her boss she'd be there, ready to start work at ten. There were no buses at this time of night so he was sending a taxi to pick her up. He was a good boss in that respect.

She wandered across the landing to Max's room. He was fast asleep in his cabin bed, snuggled up beneath his Spider-Man duvet. She climbed the first two steps of the ladder so she could look at him properly: flushed face against the pillow, one arm flung out from beneath the covers, his warm little body safe and protected.

Nothing could harm him, she knew that. He would sleep through her absence, deeply and peacefully, and when he woke, she'd be home again. She knew because she'd done it before and everything had been fine.

She leaned over and put her lips to his forehead. 'Love you, Max,' she whispered, and went outside to meet her taxi.

18

Rachel

She bumped into him on the corner, just between the marketplace and the shop that changed hands every six months, currently failing to sell cheap, faux-leather handbags. It was bound to happen eventually. You couldn't avoid anyone in Burntridge and for weeks now, Rachel had been unhealthily preoccupied with trying to orchestrate an accidental meeting with Maia. Twice she'd left work early so she could casually roam up and down the high street just after school, when Maia was most likely to be heading to Costa or Maddison's with her friends.

It hadn't happened. Instead, she'd just met Will hurrying back to his car with an armload of vegetables he'd bought from a market stall because he was a good man – oh God, he was such a good man – and committed these days to avoiding the plastic packaging of Waitrose.

She saw him notice her, then watched as his eyes darted in all directions, as if looking for a place to hide. He probably was. She was, too. But it was too late. They were there and they had to speak to each other. Those vegetables in his arms were going to serve as a good excuse for a getaway, though.

No one could stand around for long with four leeks, a bunch of beetroot and a cauliflower weighing them down like that.

'Hi,' she said.

'Hi, Rachel.' He spoke warmly. Of course he spoke warmly. He was a good man. He didn't hold grudges.

All she could think as she stood there was the fact that she knew what he looked like under his clothes – the body that had once been so familiar, but which, over the years, had slowly become less and less desired by her and more and more clothed by him, so that now here they were: standing opposite each other with a gulf between them full of awkward memories of ancient intimacy.

She wondered if he'd found anyone to have sex with yet. Unless he'd strayed during their marriage – and she was almost sure he wouldn't have done, even at the worst times, because he was a good man – then he hadn't had sex since the night they'd conceived Tess. According to certain recent (though controversial) research, this meant he was probably well on his way to prostate cancer.

She tried to shake the thoughts away. It was, after all, none of her business, and she wished she wouldn't think things like this.

'How're things?' she asked. 'How's Maia?'

'Maia's fine,' he said. 'It's great having her around.'

She nodded. Of course it was, and he deserved to have her around. It was just …

'I miss her,' she said.

'I know.'

'I understand why she left and why she doesn't want to come home. Has she told you,' she said, trying to keep her voice casual, 'why she moved out?'

'Only that she doesn't like the new arrangement. She said she didn't want the new way of life she was given and she thought she was old enough to change it if she wanted to.'

'That's fair enough,' Rachel said, and despite everything, she had a moment of pride in her daughter for taking control of her life like that, and also for not hurting her father with the details of that awful night.

Unless Will was protecting her with a lie. It was the sort of thing he'd do.

Will said, 'She's OK. I think she'll come round. She misses you.'

'Does she? Does she say that?'

'You know Maia. It's the way she works so hard at *not* saying it that makes me sure.'

'I've been worried, Will. I'm so afraid I've lost her.' She could hear the slight waver in her voice and noticed Will's raised eyebrow. In twenty years, he'd only seen her cry once, and even then it had been in anger rather than sorrow.

'You haven't lost her,' he said. 'She's fifteen and you're her mother. She'll come round.'

'She's ignored all my attempts to contact her for weeks now.'

'Look, I need to get this stuff to the car. I forgot my bags. I always forget my bags. But she's in the bookshop if you want to go and find her. I said I'd wait in the car park and drive her home.'

'Thank you,' Rachel said. 'Thank you so much, Will.'

'It's fine. And also, I wanted you to know I didn't sign that awful petition drawn up by those awful women.'

Rachel smiled. 'I never thought you would.'

He looked at her for a moment, then said, 'Have the battle lines been drawn?'

'They certainly have.'

'Oh, dear. Poor Kate Monro. I fear she doesn't know who she's taking on.'

'She'll learn,' Rachel assured him, and walked away to find her daughter.

19

Maia

James's mum was cooking again. Maia sat on a bar stool in the kitchen and watched, then caught herself. She should think of her as *Sasha*, not *James's mum*. It was against any kind of feminist principle to reduce a woman to her maternal role.

'What are you making?' she asked.

Sasha glanced up from the huge chopping board and said, '*Hashweh*. It's just rice with mince, nuts, cinnamon and dried fruit, but James loves it so I make it a lot. It's all a part of my plan to keep him coming home once he moves out. Don't ever tell him this, but the recipe I gave him for it is inferior, so he'll never be able to make it as well as I can. Eventually the time will come when he says to his mates, "I can't see you this weekend. I have to go home to my mum's for *hashweh*".' She looked at Maia for a moment and frowned. 'I hope it works.'

Maia laughed. 'I'm sure it will,' she said, 'although I reckon he'll keep coming home without that.'

Sasha shook her head. 'I doubt it. I'll need a hook, something more exciting than his tedious, ancient mother, to lure him back to the grim North.'

Maia didn't think Sasha was tedious. She thought Sasha was

great: friendly, fun, not at all strict, open to hearing ideas other than her own (unlike Maia's mother, who was enlightened and therefore always right) …

Sasha went back to chopping. Then, without looking and with a studied casualness, she said, 'I saw your mum on TV this evening.'

'Yeah, she's always on TV.' Maia rolled her eyes.

'It must be amazing, to have such a clever, successful mother.'

'Everyone always thinks that, but it's not really. I mean, it's cool that she's clever and stuff, but really, she's not as clever as everyone thinks.'

'No?'

'No. Like, she doesn't understand why I have a problem with what she does.'

Sasha looked up again. 'Really? You have a problem with it? She's amazing. All that research. She's helping to bring about real change in the world.'

'Yes, but …' Maia leaned forwards earnestly. 'Don't you think it's patronising? All these studies into poor people, all this banging on about what life is like for poor people and how bad it is. I'm sorry, but have you seen our house? My mother has shit all idea of what it's like to be poor. She went to Cheltenham Ladies' College … They must be so ashamed … But seriously, why do the people of Sunderland and Hartlepool and wherever else need my mother to tell their stories? Let them tell their own stories, manage their own protests. If I were poor and some posh woman in a fancy coat and a £100 lipstick came to interview me so she could write a bestselling book about me and keep all the money, I'd slap her one.'

Sasha laughed. 'I suppose that's one way of looking at it.'

'Seriously, though. Everyone admires my mother for *changing the world* but all she's doing is stealing other people's voices and telling their stories for them. It would be much better to get them to tell their own stories.'

'Maybe that will come next.'

'I hope so, but I bet my mother will find a way to take the credit.'

'You sound very angry with your mother, Maia,' Sasha observed lightly.

'I am.'

'James told me a bit about it. It's hard, going through all that at your age. I'm sorry it's happening to you. But you'll be OK, Maia.'

'I'm already OK.'

Sasha smiled. 'I can see that. What I mean is: you'll be even more OK.'

Her mum had caught her off-guard yesterday by bumping into her in the bookshop. Maia still wasn't sure whether it was part of a plan her dad had colluded in, or whether it had been a genuine accident. Her mother had carried the look of a huntress about her, so Maia suspected the latter, but either way, she'd walked in and found her browsing the study guide section like the sort of daughter other parents could only dream of.

'Maia,' she said.

Maia turned round and there she was, the woman she'd vowed she would never speak to again.

For a moment, they looked at each other in silence, then Maia said, 'Oh. Hi.'

'Do you want to grab a coffee?'

'Are you on your own?'

'Yes.'

'All right, then.'

They went to the café above the deli and ordered two flat whites and a slice of chocolate cream cake to share.

'So,' her mum said. 'How are you?'

'Fine.'

'I'm glad I bumped into you. I've missed you.'

Maia gazed at her coffee. She hated this. She should never have come. Even now, weeks later, she couldn't look at her mother without being flooded by memories of *that* night: the image, and the sounds. The sounds were the worst part. Maia had vowed she'd never make such revolting noises in her life.

Her mother went on, 'I understand that you needed to leave, Maia. And honestly, I admire you for taking control of a situation you were unhappy with.'

That was a well-rehearsed load of bollocks if ever she'd heard it.

'And I am sorry I caused you that unhappiness.'

To her shame and surprise, Maia felt the sudden sting of tears in her eyes. She fought hard not to let her mother see and instead concentrated on sighing and continuing to stare at her coffee. When she was sure she was under control again, she looked up and said, coolly but not nastily, 'OK.'

Her mother sighed and pushed it no further. Instead, with what struck Maia as forced brightness, she said, 'So your birthday's coming up.'

'Yep.'

'I'd like to take you out. Just you and me. Anywhere you want.'

Maia couldn't help it. She paused with her coffee spoon in

mid-air (she never drank the first centimetre's depth of any coffee, but spooned it into her mouth like soup), tilted her head to one side, smiled and said, 'Really? Anything?'

A shadow crossed her mother's face. 'Erm … Yes, I think so.'

'Even if it involved a musical?'

'Oh Christ.'

'*Les Misérables* is coming to Newcastle.'

Maia had always loved musicals, ever since she was two and her dad had shown her *Oliver!* Her mother hated them. Maia wasn't sure why, but suspected it had something to do with the cultural snobbery her mother would never admit was deeply ingrained in her. *Low art*, that's what she'd call it if she could ever bear to be honest and use such a term. Lower than graffiti, which according to her mother had an important place in some kind of rebellious subculture. But there was no excuse for musicals.

'OK. I'll book tickets.'

'Thanks Mum.'

Her mum smiled, showing a clear mixture of love and happiness and relief, and Maia felt oddly guilty, and then annoyed with herself. She'd vowed never to speak to this woman again, and yet here she was, agreeing to spend her birthday with her. Weakness, that's what it all came down to – a stupid failure to stand up for herself and make her own desires clear. What she should have said, back when they were in the bookshop, was, 'Thanks for the offer but no, I don't want to have coffee with you.'

Maia realised now that she was trapped, just like everyone else, into obedience in the face of her mother.

She drained the rest of her coffee quickly. She needed to free herself from all this.

20

Laura

Preparing Max to meet his father was a three-pronged process. To start with, she had to tell him that he had a father in the first place, and that he was a very definite four-dimensional man rather than some faint, far-flung abstraction whose face Laura could barely recall. Until now, whenever Max asked, Laura had been evasive about both his father's identity and his whereabouts. 'You do have a daddy, Max,' she'd said, 'but he was very young and ...' She never really knew how to round the story off. *He left us without saying where he was going and I don't know where he is now* would have been the honest answer, but it opened the way for too many dreamy, hopeful suggestions that they go and find him. *He might come back one day* would be giving him false hope. She ended by saying, 'We stopped loving each other and it's hard to look after a baby when you don't love each other.'

Max had taken on his usual glazed look, the way he did when faced with a concept he hadn't a hope of understanding. What she'd really wanted to say was, *Your father's an arsehole, Max. He walked out when you were two weeks old and left us on our own. He doesn't deserve anything from you and if you ever try and find him, I will knock you from here to next week.*

More than anything, it was what she still wanted to say and she understood now that this was what the rest of her life would be: a constant struggle to keep her feelings neatly on the tip of her tongue instead of letting them out, splattered like vomit all over the floor for poor Max to fall in.

He'd probably end up loving his dad more than her now, because his dad would get the good times and she'd still just be his stressed, shouty mother, trying to hold everything together and make ends meet without him. Still, it wasn't Max's fault. He didn't deserve to be told by her that his father was an arsehole. With any luck, he'd work it out for himself soon enough.

The second thing she'd need to do, after telling him his father was still around, was to let him know that his father wanted to see him and ask him how he felt about that. She'd often imagined that moment, picturing Max turning to her with eyes shining with excitement and disbelief, as if she were suggesting a trip to Lapland to meet the real Father Christmas. Now she was less sure of his reaction. For a child of five, he was already devastatingly disillusioned with life. It was possible that he'd just let the news sink in and then weigh him down, the way he seemed to do with everything else in his small, difficult world.

And after that, they'd need to meet. There was no way she could leave them alone together in case Drew decided to run off with him, so it would have to be the three of them: mother, father and child, united in sadness, anger and regret.

She waited until he'd been watching CBeebies for a while, settled on the sofa with his blanket after school. He wasn't hungry or angry. He was calm, absorbed in a world of obscenely bright colours and insanely upbeat presenters. Laura wondered what had happened to the presenters of the past – the ones you saw sometimes on those nostalgia shows, *50 Years of Children's TV* or whatever they were called – when everything was in black-and-white and they all read stories and spoke calmly to old bears, and television had been serious and nurturing instead of some outlandish fancy dress party.

She took a seat next to him on the sofa and waited for the current programme to end. Some people were dressed up as numbers, rearranging themselves into double-digits and shrieking, 'Eleven!' or 'Fifteen!' with triumphant excitement. It wore Laura out just to look at it.

As soon as the credits started rolling, she hit pause on the remote control. 'Max,' she began.

He looked at her.

'Max, I wanted to talk to you about your dad.'

He looked a little more interested.

She smiled, to show this was something to be pleased about, not worried. 'He wrote to me the other day. He's been away for a long time, but he's back now and he'd like to see you again. Would you like that?'

'Will he …' Max said, confused and hopeful, 'will he come and live with us?'

She shook her head. 'No, sweetheart. He has his own house. But if you want to, maybe one day you could go and visit him there.'

He nodded.

'So do you think you'd like to meet him? He suggested Saturday. We could go to the park and he can watch you on your skateboard and then maybe we could all go to a café and have lunch.' She hadn't meant to add that about the café. It just seemed like a nice way to finish off the scene: Max and his father in the park together, wrapped up warm against the November air, then heading off into town for a bowl of soup. She'd got herself too caught up in this fantasy, she realised. Drew wouldn't be interested in a quaint café serving soup. He'd want a pasty from Greggs. Briefly, Laura wondered what kind of rules she could lay down about Max's diet when he was with his dad. None, probably.

Finally, the excitement she'd been longing to see in him for months was roused. 'Yes!' he cried and raised his fist into the air.

She smiled and kissed him. 'That's good,' she said, then took herself to the kitchen to prepare his tea and message Drew.

Spoke to Max this evening. He said he'd like to meet you on Saturday. Come to Burntridge for 11? We can go to the park. He loves skateboarding. There are ramps and things there.

He didn't always reply immediately. She busied herself with putting bread in the toaster and microwaving a tin of beans to take her mind off the wait. The thought of seeing him again made her sick with nerves, and it worried her. She wanted to appear cool and distant, so he'd know not to come too near her even if he wanted to, so he'd regret it and regret it and regret it.

But what she feared, more than anything, was that she'd take one look at him and buckle, that she'd suddenly become twenty-one years old again, find she was still madly in love, and that all she'd want would be for him to come home with them and stay there forever.

Anger served a purpose. For five years, it had allowed her to keep on going, to keep powering through life. If she let it go now, even for a second, then the pain of losing Drew, and of losing their beautiful little family and all the dreams she'd had for them, was going to overwhelm her. She couldn't allow it to happen.

Her phone beeped and vibrated slightly across the worktop.

Cool. See you Saturday. Thank you. D x

She looked at it a while longer than necessary.

D x

The anger flared. How dare he sign off like that, as if there were some kind of familiarity between them when he'd been absent for the whole five years of his son's life? She had the urge to hurl the phone at the wall and smash his initial and his shitty little kiss to bits.

The microwave pinged to say the beans were done.

She was still angry as she peeled back the clingfilm and scalded her hand on the steam.

21

Maia

Maia had shed her virginity. She couldn't stand the term *lost*, as if something integral and good had disappeared from her and she was now going to spend the rest of her life wishing she could get it back. She wasn't. Shedding it hadn't been the most sublime experience of her life, but nor had she expected it to be. Overall, she was glad to have gone through this rite of passage so she could focus now on enjoying the sex itself, rather than worrying about whether it was going hurt and whether there would be blood on the sheets as evidence they'd have to wash away.

It hadn't hurt and there had been no blood, which made Maia wonder whether the horror stories were just propaganda to keep girls frightened of sex. When it was all over (and it was, quite quickly), her overwhelming feeling wasn't relief or love, but anger that she and her friends had been taught for so long to be afraid of this. She wanted to emblazon it across all the magazines and newspapers in the world: *First-time sex is not a bloody massacre.*

Maia knew she'd been lucky. James, predictably, was careful and tender and he'd made the build-up to it so special. The two of them had bunked off school for the day, which Maia had never done before but it was the only way they could guarantee being alone. They'd agreed James's house would be the best place because both his parents could be relied on to stay at work all day. Maia's dad had a habit of rocking up unexpectedly after lunch sometimes. 'The office was too noisy,' he'd say, 'I'll work from home this afternoon.' The possibility of her dad being in the house while Maia willingly received her first dick was unthinkable.

On the day of her birthday, a Friday, Maia stepped off the school bus and headed straight out of the car park towards the centre of town where James lived. She decided the best approach was simply to be brazen about it. She'd seen other girls play truant and they were always so obvious – casting anxious looks around them to see who was watching, stopping and hiding behind fences, laughing. Maia simply slung her bag over her shoulder and walked away with purpose, as if she were doing only what she had permission for.

No one stopped her. Of course they didn't. She was Maia Kernick. She never did anything wrong.

'Happy birthday,' James said when she arrived. He took her hand and led her into the living room, where he'd lit the fire and spread out an indoor picnic on the rug. Maia wondered whether the rug was where they were going to have sex, and also where he'd found this idea. It looked like something straight out of a magazine. *Seduce your girlfriend with an indoor breakfast picnic.*

There were plates of croissants, mini pastries, bowls of strawberries, two glasses of prosecco (even though they'd agreed neither of them wanted to be drunk for this – they wanted to be *there*, sober and present for Maia's first experience of sex), slices of smoked salmon and a loaf of sourdough. Of course fucking sourdough. It was the only bread anyone ate these days.

Maia could imagine what her mother and Erin would have to say about all this. 'What happened to the days of drinking a can of cider and losing your virginity in the car park behind the Spar?'

Her mother was always like that, full of loathing for the world that ran through her like a river. This 'I'm so down-to-earth' act was bullshit, as pretentious as the group of girls in her school who'd marked each one's first period by giving them a red, *Welcome to Womanhood* band to slip over their newly adult wrists.

In the centre of the breakfast spread was a small sponge cake with two glowing pink candles – the numbers one and six – standing together side by side. Maia's eyes were drawn to them, as if they were lights beckoning her to the adult world of carnal knowledge.

She looked from the cake to James and said, 'Is that a polite way of reminding me I'm allowed to fuck you?'

He looked crestfallen. 'No! I … We don't have to do anything if you don't want to.'

'I was joking,' she said, and sat down.

God, he was sweet. He was so bloody sweet. And now, because he was so sweet, she had to nibble politely at this breakfast picnic when what she really wanted to do was get the whole thing over and done with. She had no expectations. She was expecting it to be difficult and painful and then, after the first time, it would get better and involve multiple orgasms and deep fulfilment.

She kept up with the pretence of enjoying breakfast for about five minutes. Then she lay her plate aside, moved closer to James, kissed him and spoke words that were far more loving and sexy than the words in her head.

Afterwards, they'd slept for a while, then done it again when they woke up. It was better that time. It went on for longer, though Maia was aware of her mind drifting to her English homework, and wondered if that was normal. Probably not. She was meant to be focussing on the sensations in her body and the connection she was making with the young man on top of her, who seemed to be constantly searching for her gaze, trying to make eye contact. She couldn't do that. It was too intense and there was a neediness to it. *Look at me. Love me. Love me properly. Love me more than this.*

But Maia didn't love him. She'd never had any intention of loving him and she didn't want him to love her either. It was boring and oppressive. She was only sixteen. She didn't want the responsibility of being loved.

22

Jo

Luke had always been confident, good-looking and funny ever since he was a baby, and this meant Jo let him get away with things she would never have tolerated in her daughter. Teachers did it, too. 'Sometimes,' his year two teacher said at parents' evening, 'I go to tell him off for rudeness, but he gives me that winsome little smile and I can't help myself.' When he was eight, they'd gone to a New Year's Eve party where he'd played the guitar and amused the adults with a wit that was just on the right side of slightly-too-precocious, and Jo's friend had pulled him onto her lap, kissed him and said, 'I know boys like you. Once you hit eighteen, you'll need to keep away from my daughter.'

Right now, that very daughter was in Jo's front room, sitting with Luke on the sofa, both of them innocently drinking tea and chatting the chat of clever youths using their wit to be flirtatious. Jo had been in the kitchen when Maia turned up. She overheard their slightly insane, self-conscious reunion dialogue, which would have been funny if she hadn't been able to picture them both congratulating themselves for being so witty and then sulking because no one had discovered them yet. *Just be normal*, she wanted to say. *Life isn't a bloody performance.*

'Maia,' Luke said.

'I'm glad you're back.'

There was a pause in which they were probably hugging dramatically, for some imagined off-scene camera.

Then Maia said, 'How are you?'

He sniffed. 'I've got a bit of a nasty infection, actually.'

A cold. He had a cold.

'What? Like AIDS, you mean?'

'Exactly. I've been hanging out with too many Eighties musicians.'

'Really? I took my grade eight flute exam in June. I'm a musician now.'

'Cool,' Luke said, then added, 'Do you want AIDS?'

'No,' Maia told him, 'not really. But if I did, I'd want it from you.'

They went through to the living room, and Jo couldn't eavesdrop anymore.

He'd arrived last night on the four o'clock train from King's Cross, and she picked him up at Newcastle to save him forty minutes on the rickety slow train to Burntridge. He hadn't said much about leaving London but looked relieved to be home and she wasn't sure what had gone on. It was too soon to ask, she knew that, and too soon to push him for information about what his plans were. Luke was among the most hard-working people she'd ever met, but only if he enjoyed what he was doing. If he didn't like the work, he gave it nothing. This was fine when he was at school and university – at exam time, he'd shut himself away with his books and work through the night, fuelled by Diet Coke and a desire to be exceptional (which Jo had always taken to mean, 'not like you and Dad'), and came out with a string of As and a first-class degree in History from Edinburgh. Once all that was over, he floundered. The world of employment, he realised, was boring. There was an arrogance to all this – he considered himself too good for the bottom rung and wanted someone to fly him straight in at the top. He wasn't going to listen to Jo or his father or even his friends. The only way he'd learn was to try it, and then fail.

She reminded herself that he was young and he had time, and there was no harm in someone pausing for breath before launching themselves onto the employment treadmill, where they'd be stuck for the next fifty years. And it would all sort itself out. By the time he was forty, Luke probably wouldn't be making impulsive decisions about moving, jobless, to London to make groundbreaking TV programmes.

Maia poked her head round the kitchen door. 'Bye Jo,' she said. 'Thanks for letting me come over.'

Jo smiled and stood up from the table, where she'd been looking through the *Tes*. She always liked to see what jobs there were, especially in the independent sector, and took a small-scale dark satisfaction from stabbing the most obnoxious adverts with her pencil and defacing them.

'See you again, Maia,' Jo said.

Luke hugged his friend goodbye and they spoke about meeting next week. Luke was non-committal. 'I'm mostly just going to chill for a while,' he said.

Chill.

When the door had shut, Jo said, 'You remember I'm going to Rachel's tonight? If you want dinner, you'll need to go out and buy yourself something.'

'All right.'

'Have you got enough money?'

'For dinner?'

'Yes.'

'Yeah. Don't worry, Mum. It's cool.'

She nodded, and steered herself in the direction of other, safer topics. 'I haven't been to Rachel's for months. Remember when we used to go all the time?'

'Her parties were ace. Is she really a crazy bisexual now?'

'She's not crazy, Luke, no.'

'Yeah … But is she really bi?'

'She's living with a woman.'

'Then she's bi.'

'Fine. Yes. She is.'

He gave a low whistle. 'Wow,' he said. 'Still, it was good to see Maia again. She looks older all of a sudden.'

Jo was well aware that when he said *older,* what he meant was, *more gorgeous than she used to be.* It was true. Maia had changed, almost overnight, from gawky child to young woman. She'd cast off her glasses in favour of contact lenses, cut off her girlish plaits in favour of a sleek, chocolate-coloured bob, and carried off her unique, vintage-style fashion with the flair of Mary Quant. She stood out in Burntridge, among the teenage uniforms of jeans and drab jumpers. Jo pictured her in Camden or Brighton one day, playing her flute, commanding attention, determined to be every bit as fabulous as her mother.

'Oh, Maia's lovely,' she said. 'She's not making Rachel's life easy, though. She didn't like the new domestic set-up with Erin, so she walked out and moved in with her dad.'

Luke shrugged. 'That's the collateral damage of divorce.

Why should she put up with massive changes she never asked for?'

Jo caught the bitter edge to his voice and knew it was directed at her.

Carefully, she said, 'I agree. Rachel understands as well, but it doesn't stop her being upset. I don't know what happened exactly, but I don't think Maia moved out peacefully. There was drama involved.'

'I'll get her to talk to me about it,' Luke said. 'I always liked Maia.'

Jo had a fleeting urge to warn him away from her. *She's a child, Luke,* she wanted to say. *Keep your hands off.* She shook the thought away. They'd known each other since Maia was a baby. They were lifelong friends. She smiled. 'Good idea.' Then she added, 'You know you can stay as long as you want, of course.'

His face broke with relief and she felt guilty then, for suspecting him of planning to loaf about the family home, waiting for the world to fall at his feet. 'Thanks, Mum.'

She decided to stop avoiding the issue. 'Is it money? Is that why you're back?'

He sighed and wouldn't look at her. 'Partly,' he admitted. 'London was tougher than I expected.'

'Are you in a mess?'

'Not financially,' he told her.

She waited for more, but it didn't come.

Rachel's house really was beautiful. The rooms were endless and furnished with the sort of casual elegance Jo hadn't believed existed outside the pages of magazines in dentists' waiting rooms. It was all soft lighting, huge fireplaces, floor-to-ceiling bookshelves, chaises longues, grand pianos, expensively stocked wine racks and at least three different staircases taking them to the next floor which was, of course, more of the same. And the kitchen! Jo wasn't sure even Hugh Fearnley-Whittingstall would own a kitchen like this.

The trouble with this house, Jo had always thought, was that it was so welcoming, it could be easy to forget while you were here that it wasn't actually yours. Its layout invited you to stroll through its rooms and play its pianos and dive into its swimming pool as if you were the person who owned all this, and not your friend. But Rachel never seemed to mind. Two or three times a year, she threw open her doors and uncorked the wine and that was it: in the morning, there would be grown-up, respectable people only half-alive on her sofas, or throwing up into one of her beautiful porcelain toilets because Rachel had invited them over and said, 'Fuck it all,' in that unique way Rachel did.

Being friends with Rachel was as close as anyone in Burntridge was ever going to get to a rock-and-roll lifestyle.

This evening's bash had been a comparatively sedate and well-behaved affair but then there were only three of them present. Jo had only met Erin briefly before. Now, she was sitting opposite her, finishing off the meal she must have laboured over all day, looking extremely attractive and talking about a feature she was writing … Jo was a bit drunk now. She'd lost the thread of what the feature was about. Something to do with Glasgow. Jo put her knife and fork down then sat back and marvelled at this couple in front of her. She wondered if they might be the cleverest pair of lesbians in the country.

Rachel stood up and started clearing the plates. She never cooked. In her old life, Will had done all the cooking and now it looked as though Erin had taken over where he'd left off. What a skill it was, to make sure you only fell in love with people who could feed you. Jo wondered if it was too late to start nurturing this skill herself. But then, the thought of falling in love again was exhausting. All that trimming and waxing and shaving. She couldn't be bothered. She'd rather be independent and hairy.

It was a long way from the table to the dishwasher and Rachel seemed to be gone for ages. When she did at last return, she was carrying a wooden board piled high with cheese, biscuits and fruit. Then from out of her pocket she whipped a giant spliff, which she lit, drew on a few times and passed round.

This was what Jo liked about coming to Rachel's: the time spent discussing their children's UCAS forms, graduations and music exams was blessedly short. At her parties, Rachel was all about the dancing and the drugs. At dinners, she was all about changing the world. It must wear her out, Jo thought – fighting the country's problems and taking on all those steadfastly deaf politicians. No wonder she needed drugs.

'Anyway,' Rachel said now, 'do you ever hear from Dave?'

Jo shook her head. 'Hardly ever. He barely talked to me when he lived with me. He wasn't going to start once he'd left. We mostly just speak when the kids do something we both have to show up for.'

'Oh, God. Do they still do that? Even in their twenties? I was hoping it would all stop once the nativities were out the way.'

'It goes on forever,' Jo told her. 'Concerts, graduations,

weddings … Your children will never stop forcing you to be within stabbing distance of your ex-husband. You have to really get in control of yourself, especially when the hormones kick in, Rachel. Seriously. At my menopausal peak, I was afraid to be in the same room as Dave and a knife.'

She was exaggerating. Obviously. It was the spliff, loosening her mind. She'd never really wanted to hurt Dave; at the very most, she'd wished she could put a fire under his backside to get him moving. They had money, the two of them. She wished he would spend it. She wanted to travel the world by train – the Trans-Siberian Railway, the Pride of Africa, even just Interrailing would do. But he wasn't interested in anything. All he wanted was to enjoy the life they had at home, day after day within their own four walls, while he retreated further and further into silence. It was as corrosive as daily fighting.

Erin laughed. She said, 'It's frightening, isn't it? How easily you can see yourself shift from being an ordinary, decent person to a violent maniac. I felt like that at the end of all my relationships. I had it in me to do a lot of harm.'

Rachel put her hand over Erin's in a gesture of loving faith. 'You didn't. There's a huge gap between wanting to punch someone's lights out and actually doing it. You haven't got it in you to cross that line.'

'I have,' Jo said darkly. 'If this were America, I'd orchestrate my own school shooting. Blow down the entire PTA with one swish of my gun … Oh, dear. Did I say that out loud? I don't mean it, obviously. They're wonderful. They raise so much money. We couldn't do without them.'

'Don't worry,' Rachel said. The spliff had come back to her. 'You're among friends here.'

Jo lowered her voice, though she wasn't sure why. 'Have you had any dealings with Laura or Kate recently?'

'Not in the last few weeks. I avoid them both as much as possible.'

'I have some concerns. About Laura's son.'

Rachel raised an eyebrow. 'Oh?'

'I've been pondering it for a while now, whether to call social services or not, but it's a delicate path to tread. His behaviour is troubling. Uncontrollable fits of rage. And there's bruising.'

That was all she needed to say.

'Have you spoken to anyone?'

'No one official. Not yet. I spoke to Laura. She gave what seemed like a reasonable explanation.'

'Which was?'

'He has frequent outbursts of temper and bashes himself.' She paused and let Rachel pass her the spliff. 'What do you think?'

Rachel spoke thoughtfully. 'I'd have to see the bruises to be sure. It's possible a flailing child could injure himself, of course, but it would be a different sort of bruising to marks from a parent's fist.'

'That's what I thought. I've spoken to the deputy head – she's in charge of safeguarding – and Max's class teacher. We're keeping an eye on it.'

'And Laura? Does she have access to any support that you know of? There are groups for single parents. What about Max's father? Is he on the scene?'

Rachel was in professional mode now, making an assessment, working out how she could help so Max and Laura didn't become another statistic.

Jo shook her head. 'There's no contact with his father.'

'So she's on her own, all the time, without money, looking after a child with problems and with no respite? And let's face it, she's always furious and a little bit loony.'

'I think that's the case.'

'Then she's at risk,' Rachel declared, matter-of-factly.

'Not necessarily,' Erin intervened.

'No, of course not necessarily. But there's an insanely angry woman and a child with bruises. Sounds like a risk to me.'

Erin said, 'I saw Max in the park with her a while back. I saw what he's like when he loses control. I could see how it might hurt him, and Laura seemed pretty caring.'

Jo said, 'Yes, I know. You're right. I don't want to jump to conclusions, but equally I don't want to miss something important.'

Rachel said, 'It sounds like she could do with some help, at the very least. Tell her to go to the Sure Start Children's Centre. They'll point her in the right direction.'

Jo nodded, then tipped back the last of her wine and said, 'You know I should never have told you this. It's the booze and the drugs. Please don't say anything.'

'Jesus Christ, Jo. You know me better than that.'

She did. Of course she did. But nevertheless, she wished she hadn't spoken.

23

Erin

Today was one of those days – and they were becoming more frequent recently – when Erin felt she might be able to do this. Rachel and Will had gone together to Maia's parents' evening, so Erin had been at home for a couple of hours just with Reuben and Tess. For once, nothing bad had happened. She'd forced herself to listen to Tess's post-school ramblings about the dinosaur that had come into her classroom overnight and left footprints and an egg. This was somehow connected to a science lesson, the details of which were mercifully flimsy and which Erin couldn't even begin to piece together. But Tess had spoken with a charming sort of enthusiasm and she hadn't even backed away when, at the end of the very long story with no clear narrative thread, Erin had laughed and instinctively reached out and ruffled her hair.

Reuben, too, had been chatty and amiable. He'd just been asked by Cambridge University to send a sample of work for them to read as part of their shortlisting process. He wanted to study law there. Nowhere else would do, not even LSE or King's College London. He'd asked Erin to read one of his history essays to see if it was good enough, which she did, and he seemed grateful for the improvements she suggested, even though what she really wanted to say was, 'None of this is as important as you think it is. Your life won't fall apart forever if you forget to mention that you passed your grade six electric guitar exam with distinction. It won't matter if you don't get into the world-class institution of your choice and have to settle for some other world-class institution instead. You will get to where you need to be, look back on all this twenty years from now and realise none of it actually matters.'

But for now, it was the only thing in his life. His teachers were pushing him, his parents were supporting him. He came from a family of high achievers, where the weight of expectation sat as heavily as it did on those children whose parents paid £30,000 a year in school fees. Rachel was never going to settle for an ordinary child. It was unspoken, but sewn deeply into the fabric of their family life. 'It doesn't matter what you're brilliant at. It can be science, or it can be making cakes. But you have to be brilliant at something.'

Erin's own family had been nothing like this. It impressed and amused her in equal measure. Secretly, she wanted one of them to at least be unconventionally brilliant. Rachel wouldn't mind. She'd probably love a child who lived in a hut on the Farne Islands, with no electricity or human contact, and who befriended seals and puffins. It wasn't going to be Reuben. He was wedded to the mainstream. Maia might do it, although Erin suspected that Maia's gift lay simply in breaking her mother's heart, over and over again.

Just after eight, Rachel came home. For the first time, Tess had allowed Erin to put her to bed, to read her a story and even kiss her goodnight. It felt like a milestone. It felt like an excuse for celebratory sex.

'How was it?' Erin asked.

Rachel was reasonably upbeat. She took her coat off, then headed towards the fridge and brought out a bottle of white wine, which she unscrewed and poured into two glasses. 'OK,' she said. 'She still seems to be doing well at school, despite everything. Excelling, especially at English and music. Sometimes goes AWOL for PE but I can't bring myself to get worked up about that.'

Rachel had enough to get worked up about where Maia was concerned.

'That's good, then,' Erin said. 'She's clearly OK.'

The potential state of Maia's well-being had been a point of anguish for Rachel recently. Erin would have liked to tell Maia to get over it, to stop punishing her mother for daring to be a human being, and point out that Rachel had already spent years battling with who she really was so she wouldn't harm her children. There would be no point in that, however. Maia would simply loathe her even more, and Rachel would leap to her daughter's defence because Rachel was brilliantly, beautifully – but also slightly pathologically – empathic. She saw everyone's point of view, felt everyone's pain, needed to keep everybody well, and so Erin kept on with the sweet dishonesties that all relationships needed to uphold the bliss. 'Your children are a bonus,' she declared, from the beginning. 'I love you, so I love your children. It doesn't matter how hard it gets. I'm in this with you.'

And she was. She was in it with her. But she didn't love the children. Not yet, although it was possible she might come to.

Already she was warming to Tess, and Reuben was fine. A bit mainstream, a bit of a predictable product of his background, but fine nevertheless. He was inoffensive, and there was a lot to be said for an inoffensive stepchild.

Rachel took a seat at the island. 'Apparently, she's got a boyfriend.'

Erin looked at her, trying to read her expression. 'A nice one?' she asked. 'Or a bastard?'

Rachel shrugged. 'Will's met him. Says he's nice.'

Erin could see the sadness in her face. It was there in her eyes, etched into the brisk arrangement of her features – the way her chin jutted forwards as it always did when Rachel was trying to hold herself together and expose no pain.

'I just …' She shrugged and sipped her wine.

'I know,' Erin said, and reached for her hand.

24

Rachel

For the sake of peace, Rachel forced herself to sit through *Les Misérables* without openly retching. She hated musicals. Hated them with a passion. All that melodrama, all those abandoned women falling about the stage, wailing plaintively for the return of their cruel men, or for some other man – a better class of man, obviously – to come along and save them from poverty and prostitution.

But still. Maia loved it and that was what mattered. They'd come here to belatedly celebrate her sixteenth. Maia was too busy these days to make space for her mother in the few days around her actual birthday. Rachel had to express her interest in taking her out, and then Maia agreed to came back to her with a date during the period she unironically referred to as 'her birthday month'.

After the show, Rachel took her to Wagamama so they could sit on benches with strangers and drop food into their laps and dribble sauce down their chins because neither of them were very good with chopsticks. Again, Maia's choice.

They talked through the usual things as they ate: school, friendships, films Maia had seen recently, her plans for a weekend trip to Edinburgh. Every now and then, Rachel could see Maia looking at her oddly, and knew she was reliving that night in her head, forever unable to erase the image of her mother in the throes of passion. It made Rachel burn with shame, as if somehow she'd abused her daughter. All she could hope was that in time the memory would fade, become less intrusive and stop sitting like a solid object between them. The elephant in the room. The lesbians in the room. The child in the room. *Oh, God,* she thought. *Make it stop.*

'Dad says you've got a boyfriend,' she said, too soon, too suddenly, just so she could push that image away.

Maia dropped her gaze to her bowl of tofu ramen and said, 'It's nothing much. He's just a boy.'

Rachel nodded. 'Do you like him?'

'Yeah. He's cool. It's just a … you know … a casual thing.'

Rachel wasn't sure if this was good or bad. The thought of her just-sixteen-year-old daughter in a serious relationship was unbearable, but then she wasn't too keen on that word *casual,* bandied about to imply a relaxed lack of commitment, but usually ending in heartless sex and someone's shattered self-esteem.

Sex. Should she go near that topic? She had no idea. If Maia lived with her, she'd be able to sense it – how necessary it was to start that conversation no teenager ever really wanted to have with their mother. She didn't want to force it. What if Maia was barely kissing this boy, feeling her way through the terrifying adult world of relationships and all that they entailed, and her overbearing mother made assumptions and threw the pill at her when all she really needed was to be reminded that it was OK not to be doing this stuff, that no one ever died saying, 'I wish I'd started having sex a bit younger'?

She wondered if she needed to speak to Will about it. In the old days, before they'd fallen into their years of near-silence, they'd spoken about their children's hypothetical sexual futures and been their typically liberal selves over it. 'Better that it happens under our roof, safely and privately, than behind the scout hut,' they'd agreed, and of course the kids' boyfriends and girlfriends would be allowed in their bedrooms. Now, Rachel was less sure. She knew teenage boys and the relentless demands of their mates and their dicks. She didn't want Maia to have that kind of pressure. Her bedroom needed to be a place of sanctuary until she – and only she – decided it was OK.

Rachel studied her daughter discreetly. She looked like a child still, despite the sparkly turquoise eyelids, jet-black mascara and the crocheted cardigan with the dangly sleeves that flopped into her dinner. She felt as sure as she could be that Maia wasn't interested in sex and was sensible enough not to feel pressured into having it. She was also sure, absolutely, that if she tried to talk to her about it, Maia was going become embarrassed and defensive and quite possibly angry. She could hear it already. 'Who are you to lecture me about not having sex when you shag your girlfriend on the kitchen floor?' And, of course, it would be useless to point out that she and Erin were adults and it was therefore very different. For Maia, it was no different at all. It would just be another example of her mother's raging hypocrisy.

Instead, she said, 'So what about a job? You can get a Saturday job now you're sixteen. Help fund that trip to Edinburgh.'

'Yeah, Dad said that as well. I'll see what there is. I was hoping for babysitting, really. Everything else is boring, apart from voluntary work. There's some great voluntary work. Museums and stuff. Theatres.'

'Well …' Rachel toyed with the idea for a minute before speaking. Really, she was against anyone working for free, but on the other hand, she knew Maia was better suited to arty careers that required years of unpaid grind before anyone earned anything like a living. She said, 'If you find voluntary work that you really like the sound of, go for it and I'll pay you.'

Maia's face lit up. 'Really?'

'Yes. Of course. There's no point sitting on a checkout in Waitrose when you can do something you enjoy, and which might lead somewhere.'

'Cool. Thanks, Mum. There's this weekend thing at a National Trust property. You have to dress as a Georgian servant and cook weird old-fashioned cakes so people can try them.'

Rachel smiled. 'That sounds great, sweetheart,' she said. 'And do you want me to ask around at Tess's school for babysitting? Parents always need babysitters.'

'Yeah. Cool. Thanks.'

'I think Tess misses you.'

She was entering dangerous territory, but she couldn't help herself.

Maia sighed. 'I miss her as well.'

'Your room is still there if you ever want it. It will always be there, you know that, don't you?'

Maia looked away from her. 'I know.'

She knew she mustn't beg, mustn't say how awful it was that her child had moved out because she was so unhappy with the life Rachel had forced upon her. She said, 'I just need you to know that if you do ever want to come home, you can. You don't need to ask. You can just turn up, any time.'

'I did that once before. Look what happened there.'

It was the first time either of them had ever mentioned it. Rachel forced herself to face it. 'I'm really sorry that happened, Maia. Really sorry.'

Maia shrugged. 'It wasn't very nice.'

'I know.'

'I mean, imagine if you'd walked in on …' Maia fumbled for a name. 'Dad and his new girlfriend.'

'Has Dad got a new girlfriend?'

Maia rolled her eyes. 'His *hypothetical* new girlfriend.'

'Oh, right.' Rachel laughed. 'No, I would hate it. Of course. Anyone would hate seeing anyone in that …'

There was no right word to end that sentence on.

'And Dad likes having me around.'

'Of course he does.'

'So I think for now I should stay with Dad. You know, so he's not on his own.'

Rachel sighed. She'd never wanted this. She'd never, ever wanted her children to feel responsible for their parents. But this was what she'd done, and she couldn't tell Maia she shouldn't feel responsible for her father because Maia would then feel manipulated, as if Rachel were just feeding her a line for her own selfish reasons. So she said, 'Whatever you like. Just as long as you know you will always have a home with me if you want it.'

'Yeah, I know.'

She left it at that.

Then Maia said, 'I'm seeing Luke tomorrow. He's coming over.'

'Jo's Luke?'

'Yes. You know he's home from London?'

'Jo mentioned something about it last week. She wasn't clear on the details. Nice that he's home, though. And that you're meeting up.'

'I had a crush on him when I was little.'

'Did you?'

'Yeah. You know that time we went on holiday with them to Yorkshire? I cried for ages because he and Reuben were always going off together and Reuben wouldn't let me go with them because I was … I don't know … too little, or too embarrassing or something. But Luke was cool about it. He made me a Harry Potter wand out of some sticks and some string.'

'Then he deserves a permanent place in your heart, Maia.'

Maia appeared to be taking this comment seriously. She said, 'Do you think he's too old for me, though?'

Jesus Christ. *Yes.* She couldn't say that, though. That would be like telling her to chase him. 'That's a decision for you to make, but probably. What is he? Twenty-three?'

'Two. Twenty-two.'

'Twenty-two and sixteen … What do you think?' *Only just sixteen. A week ago, you were fifteen, which would have counted as child abuse.*

Maia grinned. 'You're right.'

'Anyway, what about this other boy? This … What's his name?'

'James.'

James. That was a steady, boring name. If she had to have

a boyfriend, then a steady, boring one was probably the best option at the moment. 'So. He's definitely nice?'

'I wouldn't be seeing him if he was horrible.'

'No, of course you wouldn't.'

'It's fine, Mum. I'm being careful.'

Rachel nearly choked. Careful of what? Careful of protecting her heart? Maia was a child. She had no idea yet that her heart would need protecting from all those emotional predators out there who might harm its tender young flesh. Rachel had always planned to punch the bastard's lights out when it happened, but now it looked unlikely that she'd even set eyes on this one. She needed to. She needed to see him, so she could get a sense of how alert her bastard-detector should be.

She meant sex. Did she mean sex? Was she really casually shagging this bloke, or was she just trying to shock her mother? Oh, God. *Don't lose your shit, Rachel.*

'Well,' she said, gulping the last of her wine. 'That's good. Good that you're being careful.'

She needed to phone Will. Right now. Right this minute. He wasn't doing this properly. Maia had to come home.

25

Maia

Maia was beginning to feel as though she liked James's mum more than she liked James, which really wasn't the way things were meant to be. Sasha was lively and interesting, while James seemed to be in a slump that had been brought about by the fact that he thought Maia didn't love him enough. 'I love you as much as I can,' she'd told him honestly the last time they'd had sex. 'But I'm just not the really loving type. It's OK if you can't live with that. I don't mind you finding someone else if you want to.'

It had been the wrong thing to say. For a while, he was speechless with shock and hurt. Then he said, 'I don't want someone else. I want you.'

At school, he started looking for her every break time when she wanted to just sit in the music practice room with Clara, talking and eating Wotsits. 'I'm not sure about him,' Maia said, and Clara asked, 'Why not?'

'Because he's gone all clingy and weird.'

As if to prove her point, the door to the practice room opened and in he strode. 'I've been looking everywhere for you,' he said, planting a kiss on her mouth.

Maia looked at Clara and raised her eyebrows. *See?*

Clara, she could tell, saw.

James draped his arm loosely about Maia's shoulders. She had to fight the urge to shake him off. She wished he'd go away.

She said, 'I was just talking to Clara.'

He said, 'What are you doing at lunchtime?'

Maia shrugged. 'Don't know yet. I'll decide at lunchtime.'

He let out a sigh of frustration.

Clara said, 'Doesn't Mr Holliday want to see you?'

Maia shot her friend a grateful look. Mr Holliday didn't want to see her at all, but she was glad to have been given this get-out and she took it with relief. 'Yes. He does.'

'Really? What about?'

She spoke more sharply than she'd meant to. 'I don't know, James.'

He looked crestfallen.

That evening, he turned up at her dad's house unannounced with a bunch of flowers. He stood on the doorstep and handed them to her. 'For you,' he said.

She sniffed them politely. 'Thanks.'

He was waiting for her to invite him in.

She said, 'I'm doing my English coursework. It's due in tomorrow ...'

He looked at her hopefully, 'You can't even take a five-minute break?'

Oh, leave me alone.

She said, 'I've only written five-hundred words. I'm really sorry.'

He sighed and turned back towards his car. She saw the exaggerated slump of his shoulders, deliberately designed to make her feel guilty, and wished she knew how to get out of this.

26

Jo

Jo headed home, thinking how glad she'd be when the term was over. A year one teacher had been signed off for three months because of long-term depression, so she had to find a supply to take her place. There was a tendency among West Burntridge parents not to trust supply teachers. Why, for example, didn't they have a permanent job? Was it because no one would employ them? Did they have the skills to guide their children through this crucial, early stage of their education, a time when one bad experience could put them off learning for life and prevent them from taking the place in the City that had been reserved for them since before they were born?

On top of that, the PTA had decided to raise extra funds this year by hosting a Christmas disco for all children from year one upwards. Jo had seen the tickets. *Dress to impress! Prizes to be awarded on the night, including best-dressed and best hairstyle!* The thought of it made Jo's stomach turn. She couldn't bear inflicting discos on children. She'd been to one before and had personally witnessed what happened to decent, wonderful kids when they went to a social event designed for people ten years older than they were. Out came the leopard print, the leather jackets, the pouts, the struts, the premature obsession with the opposite sex – all of it way beyond their emotional capability, often ending in confused tears, and all of it reinforcing some ghastly expectation that this what they had to aspire to: the tedious, gendered mainstream. Kate had already given Jo a list of prizes she was awarding. *Most likely to become a pop star* was Jo's favourite.

She would have liked to ban the whole thing, but that risked offending the PTA. The best she could do was distance herself. It was a Kate Monro Event that she, Jo, would have nothing to do with, and it was down to the PTA to chaperone it. Kate had agreed enthusiastically to this instruction and could currently be seen all over the parents' Facebook group, drumming up parent supporters, insisting they all dress in their finest so they could blast three hundred under-ten-year-olds with Katie Perry and an aspiration to have had their first snog by half-past seven. Obviously, Jo wasn't part of the parents' Facebook group, but Rachel had taken screenshots of it and sent them to her, as she always did, because Rachel was a notorious member of the parents' Facebook group and liked to occasionally throw a grenade into it. Jo still laughed about the time a mother had become overwrought about her son having picked up a piece of foil in the park just before school one morning, and stuck a panic-stricken post about it on the page. *This morning my six-year-old was in the park and picked up a piece of foil he found by the swings. He squashed it up in his hands before I had the chance to stop him. Luckily, there was nothing inside it and I just washed his hands, spoke to the school and phoned the council. I couldn't see anything else that suggested drugs, but thought I should let you know.*

There was then a barrage of parents replying about the teenagers who smoked cannabis in the park and a few laments about this being 'the world we live in and we must protect our children,' followed by Rachel wading in with, 'In all my years of smoking cannabis, I have never once used foil.' She got sixty-two laughs. It was a defence mechanism, as far as Jo could see – that endless dark sarcasm hid something underneath that was excruciatingly gentle. Jo had only ever seen flashes of it, but she knew it was there, like some lost pearl at the bottom of the ocean.

Rachel would not be volunteering to help at the Christmas disco, that much was certain, although she seemed to be showing uncharacteristic restraint on the Facebook page. All she'd said was, 'I would have loved to help, but I'll be staying in and washing my hair that night.' Sometimes, Jo wished Rachel would just admit to the fact that she bolstered the school in so many ways, but she'd never do that. To admit it would be to admit she cared, and Rachel, for some reason, did not want to be seen to care.

Jo pulled up outside her house. Maltley was looking lovely now. The lights on the village Christmas tree had been lit, and all the houses around the green had wreaths on the doors and trees in their windows. There were no garish flashing light displays here. It was almost as though the people of Maltley came together every year in an effort to demonstrate to the world the simple beauty of good taste.

She stepped out of the car and cast a quick glance towards the big house to see if any drama might be unfolding. Rachel, Jo knew, cared deeply about the fact that Maia had moved out and she'd so far been unable to bring her home, but anyone would be forgiven for thinking she didn't care at all. On the whole, she didn't talk about it much, but if it came up in conversation Rachel would simply shrug and perhaps inhale on her e-cigarette and say, 'Teenagers,' in much the same way as Jo used to say, 'Men,' in reference to her husband's most unbearable habits. It wasn't men, though. It was just Dave, or the lousy combination of herself and Dave. Similarly, this wasn't teenagers. It was Maia and Rachel, re-enacting that ancient clash of mother and daughter, those needy hearts pumping too much love, but never enough love.

Things looked quiet over there. A single light was on in the hallway, which probably meant no one had come home yet. Jo let herself in to her own house, wondering if Luke would be in, head bent over his desk, painstakingly carving out his first attempts at writing up an interview. He'd decided in the last week to become a journalist and fixed his sights on the finest training course in the country, which was going to cost Jo and Dave about ten grand between them, and which required evidence of publication to even be allowed on it. Luke was planning to politely cast aside his boyish intrigue with middle-aged lesbians and ask Erin to help him out.

He was out, and it looked as though he'd been out most of the day because the post was still on the doormat. She picked it up and flicked through it. It was mostly for her – a credit card statement, a Boden catalogue, a couple of estate agents telling her people urgently wanted her house – but then there was one plain white envelope addressed to Luke, with an official stamp across the top saying *Murray Davies Solicitors*.

Oh Jesus Christ.

The urge to rip it open right there and then was almost

overwhelming, but she managed to take it into the kitchen and put it on the table for him to find when he came home. She busied herself with boiling the kettle, making tea and grabbing a couple of fig rolls from the biscuit jar, but the whole time her eyes kept returning to that letter. Why, *why* was he receiving mail from a solicitor? She knew, she was absolutely certain, that whatever that letter contained, it had something to do with Luke's sudden homecoming. Of course it did, and it made her nauseous to imagine what it contained.

She decided to just sit there and wait for him, and then when he came home she would ask him what it all meant. Patiently, at first. Kindly. The worst thing she could be was confrontational, so although what she really wanted was to demand, 'What the hell is this, Luke? You will not stay in my house until you tell me what trouble you're in,' she knew she needed to take the supportive approach. 'Whatever trouble you're in, I can help,' she'd say, even though she wasn't sure that she could help any more. Her son was an adult, with adult problems she no longer had the power to put a stop to.

It was after six when she heard the front door open and then slam shut. He came straight to the kitchen, on the prowl for snacks, the way he always had ever since he'd started coming home from school by himself.

'Luke,' she said, before he had a chance to even say hello.

He looked at her.

'This arrived for you,' she said, and passed him the envelope.

She saw the colour drain from his face.

'What is it, love?' she asked. 'Are you in trouble? And please don't tell me it's nothing. I can see from your face it's not nothing. If you're in trouble, I can help you. Your father can help you.'

He shook his head. 'It's OK, Mum. I just …'

He was trying to hold it together, but all of a sudden his face crumpled and he started to cry.

Because she could no longer lift him onto her lap, she pulled the chair beside her out from under the table and patted it. 'Sit down,' she said. 'Sit down and tell me what's happened.'

27

Maia

Maia let her eyes roam. She was sitting in Maddison's with Clara, hoping James wouldn't suddenly leap out of a corner somewhere and demand soft kisses and public devotion. She was planning to stay over at Clara's tonight. For weeks, she'd been longing to just lounge around her friend's bedroom again, watching Netflix, talking about their rubbish lives, their tedious mothers and their plans to escape from all of it.

She was bored of this town. She wanted to get out, go somewhere new. Not long ago, she'd set her sights on studying music in London, but it was too big and too busy and there was none of the beauty she liked in the city. Maia needed to know the edges of a place, to mark the point where the city gave way to mountains or coast, and see her escape from concrete sprawl to something wilder, something more like home.

She was thinking now of Vienna. The University of Music and Performing Arts. There, she'd be able to play the flute and piano in the grand pillared buildings of the university, close to the rocky edges of the Alps, that giant wilderness beyond the city.

Maia indicated a young man with straggly hair who'd just walked in on his own. 'Look. He looks like Hamlet,' she said.

'Only you would be attracted to someone because he looks like Hamlet,' Clara said.

Maia shrugged. 'I like Hamlet. He's sexy. Also, he understands me.'

'What the actual fuck?'

'He does. We looked at that scene with his mother today. You know, where he confronts his mother about her crap choices and she can't bear to look at herself in the mirror because of what she's done. He totally gets me.'

'He's not real, Maia.'

'So? I'd still sleep with him.'

'He's. Not. Real.'

'He is. Look, he's over there.'

Clara looked, then shook her head. 'Mad,' she said.

'No. Sexy.'

'I meant you.'

'That's why we'd be so perfectly matched. I'm not messing around. I genuinely do think I'm in love with Hamlet.'

'More than James?'

Maia wrinkled her nose. 'I'm not in love with James. He's nice and everything, and a talented sax player, but he's not Hamlet. No one will ever be Hamlet. I'll have to content myself with mediocre, non-Hamlet men forever.'

'Probably just as well.'

Maia agreed. 'It is. I worry I'd fall at his feet, and you know my rules about falling at the feet of men.'

'But don't you want to, though? Really? Wouldn't you just like to meet someone amazing and ... I don't know ... marry them?'

'No, I fucking wouldn't. Shag them, yes. Marry them, no.'

'Why not?'

'You can't trust marriage.'

'But you can trust sex?'

'Well, it'll let you down at times,' Maia said, aware that she sounded more experienced than she really was, 'but you don't have to commit to one man for life. You can try out all kinds of different ones. That's what I plan to do. Forget romance. Romance is for those idiot girls at school who think they're incomplete without some idiot boy. I plan to be mostly on my own, playing music and reading poetry, shagging men who remind me of Hamlet and getting rid of them when they stop doing it for me.'

Clara looked at her with a mix of awe and concern. Maia had crossed the divide that separated everyone their age into those who'd had sex and those who hadn't. Clara was a romantic, and probably silently ashamed of her friend's casual, emotionless approach to the act they'd always been taught was wrong without love. For girls, anyway. Boys were expected to be promiscuous. *Players*, they were called. They played with girls the way they used to play with toy cars – they were too fast, too careless, too damaging. Maia liked the idea of being a player. She could be as fast and careless as any boy. She knew now that she needed to get rid of James and the next time, she'd have to spell it out from the start. *No commitment.* She liked the feeling of control it gave her – to be found attractive, enjoy herself and walk away.

'James is young,' she said. 'He's so bloody *young*.'

'He's older than you,' Clara pointed out.

Maia smirked. 'Yes, but you know what they all say about me. I'm setting my sights on real adults now, not schoolboys who pretend to be adults.'

Clara said, 'Yeah, but where do you find them? There's none at school, unless you count teachers, and you can't shag a teacher or you'll end up all over the news. Plus they're all really boring. So where do you go to meet decent men?'

Maia shrugged. 'I don't know. There must be some somewhere though. Not in Burntridge. That's the trouble. I think we need to travel far, far away from here to find them.'

'London, probably.'

'America.'

'Oh God, really? That far?'

'Maybe not.'

Clara considered all this for a while, and said, 'What about girls?'

'What about them?'

'Well, I mostly just think they're better, aren't they? More interesting. There are more exceptional girls at school than boys. Would you go for girls?'

Maia tilted her head to the side and looked curiously at her friend. 'Are you asking me out?'

'No,' Clara said. Then she added, 'I think I'm probably too young for you.'

'Ha.'

'But it would cause such a scandal.'

Maia said, 'I'll leave scandal to my mother.'

'You know there's a campaign going, don't you? About your mum?'

'*What?*' Maia asked, startled. She was the first to admit to being angry with her mother, but a campaign against her was a bit much.

Clara corrected herself. 'It's not against your mother, exactly.

But my mum knows some of the mums at the First School, and a few of them are outraged about some lesbian thing going on there. I don't know the details.'

'That's ridiculous,' Maia said. 'Women like that have nothing going on in their lives. They need to get jobs. That was always my mum's response to campaigns she didn't agree with. She'd always just say, 'These people need to get jobs.' She's probably right. What are they doing to do with the lesbians? Round them up and send them to death camps?'

'I think they're providing alternative sex education classes. You know, where they tell children that it's wrong to be gay and they all have to get married to people from the opposite sex. Then I think they throw a little heterosexual disco for them, with mock-weddings and some plastic babies to look after.'

Maia rolled her eyes. 'Oh, for God's sake. We need to get out of this town.'

She ran into Luke on her way home. Not that it was home. Not really. It was just her dad's house. It didn't feel like home in the way that the house in Maltley felt like home, or had felt like home until her mum went mad. Her room at her dad's was small, with boring magnolia walls she wasn't allowed to decorate because he was only renting. 'When I buy a place, you can have a room of your own and paint it purple if you want to,' he promised.

She didn't want to. She wanted to live in a noisy house again, to know she could wander downstairs any time and find a kitchen full of people – Reuben's mates, her mates, even Tess's mad little school friends. But she'd left that behind and she was here now, living in a small, quiet house and trying to stop her dad from being too unhappy. 'You don't need to worry about me,' he often said to her. 'You're young. Live your life.' But Maia could always see the sadness in his face. Some people, according to magazines, could be radiant with inner happiness. She'd seen the photos of her parents' wedding. Her dad looked as though he'd been radiating happiness on that day. Not any more. Now, he was the opposite, whatever the opposite was. *Darkened with sadness,* she thought, and wanted to cry.

But still. Here was Luke, standing opposite her and gazing at her appreciatively. He was good-looking. He'd always been good-looking. He had dark curly hair that he'd recently stopped taming so that whenever she saw him, he looked as though he'd just been playing sport or having wild sex.

'Hi,' she said.

'Hi.' He gave her a lopsided smile. 'How are you?'

'Cool, thanks. You alright?'

'Yeah. I've been round your old house a lot recently. Erin's helping me with my applications for a postgrad in journalism.'

Maia said, 'You're doing a postgrad in journalism? Really?'

She wasn't sure how she felt about that. Luke was clever. Really clever. He was the first person she knew to take GCSEs and A levels and he always got As in everything. His results impressed her. The way he spoke impressed her, too. He'd taken public speaking as an extra-curricular option when he was in the sixth form and she'd been there in the hall when he delivered a speech about global warming. She remembered the flare of passion and the articulacy of his words, and how the two combined to make her want to … Well, to shag him, she realised now, although at the time she'd only been eleven, so maybe she'd just wanted to look at him, or to have him kiss her goodnight. Now, though, she definitely wanted to shag him.

Speak to me with passion about climate change, darling, and I'll give you a blow job. Maia wondered sometimes if she'd been born twenty years earlier than her due date and that she was actually nearly middle-aged.

'I thought you wanted to be a film-maker,' she said. She was disappointed. Film-making required genius and creativity. Journalism was just a job for bad writers and people with no conscience, like Erin.

Luke folded his arms across his chest. 'Later,' he said. 'There's time for that later.'

He was arrogant. Maia knew that, but she couldn't help finding it oddly attractive. He did, at least, have reason to be arrogant – unlike the rest of the arrogant blokes she knew, none of whom were anything like as special as they thought they were.

He looked at her again and said, 'What are you up to now?'

'Just going home.'

'To your dad's, or your mum's?'

'My dad's. That's home. I never go to my mum's if I can help it.'

'I'm sorry you're having to go through all this. It's some heavy shit at your age.'

She shrugged. 'It's no big deal. Not really. Anyway, I like being closer to town. I can get up later, don't have to get lifts everywhere. It's cool.'

'I suppose so,' he said. 'I have a lot of spare time at the moment. I haven't got a job yet. I'm looking, but there's hardly anything around. Nothing I could tolerate, anyway. Do you want to go for a drink some time?'

She kept her tone casual. 'Sure.'

'Great. I'll text you,' he said. 'Maybe we could go to Newcastle, go to the theatre or something. I remember you liking shows. I think *To Kill a Mockingbird* is coming up here from London. Do you fancy that?'

'Fuck, yes,' she said.

This here, right in front of her, was the sort of bloke she wanted.

28

Laura

Seeing Max's dad had gone well. They'd met him in the park in the centre of Burntridge and he was already waiting for them when they arrived, which Laura saw as an improvement on the days when he used to carelessly keep her waiting, or at least a commitment to making a good start. She knew him well enough to know he probably wouldn't keep it up though. He'd always done that – behaved badly, apologised, promised to change, made an effort for a couple of days, and then reverted to his usual habits because of course, they weren't just habits. They were personality traits and attempting to change them was like pulling the moon out of the sky.

He'd had the grace to look sheepish and even slightly ashamed when he saw her. And nervous. He was definitely nervous. He hadn't waited for Laura to introduce him to Max; he'd just high-fived him and said, 'Hi there, little buddy.'

Laura imagined he'd been rehearsing it for weeks.

Max said hello and then asked, 'Do you want to watch me on my skateboard?'

For a while, they watched. Then Drew joined in because Drew, as Laura knew only too well, was a child and had so far only managed to demonstrate any lasting commitment in life to his skateboard and his motorbike. Still, she knew she shouldn't get angry, standing there in the cold watching as Drew tried out charisma for once – and managed to enchant his son – while she thought about where his next meal was going to come from.

Afterwards, they'd gone to the pub and Drew bought Max a Coke and a packet of crisps. It seemed to Laura then that Max was completely won over. He smiled and talked in the way that other children smiled and talked – animatedly, unselfconsciously, happily. How had this happened, she wondered? How could one meeting with his feckless father have transformed him so suddenly and completely? She had to fight the strange feeling of injustice she felt over this, as if her son had somehow betrayed her. All his life she'd worked to make him happy, and worried over her endless failure to do so, and now here he was: a different boy. A weight had been lifted from his shoulders. The weight of fatherlessness, she supposed.

As they were about to leave Drew said, 'Max, maybe one day, if your mum says it's OK, you could come over to my house?'

Max's face lit up. He turned to Laura and said, 'Can I?'

Laura smiled thinly and felt like taking one of the logs from the fireplace and hurling it at Drew's head. How dare he come straight out and say all that to Max without talking to her about it first? All she could say now was, 'Yes, of course,' because any other answer would have cast her forever as the villain.

Drew hugged his son goodbye. 'It's been great seeing you mate,' he said, and Laura couldn't be sure, but thought she saw the gleam of tears in his eyes. To Laura, he said, 'Thank you.'

29

Jo

Jo had always been good at getting on with work, no matter what might have been happening in her domestic life. During those years of the slow disintegration of her marriage, work had been a welcome relief from the tension. She was good at her job. People respected her and appreciated her. A handful even loved her – a couple of teachers, a few parents whose children she'd helped. At home, she was invisible. She moved irrelevantly through the house, her presence barely noted until she went away because it was then that the seamless magic of all her domestic drudgery fell apart: the teabags ran out, the kitchen floor became a health hazard, there was no one with any cash to borrow from. Her husband, though, always liked her being away. It lifted a burden for him – that burden of feeling he ought to be talking to her instead of shutting himself away in his own head.

Work was still the world that Jo escaped to, even now her marriage had ended. If she was worried about either child for any reason – Luke's impetuousness, for example; or Rebecca's horrible boyfriend – work could reliably distract her for at least eight hours every day. She was grateful to her job for giving her those things: respect for who she was, and distraction from the things that really mattered – those people she loved who could destroy her if she made them the whole focus of her life.

Today, for the first time she could remember, work wasn't enough to distract her from home. Everything was just an annoyance. A stupid little annoyance she wanted to brush away because there was no space in her head to deal with it. On Friday, Kate Monro had hosted the PTA Christmas disco and two parents had so far been in to complain about poor supervision, too many sweets and eight-year-olds having their hearts broken because, at the point where Kate asked every boy to choose a girl to dance with, two of the girls had gone unchosen and one boy had been rejected by everyone. It made Jo furious. She did so much work to create an atmosphere of acceptance in school, to make the parameters of normal behaviour as wide as she could, and then Kate Monro came along and imposed her narrow vision of normality on the lot of them.

On top of that, the homophobic parents were still raging on with their LGBTQ protest. It was all over the Facebook page, as usual. A small but vocal group of idiots wanted to set up a separate class after school so they could formally instruct their children in the art of narrow-minded bigotry. They didn't call it that, obviously. They referred to it as 'Questioning LGBTQ education and teaching the right way to live,' which would have made Jo laugh if it hadn't been so ridiculous. Rachel, as usual, had sent her a screenshot. Kate Monro sat at the heart of it, opening a post with her plans to set up this class and asking for any parents who might like to help with the teaching to contact her. Four or five had commented in support, but it was reassuring to see they were meeting a lot of resistance. *What do you mean, 'the right way to live'? The right way according to who?* Someone else had said, *I've decided the right way to live is the way I live, so I'm going to set up classes in eating donuts for breakfast and never getting dressed. #rightway*

They were right, Jo thought, to treat it this way. The only way to respond to the ridiculous was with ridicule. Besides which, Kate and everyone like her could protest as much they liked, they were never going to win. The tide of the world was turning and they weren't going hold it back. At most, they might slow it down with their petulant teaching of the 'right' way to live.

If she hadn't been feeling so upset, Jo could have laughed at that – the noble ambition of all parents to teach their children the right way to live. Isn't that what they all did? 'Let me tell you,' she wanted to say to them, 'it doesn't always work. I did nothing but teach my son the right way to live and now look at him.'

There was a knock at the office door. 'Come in,' she called. She'd been staring at the computer screen for over an hour, trying to answer emails from the county council and the universities that sent her student teachers, but she couldn't concentrate. All she could think about was how she wanted to go home and slap her son. And possibly cry.

Melissa Jenkins, a year one teacher, stepped into the office. She was young and brilliant and Jo had a soft spot for her because she was also endearingly unaware of just how brilliant she was. Whenever Jo went into her classroom and watched her teach, Melissa's face would pale slightly but she'd carry bravely on, powering through her lessons with lightning-bolt energy. Afterwards, her hands would rise to the necklace she always wore and she'd twist the pendant in her fingers and say, 'Do you think that was OK?' and Jo would smile and say, 'It was fantastic.'

Now Melissa stood in front of her and said, 'Max Spence has just told me he met his dad at the weekend. I get the impression this is the first contact he's had with him. He seems excited. I thought we should all be aware of the change in his circumstances. It's important.'

Jo nodded. 'You're right, Melissa. Thank you. How has Max seemed to you recently?'

'I haven't noticed any more bruising, and in general he's been quite calm, so that's good. Maybe this new contact with his dad will change things for him.'

Jo would have loved to share the young teacher's optimism. Years of experience told her there were no quick fixes to any of this. She smiled, 'Let's hope so,' she said. 'Thanks for bringing it to my attention. I'll make a note of it.'

Melissa left the room, and Jo's mind went straight back to Luke.

There was a young woman he worked with. Susi Lambert, her name was. Twenty-two years old. They were friends. He fancied her. He thought she fancied him. A group of them went out one evening after work. Most had gone home by nine, but Luke and Susi stayed out. They drank too much, too quickly. He lost his house keys. She invited him to sleep on her sofa. He did.

He woke the next morning, too ill to go to work, and with the darkening sense that something awful had happened but no memory of what it was. He tried to find Susi to say goodbye, but he wasn't familiar with her home and didn't want to walk in on her housemates. Instead, he sent her a text message from the bus back to Walthamstow. **Sorry I got so pissed last night. Thanks for giving me your sofa.**

She didn't reply. He went home, his housemate let him in, and he slept till the afternoon. Odd images from the night before came back to him: he and Susi kissing, his hands pushing their way up her skirt in the reckless, unattractive style of drunken passion.

The next morning, when he went back to work, he noticed an icy silence towards him from female colleagues. When he greeted them, they simply stared at their computer screens without looking up. A few blokes looked at him sympathetically, but there was no mistaking the fact that no one was speaking to him. He went to his desk and quietly got on with his work.

At eleven, his boss called him into the office.

'Luke,' he said seriously, leaning back in his chair with his hands behind his head in a gesture of arrogance, 'I'm afraid there has been a serious allegation against you from a female member of staff. Susi Lambert.'

The shock rendered Luke speechless. He let his boss continue.

'Susi has said that when you went back to her house the other night, after losing your house keys, you committed a serious sexual assault against her.'

'I ...'

He couldn't remember what had happened, so he had no power to defend himself, no alternative story to offer.

'As a result of this, you two can no longer work together

and I've taken the decision to put you on gardening leave while we sort out an alternative position for you. When we've finished this meeting, you will need to return to your desk, log off your computer, gather your things and leave. We will keep you informed of progress here and hopefully have something else for you by the end of the week. There has been some talk of Susi pressing charges, but I don't know what she has decided yet. I don't know what you want to do about Susi, or how amenable she is to talking to you. That's up to you to decide. And of course,' he added, gazing at Luke sternly, 'you know that being hungover is absolutely not a good enough reason to take a day off work. I don't expect that to happen again.'

Luke left the office with his head bowed, shaking and feeling acutely self-conscious. All he wanted to do now was pack his things, go home and never come back. But if he did that, everyone would assume he was guilty. He'd have to return and face these demons.

For the next few days, he moped around his flat, feeling anxious and frightened. How was he ever going to move past this? It would follow him around forever. He'd now always be the bloke who assaulted someone from work. Gardening leave. He remembered the first time he'd ever heard that term, when his father had referred to someone at work being on gardening leave and Luke had said, 'Sounds great. Time off, full pay.' His father had looked at him and said, 'It's not a good thing, Luke. No one wants 'period of gardening leave' on their CV. It looks very bad. It's code for being in serious trouble, one step away from being fired.'

And now Luke was on gardening leave, at the age of

twenty-two, before his career had even got off the ground. Maybe he'd have to change his name, he thought.

On the fifth day, the police arrested him, took him to the station and interviewed him for four hours. 'They were so unfair, Mum,' he told her. He'd turned down their offer of a solicitor because he was innocent and didn't think he'd need one. But he had no idea how the police worked. He talked, and they twisted his words, and trapped him in corners, and wouldn't listen to anything he said. In the end he was charged, released on bail with the condition that he had no contact with Susi, and told he had to wait for his case to reach court.

Luke floundered. He had no idea what to do, other than phone his mum and go home.

It was about the worst thing Jo could imagine, when he told her. That afternoon, when she'd sat staring at the envelope from the solicitor, her mind had gone into overdrive, imagining all sorts of foolish, reckless things her son might have been involved in: drugs, probably, or theft, or crashing someone's car. Not once had she strayed into the area of sexual assault. To do that would be to think the unthinkable. Her clever, funny, good-looking boy, accused – at best – of carelessness around consent.

As she began to process his story, she was conscious of her mind shutting down, unable to cope with the worst. Recklessness, that's what it been. Drunken recklessness.

Which was, frankly, bad enough.

She raged at him. 'Have I taught you nothing?' she demanded. 'Of all things, Luke. *Of all bloody things.*'

She had never been so furious, so appalled by one of her

children. She didn't want to look at him, and wished she could tell him to go to his room. 'Come back when you've thought about your behaviour and you're ready to improve it,' she'd say. A twenty-two minute timeout, one minute for each year of his life. He'd return to her transformed. 'Sorry, Mummy,' he'd say. 'I won't do it again.' And then she'd give him a glass of milk and a kiss and their world would be restored.

She knew now that she didn't mean *Go to your room*. What she meant was, *Get out of this house. There is no space for a sex offender here.*

She looked at him, pale and red-eyed beside her.

She wasn't ready to turn him out yet.

30

Erin

Erin caught a taxi home from the station. She'd been in London for two days, meeting an editor who'd bought her most recent feature and wanted to discuss the possibility of more, and afterwards catching up with old colleagues. Almost as soon as she'd stepped off the train at King's Cross, Erin felt like she could breathe again. Everything, absolutely everything, was within reach here. Opportunities, history, art, geography, power … And the food! She'd almost forgotten – though of course she hadn't really forgotten – that you couldn't walk a hundred yards without passing sushi or bimbimbap or shawarma, or that the Turkish bakery would still be open at 1 a.m. when she went by on her way to her hotel.

What she loved most, though, were the people – the people who went about their lives quickly, anonymously, barely looking up, not stopping her on the pavement for a chat the way they did in Burntridge, not caring who anyone else slept with or how they dressed, just as long as they didn't stand to the left on the escalator in the underground stations, or impinge on anyone's right to get on with their day. The people who hadn't voted for Brexit, the people who stood on platforms waiting for a train and heard the rise and fall of five different languages and welcomed it; the enormous man buying a sandwich on Wardour St, dressed in a tutu with his hair in a tiny top knot and all the people around him who didn't give a shit.

It was glorious.

For a day, it had been glorious. But then, on the second day, it all suddenly became too much. Everywhere was too big, too smelly, too crowded. She'd somehow managed to get lost somewhere near Charing Cross Road because she hadn't been concentrating on where she was going, and she ended up pacing the streets for half an hour, trying to find her hotel, and there was no one to share the stress of it, or turn it into a bit of an adventure with. Rachel would have done, if she'd been there with her. She'd have just shrugged and said, 'We're not really lost. We just don't know exactly where we are but we'll sort it out,' and she'd have dragged Erin into a bar and they'd have drunk white wine until their words slurred and eventually called a cab to the hotel and stumbled into bed for slightly drunken sex.

And that was what it all came down to. London was great, but it wasn't home any more because Rachel wasn't there. It bothered Erin to feel this way, to have her well-being so tied up in another person. Right now, she was happy. She was blissfully, dangerously happy and if Rachel ever left her, she was going to fall apart. She would break and become unfixable. She knew that, and she hated it. Sometimes, she wanted to take hold of Rachel, the light of her life, and rage at her, *Why have you done this to me? Why have you made me so bloody vulnerable? I was fine before I met you and now I've met you, I will never be fine again.*

God, she was so melodramatic.

But it was true. That was the trouble.

Still, for now, Rachel had missed her. She'd texted Erin earlier to say she only had one interview scheduled for this afternoon, so she'd be home on time. Erin could hardly wait to see her. All the time she was away, she'd still been aware of the lingering touch of Rachel's hand on her thigh when she'd dropped her off at the station, and the words she hadn't said because Tess was in the back, but which Erin had heard nevertheless. 'I'll be thinking of you all the time when you're gone and when you come home, we will commit some loving acts of gross indecency,' and Erin had leaned forward and kissed her, and knew her kiss carried similar unspoken words.

The taxi driver turned right off the main road and down the lane that led to the village. It was only just after three-thirty, but the sun was setting fast, blazing orange across a sky thick with dusk. Erin looked at the arrangement of old stone houses around the village green and the tiny church in the corner and for the first time since moving here, was suddenly suffused with the unfamiliar warmth of feeling that she'd come home. It was years since she'd felt this way – possibly not since she was eighteen and had gone back to her mother's house after that first term at university, knowing she'd returned to a place where there was no pressure to perform and she was loved.

She handed the taxi driver a £10 note, told him to keep the change, heaved her bag out of the footwell and stepped out onto the drive. The first thing she noticed was how cold it was here, compared to London. The second thing she noticed was that the front door of the house was wide open. Rachel's car wasn't there, so she assumed it must be something to do with

Reuben – he'd left it gaping as he lugged his guitar and his amp inside and conveniently forgotten all about it, failing to notice that the entire house was slowly freezing – but then she remembered Reuben was away on a school trip to Manchester and not due home until tomorrow, so her mind shifted immediately to burglars. She'd been burgled once before, years ago, when she house-shared in Clapham Junction, and they too had left the door wide open – like a warning, she'd thought at the time.

Erin was a wimp. She had no desire to interrupt them, preferring to just wait patiently outside and allow them to finish helping themselves to whatever took their fancy, rather than go in and risk confronting them. She was as certain as she could be that Rachel would also prefer to lose everything in the house than for Erin to have a knife through her heart or her head blown off, and even in this state of quite high anxiety, Erin could still feel the lurch of being lost in a strange world in which she mattered to someone. Her previous partners would have made a cursory pretence of being upset about it, but if Erin had ever been shot dead in a burglary, she was pretty sure they'd all secretly have been thinking, *At least it was just that Erin got killed and they didn't take my Xbox.*

She hovered for a while by the stone wall in front of the house, watching for any signs of movement inside. Her coat was too thin for a Northumberland winter and night was falling fast, so she crept towards the front door, aware that she was behaving like a madwoman and hoping no one could see her. On the doorstep, she paused for a moment and peered inside the hall. Everything was as it should be: the piano in the hall untouched; the black-and-white floor tiles immaculate; the coats all hanging neatly on the stand. No one had tampered with anything. She closed the door and headed further inside.

Everything was fine. She took herself down to the kitchen and switched the kettle on. Rachel had left her mail propped up against a vase full of white roses on the island. She flicked through a few official-looking envelopes and left them all unopened.

She wasn't imagining it. There were footsteps on the floor above her. Briefly, she considered darting out of the house again, but then they started coming down the narrow wooden staircase that in some previous century had been used by servants and linked the kitchen to the first floor.

It was Maia. She saw Erin and stopped in her tracks.

Erin stared at her for a moment. Maia stared back.

Erin sensed that Maia had been caught. She was aware that it was she who'd caught her, but had no idea what the act was that she'd caught her in. She decided the best approach was to pretend this was all completely normal and just smile. 'Oh, hi Maia,' she said, in a tone she hoped was warm and friendly.

The guilty, slightly frightened look left Maia's face and was replaced with something that looked to Erin like a cross between smugness and restrained laughter. She continued her descent, then once she was at the bottom turned her head and said over her shoulder, 'Don't worry. It's just the girlfriend.'

Erin saw legs first, as whoever it was followed Maia down the stairs. Black jeans, unmistakably male. Whoever it was then stopped, as if he suddenly realised he didn't quite have the audacity to show his face, though Maia clearly wanted him to.

She needed to stay casual. She wasn't Maia's mother, and this was Maia's home, and thank God, it wasn't for Erin to make a decision about how to deal with this. She'd need to talk about it with Rachel first. For Erin to act hastily could make the situation between Maia and Rachel even worse, and place her own relationship with Maia forever on the scrapheap.

She looked at Maia and smiled again, as if it wasn't even crossing her mind to question what Maia was doing here with a young man at a time when she expected the house to be empty.

Maia said, 'A friend from school just came to help me pick up some stuff to take back to Dad's.'

What stuff? There was no stuff. She wasn't carrying any stuff.

Erin said, 'No problem.'

'We were just going. See you soon, maybe.'

Maybe. Erin hadn't set eyes on Maia since the night she'd walked out. She said, 'That would be lovely.'

The boy on the stairs had retreated. Erin looked at Maia and said, 'To make this easier for everyone, I'll just go into the living room while you leave. OK?'

Maia looked unmistakably grateful. Erin left the room.

After they'd gone, she went back to the kitchen, sat at the table, drank her tea and wondered what to tell Rachel. She would have to tell Rachel, of course, and then help calm her worries. Although Erin had no idea who this boy was, she was as sure as she could be that it was someone other than James. She'd seen James from a distance before. He was skinnier than this boy, and from the little she knew of him, she thought he'd have been gracious and guiltless enough to come down the stairs and say hello.

Still, she shouldn't assume Maia was sleeping with this boy.

She probably wasn't. But why else would they have come here, to an empty house that Maia no longer lived in, if not to at least indulge in some clumsy foreplay?

The decision she made was quick. Without really thinking, she pushed her chair back and went upstairs to Maia's room, which had been left almost untouched since she'd moved out. Rachel had been in there once, to remove the mould-riddled mugs, make the bed and vacuum the carpet so it would look welcoming if Maia ever came home, but that was all.

The room was still tidy. On Maia's dressing table, there were still endless pots and tubes of cheap make-up, her books were still neatly lined in alphabetical order on the shelf, the door to the walk-in wardrobe was closed against the piles of vintage fashion that no doubt still covered the floor inside.

The bed, though, was unmade. On the floor beside it was a blue foil condom wrapper, ripped open and empty.

Erin recognised this scene for exactly what it was. A cold, deliberate *Fuck you* from Maia to her mother.

31

Rachel

Rachel was fed up with her children. Reuben hadn't been shortlisted for an interview at Cambridge and now the bottom had fallen out of his world; Tess had reverted to hating Erin; and Maia was refusing to speak to her because Rachel had made it clear to her daughter – her sixteen-year-old daughter, for God's sake – that she was mightily unimpressed that she thought it OK to be casually shagging blokes who weren't her boyfriend in her old bedroom.

'I'm being careful, Mum,' Maia said again, as if the fact that there was a condom involved made everything fine.

'I don't care how careful you're being, Maia. I thought James was your boyfriend. Shouldn't you have finished things with him before you started casually sleeping with someone else? It's not OK for you to cheat on your boyfriend in my house.'

'You told me last week that it's my house, too.'

Rachel was about to lose it. 'I meant it's your house to live in, if you want to. It's your house to come and stay in any time you like. But it's not a fucking brothel, Maia, and you will not treat it like one, do you understand me?'

Maia muttered something under her breath that Rachel

couldn't hear, but which she was pretty sure amounted to, 'You shag your girlfriend on the kitchen floor so actually, *Mother*, it is a fucking brothel.'

'Anyway,' Rachel continued, 'are you really being careful? Contraception is one thing, but what about *you*? You're sixteen. I know you think you're very grown-up, but are you actually tough enough to do this? To sleep with all these different boys and think you'll come out of it OK?'

Maia rolled her eyes. 'It's not "all these different boys". For God's sake, Mum. It was James and now it's … someone else. Anyway, I thought you were a feminist. I thought you always said it was OK for a woman to shag whoever she likes.'

'It *is* OK, Maia,' she said, 'but only if you can handle it. Feeling used is unpleasant. And you're being unfair to James.'

She could see Maia shutting down, tuning her out. There was no point any more in Rachel talking, but she couldn't stop. 'I have no moral issue with any of this,' she said, knowing as the words came out that this wasn't true any more. It was, until about five minutes ago. It had been true all her life that Rachel had relaxed sexual morals, but now her daughter was sitting in front of her, having slept with James and now some other boy in the space of a few days, she felt repulsed by it and found herself wanting to say, *Just keep yourself nice, darling*.

She went on, 'My concern is only that you protect yourself and you don't recklessly hurt other people.' She paused, then asked the question she'd been wondering about for days. 'Who is this new boy, anyway?'

'That's none of your business,' Maia said, looking her straight in the eye, 'And besides, I don't need to listen to this from you. Look at you,' she said, with disgust. 'Just look at you. You think it's OK to lecture me about *feelings* when you just woke up one morning and thought, 'Oh, I know. I'm fed up with my husband so I'll just go and shag some random woman and not give a shit who gets upset about it, or who *sees*. At least I do it in private. And I don't know how you can even use the word *betrayal* after what you did to Dad.'

And she'd stormed off out of the house again, leaving Rachel wondering if their relationship could ever be repaired. She also wondered who this new male in her child's life was. Someone inappropriate, no doubt. Someone she wouldn't approve of.

Then there was Reuben, moping around the house as if he'd lost all reason to live. To begin with, Rachel had been sympathetic. He wasn't yet eighteen, and this was his first real taste of disappointment and she knew how hard that was, but after a week, she wanted to shake him. 'Get over it,' she felt like saying. 'Not getting into Cambridge is one of life's non-problems. It doesn't matter. You have a place at LSE, you have a place at Edinburgh. You will be fine. You will have a career, you will earn enough money and you will be absolutely OK forever. Plus you were born with a penis, which puts you at an immediate advantage. And you sound a bit posh. And your skin is white. And you have parents who will one day gift you enough money to buy a house. So get over the fact that you haven't got into Cambridge.'

More and more these days, she wanted to take her two eldest children and bang their heads together. She wondered now if she'd spoiled them, even though she'd always hated that term. *Spoiled,* as if you could somehow ruin a child by loving them. Their well-being had always been at the heart of everything she did, every decision she made. When they were little, she'd put her career on the back burner so she could look after them, and when she did return to work, it had been gradual. They were the whole reason she'd surrendered life as a practising doctor and gone into research instead – because it was easier to fit that sort of work around school hours and she'd always had this idea that they needed a parent to pick them up, because it was only when you saw their faces at three o'clock that you could tell how their day had been and if you missed that moment, you could end up missing all that was going on in their small lives.

Her children had had good childhoods. They'd had idyllic childhoods because Rachel had been determined to do parenthood properly. She used to joke about it to Jo. 'I worry I'm giving my kids such a boring, normal childhood, they'll grow into happy, functional adults I won't be able to relate to.'

The key to all of it, she'd known from the start, was staying with their father. For years she'd managed it, locked in that loveless marriage for the sake of the children. She and Will had been brilliant at hiding the cracks. They made sure they rubbed along – no longer functioning as a unit of two, but working well as a unit of five. She'd planned to stay until the children were adults, but the time came when she met Erin and could bear it no longer, knowing she was wasting away, rotting beside a man who was rotting beside her.

And so she'd done it. She'd ended it and now the children were broken because of it. She felt guilty, of course. She felt deeply, devastatingly guilty. But amid that guilt lurked a quiet resentment because why the fuck couldn't they just deal with it? She really had to fight the urge to shout at them, *You have no idea how good you've got it. Come and see the families*

I work with. Come and see the abuse and the neglect and the grinding poverty and then tell me how bad your lives are.

It wouldn't help. Children never appreciated what they had, and why should they? It wasn't their job to be grateful. It was her job to feel blessed to have them, but she was now spotting the flaw in that happy childhood: it had left them shocked by the ordinary troubles of life, completely unable to deal with them.

She'd decided there was no point talking to Will about it. He was so grateful to have one of his children living with him again, he wasn't going to risk it by doing something wild, like imposing boundaries round her behaviour. And Rachel was in no place to say, 'She needs to come home. She needs to be with me,' because Maia had shown everyone, quite clearly, that living with her mother was bad for her.

Erin, as ever, was the only voice of reason and comfort. 'She will be OK,' she promised. 'She's doing it to get back at you.'

'Is she?' Rachel asked, craving certainty. She wanted someone to explain to her, absolutely and exactly, why Maia was behaving like this and when it was going to stop.

'Of course she is. She's angry with you. She's an injured animal, kicking out. Try not to get too cross with her.'

'I'd rather she just slapped me.'

'It's temporary, Rachel. I am certain of that. By the time she's eighteen, this will have passed. She's not an idiot. She's young, and she's having a hard time, and she's dealing with it badly.'

'Thank you,' Rachel said, knowing this was probably true. She didn't know what she'd do now, without Erin to steady her. But then, if she didn't have Erin, Maia wouldn't be behaving like this. Rachel was certain of that.

32

Maia

Maia was sitting cross-legged on James's bedroom floor, while his parents were downstairs with no idea that she was breaking their son's heart or how awful it was. She hadn't known it was going to be this bad. His face was ashen, as if she'd just bombed the life out of him. Perhaps she had. He hung his head too low and she thought he might be crying, although she couldn't be sure.

She wished she could make it stop, wished she could suddenly laugh and say, 'I don't know what I was thinking. I didn't mean it. I'll stay with you. I'll stay with you forever.'

But if she did that, she'd be trapped in this mini marriage, with all his talk of love and of abandoning his ambitions to go to the Royal Academy of Music and stay local so they could be together. She found it hard to breathe when he spoke like that. All she wanted to do was run.

After for-fucking-ever, he looked up and fixed his eyes on hers. *Oh, God,* she wanted to say, *this is why. This is why I have to end this. Stop looking at me like that. Stop looking like you want to suck me into you through your fucking eyes.*

He said, 'I don't understand … *Why?*'

He'd already asked this three times, and three times she'd answered. How long did this have to go on for? When would it be OK to get the hell out of this room? She shouldn't have come to his house to do it. She should have met him in a café, done it in a public space where they'd only have been able to talk about it for as long as it took to drink a cup of coffee.

She looked at him helplessly. 'I just … I'm sorry. I didn't realise you …'

'*Loved you?*' He practically spat the words in her face. 'Is that it? You didn't realise I loved you?'

She shook her head.

'How did you not know?'

She did know. Of course she knew. It was why she wanted to get away from him. What she didn't know was that this was the way people reacted when they loved you and you wanted to get away from them.

'I'm sorry,' she said. It was pathetic, to be sorry. She could see that.

He was silent again for a while. Then he said, 'Have you met someone else, is that it?'

'No.'

She wondered if he watched *Hollyoaks*. No one outside *Hollyoaks* spoke like this.

Oh, why was she such a bitch? She had to stop. But she'd been here an hour and they were going round in circles and she was reaching a point now where guilt was giving way to disgust.

'Why, then?' he asked again.

'I've told you. It's too much. I'm too young for this. I made a mistake.'

'A mistake,' he repeated. A blank look came over his face, as if he had no idea what she was talking about.

She nodded.

'We can slow it down, then,' he said. 'Be less serious.'

'I don't think that's possible.'

She didn't understand this need of his to keep asking why, to demand explanations. If he didn't stop, he was going to force her to tell him the truth. *I don't love you. I never loved you. And now, after all this, I don't think I even like you. Let me go home.*

She stood up from where she'd been sitting and said, 'I think I should go.'

He stared at her. 'You're just going to go? You're just going to come here, do this to me, and then fucking *leave*?'

She didn't get it. What else was she supposed to do? She'd said she didn't want to be with him any more and now she had to go. If she stayed, that wouldn't be leaving him. That would be staying with him.

There was nothing else to say. She'd explained her reasons, she'd said she was sorry. Now she needed to get out and recover from the shock of seeing what she'd just done to someone who really didn't deserve it. Poor James. He didn't deserve to be this hurt. She hadn't known. She was an idiot. She didn't understand all this. She was a bloody stupid child who'd walked into something she wasn't grown-up enough for, just because she wanted to find out what all the fuss about sex was.

How did you say goodbye to someone whose heart you'd just broken? Did you lean forwards and drop a chaste, maternal kiss on the top of their head? Did you shrug and say, 'I'll see you at school?' Dear God, what did you *do*?

In the end, she just went.

Sasha stopped her in the hall, right when she was trying to sneak out the front door without being seen.

'Are you leaving, Maia? Stay for dinner if you want.'

Maia forced a smile. 'It's OK. Thank you, but I said I'd see my mum this evening.'

'That's good. I'm glad you two are patching things up. It would break both your hearts if you didn't.'

She was about to find out that her son was upstairs clutching at his own broken heart. Maia wondered if Sasha would hate her, perhaps come after her with a knife or a rolling pin, the way overbearingly loving mothers did in books. They were usually Italian, those women, and Sasha wasn't Italian, so hopefully she'd restrain herself. But Sasha was one of the reasons Maia had stayed with James longer than she really should have done – she liked her and didn't want to upset her, or for her to despise her for hurting her son.

Maia said, 'Thanks. I really have to go.'

She knew she sounded rude and abrupt but she didn't care now. She just wanted to get outside where she could breathe again.

33

Laura

Laura was working the night shift again, thinking how much she wanted to give this up but not knowing what she could do that would earn enough money to pay the bills and give her time left over to spend with Max. Five years she'd been doing this – ever since Drew walked out and left her with nothing but a baby who needed formula to drink and a roof over his head.

She'd done it before then as well, for a year or so when she was a teenager, when she'd left home because her mother was so mad and made Laura's life miserable. It was the only work she could think of to do. She had no education, no GCSEs. Nothing. She'd spent a couple of nights sleeping on the streets until a pimp had picked her up and offered her an easy life.

It hadn't been an easy life, of course, and it took Laura too long to get away from him, but she'd done it in the end, with the help of a women's shelter. She'd found work in a shop and stayed at the shelter until she'd saved enough money and had her benefits claim approved, then moved into a bedsit. It had been damp and cold, but at least it was hers and she'd vowed then never to be a sex worker again.

But that was before she'd been abandoned, aged twenty-one, with a baby and no way to feed him. So here she was again.

Will Kernick had come to say goodbye to her, which seemed so old-fashioned and incongruously polite she hardly knew how to respond. She'd met him three times altogether, and on none of those times had he received the service he'd paid for. He simply sat there, sipped the tea she made him and sadly unloaded his torment. Then he'd kiss her chastely on the cheek and leave.

Laura had known some weirdos in her time in this job, but no one quite like this. Will Kernick, the decent family man who hadn't had a shag for years, thought he'd gratify himself by paying for sex and found, in the end, that he just couldn't do it. That's how decent he was, how charming, how respectful of women. And after he'd opened up his soul to her, he considered it only proper to come and say goodbye.

He said, 'Things have been difficult for a while. It was hard losing my wife and my kids and I didn't know what to do. For a while, I just wanted to feel better, just for a few minutes, which is why I ...' He stopped talking and shook his head, as if he couldn't believe what he'd been thinking. 'But I don't want to become one of those men who ...'

She smiled and he looked startled.

'I'm sorry,' he said. 'I didn't mean ...'

He was like Hugh Grant, she thought, all shamefaced and posh.

He went on. 'And I really appreciate that you haven't just ...' He blushed a little, but kept his gaze earnestly upon her. 'I appreciate that you've let me come here and talk to you. But it probably isn't a good idea for me to keep doing this. I feel more settled now and I don't want it to become a ... habit.'

She shrugged. 'That's fine,' she said. 'You know you're the client. You don't need to explain anything. This is just a business transaction.'

He nodded. 'I know.' He stood up to leave, 'I should say goodbye to you.' Then he leaned forwards and kissed her gently and for a moment, Laura was afraid she might sob, though whether for him or for herself, she wasn't sure.

In another life, he might have loved her properly.

It was just after two when she let herself into the flat. She was exhausted and longing for bed, longing to lie down and let her eyes close and for sleep to take her away from all this.

She dropped her bag in the hallway, then took herself into Max's room to check on him. It was when he was asleep, curled into a ball with his arms holding the covers tightly round his chin, his breath slow and deep, that she experienced the love she never seemed able to grab hold of during the day, when everything about him seemed so demanding or so worrying, and always reminded her that she was no good at this, that she should never have become his mother. But when he slept, it was different. It was possible, then, to imagine that tomorrow things would be better, that she would stop failing and he would become happy and well.

She loved watching him sleep.

His light was on, as always. She went into the room and climbed onto the bottom rung of the ladder on his cabin bed and leaned over.

The bed was empty.

He wasn't there.

34

Erin

Erin was walking alone alongside the ravine that ran through the woodland on the edge of town. Rachel had finished her interviews and the research for her new book. Now she had to start writing it and was at the stage where she welcomed anything as an excuse to put it off. She was at home, making crumpets from scratch. 'No one makes crumpets from scratch,' Erin told her.

'Then I'll be the first,' Rachel said, and tripped over the puppy who was hanging round her feet, waiting for the scraps that would inevitably fall off the worktop.

Erin decided to go for a walk and leave her to it, so now she was wrapped up against the late November wind, heading to the outskirts of Burntridge, towards the moors and hills of the North Pennines, where the landscape was frozen and the sky thick with the promise of snow. It was one of the things Rachel told her she would grow to love about living in Northumberland. There were proper seasons here. Endless daylight in summer, and guaranteed snow in winter. Sometimes, even if no snow had fallen in Burntridge, all you needed to do was drive into the hills and there it would be: miles and miles of untrodden snow, the space entirely empty of people.

Erin still wasn't sure. She understood the beauty of this far-flung county with its moorland and castles and vast sandy beaches, but even now, even after her last trip, London was what she was made of. Cut her open, she thought, and they'd find the Thames running through her veins. She missed wandering along the Southbank. She missed seeing the dome of St Paul's as she walked to work, missed crossing the Millennium Bridge, looking down at the clippers on the water, spotting the silhouette of the Tower of London in the distance. Mostly, she missed being part of the centre of the world.

Even though her life was fuller now – full of Rachel, full of family and love and all the drama that came with it – her world had shrunk to something so small, she sometimes wanted to push the edges out, let the rest of life in.

For Rachel, though, there was no 'rest of life'. She had her work and she had her children. That was her world and to her, it was enormous. 'I made it myself,' she joked. 'This whole, wide world.'

They'd agreed to try and stop talking about Maia. Last week, Rachel had given her sharp orders to get to the doctor's for the contraceptive implant and never to use her house as a slab for frivolous sex again, and that was the last time the two of them had spoken. Erin could do nothing except keep telling her she was doing the right thing, and continue with her unwavering assurances that everything would eventually be fine.

'Will it?' Rachel asked her yesterday. 'Will it really?'

'Of course it will.'

'But how? How will it be fine? My sixteen-year-old daughter doesn't speak to me and now she's shagging every bloke who fancies her. Which, let's face it, is pretty much every bloke.'

Erin couldn't help smiling at that – the love and pride still strong amid the despair. And the melodrama, of course, because Maia clearly wasn't sleeping with every bloke who fancied her. It was just James, and then someone new. She said, 'Everything will be fine in the end because everything always is fine in the end. That's how it goes. If it's not fine, it's not the end.'

'No, it's definitely not the end,' Rachel said. 'I spend my days waiting for the next shock to drop. An abortion, perhaps. HIV. Maybe genital herpes and the beginnings of lifelong shame.'

Erin knew when Rachel was in this sort of mood that there was nothing more she could say. The most effective thing she could do was get out the house for a few hours and know Rachel would be fine when she returned. Besides, today was going to be a good day because at some point, eventually, Rachel would write the first paragraph of her new book, which meant she would be happy again. Erin would sample her baking and declare it delicious, even though it was likely to be a dismal failure, and later they would light a fire and decorate the Christmas tree. Afterwards, they'd curl up on the sofa and listen to a novel, as if they were the Victorian couple Dickens never wrote about.

It was nearly ten in the morning, but full daylight hadn't yet dawned. The deep brown branches of the tree skeletons spiked against the grey sky, the icy waters of the ravine rushed below her and the path beneath her feet was hard with frost. Erin was cautious as she navigated her way over a steep section of the path. It felt a lot like the opening of one of those Emergency 999 programmes. A lone woman from London walking in icy conditions and unsuitable footwear by the side of a ravine. An hour from now, a group of youths playing truant from school would find her body, stiff and lifeless in the water.

Ahead of her, the path was blocked by a huge rock. She looked at it for a while, wondering what she was meant to do. When they'd been to the Lake District a few months ago, Erin had made as if to turn back when rocks appeared on the path, but Rachel laughed at her and said they were meant to climb them.

'Seriously?' Erin had asked.

'Yes, seriously. These are mountains, Erin. They're not meant to be friendly. You have to conquer them.'

But this wasn't Buttermere. This was ordinary Burntridge and she was barely out of the town centre yet. Why was there a rock in her way?

She shouldn't be this clueless. She was aware of being a disgrace to womankind but she just wasn't used to this sort of thing.

She could hear Rachel's voice in her head. 'Don't play the fucking ex-Londoner card, Erin,' she'd be saying. 'You have rocks in London.'

'Not *in our way*, we don't. They're not just hanging around, blocking the exit of the underground station.'

She could see that the path continued beyond the rock. It took three attempts and she was torn between wanting someone to come along and sort this whole thing out for her by giving her a leg-up, and not wanting to be seen like this: a grown woman, failing to get herself over a rock.

Slowly, she hauled herself up, using her hands as grips, then brushed the dirt from her jeans and continued walking. Ahead of her, she noticed what looked like an abandoned anorak and assumed people had been fly-tipping again. The area was rife with fly-tippers. Often, there were discarded washing machines or pushchairs caught on the steep edges of the ravine and the council had to bring in cranes to haul them away again.

As she grew closer, she realised it wasn't an anorak, but a child. She slowed her pace, feeling herself about to step into a crisis, about to take on a responsibility she wasn't sure she wanted.

But she couldn't walk away. She'd seen it. She was involved.

Erin had done basic first aid training in her late teens, when she'd worked at a kids' camp in Texas, back in the days when students could spend whole summers travelling instead of squandering them behind a supermarket checkout so they could pay their next term's rent to some filthy, tax-dodging landlord. She wasn't sure she'd remember enough of it now.

She kneeled down on the ground beside the boy, took his hand in hers and felt for a pulse. He was alive, but so cold.

'Help!' she called, recalling that it was the most important thing to do. 'Help!'

His lips and fingers were blue, his breathing shallow. Should she put him in the recovery position? She wasn't sure. 'Help!' she called again.

Beneath his jacket, he was wearing only pyjamas. Quickly, Erin took off her coat and wrapped him in it. She pulled him onto her lap to protect him from the frozen ground. Her phone was at home, lying on the kitchen table. She deliberately hadn't brought it with her. She felt close to tears and wished Rachel was here because Rachel would absolutely have known what to do.

'Help!' she called again.

She could see a park behind the trees, and beyond it a housing estate. If she could just lift the child, she'd be able to carry him and find a house where someone would let her call an ambulance.

She slid one arm under the boy's knees and the other beneath his shoulders. He was lighter than she'd expected. Slowly, slipping slightly and cursing her stupid choice of shoes, she stood up and carried him towards the houses.

She'd seen this boy before. She knew who he was. He was Max Spence, Laura's child.

35

Laura

Laura was still searching: the allotments, the path around the reservoir at the top of the hill, the park at the back of the estate. Everywhere. She'd left the door to her flat open, and also the entrance door to the building, along with a note saying *Please don't close*. She didn't care if other residents were angry about it. That was the least of her worries. On the kitchen table, she'd left a plate with four malted milks on it and a glass of orange squash in case Max came home.

The first thing she'd done when she saw that he wasn't in bed was slowly and calmly search every inch of the flat. Five times, she did it. Five times, he was nowhere to be found. She didn't panic. She was calm and ice-cold, and knew she was simply going to look and look until she found him. It didn't matter how long it took. She would find her son.

She wanted to text Drew. A nasty, accusing message. *You've taken Max, you bastard. Bring him back*. She couldn't, though, because what if it hadn't been him? He would then know that she'd left him alone at night, that she did it regularly, and that she was a sex worker. And he'd use all those things as evidence that she shouldn't be looking after a child and he should have custody of Max. And the judge would grant it.

For exactly the same reasons, she'd thought during the night that she couldn't go to the police. She would have had to explain everything and then they'd arrest her for neglect and take him away from her – place him with other parents who could look after him properly, who didn't take their anger out on him, who would love him the way he deserved to be loved. And although it had often crossed her mind that this might be best for him, she knew that if it ever happened, she would have no reason to keep going and she would die.

It had all made sense at two o'clock this morning, when she'd come home and found his empty bed and that cold, cold calm had settled inside her. She couldn't tell anyone and she would find him herself. Later, as dawn broke and she heard the murmur of cars from the main road and still hadn't found him, Laura began to think maybe she should have called the police, after all. She could have come up with a story – told them she'd been on her sofa bed in the living room (because she gave Max the bedroom), fast asleep, and when she woke up at two and crossed the hall to the bathroom, she'd noticed Max was gone.

That would have been the sensible thing to do, and now it was too late. If she went to the police now, she'd have to tell them how long he'd been missing, and then she would immediately be under suspicion. What sort of mother let eight hours pass before she bothered to report her missing child?

She'd looked everywhere and it was cold. It was so cold, and she was exhausted, but she couldn't give up. 'Max!' she called, as she climbed over a stile to the neighbouring field. 'Max!'

A lone dog walker smiled at her. 'Have you lost him?'

Laura, flustered and close to tears now, said, 'I don't know. I don't know. He was in his bed …'

'Don't worry, love. They can find their way home. Iggy here ran off after a rabbit the other day and I thought he was gone forever, but he came back. You got enough treats? I can give you some.'

He reached into his pocket and handed her a small bag of dog biscuits.

She smiled weakly as she took them. 'Thank you,' she whispered.

'Good luck,' the man said, and went on his way again.

The trouble with the police was that Laura was frightened of them. She always had been, ever since the night when she was five years old and there'd been that hard knock on the front door. Laura had watched from upstairs, spying through the bannisters in her nightdress. Her mother opened the door to two male officers, both of them grave and stern. 'We've come to talk to Michael Spence.'

'What's he done this time?'

'We'd like to talk to him. Can we come in?'

Her mother pulled the door wide and Laura saw the officers wiping their boots on the mat, respectful even when they'd come to arrest someone. They went through to the living room and Laura could hear nothing then except for the murmur of serious voices and her father saying, 'This is ridiculous.'

After five minutes or so, the officers came out into the hall again, followed by Laura's father, and they all walked down the driveway to the waiting police car. Laura watched from her window as they bundled her father into the back and drove him away.

From then on, she only saw him in prison. Every few weeks, she and her mother would sit opposite him at a table in the visitors' room, watched over by the guards, and Laura would look at the stark black-and-white clock on the wall, watching the minutes tick by, wishing they would move faster so she could get out and never come back.

No one ever told her exactly what her father had done to end up in prison, but Laura had never doubted the power of the police. If they found out that she left Max alone at night, she'd go the way of her father and then what would happen to her son? There was no one left to look after him. Her own mother was long dead and she had no siblings she could entrust him to. He'd end up with his father, the man who had no idea what it meant to be responsible for anything, let alone a child.

So now here she was, combing the area where she lived, calling his name and feeling the sudden rise of rushing panic as the cold shock wore off. In her mind, she began to travel away from the estate and over the whole town of Burntridge, then west towards Cumbria and north to Scotland, south to London …

Oh God, the world was so big and Max was so small.

She felt like throwing herself to the ground and howling. For a while, she simply stood where she was and put her head in her hands. *If someone brings him back to me, I'll start all over again. I'll be a better mother. I won't leave him. I'll get a different job. I won't be stressed and short-tempered and cruel. I'll be patient and loving. I'll do it properly.*

She lifted her head again and looked around, as if her prayer might have been answered. It hadn't. Max was nowhere to be seen.

Then she saw her. A lone woman crossing the park behind the allotments, carrying a child.

Max.

She knew it was Max the moment she saw her. Laura broke into a run.

'Max!' she said, and started to cry, loudly uncontrollably. She was aware of herself repeating his name as she sobbed.

The woman carrying him was Rachel Saunders' girlfriend.

'He's very cold. We need an ambulance.'

Laura couldn't speak through her tears. She reached out and took Max in her own arms. The woman had been right. He was freezing. She wondered if he was dead.

'He's alive. I checked his pulse.'

Laura nodded and began half running towards the flats. He was heavy. She couldn't move fast enough.

She was aware of the woman – she couldn't remember her name – following her. She wished she'd just go away, leave Laura to deal with this by herself. She didn't want other people involved, prying people like Rachel Saunders' girlfriend, who would tell Rachel, who would tell the police …

But she needed help. She needed to bring her son back to life and she had no idea how to do it.

'I'm sorry,' she said, as she carried him through her front door and laid him on the living room floor.

'He needs an ambulance,' the woman said again. She sounded agitated.

Laura took her phone out of her pocket. She had credit on

it, for once. She passed it to the woman. 'We don't need the doctors yet. Just google it,' she said. 'Google what we have to do.'

They worked together, the two of them. The website said they had to keep him still, so they cut away his wet pyjamas. Laura looked at them in a pile beside her son and all she could see was £7.50 in shreds, and no idea where she'd find another £7.50 to replace them.

They carried on. Laura found every blanket and coat in the flat and laid them over him. She didn't have many. She took the covers off the sofa and used those. Erin made a warm compress, emptying a bottle of orange squash down the sink and refilling it with hot water. She wrapped it in a cloth and Laura held it to his neck.

When he still didn't wake, Erin said, 'We have to call an ambulance.'

Laura looked at Max. His skin was pinker now than it had been, his breathing more regular. 'Wait,' she said.

She went into the kitchen and warmed a mug of milk in the microwave, then rooted in the cupboard until she found a Calpol syringe. She took them both back to the living room, filled the syringe with milk, lifted her son's head and dripped it steadily into his mouth. Over and over again, she did this, until he started moving.

They both breathed sighs of relief. Laura went on dripping the milk into his mouth.

*

When he was sitting upright again, dressed in his other pair of pyjamas and sipping more hot milk from a mug, Laura turned to Rachel Saunders' girlfriend and said, 'Thank you.'

The woman said, 'I still think you need to get him checked out by a doctor.'

'I will. I'll take him to the GP later. Please,' she said, 'please don't tell anyone about this.'

The woman spoke gently. 'Do you want to tell me what happened? I might be able to help you.'

They were always like this, the rich people. Always thinking they could help. But their idea of help was to involve social services and people who would declare Laura an unfit mother and have Max taken away from her. She'd seen it happen when she was a child. The memory of the children in the house next door being removed from their home while their mother howled in the doorway had haunted Laura forever.

Laura shook her head. 'You can't help me,' she said.

'I'm worried about your son. I want to get him to hospital. I know he seems OK now, but we don't know what happened, or how long he was out there, and what complications there might be. Please let me get you both to hospital. I can go home and get my car and I'll drive you, or we can go together in a taxi. I'm more than happy to pay for it.'

Oh, God. She was so nice. She really was, and Laura was so ungrateful.

Laura said, 'I can't take him to hospital.'

She started crying again. She wished she wouldn't. It was humiliating to be crying like this, to have lost all control of her life in front of this woman who lived in that big house and wrote those articles for newspapers about Rachel Saunders' stupid, meaningless research into the lives of people like her. 'Try living it,' she wanted to say. 'Try seeing if you can squeeze the very last of the toothpaste out of the tube so your son doesn't have to go to school with smelly breath because yesterday you bought him trainers you couldn't afford but which all the other children have and you can't cope with the guilt of depriving him of one more thing. Try going three days without food because you had to have the washing machine repaired and now there is barely enough money to feed your son. Try ...'

It wouldn't work. No one was ever going to try this life. Rachel Saunders thought she understood, but she didn't have a clue.

The woman sat beside her and put her arm around her shoulders. Laura wanted to shake it off. 'Don't touch me,' she wanted say, but that was so rude, when this almost-stranger had just saved her son's life.

Instead, she said, 'He's all I've got. I can't lose him. Please don't tell anyone. Please.'

'But ...'

'I know it's wrong. I left him alone. I work nights sometimes and I can't afford a babysitter. He's always been OK. I take care of him. I do. But if anyone finds out, they'll take him away. I need him here. I know I don't have much and I'm not like you, but I do my best and I can't ...'

She'd done it. She'd blurted it all out. It seemed to Laura that she had no choice. She either did what this woman said and took Max to hospital, where there would be prying eyes upon him, or she had to explain why she couldn't.

The woman was silent for a while. Then she said, 'I won't tell anyone. But give me your number. I might know someone who can babysit for you, free of charge, and you'll be able to work without worrying.'

'Please don't tell anyone. I know you're Rachel's ...' She couldn't bring herself to say the word *girlfriend*.

'I am Rachel's,' the woman said, and smiled.

'Please don't tell her. I know she'll want to help, but I can't have social services involved.'

'I wonder if you might have got the wrong idea about social services ...' the woman ventured.

Laura shook her head. 'I haven't. I know what they're like. They take people's kids. Poor people's kids. They take poor people's kids. Rich people are OK. They can do what they like to theirs. Please don't tell her.'

The woman put her hand over Laura's in a gesture that felt a lot like a vow. 'I won't tell her,' she said. 'We'll keep your son with you.'

36

Rachel

Erin had been gone for ages. Rachel had given up on making crumpets from scratch. It was a fool's game. She wasn't sure what on earth had possessed her to try it. She'd made a lemon drizzle cake instead. It worked and now the kitchen was filled with the aroma of lemon sponge, which felt like a small moment of triumph in Rachel's otherwise hopeless culinary life, and she was desperate for Erin to come back and try some. If she didn't come home soon, Rachel would have to stop procrastinating and get on with some work. The thought of turning on her laptop made her anxious. The start of a new book was always like this. Despite all the material she'd been gathering for months, she worried she'd never fill the pages.

Eventually, after hours and hours, the back door opened and Erin stepped slowly inside. She walked with heaviness and looked pale and sad.

'What's wrong?' Rachel asked.

Erin didn't smile. She took a seat at the island and said, 'I witnessed something while I was out that I wish I hadn't.'

'What?'

Erin appeared to hesitate. 'A car crash,' she said. 'An accident involving a child. I had to give a statement. That's why I was so long.'

Rachel bent down and put her arms around her. 'You poor thing,' she said. 'Shall I make a pot of tea, or do you need gin?'

Erin smiled. 'Tea is fine.'

Rachel busied herself making the tea. 'I made a cake,' she said. 'A lemon drizzle. I haven't done one of those since boarding school. I think it's all right. Try it,' she said, pushing the cake board and a knife towards Erin, who seemed to pale visibly at the sight of it.

'Maybe later,' Erin said weakly. 'I don't feel like eating at the moment.'

'Of course you don't. Sorry. I must remember that my baking triumphs cannot undo a car crash.' She brought the tea and two mugs over to the island and sat down beside Erin. 'What happened?' she asked.

Erin told her a story of how a car had been speeding along the housing estate on the edge of the woods and knocked a boy over while he was crossing the road. The force of the car pushed the boy several metres up the road. For a while, he lay there and seemed to be unconscious, but he was OK. Just badly shocked, so he couldn't move. Erin called for an ambulance and had to wait for the police and give a statement. 'It was awful,' she said. 'Really awful. And I'm exhausted now. I feel like I need to sleep for a week.'

'Why don't you?' Rachel said. 'Go and lie down. I'll bring you anything you need.'

Erin looked at her appreciatively. 'Thank you,' she said, but didn't move.

Rachel held Erin's hand in hers for a while, and thought

about what she'd just been told. She could picture the scene, she knew the spot. A few of the children's friends lived up that way.

She said, 'Was it anyone we know?'

Erin was silent.

Rachel felt a sickening shift inside her. 'Erin?' she asked.

Erin nodded.

'Who?'

Erin turned her face and looked at her. 'Max. It was Max Spence.'

Rachel had to let that sink in for a moment. 'Did you see his mother?' she asked.

'Yes. She was frantic, beside herself.'

'So he wasn't at school.'

'I suppose not.'

'But he was out wandering the estate on his own?'

Erin shrugged. 'Laura was devastated. I know Jo worries about things in that house, but I saw her today and I can tell you that woman loves her child.'

'They all do,' Rachel murmured darkly.

'I think we should cut her some slack,' Erin said, then walked away.

Rachel saw Laura in the schoolyard on Monday morning. She was wearing a long coat with the hood up and sunglasses, despite the fact that the sun hadn't put in an appearance in Burntridge since October. Rachel wondered if she was in disguise, trying to slip by unnoticed. Because of this – she couldn't help herself – she stood right beside her while they waited for the teacher to come out and lead their children into class.

For a long time Laura ignored her, holding fast to Max's hand and staring straight ahead. Rachel, who'd let go of Tess and wasn't entirely sure where she was, said, 'Hi.' Then she looked down at Max and asked, 'How are you, sweetheart?'

Max stayed silent. Laura looked at her, as if unsure of what to do.

Rachel said, 'I'm glad he's better. Erin told me about the accident.'

Laura's face paled and she cast an anxious glance around her. She cleared her throat. 'What did she say?'

'That she'd witnessed Max being hit by a car and you were distraught. No wonder. I can't imagine how traumatic that must have been for you.'

Laura nodded and seemed to be thinking carefully about her words. 'He was just going to the shop for some sweets. I let him do that. It's not far.'

Rachel noticed she was wringing her hands while she talked. 'You must have been frantic.'

'I was. But I ...' She shook her head and didn't finish the sentence. Instead, she said, 'I asked Erin not to mention it to anyone. I understand she had to share it with you. But it's difficult, you know. I'm a single mother and people blame us when things go wrong. I feel so awful about it ...'

Rachel softened her tone. 'It's not your fault, Laura. Accidents happen.'

'I know. But I'd appreciate it ...'

'Of course. I won't tell anyone.'

'Thank you,' Laura said.

The bell rang. They each shepherded their children into line and into school.

37

Jo

Max Spence had come back to school today after being off for nearly a week. He was bruised, had a nasty cough and looked underweight to Jo. Then, at lunchtime, Melissa Jenkins grabbed Jo in the staff room and told her she'd overheard Max saying he wasn't allowed to tell anyone why he'd been off, or why he was ill. 'He stopped when he realised I was listening,' she said. 'I tried talking to him, but I couldn't get anything more than that.'

Jo nodded. 'I'll phone his mother,' she said. 'I'll ask her to come in.'

Jo tried all afternoon to contact Laura, but she wasn't answering her phone. She wanted to refer Max to the educational psychologist, but she'd need Laura's consent and she wasn't sure she'd get it. Also, those bruises worried her. She was ready to act.

'I've never seen Max in the midst of an episode,' she said to Melissa. 'Do you think he could be hurting himself that way?'

Melissa nodded vehemently. 'Oh, without doubt,' she said. 'I've seen him do it.'

'OK,' Jo said, but she still wasn't sure. Something gnawed

away at her about this child. The trouble was, unless he spoke, or unless she moved in with him for a week, she couldn't tell how seriously she needed to listen to her paranoid instincts. She wished she had an invisibility cloak and could sweep through town, spying on every family with problems.

She decided to try and catch Laura in the yard after school when she came to pick him up, but it was Max's father there today, and she couldn't be seen to be going behind Laura's back. She wanted to ask Laura to consider – once again – the possibility of the educational psychologist. Jo knew Laura's type, though. She'd seen it before in other schools. Laura was conscientious. She wanted the best for her son, she worked hard to bring him up, but she struggled and the fact that she struggled made her hypersensitive to anything she might perceive as criticism. When Jo said, 'I'd like to consider referring Max to the psychologist,' Laura didn't hear, 'I'd like to help your son achieve his fullest potential.' Laura heard, 'You're an appalling mother. Your son isn't doing well at school. We're sure you're causing him problems and we're going to get someone in that he can tell all his terrible secrets to.'

Jo drove home and her mind drifted to Luke again. It never stayed away from him, and the story he'd tried to keep from her, for long. She was desperate to talk to someone about it, but the shame was too deep. How could she ever admit that her son had been accused of sexual assault? He'd barely even denied it, which she supposed was a good thing. He simply said he couldn't remember because he'd been drunk. Perhaps he was just letting that fact sit there between them, hoping his mother would grab hold of the unspoken possibility that this girl was making it all up.

It was a thought Jo was desperate to grab hold of, to find evidence for, despite the fact that she had always believed in believing the victim and that to do anything else would be her own small, yet unforgivable, contribution to halting progress.

But what if she *had* made it up? People did make false allegations sometimes. Maybe she was competing with him for a promotion at work, or maybe there had been a relationship there that turned sour and this was an act of revenge.

Maybe.

It was just so hard to believe Luke could have done this.

She should speak to Dave about it, she knew that. If his son was facing court, he needed to be told. And Jo could do with sharing this burden. She was tired of lying awake at night, imagining all the worst possible outcomes. Dave would be calm and stoic and practical. He always was. It was what she'd once most loved about him, and then, eventually, most loathed.

She drove into Maltley, and saw Rachel's car on the drive of the big house and decided to call in. She needed advice about Max, she wanted to talk about Luke, and she knew Rachel was the only person she knew who would listen without judgement.

Tess opened the front door. 'Muuuuum! It's Ms Fairburn!'

Jo smiled. 'It's alright, Tess,' she said. 'You can call me Jo when we're not at school.'

Rachel called back from wherever she was, 'Ask her to come in, Tess.'

Tess stood back from the door. 'Mum says come in.'

'Thank you,' Jo said, and stepped inside.

Tess walked alongside her as she headed down the hall towards the living room. 'I haven't done my spellings yet.' She said this boldly, as if someone had dared her.

'Never mind.'

Rachel came down the stairs. She smiled at Jo. 'Hi, lovely,' she said. 'What brings you here?'

'Have you got time for a cup of tea?'

'Always. Tess, go and practice the piano.'

'I hate piano.'

'Watch TV, then.'

'OK.' Tess skipped away.

Jo followed Rachel down to the kitchen and leaned against the island while she made the tea.

Rachel said, 'So what's wrong? You look knackered.'

'I want your advice about Max Spence.'

A shadow crossed Rachel's face. Jo assumed it was to do with the LGBTQ protest.

'Are you still concerned about him?'

Jo pulled out a bar stool and sat down. 'Yes. He was off school for a few days, and now he's back with new bruises and a secret.'

'A secret?'

'He's not allowed to tell anyone why he was off.'

'Right.'

'Does that sound dubious to you?'

'It doesn't sound good.'

'His mother is so bloody uncooperative.'

'She's frightened.'

'Of what?'

'Of losing him. Listen, this is confidential, but Erin witnessed an accident involving Max last week. It so clearly wasn't Laura's fault, but Laura blames herself and is terrified of it getting out. I've seen this sort of thing so many times. Women with no confidence, paranoid that the world is judging them ...'

Jo frowned. 'What was the accident?'

Rachel told her a story about a speeding car and Max walking alone to the shop when he should have been at school. It still made Jo uneasy, but Rachel was insistent. 'Erin said Laura was distraught and terrified people would blame her because she lets him cross the road by himself.'

'That's ridiculous. I mean, it's possibly not the wisest move, but people do it.' She paused for a moment, then said, 'What's the worst thing you've ever done as a parent?'

Rachel didn't hesitate. 'End my marriage and get it on with another woman.'

'Really? Is it really that bad?'

'It seems to be. For Maia, especially. She's not going to be coming back to live with me any time soon. And she's …' Her voice trailed off and she shook her head, as if she couldn't bear to talk, or even think about it.

'What?' Jo asked.

Rachel said, 'It doesn't matter. It's fine.'

Jo checked her watch. 'I should be getting home. We'll have a proper night out soon,' she said, picking up her bag and heading to the door.

Rachel saw her out. It was raining and dark outside and Jo went quickly across the green to her own home. The front door was unlocked. She braced herself for the sight of her son moping about, watching TV, worrying about his future.

If he *had* assaulted that girl, he was completely unconcerned about her. He hadn't expressed a word of remorse, or given any indication that he understood the impact of his actions. His only fear had been for himself.

It made her nauseous to think that could be the case.

Her rising anger rose even further when she walked into the kitchen and found all his empty bowls, plates and mugs spread all over the worktop. For God's sake. She started clearing away, then stopped herself and slammed a mug back down so hard she chipped it. 'Luke!' she called.

He didn't answer. She stormed up the stairs. 'Luke!' she called again. 'Can you come and clear up your bloody mess?'

His bedroom door was closed. Recklessly, she threw it open. 'Luke,' she began again, and then stopped.

His music was playing, and he was lying on his back in bed. She couldn't see his face, but sitting astride him was a young woman.

Maia.

38

Erin

In the old days, before she'd moved in here, Erin had vowed never to be that kind of step-parent who competed with the children for the most significant place in her partner's heart. For a start, she knew it would be a losing battle and besides that, she wanted it to be a losing battle. One of the many hundreds of reasons she loved Rachel was because she'd seen her love for her children. It impressed Erin – the steady tower of unwavering devotion that could be relied on never to fall. It evoked the same awe in Erin she felt at the sight of magnificent buildings – a sense of wonder, and a certain knowledge that she could never produce this herself.

Today, Maia had come over for Sunday lunch. She'd given no warning, just turned up in the kitchen, much like she had that evening she'd caught Erin on the brink of orgasm and triggered her mother's lifelong shame. Now, as Erin sat there at the table with all three children together and watched Rachel beam as though their presence had lit a happiness inside her that Erin herself could never touch, she became aware of the creeping darkness of something that felt like jealousy around her heart.

You're not jealous, she told herself. *You're an adult, and you're better than this.*

She couldn't put her finger on the feeling.

Maia reached over the table for more roast potatoes. When she bit into one, an expression of exaggerated ecstasy crossed her face. 'No one makes Sunday lunch like you, Mum,' she said.

Rachel smiled with a love that came close to breaking Erin's heart. 'That was always my plan,' she said. 'I started when you were little.'

'What plan?' Reuben asked.

'My plan to keep you coming home.'

Maia said, 'That's hilarious. James's mum had that plan as well. She told me about it. God, mothers are all so needy.'

Erin could see Rachel stopping herself from speaking. She knew exactly what she would say if she could, if motherhood hadn't gagged her from expressing her own needs. 'Yes, we are. We are so bloody needy, Maia. We love you more than you will ever know or understand, more than you will ever love us in return, and sometimes, we ask that you stop smashing our faces in for our mistakes and spend some time with us because you grow up and we miss you.'

Rachel didn't say that. She said, 'How is James?'

Maia made a face. 'No idea.'

From that, Erin supposed, they were to infer that James was no longer Maia's boyfriend. It seemed hardly surprising, given that Maia appeared to have been sleeping with someone else while she was with him. Erin shouldn't judge her, she knew that. She herself had slept with more men than she could count, but at least she'd waited till her twenties, and at least she hadn't broken anyone's heart, as far as she knew. But there was a ruthlessness to Maia that she didn't like. A willingness to hurt. A desire to hurt.

Erin couldn't help it. She was suspicious of Maia and her

reasons for rocking up here today. There was a shamelessness to it, to the fact that Erin had caught her using this house as a place to cheat on her boyfriend, and yet she could still quite brazenly walk in and flaunt her beautiful face as if nothing had happened.

She realised now, as she sat there noting Maia's carelessness with the hearts of everyone around her, that it wasn't jealousy she was feeling but resentment. She resented this child for her anger towards Rachel, and for the way she was now rampaging through the world creating victims out of her desire to punish her mother. Her only saving grace, as far as Erin could see, was that she didn't really understand what she was doing. How could she? She'd never loved. She had no idea.

Erin tried to shake the thoughts away. She didn't like herself for thinking them and the reality was that Maia had been disarmingly lovely ever since she'd arrived. She'd patiently played games with Tess, she'd been warm towards her mother for once and her conversation about school had been amusing. The girl was undeniably clever. It was a lively, socially confident cleverness, like her mother's, and if Erin were feeling charitable, she might see it as a point of vulnerability. A mature, insightful intellect and an inexperienced heart – bound to lead to disaster.

Reuben said, 'James is pretty angry with you. You should hear the shit he's saying about her, Mum.'

Maia shot him a look.

'What shit?' Rachel asked.

'Nothing,' Maia said. 'Just the kind of rubbish people talk when they've had their egos bruised. It's just lies. He's only making himself look like an idiot.'

Erin glanced at Rachel and saw her concern at the thought of her daughter being slandered. Erin wondered what he was saying – that Maia was a bitch, probably, and that she'd cheated on him with another boy.

Erin understood James. She understood the feeling of being wronged and how strong the urge for vengeance could be. That was the trouble here. She wasn't Maia's mother. She wasn't automatically her ally.

Erin wondered if this resentment she was feeling might be crossing the border towards loathing.

After Maia had left, Tess was in bed and Reuben was upstairs revising for the mock exams he faced after Christmas, Erin poured herself and Rachel a glass of wine and said, 'Would Maia be interested in babysitting work?'

'I'm sure she would.'

'I didn't want to mention it while she was here. I wanted to run it by you first.'

'You nutter. It's fine with me.'

'It might not be, when I tell you my plan.'

Rachel leaned forwards and kissed her. 'You are a woman of mystery, Erin,' she said.

Erin didn't smile. She said, 'Laura Spence needs help. She works nights sometimes and she doesn't have anyone to look after Max. If she can't find someone, she'll have to quit her job. She's terrified of losing him. I wondered, if I paid Maia, would she babysit free of charge for Laura?'

Rachel was quiet.

After a while, Erin asked, 'What do you think?'

'I don't know,' Rachel said.

Erin knew what that meant. It meant Rachel was still too

furious about the LGBTQ protest to be able step in and help this woman. Erin understood that *I don't know* meant *No way*.

She said, 'What if I ask Maia myself? Explain the situation and let her decide?'

'Oh, Maia would love that. Anything to piss off her mother.'

'Rachel, please …'

'Look, I will probably come round. You just need to give me a few days. I don't like that woman. I can't bear her prejudices, but I accept that you might have a point. I can hardly refuse, can I, given my work?'

'Not really,' Erin said.

Rachel laughed. 'All right. Talk to Maia. I'm sure she'll do it.'

'Thank you.'

Erin looked away. She'd lied to Rachel, and the weight of it bore on her heavily. She hadn't meant to lie. She'd just wanted to keep Laura's secret, but she found herself unable to keep it completely, so she made up the story about a car accident, and then said Max had been the victim. Now, she put it down to the after-effects of shock and trauma. She hadn't been thinking properly, and she felt so awful for Laura, who clearly had so much love for her son and was only trying to do what all the other parents in the world were trying to do: keep a roof over his head and food on the table. Laura was desperate, that much had been clear. Erin wanted everyone to get off her case.

But now she'd said something that wasn't true and she'd dug herself into a hole she couldn't find her way out of. She had a horrible feeling now that this wasn't going to disappear with time, but would grow and keep on growing.

39

Laura

Laura pushed Max into his line and kissed him goodbye, then hustled away as quickly as she could without meeting the teacher's eye. *Look after him,* she wanted to say. *Please take care of my boy,* but how could she say that when everyone knew now that she barely took care of him herself? She could feel her cheeks flame as she walked out of the gate and into the park. Ever since that awful night when she thought she'd lost him, she'd barely been able to leave the house. Whenever she stepped outside she felt the weight of everyone's eyes upon her, their questions, their appalling judgements: what a terrible mother Laura Spence was to leave her child at home alone while she worked.

Everyone knew. She felt sure of that. Erin had told everyone. She hadn't told them the truth. She'd changed the story and Laura had no idea why. Why would anyone do that?

The day afterwards, Laura had sat and talked to Max about what had happened. He said he'd woken up and she wasn't there, and so he'd gone out into the night to find her, and then he'd got lost. He sat down and cried for a while, and hoped someone would find him, but no one did. In the end, he must have just fallen asleep.

Now, because of that night and because Jo Fairburn had overheard snippets of Max's conversation with another child and leaped to conclusions, she had to go into school yet again to discuss things.

She knew the questions would be about the bruising again. It didn't matter how often she explained it, no one believed her. They thought she beat him. It was too much of a coincidence that a child should have all these problems, that his mother was struggling to make ends meet and that he should have bruises for some reason other than that she couldn't control her fury with life for dealing her this crappy hand.

She needed to get away from the schoolyard before she lost it. She took her hat out of her coat pocket and pulled it as far down over her head as she could, hoping she'd be able to hide behind it as she headed into town where she was meeting Kate Monro for coffee. They still had to pull everything together for the Christmas fair next week and Laura had done nothing at all to help recently. She didn't want to see anyone, and would have quietly withdrawn from the fair if Kate hadn't bombarded her with text messages the evening before, cajoling, encouraging and, finally, demanding.

Meet me for coffee at the deli tomorrow after drop-off. Lots to sort out for fair. Won't take no for an answer. Still need to sort out the LGBTQ protest group as well.

It was the mention of the LBTQ protest that triggered Laura's resolve. She would go. The café at the deli was small – only four tables – and West Burntridge parents didn't usually go there. A long flight of steep steps led from the shop up to the café, which excluded anyone with younger children and those with older children were mostly back at work by now. She could probably go there unnoticed by anyone, and the LGBTQ protest still mattered to her, even more since ... Well, since Max had disappeared and Rachel bloody Saunders' lesbian girlfriend had found him. Of all people, it had to be *her*. Laura had been grateful, of course she had, but why couldn't Erin have kept her mouth shut like she'd said she would?

Laura had tried to ask Rachel not to tell anyone. 'I'd appreciate it ...' she said, and then her voice trailed off because the trouble with Rachel Saunders was that even if you couldn't stand her and had hardly any respect for her, she was intimidating. All that success, all that confidence. You could tell just by looking at her that she thought she was better than everyone else, despite all that endless howling for equality. And really, where would Rachel Saunders be without inequality? Not in the lofty position she was in now, that was certain. She'd made a bloody fortune from banging on about poverty.

Rachel had reached out and touched her arm, in a gesture that for a moment felt like genuine affection. 'I can promise you complete confidentiality, Laura,' she said, and Laura stiffened at the way she used her name like that, as if for added seriousness. 'What happened will go no further.'

The woman was a doctor. The country paid her to keep other people's secrets. But Laura didn't trust her. She felt as though her whole world was now in jeopardy. She wanted to reignite the LGBTQ protest, get the whole thing moving, put some momentum behind it, let Rachel Saunders know how it felt to have the whole world looking at you, judging you, talking about how you lived the wrong sort of life.

Laura checked her thoughts as she walked into the deli and up the stairs to the first-floor café that overlooked the cathedral.

Of course she was grateful to Erin for saving her son, but when she told Rachel about it, she'd slipped a time bomb into Laura's life, and Laura could hear it now, beating away the minutes, ready to smash her world to pieces.

Kate was already there, sitting at a table by the window, two lattes in front of her. Laura draped her coat over the back of a chair and sat down opposite her. She was looking galvanised and full of purposeful, angry energy.

'I ordered you a coffee,' Kate said, pushing a cup closer towards her. She looked at Laura for a while, then said, 'You look like you need it. You look tired. Are you OK?'

Laura smiled thinly. 'I'm fine. Max hasn't been well,' she said, then added, 'Did you ... did you hear about that?'

Kate shook her head and looked concerned. 'No. Not a word. It wasn't serious, was it?'

Laura felt relief flood through her. Kate Monro was the barometer by which anyone could measure schoolyard gossip. If she didn't know something, then it was likely no one else would know it either. Rachel, so far, had kept her word.

She said, 'Nothing awful, and he's fine now. I had to keep him off for a few days, that's all.'

Kate smiled sympathetically. 'Exhausting, isn't it, when they're ill? And I can only manage the Florence Nightingale act for the first hour or so. After that, I'm all just, "Stop moaning and go to sleep."'

'I know. Me too.'

'I bet Rachel-the-lesbian is brilliant with her kids when they're ill. I bet she makes all those soothing noises and brings them homemade chicken soup on their own personal sofa.'

Laura sneered. 'Just because she's a doctor doesn't mean she looks after her own kids. They never do, do they? These professionals never manage to make it work at home. Teachers always have badly behaved kids, shrinks have mad kids, judges have criminal kids ...'

'Really?'

'I don't know. I'm making it up. But I once knew a teacher whose kid was expelled from school. So Rachel might be a doctor but that doesn't make her a perfect mother. That's all.'

Kate sipped her coffee, then leaned back in her chair and said, 'You know about her daughter, right? The elder one?'

'Yeah, she left home.'

'Apparently, according to my friend with kids at the high school, she walked in on Rachel and Erin having sex. They were going at it on the kitchen floor. The kitchen floor! When there are three children in the house.'

'No way!'

'Can you imagine that? Can you imagine shagging anyone in the kitchen when you have *three children* in the house, let alone it being another woman? She must have known – of course she must – that any of them could have walked in at any moment. Imagine if it had been Tess, that poor little one. How do you explain that? "Oh, Mummy's just going down on her friend, darling." It's ... it's not far from child abuse.' She shook her head in disgust.

'That's awful,' Laura said, and felt the old resurgence of anger. Why didn't anyone threaten to take Rachel's children away? She was hardly an example of great parenting – throwing their dad out and then inflicting live homosexual pornography on her children. She wanted to spit in that woman's face. The only reason Rachel got away with it was because she had money and everyone knew money could cover up all sorts of domestic crimes. And it was money she'd made writing about people like Laura, when Rachel didn't have a clue what it was like to be a person like Laura. Not a clue. How dare this woman waltz onto Sunderland council estates in her expensive coat and start flinging words like *deprivation* around the world, claiming to speak on everyone else's behalf because they were all too stupid to string a sentence together? That was what she really thought, Laura was certain.

'Anyway,' Kate went on, 'now Maia is pregnant.'

'What?'

'That's the rumour, anyway. She hasn't been at school for a few days and everyone knows she's been sleeping with any bloke who'll go near her. So now there's word going round that she's pregnant. Her mother will force an abortion on her no doubt, then sweep it under the carpet as if nothing ever happened.'

Laura couldn't believe it. She knew Rachel's eldest daughter only by sight: slim, gorgeous, always startlingly dressed. She'd always seemed like such a nice girl, and Laura had an inexplicable urge now to find her and look after her, to steer her away from this terrible path towards shattered self-worth and lone parenthood and set her upright, away from all this.

Even as the thought took shape, Laura was aware of the absurdity of this sudden tenderness towards a child she didn't know, the daughter of someone she loathed, and she knew, in some deep recess of her heart, that it wasn't Maia she wanted to save, but herself.

40

Rachel

Rachel couldn't help it. She was a fighter. Not an aggressor, no one would ever call her that, but a defender. If something offended her – personally, locally or globally – she fought it as hard as she could. It wasn't necessarily an admirable quality, she was aware of that. It meant she talked too much (*ranted* was the word her children used); it meant she expended energy on things she couldn't change; and it meant people were either afraid of her, foolishly admiring of her, or determined to put her in her place. There was no in-between.

'Oh, how can you be bothered?' her mother used to ask, when Rachel appeared on the news, ranting about her latest research into health inequality. 'How can you be bothered to fight other people's battles?'

'Because it's everyone's battle, Mum,' she'd say. 'The battle for a decent world is everyone's battle.'

Other people would throw adjectives at her. 'Amazing,' they'd say. 'You're incredible. How do you do it?'

She never really understood that. 'How do you not do it?' she wanted to respond. 'How can you live in the world and not be fucking furious?'

Then there were the others. The haters. The people who assumed that because she was confident and passionate, she must also be arrogant. The people who would like nothing more than to see her fall because, as far as they were concerned, nothing had ever been hard for Rachel Saunders and therefore she deserved a good kicking.

Kate Monro was one of those, and now here she was, striding towards Rachel and Erin in the schoolyard with that trademark red clipboard tucked under her arm. God, she was bold. She was shameless. Last night, she'd posted on the parents' Facebook page again, *We are pleased to have so much support for our #rightway campaign, but we still have a battle on our hands to make our voices heard. Come and join us in the Queen's Head at 8pm on Wednesday to discuss the way forward. #rightway #westburntridgefirstschool*

It was all such bullshit. They didn't have 'so much support'. They were a handful of idiot mothers trying to fight a battle they hadn't a hope of winning. The reason they had to meet in the pub was because Jo had vetoed it as a topic for discussion in school. She wouldn't have it mentioned in PTA meetings, and she'd refused to lend them a classroom after school for them to host their alternative sex education lessons.

'Give in,' Rachel wanted to say. 'Accept that the world is changing. Accept that homosexual marriage is now enshrined in UK law and get over it.'

She braced herself internally for the inevitable argument. It wasn't that she enjoyed arguing. She didn't. She'd much rather have a peaceful life. It was that she simply couldn't just stand there and passively accept other people's shit the way everyone else did because everyone else was too middle-class, polite and frightened to fight back.

Kate's blonde hair bounced about her shoulders as she approached. 'Morning, ladies,' she said brightly.

'Hi,' Rachel murmured, without smiling. Erin said nothing.

Kate pulled the clipboard out from under her arm. Rachel wondered how important that clipboard made her feel and had the urge to stamp on her, to squash her.

Kate smiled and went on speaking. She'd adopted the tone of a woman selling make-up. 'It's that Christmas fair time of year again,' she said. 'So I'm just seeing a few parents and asking whether they'll be contributing to the raffle again.' She checked her clipboard which, as far as Rachel could see, had nothing on it except for a blank piece of paper. 'I know you've always given very generously in the past, Dr Saunders.'

Coldly, Rachel said, 'I'm afraid I won't be making a donation this year.'

Kate raised her eyebrows in surprise. 'What about a stall, then? Could you help run a stall? There must be so many things you could do. A woman of your talents.'

'I'm afraid I take offence at the campaign you are running against sex education, which means I won't be supporting the PTA at all this year. Not in any way. Please don't ask me again.'

For a moment or two, Kate looked taken aback. 'It seems a shame to mix the PTA with the campaign, Rachel. They are, as you know, separate things.'

'They are run by the same people.'

'But to punish the school because you don't like the campaign ...'

'I know. It's a shame for the school to miss out on funds.

But I will not be seen to support you or your ideas and I want that to be absolutely clear.' She felt her anger rise as she spoke. 'In fact, *I'd* like to start a campaign, Kate. I'd like to set up a petition in protest at those parents who allow their six-year-old daughters to have their own YouTube channels, where they dress in leopard-print miniskirts and belt songs into phallic-looking microphones and carry on like some fucking paedophile's dream …'

Kate gasped.

So did Erin.

Rachel stopped talking. She'd gone too far. Even she could see that. But she was so angry.

Kate's face was red with fury. She turned and walked away.

This, Rachel knew, was not the end.

41

Maia

Maia liked him and it had taken her by surprise. She didn't especially want to like him, not in this way, and she was annoyed with herself about it. She found that she was having to fight the urge to send him text messages or, even worse, walk casually past his house and hope he saw her.

That was why she'd ended up going home for Sunday lunch at the weekend. Luke told her he needed to use all his spare time at the moment to put together his application for journalism courses and although she wanted to be cool about it, she missed him. On Sunday, she asked her dad to drive her back to Maltley so she could drop in on her family. Her dad agreed – he saw it as a positive step towards the reconciliation with her mother that he felt sure Maia was in desperate need of.

Really, she'd just wanted to run into Luke. She spent half an hour wandering round the village, pacing the footpath between the church and his house, hoping he'd appear at a window and come outside.

He didn't.

She wondered what James would think if he could see her now, chasing after a bloke in a way she'd never chased after him. The thought of it made her smirk inwardly. Somehow, he'd found out about Luke and he'd responded by slandering her. At least, that was where Maia assumed the lies had all started because she had no other enemies at school. His friends were talking about her now, using words Maia couldn't repeat, not even to herself, because she'd always been taught to believe words like that only existed to shame women, and shaming women was wrong.

She didn't care about the rumours. She could shrug them off. She had her mates and they were on her side.

She stopped pacing the village as she realised she was behaving like an obsessive, lovesick idiot. Then, promising herself never to do this again, she headed over to her old house, knocked on the door and surprised everyone with a visit. Her mum was tragically delighted. She obviously thought the fact that Maia had dropped round suddenly meant she still saw this place as her home, and that she missed it. Maia had no choice for now but to let her think that.

Erin was suspicious, though. Maia could see that. *Oh, fuck you*, she thought, every time she looked up and caught Erin watching her with that weirdly pissed-off expression on her face. As far as Maia was concerned, the woman could hurl herself under a bus. Maia had as much right to be in her mother's house as Erin did. More, in fact. She'd been there longer. And also: she was her mother's child and therefore more important (even if her mother didn't seem to realise this at the moment).

She didn't stay over. She left just after seven, because she had a maths test tomorrow and needed to revise. This was true. She wished her mother would acknowledge what a brilliantly good daughter she had, but she never did. Maia knew perfectly well that all over the country, right now, right this minute, parents were on the floor begging their children to revise for tomorrow's maths test. They were bribing them with promises of cash, new iPads, Xboxes, whatever the hell they liked as long as they just did some bloody work. Maia's parents had never had to do this. 'I wouldn't do it anyway,' her mother had remarked when Maia pointed it out to her. 'I expect you to work hard and do well. I'm not rewarding you for doing the things I expect.'

'Not even if I get all A stars?'

'Not even then.'

'What if I was really stupid, predicted Fs and managed to get all Cs? I bet then you'd pay me.'

'If you were a struggler, it might be different.'

Her mother was always like that. Always. She saw such nobility in struggling. A genius child was wasted on her.

Luke said his mum was the same. He'd achieved all As in his GCSEs and A levels, plus a first-class degree from a top university, and his parents hadn't given him anything apart from a few celebratory meals. 'Mum says hard work is its own reward, and what more do I need than the results? Well, you know, a bit of the old Mum-and-Dad pride wouldn't go amiss,' he said.

'Exactly,' Maia agreed, and they understood each other.

They'd gone to see *To Kill a Mockingbird* a few evenings after Luke first suggested it. Maia had never done something so expensive with a friend before. The tickets were fifty pounds each, but her dad gave her the money because going to the theatre fell into the category of Things That Are Good For You and her parents had always paid for Maia to do the things they approved of. She didn't tell him she was going with Luke.

They held hands through most of the performance. Maia tried to hide the fact that she was crying at the end of Act One, when Jem and Scout were lying in bed talking about their dead mother. But Luke sensed it and without looking at her, reached into his jacket pocket and handed her a packet of tissues. She didn't feel that he was laughing at her, or thinking she was sweet and in need of comfort in the face of her endearing feminine emotion. She felt simply that he understood that she'd been moved.

She liked him. That night, she started to really like him.

He drove her home and they spent a while snogging in his car round the corner from her house, but she couldn't actually have sex with him yet. She drew the line at shagging him in the back of his car. That was for later, not their first time together.

Their first time together was at her old house when everyone was meant to be out, but then Erin had come home suddenly and almost caught them. Maia didn't care. She had no need to hide it. But Luke was embarrassed. Endearingly, charmingly embarrassed. He'd come halfway down the stairs, then turned and fled. 'How could I stand there and face her?' he said. 'She's done all that work, helping me with my journalism applications, and then I show up at her house and …'

Maia understood. Beneath his arrogant swagger, he was humble enough to feel shame. She realised afterwards that in her rush to get out, she hadn't cleaned the evidence up from her floor. At first, she'd felt respectably embarrassed about it, but then she thought, *So what?* Her mother and Erin had never had any shame. Why should she?

The next day, Maia walked out of school at lunchtime, caught the bus to Maltley and went to Luke's house. They drank tea and ate cheese, then went to bed for the whole afternoon. Luke was different from the others. More confident, more mature, and he definitely knew his way round the female body and how to bring her to a gasping climax.

This, she realised, was what the fuss was all about.

'Where did you learn to do that?' she asked.

He grinned. 'I've watched a lot of porn.'

That wasn't the answer she'd wanted. Still, she supposed it had been a stupid question. There was never going to be a welcome answer to it, unless he'd said, 'I just knew what to do because it's you.' Which would have been a lie.

She slapped him. Not hard, but hard enough to make her feelings clear.

He looked shocked, then amused. He held a hand over his cheek and said, 'What was that for?'

'For watching porn.'

'Darling Maia, you don't want to waste energy getting uptight about that one. All blokes watch porn.'

'Well, they shouldn't.'

'Sorry,' he said, and grinned. 'I am sorry. But you can't deny that you just benefitted from it.'

Oh, he was such an arrogant bastard. She pushed him down on the bed and climbed on top of him.

It was when they'd been in that position for about ten minutes that his mum walked in.

She'd walked out again almost immediately, but not before Maia had recklessly turned her head and, in doing so, put an end to any hope of mystery surrounding the girl her son was shagging. Maia hadn't meant to do that – it was just intuitive. Someone had walked in suddenly, so she'd turned to see who it was.

Luke was angry. Maia was mortified. The moment was ruined. She eased herself off him, sat down on the bed and covered herself with the duvet, feeling an ironic sense of déjà vu.

'I'm so sick of this,' Luke said, balling his fist and punching it into the pillow. 'There's no fucking privacy here. She shouldn't have done that. She shouldn't have just walked in like that.'

'No.'

'I need to get out.'

'How?'

'I don't know. I need a job.'

'But what will you do? You hate all the jobs. They're boring. They drive you mad.'

'Yeah, but I can't go on like this. She'll have a go at me now. She'll say you're too young …'

'I'm sixteen.'

'Exactly. Sweetheart, it's so young.'

'It's not illegal.'

'It won't make any difference to her. She's known you since you were a baby.'

Maia laughed and glanced towards the door. 'How am I going to get out without seeing her?'

'You shouldn't have to. You've done nothing wrong. We were just … you know. Doing what people do.'

It didn't sound particularly special, when he put it like that. She let it go. She said, 'I'd still rather not bump into her.'

'Don't worry. She'll hide in the kitchen till you've left.'

'I should probably go now,' Maia said, standing up and reaching for her clothes, which were strewn around the bedroom floor. She wondered if Jo was going to tell her mum. Not that it mattered. Her mum needed to realise Maia could do what she liked now. But she didn't relish the lecture she knew would be waiting for her, the same one she'd heard several times over the last few weeks. God, it was so embarrassing, having her sex life scrutinised by her mother. She wished she could move far away from here.

Luke fixed his eyes on her while she dressed, and she heard his deep sigh of frustrated desire. He reached out his hand and brushed his fingers against hers. 'Don't go yet,' he said, pulling back the covers to show her he still had a hard-on. 'I haven't finished.'

She hesitated. This was hardly sexy any more, but he was so bloody good-looking and so clever, and he'd been reduced to something helpless and tormented, with his unyielding erection and Maia, half-naked before him.

She gave in, and got back into bed.

42

Laura

A cold, sunny morning in early December. Drew had taken Max to the local cinema for the Saturday-morning showing of an old Disney film. He asked Laura if she wanted to go with them, but she'd said no. There seemed little point in spending extra money on a seat for herself, when Max would be happy enough alone with Drew. 'I'll meet you afterwards. We can go to the park.'

Max loved having a dad, as Laura had always known he would. Every morning now, his first question was always, 'Am I seeing Daddy today?' and it made Laura feel at once uplifted and furious. It delighted her to see animation in her son's face at last, the enthusiasm for life that had always been missing, but she felt it like a hard slap in the face. Drew, absent for nearly the whole of his son's life, had suddenly returned and was able to make their son happy in a way Laura, battling on alone, had never been able to.

'I'd like to have him for a weekend soon,' Drew had said the other day, 'if that's OK with you.'

She wanted to say no. She wanted to say, 'You can't just abandon him for his whole life, then come back and pick and choose which parts of fatherhood you get involved in.'

She didn't say that. She said, 'Of course. Max would love it.'

He said, 'I want to be a proper dad.'

She said, 'OK. I'd like you to be a proper dad as well.'

'I'm not the waster I used to be. I've got a job. I've had it a couple of years now.'

This was an improvement. When she'd known him, he'd never held on to one job longer than three months.

'And I hope that soon I'll be able to start paying maintenance and buying some of the things he needs.'

'That would be a big help,' Laura said, although she couldn't afford to believe a word of it.

He looked at her earnestly. 'I really mean this, Laura. I have so many regrets …'

'OK,' she said, because she drew the line at offering him comfort.

When they came out of the cinema, Drew was holding Max's hand and Max was smiling broadly, high on his father's company and too much popcorn.

She smiled at them. 'How was the film, Max?' she asked.

'Brilliant,' he said.

She took his other hand and together the three of them headed to the park.

Laura shivered. Drew had persuaded Max to stand on a swing with him, and now he was lurching him into the air, higher than Laura felt was safe, the chains on the swing buckling with each ascent. Max was screaming. 'Higher, Daddy!'

Laura couldn't bear it. All she could see were the consequences: the two of them flung to the ground, faces smashed, limbs broken.

But she couldn't break up this fun.

It was cold standing on the sidelines, watching. Her mind drifted to what she should give Max for lunch.

Drew was so good at this, she thought. He was so good at engaging a small boy because he was, at heart, a small boy himself. If only he'd stuck around, then they could have worked together to give Max what he needed: her focus on the practical, and Drew's sense of fun and adventure.

She felt a sob rise in her throat at the thought of all they had lost.

43

Jo

It was the last week of term, so here Jo was at another PTA meeting when what she really wanted to be doing was bashing her son's head against the wall. Maia. Sixteen-year-old Maia. Her best friend's daughter. Jo didn't believe for a minute that he really cared about her, and this knowledge was chipping uneasily away at her willingness to believe he was innocent of the assault Susi Lambert had accused him of.

They were different things, she told herself. The fact that he'd slept with Maia didn't make him guilty of assaulting someone else. But still. It wasn't helping.

She forced herself to concentrate on the meeting. The focus today was the Christmas fair, the second most important fund-raiser of the school year. Jo had her suspicions that Kate Monro was determined to make this the most spectacular Christmas fair the world had ever known, purely to prove to Jo how much she needed her, and how she ought to take note of all Kate's suggestions for the successful running of the school. Otherwise, Kate would extract herself from fundraising, the school would lose over £60,000 a year, and the whole place would fall apart.

At the moment, there was concern about whose husband was going to be Father Christmas. Kate's husband had dutifully taken on this role for the last three years and the time had come for some other dad to play his part. No one was especially keen. It seemed that most of the women of the PTA had married a load of joyless men, whose seriousness in the world could not be compromised. Jo wondered if they were all like this in the bedroom as well – in charge, on top, no playing around.

Kate sat beside her. Jo saw her take her black biro from beneath the clip on her red clipboard and scrawl across the paper, *Find Father Christmas*. Then she took a green biro and added an exclamation mark, no doubt to remind herself that this was an urgent matter. *Get a job*, Jo pleaded silently. *Just go and get a bloody job*.

The talk moved on to the rest of the fair. They needed to arrange stalls selling homemade chutneys and pickles; another few stalls selling those strange, hand-knitted angels that often appeared hanging in trees around town, for reasons Jo had yet to decipher; and a place where someone's ecologically enlightened mother could teach the less enlightened how to make wreaths out of nothing but some orange peel and a blade of grass. There also needed to be a space for children to make stars. And through it all, the choir would sing carols, led by the magnificent Mr Hunter, the school's only male teacher who was two years out of his PGCE and in the eyes of the parents, already well on his way to taking over the headship when Jo retired because according to everyone, he was amazing.

'Of course he bloody is,' Rachel had said recently, when Jo commented on the Mr Hunter phenomenon. 'He's a bloke. He can cruise by with nothing but a dick and a guitar. A female teacher would have to be five times as good to get anything like that level of adulation.'

She was right. Novelty and sexual attraction worked wonders at making the mothers think a man was excellent at his job.

Kate went on, 'As usual, it will be the raffle that brings in the largest chunk of the money. I've sent a tenner's worth of tickets home with each child, along with a list of prizes so far. If every family spends ten pounds on tickets, we should make 4,000 pounds. I've already bagged a weekend at the Manor House, two tickets for the spa, and a luxury hamper from the deli. The toy shop has promised a wooden doll's house and the photography shop is giving us a mid-range camera. It's pretty impressive stuff. Unfortunately, our most generous parent contributor is refusing to contribute this year.'

Here she looked pointedly at Jo, as if this were her fault.

Jo tried to ignore the comment, but someone else asked, 'Who's that?'

Kate sighed. 'Rachel Saunders. She's usually very generous in her donations. Last year, she gave us a brand-new child's bike and the year before she gave vouchers. But she's refusing to donate anything at all this year because she is *offended* by the LGBTQ protest that a few of us are spearheading.'

Jo noticed a couple of smirks. Then someone said, 'She's gay, right?'

Kate shrugged. 'Seems that way. A recent thing.'

'That'll be why, then.'

Jo said, 'Please can we keep the conversation focussed on the fair?'

But already they were off and there was no stopping them.

Kate stood up and crossed the room to one of her friends, presumably to give the impression of wanting to keep her talk away from Jo's ears, but speaking in a voice deliberately loud enough for her to hear.

'I approached her in the yard the other day,' Kate said. 'I swear, I did *nothing* to provoke her. I just explained that I was talking to certain parents who had been generous in the past and was asking if they could donate to the raffle. She said she was refusing to donate anything this year because of the protest, and *then* … you won't believe what she said. It's almost unrepeatable.'

Only almost, Jo thought. *If I were a gambling woman, I would put my money on your repeating whatever it was Rachel said within the next forty-five seconds.*

'She said she would like to protest against the sort of parents who allow their children to dress in leopard print and set up their own YouTube channels where they sing and dance like … like a …' Here she lowered her voice to a stage whisper, 'Paedophile's dream.'

Jo couldn't help herself. She laughed, and hastily tried to turn it into a cough. She loved Rachel for her uncontrollable mouth, for the fact that she could be relied on to say what everyone else was thinking. Jo would have said it herself if she could.

Another parent said, 'That's outrageous.'

'Isn't it?' Kate agreed, and dabbed at her eyes. The memory had upset her. 'She shouldn't be able to get away with speaking to me like that.'

'She's unbelievable,' another woman said. 'So superior. But you know she has no reason to be. Look at the mess she's made with her own kids. Her daughter ran away from home because of the new lesbian lover. Actually ran away. It took them days to find her.'

Kate said, 'Oh, she's really troubled. Someone told me that the new lesbian lover is abusive. You know, physically. She doesn't like the kids and so …'

Jo had reached boiling point. She couldn't tell them Rachel was her friend, or they'd see her as not being on their side (which she wasn't, but she had to pretend impartiality). She spoke loudly, to interrupt. 'I'm not sure that anything you're saying here is true,' she said. 'Repeating things that aren't true, or for which there is no proof, is dangerous. Please don't do it in my school. Can we bring the focus of discussion back to the Christmas fair?'

Kate stood up and returned to her seat and Jo could feel the intensity of her outrage. It was both personal and moral. The worst kind of outrage to have directed at a school.

44

Erin

Erin had seen Laura in the schoolyard this afternoon and approached her. 'Laura,' she said, 'I was meaning to phone you.'

Laura stared at her, hurt and ice-cold.

Erin went on, 'I'm so sorry. I wanted to tell you what I said to Rachel. I couldn't keep it completely to myself because she was at home and I'd been gone for so long and when I came back I was ... Well, I think I was in shock. So I had to come up with something. I wasn't sure what to say, so on the spot I made up a story about witnessing Max being hit by a car. I'm really sorry. It was stupid, but I was at a loss and I didn't know what to do. But I can promise you that neither Rachel nor I will ever repeat it.'

She saw Laura thaw slightly. 'OK,' she said. 'That makes sense now. I thought ...' She let her voice trail off and didn't finish the sentence.

'How is Max now?'

'He's fine. Really fine. I wanted to say ... I mean, I'm grateful to you for helping me that day and not ... for not going to the authorities.'

The authorities. Erin wasn't sure who they were. The police, probably, or social services. She said, 'I spoke to Rachel's daughter, Maia. She said she'd be happy to look after Max when you work at night. She wants to work with children, so she just needs the experience. You wouldn't need to pay her. Do you want her number?'

That was another lie. Maia didn't want to work with children at all. She wanted to be a musician. But Erin couldn't say, 'I've managed to get everyone feeling sorry for you. We're a lovely family of middle-class do-gooders. Please let us save you.'

Laura looked at her suspiciously. 'Really? And Rachel's OK with that? I mean, after the …'

Erin knew. *After the LGBTQ protest that I am still at the heart of.* She said, 'Rachel's fine. She's a good woman, despite being a disgusting lesbian.' She smiled to show she was joking, but she couldn't let it sit between them unaddressed, the elephant in the schoolyard.

Laura looked away.

Erin pressed Maia's phone number into Laura's hand. 'Call her,' she said.

45

Laura

The young man was back with his weird sexual fantasies, and Laura could barely do it any more. He wanted live shows from her, while he stuffed his head in a plastic bag and wanked. Cutting off the oxygen to his brain (did he even have a brain, Laura wondered?) apparently increased the intensity of his climax, but it looked like dicing with death to Laura, and when he came back the next night with the desire to strangle her while he thrust away on top of her, she found no pleasure in it whatsoever. Not that there was ever pleasure to be had in this job, apart from when Will Kernick had been her client, but this was extreme, and not even the extra money he paid for the privilege of nearly killing her was enough to make it worthwhile.

'I don't want you to come back again,' she said, just before he left.

'Why not?'

'I don't feel happy with these practices. They're dangerous.'

'They're fine, if you do it properly. I told you the sign to make if it became too much.'

That was true. He had. If she felt like she was about to die, she needed to raise her right hand above her head. It wasn't always that easy with fourteen stone of male muscle on top of you.

'I don't want you to come back again,' she said, more forcefully.

'Suit yourself,' he said, and left.

She poured herself a glass of water and sat on the edge of the bed to drink it. This was so wrong, she thought. She needed to give this work up. Maia Kernick – of all people – was at her flat right now, looking after her son for nothing, believing Laura was working at a call centre for a bank, while all the time Laura was risking everything by acting out some revolting young man's pornographic fantasy.

Erin had been kind to her. It was the first time anyone had shown her kindness for years, and it left her feeling guilty. She didn't deserve it.

She wondered what Jo Fairburn would do if she knew about this. Or Rachel Saunders.

46

Rachel

Rachel lay in bed, unable to sleep. Erin was lying to her, or keeping something from her, or at any rate wasn't telling her the whole truth about something. Rachel knew this. A barrier had come down between them, and it was the barrier that formed when one person had stepped away into a world of secrets. She knew it had something do with Max Spence's accident, but she couldn't put her finger on what, exactly. Sometimes, she'd wondered whether it had been Erin who'd hit him, but that was impossible. There would have been police involved if she had, and Erin didn't speed. She wasn't necessarily a good driver, but she didn't speed. Besides that, Rachel was sure Erin would have told her.

Maia was babysitting for Laura this evening. Rachel had spoken to her on the phone earlier, and she'd said she was taking her copy of *Hamlet* over to Laura's and would finish Act 5 while the child slept. *Hamlet* was part of Maia's enrichment class, aimed at stretching the most able to prepare them for their eventual Oxbridge entrance. Maia was scornful of Oxbridge, and said she had no intention of going. She wanted to be stretched for the purpose of being stretched. There didn't, she argued, always need to be a tangible outcome to deeper thought in order for it to be worthwhile. God, she was her mother's daughter, however hard she tried not to be.

Rachel reached for her phone on the bedside table and sent her a daughter a text message. **How's it going?**

A bit weird.

In what way?

The kid's insane.

Are you all right?

I think so.

Call me if you need help.

It's all right. Dad's here.

She went on lying there, grateful that Will had gone to save her.

This was what happened when you got too involved in other people's lives. She should have said no when Erin asked.

47

Maia

Maia had never been to a place like this before. The kitchen was tiny, furnished only with a small garden table and two foldaway chairs propped up against the wall. A microwave took up all the worktop space. The living room had only a two-seater sofa, a small chest of drawers and the smallest television set Maia had ever seen, and there was only one bedroom. She couldn't work out where Laura slept. The bedroom was Max's. It had a cabin bed, but the wood in the frame was cracked and splintered and it looked as though he might cut his face if he rolled over in the night.

There were no books, no musical instruments, not even any pictures on the walls. There was no food, either. The whole purpose of babysitting, as Maia and her friends saw it, was that you got paid to be bored while eating someone else's snacks, but when she'd opened the cupboards to find them, there were none there. There were two potatoes, a bag of pasta, two tins of economy beans, a bottle of orange squash and a loaf of economy white bread. That was it. She opened the fridge. A pint of milk, a jar of strawberry jam and a small block of economy cheese. Nothing more. She couldn't quite work it out.

She wasn't sure if she should put the TV on. What if Laura couldn't afford it? She sat down on the sofa and read *Hamlet* in silence, answering the questions on her worksheet as she went. Then, suddenly, she looked up and saw the boy standing silently in the doorway, watching her. It freaked her out. She wondered how long he'd been there.

'Hello, Max,' she said. It was nearly 11 p.m. She'd started here at 9.30. He'd been asleep when she arrived.

'Where's Mummy?'

'She's at work, so I'm looking after you.'

With no warning whatsoever, the child went completely insane. He let out a low moan and hurled himself to the ground, bashing his face on the edge of the door frame as he landed. It made Maia wince to see it. Then he just lay there, head down, and kicked his arms and legs. There were limbs everywhere, banging against the wall and the floor. Maia wondered if she ought to try to move him, but there was no space big enough to put him in safely. She was scared of him, too. She'd never seen anything like this before.

Laura had left her mobile phone number. Maia sent her a text message. **Hi Laura. Max woke up and I don't think he liked the look of me, as he is now lying on the floor, kicking and screaming. I'm not sure what I should do.**

Fifteen minutes passed before she replied. **Sorry. Only just saw your message. Is he calm again now? You just have to leave him to it. I'll be home asap.**

Maia did as Laura said and left him to it. She sat on the sofa and watched him. He pulled at his hair and hit himself with his fists. Time passed and his mother didn't come home. Maia sent a text to her dad. **Dad, can you come** and help me? The child is going mad and I don't know what to do. It's kind of frightening.

His reply was immediate. **Be right there**.

Five minutes later, she heard his car pull up outside and went to the main door to let him in. She had to step over Max.

'What's up?' her dad asked. He looked tousled, as if he'd had to get out of bed for this, and Maia felt bad.

'Come and see,' she said.

They walked through to the flat, where Max was still howling and thrashing.

Her dad looked at him. 'Good grief,' he said. It was as beyond him to know what to do as it was Maia.

Maia said, 'Can you stay with me?'

'Yes. Of course. You should never have been asked to look after a child like this. You're too young. You haven't got the experience.'

Maia shrugged. 'Erin wanted me to. His mum works nights and can't afford childcare, but if she doesn't work, she'll have no money to feed him.'

Her dad nodded. 'That's difficult. Erin probably meant well, but it's not your problem.'

Maia was relieved. She didn't want to come here again.

Laura did come home at last. It was nearly 1 a.m. 'I'm really sorry,' she said, as she walked through the door. 'I couldn't …'

She stopped speaking suddenly as she saw Maia with her father, and Max, fast asleep on the floor, where he'd eventually worn himself out.

She was silent, speechless for a while.

'What's going on?' she eventually asked.

Maia's dad stood up and held out his hand for Laura to shake. 'I'm Will,' he said, 'I'm Maia's father. Maia had some difficulties, so I came over to help her.'

Laura wouldn't take his hand. He ended up putting it back by his side.

She looked really embarrassed. Flustered. Afraid. Eventually, she said, 'I'm so sorry. I thought he'd be OK. I'm sorry. I shouldn't have …' She shook her head.

Maia was watching her father. He was looking at Laura strangely, as if he knew her from somewhere and was trying to work out where. Then he made a movement towards her, and suddenly stopped himself. Laura wouldn't look at him.

Maia wondered if maybe they'd met on Tinder or something, and hadn't got on.

Her dad cleared his throat. 'I'll take Maia home now,' he said. 'She's got your number, hasn't she?'

Laura nodded, but still wouldn't look up.

'She'll be in touch. I hope you're OK.'

Maia noticed he touched her arm as he walked past, but then when they were in the car he said, 'You're not to go there again, Maia, do you understand?'

'All right, you don't need to be like that. I was just doing someone a favour.'

'I'm sorry,' he said. 'But there are problems there, and you don't need to be involved.'

He drove home in silence.

48

Jo

It wasn't until the following Monday, when she was driving home after school, that it occurred to Jo that Laura Spence hadn't been at the meeting about the Christmas fair. She seemed to have bowed out of school life completely. She used to be such a huge part of it, and she'd stood out to Jo because she wasn't an easy fit among the other mothers there. The others were mostly women who didn't work, women who'd walked out on careers that demanded too much time and energy, and now they were professional parents instead. It wasn't enough for them to simply know they were the best, most devoted mothers in town. They needed to make sure everyone else saw them that way, too. Otherwise, what would be the point? They could have just stayed at work, been rewarded with hard cash and recognition.

Jo had assumed – when she thought about it at all – that Laura's reasons for being on the PTA were purely social. Clearly there was some kind of bond of shared prejudice with Kate Monro, and without the monthly meetings, Laura could probably go for too long without seeing another adult. When Jo met with Max's class teacher the other day, she'd said it wasn't Laura who'd come to the previous evening's parents' consultation, but his father, and that Laura was no longer appearing in the yard very often.

Jo was cautious in her response to this, hesitant as always to leap to conclusions and create a fantasy melodrama out of a minor detail. 'Well,' she said, 'it's a positive thing that the father seems to be stepping up.'

Melissa Jenkins agreed. They would simply keep a quiet eye on things.

Jo parked the car in her drive and prepared herself to face her own son. 'We all have problems with our children,' she wanted to say to Laura. 'Don't let the shame take you over.' She could never say such a thing, though – could never overstep the professional boundary that allowed other people to think Jo Fairburn was a strong, mysterious woman whose life was so together she could devote her time to diagnosing the flaws in everyone else's.

Luke, unusually, was in the kitchen when she walked in. She just about managed a smile.

'Good day?' she asked, more coldly than she'd wanted to.

'Yeah,' he said. 'I had a letter from Susi's solicitor. She's dropped the charges against me.'

He looked at her expectantly, waiting for her joy.

Jo said nothing.

'Susi has dropped the charges against me,' he said again.

'That's a relief. Did she say why?'

Luke shook his head. 'There were no reasons given. Just a letter from her solicitor saying charges had been dropped.'

'You must be relieved.'

'I am,' he said. 'Aren't you?'

Jo sighed and then smiled. 'Yes, I am. Of course I am. I'm sorry. This is excellent news.'

'She just knew she couldn't win.'

'Looks like it.'

'Mum, I know this has been really hard for you. I know it's really hard not to believe the victim and I understand that. I usually believe the woman in cases like this. It's really important. But I didn't do it. I know I didn't. I never would. And sometimes, people do make things up. I don't know Susi very well and I don't know why she'd do this, but ...'

'It's OK, Luke,' Jo said. 'I believe you.'

Even as she said it, she wasn't sure.

Carefully, she said, 'And what about Maia?'

He shrugged. 'What about her?'

'She's sixteen, Luke.'

'She's a mature girl.'

'She's my best friend's daughter and you've known her since she was a baby. It's ... I just feel unhappy about it. She's young. She's been through a really hard time and however mature she might be, and how smart, she's vulnerable.'

'She's fine. She's stronger than you think.'

'She's a child, Luke. What I saw ...'

His voice rose. 'Was none of your fucking business.'

She turned away from him. At that moment, she would have liked to slap his arrogant face. She'd spoken to Dave about the case soon after she found out. She broke the news to him over the phone, and listened while he silently took it all in. It was in that silence, Jo realised, that they both began to experience guilt. Was it their fault this had happened? Was it because they'd separated, destroyed his home, left him feeling he had nowhere to turn, or that he was powerless? They needed to come together now to sort this out, to put right what they'd done so badly. But it was too late. And besides, he was an adult and ought to have adult coping strategies. He didn't need to go round assaulting people to prove his worth.

Now, when she'd gathered herself together, she turned back to him and said, 'It is my business. You are my son, you had a charge of sexual assault against you and you have been sleeping with my best friend's sixteen-year-old daughter. That is my business.'

'Yes, Mum,' he said scornfully. 'Sixteen. Perfectly legal.'

'You are twenty-two.'

'So?'

'How do you think that would have looked in court, Luke? Any prosecutor worth their salt could easily paint you as someone who takes advantage of young girls who don't know what they're doing.'

'It's not going to fucking court any more. And God, you say you're a feminist and you take the girl's side, but taking the girl's side in stuff like this seems to involve turning all females into these vulnerable little things who can't think for themselves. Why is it always assault? Or if she's consenting, why does it always have to be that she doesn't know what she's doing? Treat Maia with some respect, Mum. She's an intelligent girl and perfectly capable of making her own decisions without me having to *take advantage* of her.'

'I'm sure she is, Luke, and if I believed for one minute that you were serious about her and had some affection for her, I'd be less bothered by it, but bearing everything in mind, I don't like what I'm seeing here. I don't like it at all.'

'Oh, thanks for that, Mum. Thanks a lot,' he said.

'I want you to stop seeing Maia.'

'You can't say that.'

'Oh, I most certainly can, young man. You stop seeing her, or you get out of this house. And while you're at it, you can get a job. I've put up with this long enough. If you're going to stay here, you need a job and you need to start paying me rent. I will give you two weeks.'

'Two weeks or what?'

'Or you can leave. I don't want to hear that everything's boring or that you're overqualified and too bloody good for whatever's out there. You're not too good to face the realities of life, Luke, which are that you pay your own way and you don't sleep with children.'

She shouldn't have said that. That really was going too far.

She'd rendered him speechless. He stared at her, his face rigid with hurt, then he left the room and the last thing Jo heard was the hard slam of his bedroom door.

49

Erin

It had all turned out to be disastrous for everyone, which hadn't been the plan in any way. Erin hadn't realised how late Laura worked. She'd assumed a night shift was something like eight till midnight, but it turned out to be from ten till two, which meant Maia didn't even start babysitting until not long before she'd usually be going to bed. When she heard about that, Rachel – who was a firm believer in the power of sleep to keep her children pleasant – had taken it as the first sign that things weren't going to go well, and had even said to Erin, 'What job can be worth putting in a four-hour shift at that time of night?' Erin shook her head. Who knew?

And then Max had woken up, lost his shit and frightened the life out of Maia, so Will went along to rescue her, and now he was on the phone to Rachel, adamant that Maia must never go back there again.

'I know, Will,' Rachel was saying. 'It was a mistake. I'm sure she'll get over it, though.'

There was a pause while Will replied, then she said, 'Do you think you might be overreacting a bit? Maia will get over this. It's unfortunate, but it's hardly going to traumatise her for life.'

Another pause. Then, 'Oh, for God's sake. She's not three years old.'

Erin could see her losing patience while Will kept on making his feelings clear. In the end, she snapped, 'I get it. I don't know why you keep shouting at me. I agree with you. We've said everything. There's no point continuing this conversation. I'm going now, Will. I'm gone.'

She ended the call. 'Jesus Christ. He's so fucking worked up.'

'I'm sorry,' Erin said.

Rachel reached out and put her arm around her. 'It's not your fault. It's just one of those things. Poor Laura. She's got a lot on her plate.'

'What do you think's wrong with Max? It sounds really serious.'

Rachel sighed. 'He hasn't got the language skills of most children his age. That's probably part of it. Kids who can't express themselves in words will make themselves heard in other ways.'

Erin's mind went back to the morning in the woods, when she'd found his near-lifeless body on the ground. She hadn't asked Laura at the time what he'd been doing, why he'd left the house in the middle of the night while she was at work. It wasn't the right moment to ask, although she'd wanted to know. Now she wanted to know even more. She wondered if he'd run away, and if he had, what it was he'd been running from.

She hated this. She hated keeping this secret from Rachel. But she'd witnessed Laura's distress and she'd promised her she wouldn't say anything. It was such a cliché that some secrets were better not kept – the sort of thing you had to tell a child, because adults weren't usually stupid enough to keep secrets like this.

Rachel's words came back to her. *They always love their kids. It doesn't stop them abusing them.*

Erin opened her mouth to tell her the truth about that day, 'Rachel,' she said.

But Rachel's phone rang, and it was Maia, and the moment was lost.

50

Laura

Tomorrow would be Max's birthday. Laura couldn't do it. After that excruciating night with Rachel Saunders' daughter, when Max had had one of his scenes and Will bloody Kernick ended up here in her flat (in her flat!) and so clearly knew exactly who she was, she'd stopped going to work. She had to. She felt she was living on a knife-edge. Soon word was going to be spread all over town that Laura Spence was a whore. Her only hope would be that Will Kernick was so deeply ashamed of even setting foot in her room, he'd keep her identity to himself. She wasn't sure, though. She could see Erin on one side, Will on the other, each of them knowing Laura's worst secrets. All they had to do was open their mouths, let the words out, and there it would be, right in the hands of Rachel Saunders. Rachel Saunders and her heroic insistence on doing the right thing.

If she at least gave up work, she'd have some defence. She could deny it.

But now there was no money. Sex work was well enough paid, but Laura had always hated it and did as little of it as she could – just enough to keep the rent paid and food on the table. And there were always clients who walked out without paying, leaving her skint.

She couldn't afford the sort of extravagant birthday party Max's classmates always had, where parents would pay to shut down the local cinema and take the whole class to see a film; or hire dancers from a theatre company who'd have two hours to teach the children to perform key scenes from *Frozen*; or even just parting with a hundred pounds to haul everyone to soft play.

All she could really afford was the sort of party she used to have when she was little, where a friend or two would come over for tea, but Max didn't seem to have friends any more. He was the odd one out, the weird kid, and other children kept their distance. Besides that, Laura thought she would rather do nothing at all than throw her son a pathetic little gathering nowhere near to what others expected and expose him to comments that he and his parties and his mother weren't good enough.

She had no energy for any of it. The thought of the shopping she'd have to do, the bread she'd have to butter, the pass-the-parcel she'd need to wrap … It made her want to close the curtains, crawl into bed and hide.

It was so hard, this game of pretending.

She looked at Max lying on the floor, absently watching TV. He was so unhappy, she thought, so troubled. She remembered his little face when Drew brought him home on Sunday after their first weekend together – smiling, streaked with dirt, as if every hour from Friday till Sunday had been lively and carefree.

There'd been mud all over his trousers. Laura tried not to let him get too dirty when they went out. She had to make his clothes last as many days as she could, to spare the expense of doing the washing. It kept her on edge, everywhere they went. Always, she was watching him, 'Don't do that Max,' she'd be saying constantly. 'You'll get dirty.' And then he'd do it and he'd get dirty, and she'd shout at him, make his life a goddamn misery.

'Sorry about the mess he's in,' Drew said cheerfully. 'We did an obstacle course and there were no spares in his bag.'

'Never mind,' Laura said. Of course, he'd made it her fault their son had spent half the day in muddy clothes that had no doubt been wet for several hours, too. Of course, it was beyond him to think of going to Tesco and buying another pair for a fiver. No – let the boy spend the afternoon in wet trousers and make it his mother's fault, even though she'd hadn't even bloody well been there.

'Has he had tea?' Laura asked.

'We went to my mum's. He had a huge Sunday lunch.'

They'd been to his mum's. So now Max had a grandma to dote on him and feed him and love him and do all the things Laura failed at. No wonder he looked as though he was about to cry at the thought of coming back here.

She turned her attention to her son. 'Did you have fun, Max?' she asked.

Max didn't say anything.

'We had a great time, didn't we, buddy?' Drew said.

Max nodded.

'Shall we do it again next weekend?'

That wasn't the agreement they'd come to. They'd agreed Drew would take him every other weekend and Wednesdays.

'Yes!' Max said.

'Brilliant. I'll see you on Wednesday, as usual.'

'How many days is that?' Max asked.

'Just three days. I'll pick you up from school, shall I? We'll go to a café for tea.'

Laura wondered where he found money to eat in cafés when he couldn't afford maintenance payments.

Hesitantly, Drew said, 'Is that all right with you, Laura?'

She smiled thinly. 'Fine.'

Drew kneeled down on the floor so he could hug his son goodbye. Laura pretended not to notice how Max returned his affection, or the tears in his eyes.

She was angry that Drew found this all so easy. 'Take him,' she wanted to say. 'He'll be better off with you.'

Now, she thought about Max waking up here tomorrow morning, his sixth birthday. All she'd bought him was a CBeebies comic. It came with gifts – plastic sharks, stickers, a few craft materials. It would keep him happy enough for ten minutes, but it was hardly special. She hadn't even made him a cake.

'Max,' she said, 'do you want to go to your dad's for your birthday?'

He answered with enthusiasm. Slowly, she'd recently been accepting that Max was happiest with Drew. Why wouldn't he be? Drew was everything Laura wasn't: fun to be with, slow to anger. He wasn't suffering from the accumulated tiredness of six years without enough sleep, six years of worry, six years of battling on with something she was just no good at, however much he wanted to be. Drew was right at the beginning of his parenting tether. Laura was far, far beyond the end of hers.

Drew picked Max up at 6.30. He looked as though he could hardly believe his luck, that his son was going to wake up with him on his birthday. When they left, he was promising balloons, cake, presents, fireworks, the earth and everything on it.

Laura sat on the sofa and cried.

She hardly slept. In the morning, she woke up with the shame of knowing it was Max's birthday and he wasn't here with her because she'd sent him away because she found him too difficult and couldn't bear the thought of looking into his face over breakfast, seeing only sadness and longing there – that longing for his father, who'd abandoned him as a baby but had now waltzed back into his life and was doing such a good job of making up for lost time, of putting right the terrible past.

But it was Laura who'd made the past terrible. Drew had barely even been there.

51

Rachel

She should probably apologise to Kate. Rachel knew she'd been out of order in the schoolyard the other day, and Kate was never going to let it go. It had been like handing her a rifle and giving her a reason to shoot. Also, it was making Jo's life difficult.

Rachel was thinking about trying a new and unfamiliar approach, which was to remain calm and generous in the face of persecution. Erin's idea. 'Instead of fighting, why don't we support her?'

'Support her? Fuck off.'

'No, I don't mean that. I mean just keep proving to her, again and again, how stupid this protest is. Invite her over, let her see that you are a perfectly ordinary person, living a perfectly ordinary life, and who you sleep with is of no consequence whatsoever.'

'I draw the line at inviting her over.'

'Fine. But instead of being angry, be nice. Kindness is the best weapon you have. Eventually, she'll start wondering what it is she's fighting here.'

It made sense. It really did.

A few days later, she armoured herself with the sort of smile she usually reserved for distressed patients, then approached Kate again outside school. She was there with Laura. Erin thought that might make a difference, that Laura might already be thawing her approach to the disgusting lesbians on the grounds that one of them had helped her when her son had been in an accident. Rachel knew better than that. She said, 'If there's one thing I've learnt in all my years as a doctor, it's not to expect gratitude or respect. You'll never get it. Laura Spence hates gay people. She won't change just because one gay woman helped her when her son was hurt.'

Rachel was certain of this, although Erin still seemed to be holding fast to a belief in the power of heroic deeds to produce heroic changes of attitudes. 'It won't happen,' Rachel said. 'I promise you. Laura Spence will no more stop being disgusted with homosexuality than I will start believing in Santa. Trust me. This isn't Hollywood.'

Still, she tried it. 'Hi Kate,' she said, with a smile for Laura. 'I want to apologise for what I said to you the other day.'

Kate looked at her. So did Laura.

Rachel went on, 'It's very difficult for me, when I see people judging the way I live and thinking that it is somehow wrong. Also,' she was about to get personal, which was never easy for Rachel, but perhaps it was a better approach than fury, 'I struggled for many years with who I really was. Lots of people do. It's incredibly hard to live your life as one thing, knowing all the time that you're really something else. And then I met Erin and I couldn't hide it any longer, and I made the decision to be honest. I have hurt some people with that decision, but in the end, I would have hurt them more by keeping this secret. It has been a really difficult thing to do, and when I heard about your campaign, I was ... Well, I was hurt by it and worried to think how my daughter would be singled out and possibly targeted by other children. I wanted to believe we now lived in a world where people would allow others to love passionately and honestly and openly, so I was disappointed – really disappointed – to find that we don't. And it came out as anger, and I'm very sorry.'

There. That should do it.

Laura cast her eyes downward. She preferred to act as angry fuel, rather than fight head-on. This conflict was hard for her to face, Rachel could see that, but she would probably seethe in silence for months.

Kate nodded, then allowed herself a small, peaceful smile towards Rachel, the woman who had just admitted that she suffered sometimes, and she hurt. She said, 'Thank you for apologising. I suppose I can understand why this upset you. It's not personal, though ...'

It fucking is.

'Please don't see it as an attack on you or your daughter.'

'It's quite difficult not to see it as that, though. It is an attack on what I am.'

'Well ...'

'And really,' she was keeping her tone polite but God, it was a struggle, 'all I am doing is loving someone. It isn't hurting you, or anyone else in Burntridge.'

'No ...'

'I have a suggestion.'

'What's that?'

'Perhaps, when you've got your classes under way and

taught children about the right way to live as you see it, I might be able to come and talk to them about what it feels like when you know yourself to be different and struggle to fit in. It might help those children who already feel themselves to be different.'

'That might be possible,' Kate said, in a tone that was incredibly doubtful.

'Let me know,' Rachel said, and smiled again.

She'd done it. It probably wouldn't make the slightest difference yet, but she could see she'd at least made Kate feel awkward.

Erin was right. She'd break these women with politeness.

52

Maia

Luke didn't like Maia as much as she liked him. That was clear. It had always been clear, ever since they first got together. She wasn't even sure they had got together, or at least, that Luke ever thought of them as being together. He'd never called her his girlfriend, never seemed that bothered about seeing her, and she was sure his mind wandered when they had sex. It used to drive her mad, the way James always wanted to look into her eyes and seize every shred of intimacy from their encounters. Now she wished Luke would do that. He never did. He looked anywhere but at her.

She wanted to ask him, 'Do you actually like me, Luke?' But it was such a pathetic thing to say. She should probably just walk away, the way strong women did in books, knowing they were worth more than this. But there was something about the fact that Luke withheld his affection that made her want it more. If he just threw himself at her, the way James had done, she probably wouldn't give a shit about him. That, she realised, was how bastards operated, and why so many women couldn't get enough of them.

They were at her dad's house. He was out for the night, and

Maia didn't feel comfortable going to Jo's any more, not after last time. She expected Jo to tell her mum. They were friends. She'd consider it her responsibility. Maia didn't care. Her mum could get as worked up about it as she liked. It was still none of her business.

They'd just had sex and now Luke was lying on his back in her bed, scrolling through his phone. He tossed it aside, then stood up. 'Just going for a piss,' he said.

She watched him as he walked, naked, to the door. He had such a good body – toned and muscular, with chest hair. James hadn't had much in the way of chest hair. It hadn't bothered her, but now she had Luke, she realised she liked it. There were probably lots of girls who liked it, who liked him.

Without really thinking of what she was doing, she picked up his phone. It hadn't gone into sleep mode yet, so she didn't need to know his passcode to get in.

It was open at his photo album. He always took photos of her and she let him. Sexy, nude photos that were never too graphic. He wanted them to be more graphic, he said, but she refused. She wasn't a porn star. She drew the line at that.

But someone in his life was. She realised that as she scrolled through his album, knowing he'd have done exactly the same with previous girlfriends, but assuming he'd have had the decency to remove the evidence from his phone. And his head, for that matter.

She wanted to see more closely what this woman looked like. She expanded the photo to her face.

'Who's this?' she asked, when Luke came back in.

'You've been going through my phone?'

She shrugged. 'You left it here.'

'That doesn't give you the right to go through it. Jesus Christ, Maia. I didn't think you were like this. I didn't think you were one of those pathetic, insecure girls who …'

'Who is she?'

He snatched the phone out of her hands. 'She's no one.'

'She's clearly someone.'

'She's just …'

'Go on …'

'Fuck off, Maia.'

'This is my bedroom, mate. I think you'll find it's you who needs to fuck off.'

He was silent.

'I know this woman,' Maia said.

'You do not.'

'I do. I babysit for her.'

He went a little pale.

'So,' Maia said, 'how've you ended up with pornographic images of Max Spence's mother on your phone?'

Maia listened to him talk. 'She's a sex worker,' he said, as coolly as if he were letting her know that Max's mother operated a checkout in Tesco.

'Right. So you've been …' She couldn't finish the sentence.

He laughed. 'Oh, Maia. It's no big deal. All men do this sort of thing.'

All of them?

Her mind drifted to her father, and how he'd seemed to recognise Laura when she came home that night. For now she pushed the thought away and blocked it from becoming too clear. But it was going to come back and haunt her, she knew that.

She turned her attention to Luke again. 'Why?' she asked.

'Why did I do it, or why do all men do it?'

'Why did you do it? I mean, why did you do it in the first place, and why did you do it when you're with me?'

He lay beside her and ran his fingers over her cheek. 'Oh, sweetheart. I didn't realise you saw it like that.'

'Like what?'

'Like something serious. I thought we were just having fun. I thought that was what you wanted, and why you got so tired of your boyfriend.'

That was true. That was what she'd told him and it was the way she'd started out. She hadn't realised, at the time, that she was going to feel this way. It wasn't love, she knew that. It was a desire to be the only one he was sleeping with. Just for a while. Just for now.

She didn't want to be like this. She didn't want to be so easily shockable, so naive as she navigated her way through this new, shadowy world.

All men sleep with sex workers.

Did they?

Really?

'So what's the appeal?' she asked. She was prepared to listen. She was interested. She needed educating.

He shrugged. 'There are things it's not always easy to ask women to do, especially when they're so young and beautiful. They're enjoyable things,' he added hastily. 'I don't do anything disgusting. I've done it with a couple of other girls and they liked it.'

'What sort of things?'

He looked at her curiously. 'You want to know?'

'Sure.'

'I'll show you,' he said. 'I promise you, you'll like it, but you need to trust me, sweetheart.'

53

Erin

It was evening, and Erin and Reuben were sitting on separate sofas in the softly lit living room, each working on their laptops in companionable silence. Erin's feature was due tomorrow and Reuben was writing a history essay about Thatcher and the miners' strikes. His disappointment about being rejected by Cambridge seemed to be wearing off, although Erin suspected he was going to become one of those men who carried a chip on his shoulder about it until at least middle age.

Rachel was out, giving a public lecture at Newcastle University. She'd written it earlier that day, in less than an hour. It would undoubtedly be sharp, brilliant and also very funny because Rachel couldn't be anything else. 'How do you write this stuff so quickly?' Erin had asked her, envious and slightly awestruck.

Rachel shrugged. 'I just know my shit,' she said. No big deal, as always.

It reminded Erin of the time, shortly after they'd met, when Rachel had given a guest lecture to a group of first-year medical students in London. They'd been sent for a one-off professional practice talk, to be followed by a session in a hospital or clinic.

This particular group were given paediatrics, which had been Rachel's specialism and for which she felt they ought to be grateful, but when Erin met her afterwards in Leicester Square, she was fuming. 'They were a bunch of self-entitled, arrogant shits,' she said. 'Two of them were stretched out across three seats, yawning, because obviously they didn't come to medical school to deal with something as trivial as *children*. They were bloody lucky to be there, the tossers. They could have been sent to the ingrowing toenail clinic. How dare they yawn through a lecture I took time to write for them?'

'Did you throw them out?' Erin asked.

'No. But I did punish them.'

Erin raised her eyebrows with interest. Rachel continued, 'Afterwards, I took them to the neonatal ward for their work experience. Told them it was really exciting and they were really privileged to get this hands-on experience so early in their careers. The sister there is a great friend of mine. Brutal, she is. *Fucking brutal.* I handed her these two lads and told her they needed the goddamn self-entitlement knocked out of them and she was to show no mercy. So she took them down to a ward full of babies whose heads are the size of testicles and told them to feed them. She was brilliant. Each boy sat there, dripping milk down the throat of a see-through baby, looking absolutely petrified. 'Careful you don't choke them,' she was saying. 'It's a very important and difficult job.' She didn't mention the only reason they had to do it was because she didn't have any poles to tie the milk bags to so it could be administered mechanically. It was bloody brilliant.'

Erin laughed out loud at the memory. Reuben looked up from his laptop. 'What are you laughing at?' he asked.

'I was remembering the first time I saw your mum give a guest lecture. That's when I realised she's not a woman to be messed with.'

'Yeah. You should try being her kid.' He gave a low, American-style whistle, as if to emphasise the fact that being the child of Rachel Saunders was an experience beyond the imagination of most people.

Erin knew, and Rachel knew, that the hardest thing about being Rachel's child was living in her shadow. Most of the parents of Reuben and Maia's friends had reached the peak of their life's achievements and moved over, let their children come in and take their places while they started slowing down. Their purpose now was to watch their children go forwards and hope they'd do more than they themselves had ever managed. But Rachel was never going to slow down and she was never going to peak, either. And the chances of her children ever achieving more than she had were remote. 'I'm glad I've got Dad's surname,' Maia had remarked one day before she moved out. 'Otherwise, people would just look at me and say, 'Oh, are you Rachel Saunders' daughter? And they'd expect me to whip some kind of magic trick out of my arse.'

Rachel had been unconcerned. 'They'll find their own paths,' she said.

Erin said, 'I'm convinced it's partly why Maia's so resentful, though. No matter how brilliant she is, you'll always be better.'

'It's not a bloody competition.'

'No, but she's young. She's trying to carve out some kind of identity for herself, but she's always overshadowed by this bloody amazing mother. All her friends' mothers are just sitting around in their offices, amazed that their kids can point to

Outer Mongolia on a map. You're harder to impress. You just assume they'll be outstanding because it's normal for you.'

Rachel shrugged. 'You're probably right. You know, I never put their artwork on the walls when they were little. I always said to them, 'When you produce something truly amazing, I'll put it up.' And I did, but it took Maia till she was ten and Reuben till he was twelve. But Jesus Christ, there are enough deluded fools around without me producing more. Don't inflict shit on the world, that's what I say. And look, they've both survived.'

There was a sudden knock at the front door. Erin glanced up from her work towards Reuben, who showed no sign of having any intention of answering it, even though any visitor at this time of the evening was far more likely to be for him than her. She moved her laptop aside and headed to the door.

Maia.

She stood before Erin, pale-faced and looking slightly shaken. 'Is it alright if I come in?' she asked.

Erin opened the door wide. 'Of course.'

Maia stepped inside and looked around. 'Is Mum in?'

'She's not home yet. She'll probably be back in an hour.'

'Do you mind ... Do you mind if I stay tonight?'

Erin smiled warmly. 'Not at all. You're always welcome. You know that.'

'Thanks.'

They went through the hallway and into the living room. Brightly, Erin said, 'Visitor, Reuben.'

Reuben looked up at last. 'Oh, hi,' he said. 'Haven't seen you round these parts for a while.'

Maia barely smiled. She looked shocked, as though

something awful had just happened. She said, 'Would you mind if I had a bath?'

'You don't need to ask.'

Erin knew what this was. Some bastard she'd been pretending not to be in love with had just hurt her. She recognised the signs. She'd been there herself, too many times. *The first cut is the deepest,* her mother had said, years ago, and Erin believed her. It turned out to be another meaningless platitude Erin wasn't about to inflict on the stricken young woman now standing in her living room. *The first cut is just the start, love. Get used to it.* She probably shouldn't say that, either. Not at the moment.

She said, 'Are you all right, Maia?'

Maia nodded and headed up the stairs. Erin could hear the bath running, then silence. Maia stayed there for a long time.

The longer Maia spent locked in the bathroom, the more uncomfortable Erin began to feel. Had she been attentive enough when she came home? Probably not. She should have offered to make her a cup of tea, sat with her, encouraged her to talk. But then, Maia didn't like her, which made it difficult to offer an understanding ear.

She glanced at Reuben, deeply lost in his laptop, oblivious to crisis of any kind.

Just after nine, she heard Rachel's car pull up. She went to corner her in the hallway, so they could talk without Reuben overhearing.

'Maia's here,' she said.

Rachel took her coat off and slung it over the stand. 'Good mood or bad?' she asked.

'I think something's wrong. She seemed upset. She was looking for you. I asked if she was OK, but I don't think I asked hard enough.'

A brief moment of something that looked like comfort crossed Rachel's face. She replaced it quickly. 'Really?' she asked. 'She still needs hot chocolate and a chat with her mother after a bad day? That's something, I suppose. Where is she?'

'She's in the bath. She's been there a while.'

'It'll be some bloody bloke, won't it? Do I need to get ready to stab him, do you think?'

'She did seem very … not upset. Shocked.'

'Ah, yes. The first experience of a bastard. It'll do that to a sixteen-year-old. For fuck's sake. I told her. I *told* her it was no good to shag a hundred different men a week. I had no idea I was so traditional, but it turns out that I am when it comes to my children. No one can handle that at sixteen. You have to be tough. But she thinks she is tough, just because she's survived her parents' divorce. God, she drives me mad.'

Erin raised her eyebrows. 'Is that what you're going to say to her?'

'No. I'll be lovely, of course. For now. But tomorrow …'

She leaned forwards and kissed Erin briefly on the lips, then went upstairs to begin the long process of finding out what had just happened to her daughter.

54

Laura

Sunday night. The flat was cold. Max had spent the weekend at his dad's, so Laura had turned the heating off. There was no need to spend money on keeping warm if he wasn't here. She'd spent all of Saturday and Sunday lying beneath her duvet on the sofa, mostly sleeping to escape the emptiness of Max's absence and her expanding fear of the future.

If Rachel Saunders or Jo Fairburn found out how she'd earned her living, or that Max had gone missing for eight hours and she hadn't called the police, they would call social services. Thinking about the things the world could unearth about her made her shake.

Prostitution.

Her criminal father.

The postnatal depression that seemed to be dragging on, when it should have been over years ago.

The fact that she'd been expelled from school.

Her habit of being with abusive men.

Her insane, all-consuming rage.

Her inability to look after her child properly, even though she'd tried and tried.

And now, there was unemployment to add to the list. Unemployment, bare cupboards and an empty fridge. And the kitchen floor needed cleaning. It was covered in Rice Krispies. And Max's cabin bed frame was split. Splintered wood now threatened to cut him in his sleep, and the whole thing might fall down any minute. She ought to move his mattress to the floor, but his room was small and there wasn't much space. Really, the whole bed frame needed hauling to the tip, but she didn't have a car. She'd need to break it down and take it, piece by piece, on the bus. It would be hours and hours of work.

The thought of everything she had to do made her want to cry.

She stood up from the sofa, went to the boiler cupboard in the hall and turned the heating on for Max. She'd missed him so much, but she didn't want him to come home. She had nothing to feed him, nothing to give him, and every noise he made at the moment felt like someone clawing at her nerve endings. She'd end up shouting at him and he didn't deserve it. He never deserved it.

She wished someone would just take her away for a while.

55

Rachel

Rachel took her Fleetwod Mac *Rumours* record out of its slipcover, blew away the dust and placed it on the record player. She'd been collecting vinyl for a year now, ever since she and Erin had borrowed a friend's house in Cornwall one weekend and there'd been an old record player in the living room. The sound when they played it was completely different to the sound they were used to on CDs and Spotify – warmer, richer. Better. She wondered why the world had ever done away with it in the first place.

Stevie Nicks' voice blasted the room and Rachel turned it up. *Bastard*, she thought, reaching for the granite cleaner and pumping more than she needed over the worktop. *Bastard, bastard, bastard.*

What was it he'd been accused of? Nothing criminal. Nothing anyone could arrest him for. Nothing, in fact, that Rachel was even sure of. Maia hadn't said very much about it and Rachel had been piecing things together based on the little she had told her, while filling the gaps in the narrative herself with imagination and instinct.

Erin had been right that night, when she'd said Maia looked

shocked. When Maia did finally drag herself out of the bathroom after Rachel had knocked on the door and offered to bring her hot chocolate in bed, she was pale and puffy-eyed, wrapped up in the old dressing gown she'd left behind when she moved out.

'What brings you home this evening?' Rachel asked gently. 'Are you all right?'

At the sight of her mother, Maia crumpled and began to cry. She'd always been like that, always able to hold back the tears until the knife of maternal tenderness came along and cut her in two. Rachel put her arms around her.

Maia was working to get herself under control. 'It's OK,' she said. 'I'm all right. I'd just like to stay here tonight, if that's OK.'

'Of course that's OK.' She looked at Maia seriously for a moment, noting the shock and the look on her face that seemed like confusion, and said, 'Has someone hurt you?' She meant *assaulted*. She meant *raped,* but those words were too strong to hurl about at this early stage.

Maia shook her head. 'Not really. A bit.'

'A boy?'

'Yes.'

'Do you want to go and get into bed? I'll make you a hot chocolate if you like.'

Maia nodded feebly and headed down the landing to her room. Rachel watched her and thought, though she could have been imagining it, that she walked like somebody injured. A feeling of sickness came over her and then guilt, because if Maia had still been living with her, none of this – whatever *this* was – would have happened. She was as sure of that as she was of anything.

This, it emerged later, was to do with sex. Rachel had already known that, but it still hit her with the full force of a brutal shock. She took Maia a hot chocolate and a biscuit up to her room, then sat on the edge of her bed, smoothed the hair back from her face and said, 'What happened, Maia?'

Maia turned her face away. 'It's nothing, Mum. Just some lad …'

'Do I need to beat him up?'

'*Mum* …'

Rachel raised one hand in surrender. 'OK, I'm sorry. I won't. Can you tell me who it was?'

'Luke.'

Rachel paused for a moment. Luke, her best friend's son. She needed to be careful not to react too strongly.

'Luke?' she repeated, buying herself time.

Maia nodded.

Luke was so much older. He was practically a man. Maia was still a child who didn't know what she was doing. Rachel had broken her heart and now she was messing around with boys and sex when what she really needed was her family back together and the unending love of her mother.

'Did he do something you weren't consenting to?' she asked. It was a minefield, navigating the rocky waters of her daughter's sexual encounters. *Just stop it*, she wanted to shout. *Just stop shagging. Come home and live with me and I'll bring you hot chocolate in bed every night and smother you with maternal devotion. Just stop having goddamn sex with people old enough to be …* Well, all right. That was going too far. Luke wasn't old enough to be her father, but he was in his twenties

302

and Maia was still a teenager. That was a generational leap, as far as Rachel was concerned.

Maia said, 'Not exactly. It was just ...' She shook her head again, her cheeks flaming with shame.

Rachel pursed her lips. 'I see,' she said, and she thought she did see. He'd found a naive, vulnerable young girl who thought she was tough enough to fling herself into the adult world of relationships, and he'd taken advantage of that because he was cool and good-looking and thought he had the right to. Maia wasn't going to say much more than she'd already said, but Rachel could guess what had happened. He'd subjected her to something brutal, or at least, something more brutal than she'd thought she was entering into, and now here she was: ashamed, uncertain and injured.

'You know,' Rachel cleared her throat, trying to tread carefully, 'if he did something to you that you didn't want him to do, it counts as assault. He didn't need to know you weren't consenting. If he was reckless about it, then that's enough.' She looked at her daughter. 'Was he?'

'No, not really. I don't know. I just want to forget it now.'

'OK,' Rachel said, and kissed her. 'But just think about what I've said. I know you don't want to share the gruesome details with your mother. I understand that. But if he's hurt you, deliberately or not, it's wrong.'

She had to fight every urge to tell her daughter to just get in the car with her and go to the police. They could get the bastard arrested. Get him thrown in custody. Wreck his life. But one look at Maia's face told her she wasn't up to that. She was brutalised, traumatised ...

Oh God, but she really should go to the police. There would

be lovely female officers there who'd be sympathetic and gentle. They'd sit her down in a comfortable room and bring her tea and help her tell her story, and it would be so much easier for Maia to tell her story to kind strangers than to her furious mother.

'Maia,' she tried. 'You know, if he hurt you, we can take this to the police …'

'No, Mum.'

'They'd be able to help you. Even if you don't want to press charges, they'll have support you can access and …'

'Please stop,' Maia said, and Rachel could see she was close to tears again. 'Please don't. I don't want to talk about it. It's nothing really. I'll be fine in the morning.'

More than anything, Rachel wanted this to be true. It wasn't, though. She could see that very clearly and she couldn't let it go. 'Maybe I can phone and ask if they'll send someone out to speak to you. A woman, someone kind and understanding. You'll be able to talk to her about what happened.'

Maia didn't answer. She rolled over and buried her face in her pillow. She wasn't crying, Rachel knew that. She was just fed up with her interfering mother.

She needed to respect her daughter's distress and back off from all her talk of assault and the police. It was too soon, except that if Maia left it any longer, it was going be too late to press charges. They needed the evidence now. They'd needed it hours ago, before she'd even stepped in the bath.

She stood and looked at her daughter, face-down on her bed, and didn't know what to do.

She should give her space, perhaps. She should step back, leave her alone for a while and hope her feelings might overwhelm her and spur her to act. Let her get angry and want to destroy him. Let her despair and long for support. Let her do anything, as long as she fought back.

Rachel didn't care that Luke was her best friend's son. The preservation of friendship was unimportant in the face of this. In her mind's eye, she witnessed Jo falling off a cliff edge. A sacrifice she was prepared to make.

56

Laura

It was Wednesday, which meant Drew had picked Max up from school and taken him back to his house for tea. His house, apparently, had a backyard with enough space for them to play Swingball, which was Max's favourite thing to do, despite the cold. 'I just wrap him up,' Drew said blankly to Laura when she questioned him about it. 'No such thing as bad weather, just bad clothing.' Of course.

At exactly six-thirty, he rang the buzzer for the flat. 'It's Drew,' he said, when Laura answered. 'Bringing my boy home.'

Laura pressed the button to let them in. He was good, she thought. He was making a real effort. Not once had he been late picking Max up or dropping him home again. He agreed to the timings Laura insisted on, always making sure he was back by six-thirty so he could be in bed at seven. At first, she'd wanted him home at six, so he could have his bath and get ready for bed, but then Drew said, 'What if I bath him at mine and bring him home in his pyjamas? Then can I keep him half an hour longer?'

What could she do but agree? Half an hour was precious to a man who had already missed out on nearly six years.

They came in. Laura hugged her son and said, 'Did you have fun?'

He nodded enthusiastically. 'We had a Subway for tea. Steak and cheese.'

'Delicious,' Laura said.

Drew motioned as if to go. She said to him, 'Why don't you stay for a cup of tea? Put Max to bed if you like?'

Max spun round to face him. 'Please, Daddy,' he said. '*Please*.'

'Alright, buddy,' he said.

The three of them sat together on the sofa, watching CBeebies till seven, then Drew ushered Max to his room and Laura listened while he read him a story. He was a decent reader, she realised. Better than she was. She'd been OK when Max was tiny, but now he was older, the books were harder and she wished she'd paid more attention in school. She struggled, though she wouldn't dare admit that to anyone.

Drew came back in. For a moment, he looked at Laura, then said, 'I suppose I should go.'

'Wait,' she said. 'I just wanted to talk to you, if that's OK.' She worked hard to keep her voice level, not to fill him with fear of confrontation. She didn't want a confrontation. She just wanted to talk.

He shrugged. 'All right.'

He had to sit beside her on the sofa. It was the only seat in the room. They each made sure there was space between them.

She said, 'Why did you leave us, Drew?'

He shook his head, as if he couldn't bear to think about it. 'Because I was an idiot,' he said. 'That's it, Laura. I can't make any excuses. I was just an idiot, and it's something I am going to regret for the rest of my life.'

She hadn't expected that. She'd expected him to say he was a kid, he couldn't cope, he hadn't been ready.

He sounded sincere.

She said, 'But you were gone for nearly seven years. Seven years. It has been so hard …'

'I know.'

'Why so long?'

'I thought about it for a long time. At first, I thought you wouldn't want to hear from me, so I stayed away. I couldn't face it. Then I decided I wanted to know my son, but I knew I'd need to show you I wasn't a waster anymore. So I got a job and a place to rent. I wanted to be decent. I wanted you to see I was decent.'

She nodded. 'OK. So what about money now?'

'I need to start paying you maintenance, I know that. I'm going to do it, I promise you. I want to be a proper dad to Max. I don't want to just take him out and have him for weekends. I want to provide for him, too.'

'Thank you,' Laura said, and she believed him. He had changed.

57

Erin

Erin let her coffee go cold while she listened and bore witness. Rachel was out, rampaging over the hills. 'I'm going to work off my fury in the wind,' she'd said, 'like a Victorian madwoman.'

Erin said, 'OK.' Then she added, 'You know, Maia might talk to me.'

'Are you going to try?'

'I'd like to. It might be easier for her to speak to someone who isn't her mother.'

'You mean someone who isn't me?'

Erin smiled. 'Yes,' she said. 'Someone who isn't you.'

'Then try it. She can't keep this to herself.'

'Listen, I want to be able to tell her honestly that I won't share anything she'd rather you didn't know. Can I do that?'

Rachel looked at her, as if weighing up what Erin had just said and how she felt about it. Finally, she sighed. 'Yes,' she said. 'Yes, you can do that.'

After she'd gone, Erin made herself a cup of coffee and Maia a cup of tea and took them up to her room.

'Maia,' she said. 'I've brought you some tea if you want it.'

Maia was sitting upright on her bed, staring into the near distance. 'Thanks,' she said.

'Can I sit with you for a minute?'

'OK.'

Erin took the seat at Maia's desk. 'I know …' she began. 'I know things have been difficult between us. I know you never asked for this to happen to your family and I do understand why it's been hard for you to accept me. I really do. And I haven't always known the best way to deal with it, either. I've never had my own children. I've been feeling my way through this as much as you have and sometimes it has probably felt as though I don't care, or that I'm only on your mum's side, or that I was happy you moved out.'

She paused for a moment to test Maia's reaction. She was listening, and her face was free of its hard edges.

'Sometimes, I've thought it's best if I just stay in the background and give you space to work things out with your mum. Maybe that wasn't best. Maybe I should have come to you and spoken to you before this, to try and make things better between us.'

Maia stayed silent, but still she was listening.

'I am sorry you've just experienced something so awful you feel unable to share it with anyone, but I want you to know I can listen to you if you ever feel ready. And I won't share it with your mum if you don't want me to. I can …' She paused, looking for the right words, 'I can be your friend.'

Maia's eyes filled with tears. She whispered, 'He hurt me.'

58

Rachel

Rachel was attacking the oven with a scourer when Erin walked in. Never before had she cleaned anything with such vigour. She felt as though this rage might never end, and she'd just be here, on her hands and knees in front of the oven, for the rest of her life. If she ever stood up, she was at risk of opening the front door, striding across the village green and killing that bastard who'd done this to her child.

She was aware of Erin watching her in silence. There was so much silence in this house now. Something too big for anyone to cope with had happened, and no one knew what to say to make anyone else better.

Maia had told Erin, and Erin hadn't shared the details with Rachel. 'She needs to know she can trust me. We have to do this so carefully, Rachel.'

'I know we do.'

'She will tell you. Just give her time. We can't force it.'

'I want her to go to the police. That's all I want.'

'She might.'

'She needs to do it now.'

'This fury isn't going to help her, Rachel.'

Rachel hurled the scourer at the wall. She knew Erin was right, that they couldn't force Maia to do something she thought would increase her trauma, but Rachel was convinced that her daughter's healing lay in taking back some control over what had happened. Allowing herself to be silenced would make it worse, not better. Maia wanted to put it in the past, push it away, carry on as though it had never happened, but Rachel knew it would never work like that. Sexual assault refused to be buried. It would rise up and find new and brutal ways to hurt her for years, perhaps forever.

'I can't let this go,' she said. 'That arsehole needs to pay for what he's done to my daughter.'

59

Maia

Maia had barely cried, and she wasn't going to cry. She played the flute instead. Last summer, she'd taken her grade eight exam and now she went over and over those pieces, as if the music were a pool she could plunge into and the water would wash her away.

She would go to Vienna. She'd live in the city, burrowed inside the rocky edges of the mountains, and no one would ever come near her again. She'd become a world-class solo flautist and she would play on the finest stages in the finest halls, and critics would comment on the depth of her performance and everyone would question where this excruciatingly beautiful yet angry sound came from and only Maia would ever know.

Until then, she was going to work and work, and hammer out the life that was waiting for her.

The night came back to her in dreams. He was promising love, promising something exquisite, promising something beyond her. She lay back, trusting, so trusting. His mouth murmured beautiful words by her ear. And then his hands gripped her throat, and she couldn't breathe, and she had no voice to say no, and his words switched to something poisonous and she couldn't move her head away from them, and she had no way of moving from beneath him, and all she could do was know she would die.

But she didn't die. She woke up, gasping for breath and bruised, with no idea how long she'd been out for.

He sat on the bed, gazing at her. 'There,' he said. 'There,' and she didn't know what he meant.

She put her clothes on and went home.

She didn't want to be seen.

In the days that followed, she was mostly silent. She took herself to school and reclaimed her place at the top of the year. She wrote an essay about the nature of love between Heathcliff and Catherine, discussed violence and love addiction, and her teacher passed it to the head of sixth form, even though Maia was only in year eleven. 'What can we do with this star?' they asked, and gave her extra books to read, extra ideas to consider.

Her mother asked her questions. She didn't answer them.

She spent her evenings in the bath.

At school, there were rumours about her. Some said she was pregnant. Some said she'd had an abortion. Almost everyone used words that Maia's mother had always told her were despicable, and no woman should be shamed for having sex with anyone she wanted to.

But Maia was ashamed. She'd hurt James and she'd slept with someone else, and now she'd been punished, like one of those terrible women in Victorian novels who had to be virgins or die.

She couldn't say that, though. She couldn't say that was how she felt. It was so old-fashioned to feel that way.

She didn't tell anyone what had happened. She wasn't even sure herself. All she knew was that he'd strangled her and she'd passed out and when she woke, he told her it was normal, and most women liked this sort of thing. The prevention of air was meant to increase the intensity of the experience.

She hadn't liked it.

For several days, she ached and bled. She wasn't sure why.

She wondered if her mother would kill him if she knew. It didn't seem impossible. Sometimes, Maia thought about killing him herself. She wanted to pin him down to a bed, sit astride him so he couldn't move, put her hands to his throat and let go only when she knew the breath was gone forever.

She wouldn't do it. She didn't have the strength.

Her old naivety made her angry. It was obvious now, what sort of man he'd been from the start. Seductive, entitled, shameless. After that first night, he'd never even pretended to care about her. She should have walked away weeks ago, but his arrogance attracted her, made her long to be the girl who held on to him.

She'd been an idiot, and now this had happened.

She started to think she was too young for all this. She remembered watching a sixteen-year-old giving birth on TV once, and her mother saying, 'Someone needs to give her an epidural. She's too young to cope with that pain.'

That was how Maia felt now. She was being devoured by the anguish, and too young to cope. She wondered what would happen if she made it out of this alive.

After a while, she decided she would make it out alive. She wasn't going to let him destroy her. She knew her mother would have wanted to go to the police, but Maia couldn't face that – describing what had happened when she barely even knew herself, going to court, being judged, being talked about. She imagined James taking silent delight from the fact that she'd slept with someone who wasn't him, and now she'd been punished.

She thought that if she could, she'd like to go back in time now and appreciate him more. He hadn't been exciting like Luke, but he was good and kind and generous, and he'd loved her. She felt she understood now, how rare that was, and how important.

60

Erin

Erin had been right, of course. They gave Maia space and she began to open up. She allowed Erin to share with Rachel the details of what had happened, as long as Rachel promised not to try to talk to her about it, or go mad and kill anyone. They just allowed the truth to hang there between them, all of them knowing and understanding, but letting Maia decide what to do with it.

To Erin, Rachel said, 'You know we can't ignore Jo forever.'

'No.'

'I need her to know about it. I can't live opposite her, pretending this never happened.'

'I know.'

'Will you speak to Maia? Ask her if it's OK?'

Erin spoke to her and she said it was OK. 'But Rachel, you can't see her while you're this angry.'

'I've got no choice. I'm never going to stop being this angry.'

'Shall I talk to her instead?'

Rachel felt as though she'd just been handed a gift. 'Would you really do that?'

'Yes, if you want me to.'

'That might work better. It's going to fall apart, we know that. The friendship, I mean. But maybe it'll fall apart more quietly if you take charge.'

Erin smiled. Rachel had to turn away from her. She couldn't cope with gentleness now. A smile, a loving touch, a hug … they would break her. She had to stay angry. She had to stay half-insane with rage because if she didn't, if she didn't direct all this fury towards Luke, she would have to face the fact that none of this would have happened if Maia had still been living here. None of it. Rachel would have jumped in and solved it months ago. Instead, she'd let her daughter down. Over and over again, she'd let her down …

She felt a sob rise from somewhere deep inside her. A grief she couldn't bear to look at.

From the kitchen window, she could see across the green to Jo's house. Ever since that night, she'd been keeping an eye on it, checking to see if Luke was emerging from inside, getting on with his life as if he hadn't just destroyed a sixteen-year-old girl and all her family.

So far, there had been no sign of him. Rachel wondered if he was hiding.

61

Jo

Things seemed to be slowly improving. Luke had found a job at last – a temporary job, but a job nonetheless. He'd been offered a twelve-week contract with a wildlife conservation charity in Newcastle, and had to phone people with a record of previous giving and ask if they could reinstate their direct debits. 'It was practically an audition,' he said proudly. 'I wasn't allowed to sound like a businessman. I had to sound caring, compassionate and grave about falling wildlife numbers.' He lowered his voice and adopted the required tone, 'You probably already know that we have a third less wildlife in the world than we did in 1970 … The boss was impressed. He offered it to me on the spot.'

Acting. Pretending to care. Persuading people to part with their money. He'd be so good at it.

Jo wished she wouldn't think like this. He was doing his best.

As far as she could tell, he also seemed to have stopped seeing Maia. He'd kept things going with her for a while after Jo had spoken to him about it, but now it looked as though things had fizzled out. Maia hadn't been over for days. Jo didn't want to ask Luke anything about it. All she hoped was that he hadn't hurt her. She knew what Luke was like with women. He became infatuated with some idea of perfection that he'd found, everything would be intense and wonderful for a while, and then he'd realise she wasn't perfect after all, and that would be that. Over.

She turned the radio on and thought how she really ought to be feeling lighter than this. Her son was no longer charged with assault, he had a job and he'd stopped sleeping with Rachel's teenage daughter. He'd also just had a letter inviting him to an interview for the journalism course he was striving for and Jo knew he was more than likely to be offered a place. She'd read the articles and interview he'd sent in with his application. They were good. This time next year, he'd be back in London, moving forward with his life.

Jo had so many reasons to be upbeat, but all she could really feel was a persistent sense of dread, as if the anxiety of the last few weeks wasn't really over, but had just temporarily abated and was going to return again in full force.

On top of that, there was less than a week till Christmas and she was completely unprepared. Luke said he and Rebecca were both going to their dad's, and Jo hadn't got round to inviting herself anywhere else. Most people were more organised than she was, she'd always known this, which meant they would probably all have ordered their turkeys and planned their meals by now, so Jo was faced with the slightly unwelcome prospect of Christmas Day alone, turkey-less and childless, with nothing but an open fire and a few nuts to mark the day.

Maybe she should volunteer at a homeless shelter in Newcastle, or at the community centre in Burntridge, where those who were old and alone for Christmas could tuck into Bernard Matthews turkey slices and some soggy roast potatoes free of charge. It wasn't the turkey or the potatoes they went for. It was the company of other people, lonely souls like themselves who'd been alone for so long they'd forgotten how to be sociable and mostly just sat in silence, but at least on Christmas Day they could sit in silence together, in paper hats.

Jo wasn't sure she had it in her to do it, though. There was something deeply depressing about trying to convince people with unimaginably miserable lives that they could just pull a cracker and be jolly.

She knew Rachel would have her, if she mentioned it. Christmas Day at Rachel's was always fun. The champagne came out at breakfast time and didn't stop flowing until the last person had passed out or gone home. And the food was always incredible. There were four-bird roasts, sticky toffee puddings, homemade petits fours, luxury mince pies that were like no other mince pie Jo had ever tasted …

She'd mention it to Rachel when she saw her next. She wouldn't need to say much. 'The kids are going to Dave's for Christmas and I haven't sorted myself out' would be enough for Rachel to pounce on her with an invitation. That was what Rachel did. She filled her home with her friends, especially at Christmas. 'Too much intense family time is no good for anyone,' she'd said a couple of years back.

Jo hoped this wouldn't have changed, now her miserable marriage had come to an end and time at home was no longer strained and endless.

There was an unexpected knock at the front door. She could hear Luke's bedroom door flying open and Luke bounding down the stairs, as if he were expecting someone. Jo stayed where she was in the kitchen and let him answer.

She heard the low murmur of Luke's voice and the louder, more distinct words of the woman he was talking to. It sounded like Erin. Jo's immediate thought was that something must have happened to Rachel, because why would Erin come over here by herself?

'I need to speak to your mother, Luke,' she was saying firmly. 'Please let me in.'

Jo walked out to the hallway. Luke was standing at the door, looking the way Jo imagined she herself always looked when she knew she was about to be taken hostage by Jehovah's Witnesses – polite, but determined to push them away before they opened their mouths.

'I'm here, Erin,' she said. 'Come in.'

Erin didn't smile. She stepped inside. Without saying a word, Luke walked out through the front door, got into his car and disappeared.

It was like listening through the blaze of a low-flying aircraft. Jo had to keep asking Erin to repeat what she'd just told her, over and over again. Then, for a while, she would go back over the story, checking the details, making sure she had it right.

Maia had been sexually assaulted.

Definitely.

And it was Luke who'd done it to her. She'd been consenting at first, but then it changed. That was her story.

Jo shouldn't have been this shocked. She realised that for days she'd been expecting this, that in some distant part of her, she already knew. Her son had assaulted her best friend's daughter.

322

'I'm sorry,' Erin said. 'But we both felt we had to tell you. We couldn't let things go on as usual, as if this had never happened.'

Jo shook her head. 'No, of course you couldn't.' She paused for a while and added, 'I'm sorry Rachel felt unable to speak to me.'

'Rachel is ...'

'Furious, I should imagine.'

'Yes.'

Jo fell silent for a while. She wasn't furious yet, but she knew it was on its way. That bloody boy. That entitled piece of shit. Her beautiful son, who she hadn't brought up to be like this. She said, 'Is Maia ... Is she going to take this to the police?'

Erin sighed. 'She doesn't want to. She says it won't help anything. She says she wants to put it behind her.'

'Do you think she can?'

'I think she can. It will take time, but I think she can.'

'I know she hasn't been easy for you ...'

'No.'

'But she's always been such a lovely girl. You haven't known her at her best.'

'Oh, I've only really known her at her worst, I think,' Erin smiled.

'I'm sorry about what my son has done to her,' Jo began, and then stopped because she couldn't go on. Never in her life had she known shame like this. She had to fight to stay on top of it, to keep it firmly in her head as something real that Luke had done. The urge to push it away, to deny it, to blame someone else for it was strong. It was really strong.

She would not allow those horrible thoughts about Maia to

take shape. She would not. Erin had described Maia's behaviour the night it happened, and for the days that passed afterwards, and Jo knew it was the behaviour of a victim, not of a liar, not of a troubled girl who had made something up for sympathy or attention.

'I knew …' she began, 'I knew they were having some sort of relationship. I wasn't happy about it. I told Luke to break it off. I didn't tell Rachel. I should have done.'

She'd planned to tell Rachel. She really had. But they were all so busy and there was never any time to find.

Erin said, 'It's not your fault.'

Jo said, 'He's my son.'

'It's not your fault.'

Eventually, Erin went home. As she left, she turned suddenly and embraced Jo. She said, 'I'll tell Rachel to give you a ring.'

Jo nodded. 'I'd like to speak to her. I'd like to see her, when she's ready.'

Erin left then. Jo paced the ground floor of the house, waiting for Luke to come home. An hour or more passed. It crossed her mind that he might never come home. She wanted him to, purely so she could tell him how sick he made her and then throw him out again. She went up to his room and packed his things. He was no longer welcome here. He'd have to find his own way through life now.

She worked in a frenzy, flinging his belongings into his backpack, not bothering to fold anything. Let him sort it out himself. Let him wear creased clothes to work. Let him work out how to use a bloody iron if he cared about being present-able.

When she'd finished, she dragged the backpack down the stairs and left it in the hall by the front door. She picked the phone up from the table and dialled 101.

The answer was automated. She hit option two. *Report a crime.*

62

Erin

From upstairs came the sound of Maia playing her flute. Erin knew nothing about classical music so she couldn't name the piece, but she knew enough to know that Maia played exquisitely. She also thought, though she might have been imagining it, that something had changed in her music since that night. There was a depth to it now, a richness, as if it were being played by someone who had slipped into a world other people couldn't enter.

Rachel, too, seemed lost in another world and it felt to Erin like a place where she'd never be able to reach her again. It looked like grief – that wild whirl of uncontrollable feeling that kept plunging her further and further downward. Erin knew she was trying with all her strength to fight it, to stay afloat, but for now, it was stronger than she was.

Erin said, 'Jo would like to see you.'

'What for? If she's going to point the finger at Maia ...'

'She isn't. She's as disgusted by Luke as you are.'

'I doubt that.'

'She's on our side.'

'Did you see him when you were there?'

'Briefly. He left almost as soon as he saw me.'

'Well, that's something. He's got a guilty conscience, at least.' She drew on her e-cigarette and exhaled before adding, 'He knows what he's done.'

Erin nodded. 'Yes. I think he does.'

'I don't know if that's better or worse.'

The sound of the flute playing above them stopped. A few minutes later, Maia appeared in the kitchen, dressed in leggings and an old hoodie. 'Is there any tea left in that pot?' she asked.

Rachel leaned over the island and lifted the lid. 'It's lukewarm. I'll make some more,' she said, heading towards the worktop and flicking the switch on the kettle. Idly, Erin wondered how much that kettle had cost. It was bright pink and retro-looking, to coordinate with the Smeg fridge.

Maia took a seat at the island, beside Erin. She looked OK. She looked as though she was recovering.

Because she could think of nothing else to say, Erin said, 'I loved hearing you play just now.'

Maia smiled. 'Thanks. I know it's early to be thinking about all this, but I'd like to apply to music colleges abroad. Maybe Vienna or Rome. Somewhere like that.'

Rachel brought the refilled teapot back over and set it down on the worktop. 'That would be amazing,' she said. 'But maybe not Rome. Vienna sounds good.'

Erin knew exactly what Rachel was thinking. She was thinking of all the Italian men, bare-chested, charming and powerful, lurking in corners, waiting to do terrible things to her daughter. Not even Rachel was beyond the influence of cultural stereotypes at times like this.

Maia rolled her eyes, as if she also understood where her mother was coming from. 'There's still loads of time,' she said. 'I don't even have to apply for another year or so.'

A white car pulled up outside. A man and a woman Erin didn't recognise stepped out. Rachel looked up and said, 'Jehovah's Witnesses or scammers? Which do you think?'

'Jehovah's Witnesses wouldn't drive, Mum.'

'Wouldn't they? I'm sure they would.'

'Not to someone's front door.'

Rachel left the room to find out who they were and what they wanted. Erin said, 'Vienna's beautiful. I spent some time there when I was younger.'

'Cool,' Maia said. She pulled her phone out of her pocket and turned her attention to whatever was on it.

As she looked at her, Erin dared to believe that Maia was getting better, that she was going to be OK.

Rachel came into the kitchen, followed closely by the two strangers who'd got out of the car. She cleared her throat. 'Maia,' she said.

Maia looked up from her phone.

'These people are police officers. They'd like to talk to you about Luke.'

Maia looked shocked. 'You went to the police?' she asked.

Rachel shook her head. 'I didn't,' she said. 'Jo did. Will you speak to them, love? It doesn't have to be here. You can go somewhere private. They just want to find out what happened.'

Erin could hear the desperation in Rachel's voice and how close she was to begging. The police officers smiled benignly. They were here to help.

Maia paused for a moment, then sighed and said, 'All right.'

Rachel took everyone through to the living room. Erin couldn't help it. Her heart went out to Jo Fairburn.

63

Rachel

Rachel was as proud of Maia as she'd ever been. The police officers had managed to ease her fears, she'd told them what happened and now she seemed fuelled by a desire to stop Luke from doing the same thing to anyone else and for anyone else to suffer in the way she had suffered – and was continuing to suffer, as far as Rachel could see, though she tried to hide it behind a facade of hard work and ambition.

It was becoming evident that Maia's response to personal crises was not to let them quash her, but for them to drive her onwards, ever more determined to make a success of her life. Maia was going to grow into one of those women who remade themselves after a messy relationship break-up, or a divorce, or whatever other emotional dramas were lurking in her future. It reassured Rachel, who suspected that Reuben would be the opposite and probably sink into years-long depression after every experience of heartache and she'd have to fight the urge to bring him home and look after him, or slap his face and tell him to get over it. Rachel was well aware that as a parent facing her children's life crises, she seemed to veer between extremes of gentle nurturing and frustrated impatience, and occasionally wondered if this might be the root of all their problems. Then she decided it probably wasn't.

It was Saturday, a week after the police had first come over to talk to Maia, and Rachel had agreed to meet Will in Burntridge for coffee and to fill him in about his daughter's current well-being. There had been no discussion so far about Maia's living arrangements and everyone seemed to silently understand that Maia could do whatever felt best whenever she wanted to. For now, the process of putting herself back together meant being in her old home, surrounded by familiar comfort and the love of her mother who, for all her flaws, was easier to talk to about being a victim of forced erotic asphyxiation than her father was ever going to be.

He was already there when she walked into Costa. He'd selected a table in a darkened corner, where they wouldn't be overheard. Rachel ignored the familiar faces of other parents as she navigated her way through the Saturday morning labyrinth of overcrowded tables, high chairs and too many people carrying too many trays. Through it all came the endless drone of the coffee machines, the whirl of the milk frothers and the constant bang of sullen baristas emptying used coffee granules from the filter baskets.

God, there was nothing relaxing about this.

She took the seat opposite Will. 'Hi,' she said.

He pushed a mug of latte her way. He'd texted her five minutes ago to ask what she wanted. He was good like that.

He didn't waste time with politenesses and small talk. 'How's she doing?' he asked.

Rachel sighed. 'OK. Better than me, I think.'

He smiled. 'Of course.' Then he said, 'Any word from … from him?'

Rachel understood that he could no longer say Luke's name. She couldn't either. *The arsehole* was how she referred to him in her head and to Erin, or *The bastard*. To other people, she just said *him*, the same way Will did.

She shook her head. 'He's gone AWOL. The police are confident they'll catch up with him, though.'

'And what about Jo? Have you spoken to her?'

His fist was clenched, his face set hard. He was as furious as she was.

'Not yet. When I'm ready. I'm really grateful to her for doing what she did, but I just … She needs a supportive friend and I can't be one over this. I just can't.'

'No.'

'Maia has spoken about leaving school.'

'*What?*'

Hurriedly, Rachel added, 'I mean she wants to try and get into one of those specialist music colleges for the sixth form. She wants a fresh start. She wants to go to university in Vienna and it would be good training for her.'

'Private school? Rachel, we agreed from the very start …'

'They're not private schools, not exactly. You're selected by musical ability, not ability to pay for it.'

'Right. But you know this goes against all your principles, don't you? I thought you were against any sort of selective education, anything that keeps the top at the top and the bottom at the bottom. I thought …'

'That was before my daughter was sexually assaulted, Will. It was before she started feeling that everyone at school was looking at her and talking about her, and wanted nothing more than to get the hell out of there. I don't blame her. I think she'll thrive at a music school. I can put my sanctimonious principles aside in this one case.'

She saw him thaw and understand. 'OK,' he said. 'It probably would do her good.' But there was a flatness to his tone that betrayed a lack of enthusiasm. She wasn't sure whether he was just going to go along with Maia's wishes, or if he was simply finding it impossible to feel upbeat about anything at the moment.

She said, 'How are you coping with all this?'

His fist clenched again, and he spoke like a man barely in control. He said, 'Every day, I have to fight the urge to hunt down that arsehole and kick the shit out of him.'

Rachel nodded. She understood. Oh, how she understood.

He carried on. 'I have never been violent in my life. Never even been tempted, never really understood the urge to bash someone up. But this is huge. I can see why people shout for the death penalty. I'd love to watch that bastard hang after what he did to her.' He took a sip of his coffee and said, 'I thought I was a good, enlightened liberal thinker, but it turns out I'm as brutal and primitive as everyone else.'

'We all are. I'm so glad she spoke to the police. I couldn't have gone on, knowing he was getting away with it.'

'I wish they'd hurry up and find him.'

'They will.'

'How do you think Tess and Reuben are managing?'

'Tess is fine. She knows someone did something horrible to her sister and she's outraged and appalled, but she's a good distraction for Maia, I think. Reuben's too embarrassed to say anything about it, but he's quietly supportive. They both know I'm completely mental about it.'

Will smiled then. 'How does Maia feel about your fury?'

'She's grateful for it,' Rachel said. 'She doesn't realise that yet, but she is.'

'Right.'

'She hasn't said as much, but I can see there's guilt and shame ticking away in there, waiting to come out and get her in time. I want her to speak to someone. The police have put her in touch with a few organisations and I think someone will be coming to see her. She doesn't like it, though. Doesn't like all the fuss.'

'I'll give her a ring later. I'll take the three of them out somewhere, just to do normal stuff. Sounds like it could be what she needs.'

'I think that would really help,' Rachel said. 'Get her away from her murderous, over-protective, furious mother who can't think of anything but how she wants to squash the life out of that piece of shit.'

Will laughed, as if Rachel were just being her usual, over-dramatic self.

64

Maia

Maia hadn't told anyone about it, but this was Burntridge and word spread fast. It was all over school. No one spoke to her about it, but they all spoke to each other and it turned out that most people thought she was lying, or perhaps mistaken. Maia didn't know why they would think this, other than because it was too big and too dramatic for them to process, so in their heads it couldn't have happened. But the bruises were still there around her neck and on her chest. She wore a scarf to cover them up.

All she could do was shrug off the gossip, knowing that she knew the truth and other people didn't matter. She only had to get through at this place until July, then she'd be gone. She'd sent in her application for Chetham's in Manchester and the Purcell School in Hertfordshire and knew she stood a good chance at the auditions. Even if she didn't get into either of them, she wasn't going to stay here for the sixth form. She'd go to a college in Newcastle, or Durham, anywhere but here.

She hadn't told anyone what Luke had said to her about Laura. She'd hardly really thought about it, but now and then it drifted back to her and she wasn't sure what she should do, or if she should do anything at all.

James had barely spoken to her since the day she'd finished things with him. She often caught him watching her during orchestra practise when he thought she wasn't looking, but he never smiled and she never did, either. He'd spread such horrible rumours about her. She wasn't sure what he'd think if he knew about Luke. He probably wouldn't accuse her of making it up, but he'd say it was her fault because she'd slept with him in the first place, and because she was too willing to shag anyone who even looked at her, and because Luke probably assumed she wouldn't mind being strangled since she didn't seem to mind anything else.

Today, when they were packing away their instruments after orchestra practise, he slung his saxophone case over his shoulder and came up to her. 'Maia,' he said.

She looked up from her flute, which she'd been concentrating too hard on dismantling. 'Hi,' she said.

He shifted awkwardly. 'I heard about what happened.'

She flushed and looked back down and pretended to dust her case, something she never did and James knew it.

He said, 'I'm really sorry. I hope you win the court case.'

She looked up again and smiled this time. 'Thank you.'

'Also, I didn't mean those things I said about you. I don't know what I was thinking. I was … It was stupid of me. I'll put it right.'

'I'd appreciate that.'

He was quiet for a while, then said, 'I heard you're leaving.'

She shrugged. 'I'm going to audition for music school.'

'You'll get in.'

'I hope so. If not, I'll just do my A levels somewhere else. I can't stay here.' She let the weight of what she hadn't said sink in. She couldn't stay here because James had said awful things about her and now no one believed her when something terrible had happened.

'Could we maybe meet up one day?' he asked.

She shook her head. 'No.'

He let his disappointment show, but she wasn't going to change her mind.

65

Rachel

The Christmas fair. Rachel's heart wasn't in it, not in any way, but Maia had insisted they come. 'We need to get back to normal,' she'd said, in that forceful way she had. 'Tess wants to go. All her friends will be there. What if I come with you? I can take her round the stalls. You can just sit and drink mulled wine or whatever.'

'Are you sure? What about Jo? You know she'll be there.'

Maia faced her squarely. 'That's OK,' she said.

Rachel sighed and gave in. Not once in her children's school lives had she missed the Christmas fair. It was a crucial event in the year and the message from the PTA was clear: you were expected to donate a significant portion of your soul to it. If you really couldn't spend your whole year knitting nativity sets for the craft stall, you could at least give up this one evening of your life to stand dutifully behind the tombola and smile at the children who won someone else's unwanted three-pack of sparkly tights. And finally, if you really were so feeble that you couldn't run a stall, you had to show up on the night and spend as much money as you could. Any absences would be noted and talked about. Long-term grudges would be held.

Rachel just wasn't ready for it, not yet. Jo would be there, gold tinsel in her hair, tiny Christmas trees dangling from her ears, a beatific smile on her face as she drew the raffle and bestowed extravagant prizes on happy winners, while trying not to think about her son, the sex offender.

Rachel hadn't spoken to her since it happened. She knew she needed to. They'd been friends for twenty years. They'd seen each other through some of the toughest times in their lives, and although this crisis wasn't one that could be easily healed, their lives would continue to overlap. They would still be neighbours. Jo would still be Tess's headteacher. And besides that, Rachel knew that Jo was trying her best to do only what was right in this situation. Not once had she defended her son. She'd turned him into the police. She was as much a victim as anyone.

Rachel had to talk to her, but it was hard. It was too soon. But now the Christmas fair was upon them and if Rachel went to it, they were going to be forced into a public space together before they'd had a chance to meet in private. There'd be awkwardness, avoidance, rawness, hurt feelings …

For once, Rachel didn't know what to do. Only time could bridge this gulf, and hardly any time had passed yet. Maybe she should stop off at the petrol station on the way to school, buy Jo a poinsettia and hand it to her at the fair to show that she wasn't angry with her friend. She merely hated her son and would gleefully swing him round by the penis until it snapped away in her hands and he went flying through the air to his death.

Rachel spent an unhealthy amount of time imagining what she would do with Luke Fairburn's dick, given half the chance.

She decided against the poinsettia. It was too trivial, and the situation demanded more than just tokens. She'd have to either seek Jo out, or avoid her completely. Besides, she thought, it was possible Jo wouldn't even be there. The deputy head could easily stand in for her.

Things were in full swing by the time they walked in, just after five. The school hall had become a marketplace. There were craft stalls; seasonal cake stalls; stalls selling diligently-made winter chutneys; stalls selling enormous white candles and bunches of twigs lit with fairy lights. At the back of the room, the choir stood in front of the Christmas tree and sang *Silent Night,* accompanied by two girls on violins. Rachel recognised one of the girls as Kate Monro's daughter and made up her mind not to be impressed.

At the far end of the hall, as always, a woman was teaching a group of mothers how to make mantelpiece decorations out of nothing but some old leaves and a piece of dried-up orange peel. All of them were concentrating hard, their neat little heads bent over their work, arranging things in bunches, tying them with ribbons. Their teacher offered her artistic guidance, always with a serene smile on her face. Rachel supposed that when the meaning of your existence was decoration making, you probably had no reason not to smile serenely. The woman was on another plane, closer to Nirvana than Rachel would ever be, liberated from the tyranny of giving a shit about things that actually mattered.

Somewhere inside her, she felt a rumble of deep hostility and an urge to slap the face of every one of those women – women who could sit there arranging conkers in baskets; women whose minds were able to focus on the aesthetic importance of ribbons; *women whose daughters hadn't been sexually assaulted.*

It was wrong to have come here. She wasn't ready to witness all this excited anticipation, all this fucking happiness. She wanted to bolt. She wanted to stand outside in the dark and smoke a whole packet of Marlboro and feel the satisfying burn in her throat.

Tess tugged at her hand. 'Mummy, can we see Father Christmas first?'

Rachel jerked to attention. 'Where is he?' she asked.

Tess pointed towards the corridor, where a long line of children stood impatiently waiting. 'In the gym,' she said.

'Let's wait a while for the queue to go down. Shall we get a cake?'

Over by the cake stand, Rachel noted, was the mulled wine stall. She could do with taking a seat and drinking a whole jug of it to herself. In fact, what she really wanted to do, she suddenly realised, was get disgustingly drunk and smash this Christmas fair and all its offensive joy to bits.

66

Erin

Erin kept scanning the room for Jo. There were other teachers she recognised, all doing their bit – helping children make tree decorations, leading the singing, keeping the queue for Father Christmas from becoming too rowdy. But Jo was nowhere to be seen. Erin wondered if she'd stayed at home. It would be preferable to standing among this throng of parents, not knowing who'd heard the news that the headteacher's son had assaulted Rachel Saunders' daughter.

Erin was beginning to wish they'd stayed at home themselves. She'd never known Rachel so uptight. There was violent energy swelling inside her, and Erin could almost see it: the waves of incoming madness, rippling just beneath her skin.

Rachel said, 'I haven't bought my raffle tickets yet. I need to get some.'

Erin braced herself. Kate Monro was reigning triumphantly over the most important stall in the room. It was the raffle that everyone had come here for. They wanted to see if their tickets had won them a week in someone's second home in France, or dinner for two at a castle, or a year's free gym membership. They also wanted to see if the top prizes went to people they considered undeserving of them. There was nothing they could do about it, but it would give them a topic – The Outrageous Injustices of Life – to talk about for a few weeks afterwards.

'Really?' Erin said. 'Do we need to do this?'

Rachel looked confused. 'Do what?'

'Buy raffle tickets.'

'Course we do,' Rachel said, steering Tess through the throng of parents and children towards Kate Monro.

Erin glanced behind her at Maia, who gave a helpless shrug and followed.

On the table, ever-close to its owner, was that odious red clipboard. Erin wondered what it contained today. Signatures to have her removed from town, perhaps, to have her sent back to the city where people had no morals and would turn a blind eye to the sexual deviance that Burntridge couldn't cope with.

'Afternoon, Kate,' Rachel said briskly.

Kate gave her an energetic smile, which immediately made Erin feel exhausted. She had no idea how the woman kept it up.

'Tickets are still selling fast,' Kate enthused. 'I think this year might be our best raffle yet!'

'What a triumph,' Rachel said. 'Your first raffle with the new headteacher at the helm. You show her how indispensable you are to this place and she might start taking your petition seriously.'

Oh, dear God.

Rachel went on. 'Can I have another ten pounds' worth of tickets, please? And I was wondering whether you'd given any thought to my offer to come and talk to the children in your Right Way to Live class yet?'

Kate looked flustered. Erin didn't want to be a part of this, but Rachel was fired up, desperate for a fight, desperate to outpour all that anger over someone. Over anyone. There was no stopping her when she was like this.

'Tess,' Erin said. 'Tess, why don't we see if the queue for Father Christmas has gone down?'

Tess came towards her willingly, and Erin took her hand and led her away. Kate had obviously answered Rachel's question, and now Rachel had switched to apparently safer ground. She was telling Kate how much she admired her daughter, over there playing the violin. 'Oh, we're so lucky,' Kate was saying, 'that the school helps out with music tuition for all children.'

Don't do it, Rachel, Erin pleaded silently. *Just don't.*

The queue for Father Christmas was no shorter than it had been when they arrived. Maia, who'd followed her and Tess away from the raffle stall, said, 'Tess, why don't we have a go at making fridge magnets over there?'

'All right,' Tess said. Then she looked towards the stall and added, 'Max is there. Hi, Max!'

Oh, this hell was never-ending.

Beside her, Erin was aware of Maia bristling as she caught sight of Laura, but it was too late now. They'd walked into this and the only way out of it was through it.

Erin forced a smile on her face and warmth to her voice. 'Hello, Laura,' she said. 'How are you?'

Laura returned her smile. 'Fine, thank you.' She turned to Maia and said, 'I wanted to apologise to you, Maia, for what happened when …'

Maia said nothing.

Time dragged between them like rope.

344

Eventually Erin said, too brightly, 'Tess wanted to make a magnet.'

'Of course. Max, why don't you help Tess? You can show her what to do, can't you?'

The two children sat down together.

Erin wasn't sure what was happening, but beside her, Maia seemed to be losing her breath. She was holding on to the edge of the stall, head bowed, gasping for air.

'Maia,' Erin said. 'Maia, are you all right?'

The words weren't coming out. Maia gazed at Erin in terror.

'You need to sit down,' Erin said, putting an arm supportively round her shoulders and guiding her to a seat, where she knelt in front of her. 'Breathe, Maia,' she said. 'Just breathe slowly. That's it …'

Laura stood back and watched. 'Can I get you anything?' she asked, looking helplessly around her stall for something that might help. There were only cardboard stars and magnetic strips.

Erin knew the worst thing for Maia would be for everyone to witness this. She needed to minimise the drama, keep Maia invisible. She shook her head. 'Just carry on as though we aren't here,' she said.

'Is it asthma?' Laura asked.

'No.'

'I'll get her some water.'

Laura walked away. Erin went on talking to Maia. She knew a panic attack when she saw one.

Slowly Maia's breath came back and she was calm again, and the room was busy enough for them to have been shielded by the crowd.

Laura returned with water.

Erin passed it to Maia. She drank it gratefully.

Erin said, 'What triggered this, Maia?'

'I can't tell you here.'

Erin glanced around the hall. Rachel was still at the raffle stall, talking animatedly to a shamefaced-looking Kate. She said, 'Let's head somewhere quiet. I'm sure we can find someone who'll let us go to a classroom or something.'

Laura pointed to a door at the side of the room, 'Use the PTA storeroom. It's just down there. It'll be empty. I'll keep an eye on Tess.'

The room, once they finally reached it, was really just a large store cupboard with a couple of chairs and water cooler in it. They both sat down and Erin said, 'What happened?'

Maia said, 'It was her.'

'Laura?'

'Luke had ... Luke had photos on his phone. Of her.'

Erin's mind was unable to keep up.

'She was unconscious ...' Maia was saying. 'She had rope tied round her neck and ...' She shook her head, unable to describe it. 'He said she's a sex worker. That's how he got the pictures ...'

It was as though the whole world finally began to make sense. Laura's late shifts at work, her reluctance to go to the police when Max went missing, her secrecy ...

'Holy crap,' Erin said.

Maia smiled wanly. 'And that night at her flat, when I babysat, I thought ... I thought Dad seemed to know who she was.'

Erin said, 'Oh, Maia.' Then, 'Shall I get your mum?'

346

Maia nodded.

'Wait here,' Erin said, and stepped out into the hall again.

Rachel was still at the raffle stall, arguing with Kate. Then, all of a sudden, as Erin was heading hurriedly towards her, Rachel leaned over the neighbouring cake stall, grabbed a beautifully iced snowman cupcake and hurled it straight into Kate's face. 'There!' she shouted. 'Fuck you and your petitions. This school doesn't need you quite as much as you think it does.'

For a moment, Kate simply stood there, speechless. Then she, too, reached for a cake. The people hovering by the raffle stall began to notice and stepped back to watch. Some of them looked shocked. Others laughed. Further away, the rest of the fair continued as usual, but it would only be a matter of time before everyone began to witness this.

Erin closed her eyes in dread. This was the downside to life with the brilliant, shameless Rachel Saunders.

67

Laura

Laura had never known a school event so full of tension. It started when Rachel Saunders walked in with her girlfriend and daughters. She didn't need to speak. Anger shone around her like an aura. *Come anywhere near me, ask me a single question, and I'll slap you.*

Everyone in town knew Maia Kernick had been assaulted by a bloke in his twenties. Gossip was flying about like litter but no one seemed to have a clear grasp of who he was or what, exactly, his crime had been. Some said the bloke was a stranger, others said he was Jo Fairburn's son. Whoever he was, Rachel Saunders was after him. He'd harmed her daughter. Raped her, maybe. There'd been violence involved – a knife to her throat, some said, or perhaps a post-coital beating. Some said she was his girlfriend at the time, so how could it be rape? Others murmured darkly how everyone at the high school knew Maia Kernick slept with any boy who asked her, so whatever had gone on probably wasn't that simple and they should hold off in their judgements.

Laura knew, though. Laura knew who it was.

It was that young man with his love of asphyxiation. She

had no proof, no real reason to believe it, but the moment Kate Monro told her what had happened, she knew. She knew it with absolute, deep-soul certainty. He was the man who had assaulted Maia.

And then this afternoon, Laura realised Maia knew who she was, too.

Now her eyes followed Maia around the room. She was a beautiful girl, but changed. Whenever Laura had seen her before, she'd always been boldly dressed, always carried herself like someone who knew she'd be looked at and was comfortable with the attention. Today she wore black leggings and a grey hoodie, as if she just wanted to slip through the world unnoticed. And she'd had a panic attack. Quite clearly, Maia had taken one look at Laura and the sight of her had made her fall apart.

Right then, Laura realised that she knew. Maia knew her boyfriend had paid Laura to act out the fantasies he later inflicted on her.

She wished she could reach out to her in some way, sit her down and talk to her, tell her she was sorry she hadn't done something about this horrible man before he'd got his hands on her. She felt deeply, disgracefully responsible.

But then there was the issue of Will. Did Maia know about Will? Laura wasn't sure. She hoped not. She hoped the girl could be spared that much.

'Mummy,' Max said, his voice rich with fear. 'Mummy, look.'

Laura turned and looked where Max was pointing. There was shouting, and people were backing away from the centre of the room, standing against the walls, watching.

A fight had broken out at the raffle stall.

349

68

Jo

Jo was late. It had taken all the drive and energy she possessed to force herself out of her office and down to the hall for this. She was wearing a fifties-style snowman-print dress with a net petticoat underneath. It had only cost a tenner on eBay and she knew the kids would all love it. She tried to be enthusiastic. She was meant to dazzle and smile and at the end of the evening, it would be her job to draw the raffle and bestow extravagant prizes upon happy winners.

She wasn't sure she could do it. She'd come close to asking her deputy to take her place, but in the end she decided she had to be there. It would be frowned on for decades if Jo Fairburn failed to show her face at her first ever Christmas fair as head of West Burntbridge First School.

More than anything, she hoped Rachel wasn't going to be there. It seemed unlikely. Jo was sure Rachel would have been over to see her if she'd been planning to come this evening. It was the sort of thing Rachel would do – smooth things over, make sure everything was OK before they were forced together in public. She must have understood that the first move was up to her, that there was no way Jo could impress herself on the family of the victim.

Over a week had passed since the bomb dropped into her life and sent all the pieces flying. She hadn't even begun to pick them up yet. She was behaving like a woman in the throes of deep, mad grief. She couldn't eat or sleep. She lurched from tears to anger to despair and had no control over any of it.

In a fit of fury on Wednesday afternoon, she'd phoned a locksmith and had him come over to change the locks. Eventually, she felt sure, Luke would be back. He'd stay away long enough to think it had all died down and then he'd appear again, wanting his room back and the everlasting love of his mother.

He wasn't going to get it. She'd turned him in to the police because as far as she was concerned, it was the only thing to do. Luke needed to know she wasn't going to support this, that he couldn't go round assaulting women and think his parents would turn a blind eye. She'd told them about Susi and how she'd dropped the charges, but they said they would already have a record of that. She wondered if any other women were going to step forward with allegations against her son and became fearful. Just how bad was it? In her head, she devised a scale ranging from men on building sites to Jimmy Savile, and tried to work out which point on the scale would tip her over the edge. She already felt as though she'd reached her limit, that one more shock would see her broken, beyond repair.

Her son. Her funny, charming son. She lay awake at night travelling back through his life in her head, trying to mark the points when it might have started going wrong. She hit on lots of different things – the first time he'd had his heart broken, aged seventeen, and had been depressed for months, refusing to accept it was really over; the day his maths teacher had humiliated him in front of the class for no other reason than that she didn't like him; the time his father had finally lost his temper and lashed out when he was fifteen – but really, none of these incidents were enough to create a sex offender.

She came to the conclusion that this must just be the way he was, part of his personality. It gave her no comfort. She spent the next night ransacking her memories again. She'd let him get away with too much; she'd loved him too much; she'd done too much for him and now he'd grown up with a sense of entitlement and no respect for women.

But it wasn't true, she knew that really. She'd brought her son up to be … *not like this.*

She wondered if it was going to drive her mad, and if he knew or cared about the mess he'd just made.

She walked into school just before six, to be greeted at the front entrance by a stressed-looking member of the admin team. 'Ms Fairburn,' she said. 'Thank goodness you're here. There's a fight going on in the hall.'

Jo looked at her blankly. 'A fight? Are you sure?'

'Quite sure.'

She hurried to the hall. Parents stood on either side of the room, their stalls abandoned. The floor by the craft stall was awash with glitter, there were cupcakes squashed into the white linen tablecloth on the cake stand, the choir had stopped singing and Mr Hunter was trying to prop up the enormous Christmas tree, which was in danger of falling over and was too big for one man to muscle back upright alone. A single silver star fell from a branch, taking its place among the debris of the Christmas fair. Mr Hunter went stoically on.

The fight was between Rachel Saunders and Kate Monro. Of course it was.

It wasn't a real fight, with fists and boots. It was a feminine fight, with whiplash tongues and sponge cake.

'You know those violin lessons your daughter has that you don't have to pay for? *I* pay for those.'

Rachel went on, listing it all. The food at the breakfast club, the donations, the weekend residential course for year four. The indisputable fact that Rachel Saunders was as big a financial force at this school as the whole PTA, who'd done nothing but campaign against her for months.

She'd lost it. Rachel had completely lost it.

Kate Monro had been rendered speechless. There was green icing in her hair and sponge cake round her face. The raffle table had been unfortunately placed by the cake stand, and Rachel went in for the kill again. This time, it was a Yule log, rich and perfectly iced, topped with a fondant robin.

'Wait!' a male voice bellowed. 'My wife spent four hours on that and we've got twins. You can't just …'

Oh, but she could.

The beautiful chocolate log with the fondant robin flew briefly through the air and came to a splattered landing across Kate Monro's bust.

Jo needed to intervene and break this up. She was the headteacher and now she was finally here, people were expecting her do something.

She couldn't do it.

She couldn't go up there and manhandle her friend, this

woman who had gone temporarily insane. *It's me you're angry with*, she wanted to say. *It's not Kate. It's me and my son. Hit me instead. Hurl cake at me if you want to. Just stop doing this.*

She scanned the crowd for Erin. Maybe she could help put a stop to this. More cake was flying. Kate was hurling it now. The PTA's chocolatey profits, straight into Rachel's face.

Eventually, Jo saw Erin, standing as far back from the drama as she could, visibly mortified. She had her arm around someone. Jo stared for a long time. Was it …?

Maia. It was Maia.

Her son's victim was right here in this room.

Jo couldn't face it. She had to get out. She would let the cake continue to fly.

She headed for the door. She couldn't do this. Someone else would have to end the fight. Someone else would have to draw the raffle. Someone else would have to …

She'd made it halfway across the room, and then she saw him. Right there, walking straight towards her, was Luke.

For a while, all she could do was stare at him.

'Hi, Mum,' he said.

'Why are you here? It's the Christmas fair. The whole bloody school is in this room.'

'I went home. I couldn't get in. My key wouldn't work.'

'I changed the locks, Luke.'

'You did what?'

'I changed the locks. I'm not supporting you through this one. You're on your own. I won't have a sex offender in my house.'

'I can't believe this. There isn't any proof. Susi dropped the

354

charges against me and you still want to take her side. You don't even know her. You've never met her. She's mad, Mum. Everyone says so.'

'I'm talking about Maia.'

Oh, he did such a persuasive job of looking bewildered.

'*Maia?*'

'Yes. Maia. You forced her to …'

He snorted. 'I did not force her to do anything. Jesus Christ. I'm not standing here and taking these accusations. From my own mother. I can't believe it. Can you just give me your key and let me go home?'

For a moment, Jo hesitated. Then she shook her head. 'No, Luke. What I'm going to do is phone the police.'

69

Maia

Maia opened the door and stepped back out into the hall. Erin had been gone for ages and she was bored now, sitting there in the PTA room. She'd come here because she was longing for the old, old comfort of her first school, where people looked after each other and teachers remembered her and the atmosphere was warm and festive, and she could smell the spices and magic.

She wanted that at this point in her life. She wanted magic and the soothing warmth of it. And she'd wanted to see Jo, and thank her for calling the police because it had been good for her, in the end, to tell them what happened and hear them say it wasn't her fault, that Luke was a criminal and they'd find him and punish him. People were on her side. The police were on her side. Luke's mum was on her side.

She hadn't seen Luke since it happened and hoped she'd never have to see him again, but she wished she'd never come here and had to face Laura. Seeing her face again brought back all the memories of that night, which had started when she saw those photos, those awful photos that Luke had taken when she was unconscious and probably had no idea what he was doing to her.

Maia had thought coming here would be a lovely thing to do. A healing thing. But it wasn't. It was awful, and now …

Oh, Jesus. What was the hell was happening?

Her mother had gone insane. She was over there at the raffle stall, shouting and throwing sponge cake at Kate Monro because Kate Monro had upset her months ago with her petition against LGBTQ lessons. Maia knew perfectly well that this humiliating awfulness had nothing to do with Kate. It was because her mother was furious with Luke Fairburn and Kate had just happened to be in her way.

Maia had never, ever seen her mother like this. Everyone was watching. Some were laughing. 'Go for it, Rachel!' a woman's voice called.

Others were shocked. Children stared. A handful were crying, but most seemed to think it was fun, all part of the event. Splat the Rat. Hunt the Thimble. Hurl the Cake.

After far too long, Erin stepped into the affray. She grabbed hold of Rachel and said, 'Will you stop this? Your children are here in this room.'

The cake throwing stopped. Both women looked shamefaced, then Kate Monro began to laugh. She dusted herself off, then turned to the hall and said, 'I think we can all agree that this woman here …' still laughing, she gestured to Rachel, '… this woman here owes the PTA a hundred pounds for lost profits from the cake stall.'

Rachel said, 'Guilty as charged,' and opened her purse.

People started clapping.

Maia sighed. Her mother was a nightmare. A total nightmare. She was ready to leave now. The whole fair had been a disaster. She wanted to be at home, curled up in her bed with a book. She had no idea where Tess was. Probably still sitting with Max, making magnets.

She headed to the raffle stall. 'I'm going,' she said coldly to her mother. 'I'll wait for you outside.'

She didn't wait for her response. She just walked away, towards the door.

And then she saw him.

He was here.

Luke was here, brazen as anything, standing beside his mother. For a minute, Maia wondered if Jo had brought him. Maybe she wanted to show him off to the other parents. 'This is my son,' she'd say. 'My gorgeous, clever son. Look!'

Jo saw her then. She looked at Maia and said, 'It's all right, sweetheart. I'm dealing with it.'

Maia watched as Jo walked past her, closed the door and pulled the bolts across it.

All over the hall, people were starting to realise that something else was happening. The excited buzz of the cake fight slowly dwindled to a dramatic silence.

Jo was on her mobile phone. 'Luke Fairburn. He's wanted for assault … I've got him here … West Burntridge First School … Yes, I'll keep him … Please come quickly.'

The door was locked. No one could get out, even if they wanted to.

A quick-thinking young teacher clapped her hands together and said, 'Why don't all the children come to the gym to see Father Christmas? No need to queue any more. All the children to the gym!'

Hardly anyone moved. The teacher's cheeks flamed and she shuffled away.

Luke looked as if he didn't have a clue what was going on, or why.

He was good at this, Maia thought. He was so good at innocence.

'What are you doing?' Luke demanded again. 'What is this?'

Jo's voice was crisp and professional. 'The police will be here soon. They'll explain it all to you if you don't know.'

Maia was almost expecting Jo to stand and calmly address the school. 'I'm sorry about the lull to this evening's proceedings,' she'd say. 'This is my son and he assaulted Maia over there, so we're just waiting for the police to come and arrest him and then we can carry on.'

She didn't. She turned away from her soon and stood beside Maia.

Maia looked towards her cake-sodden mother and fixed her eyes on her. *Please don't cause a scene*, she pleaded. *Please don't cause a scene.*

Her mother was tranquil, as if the fight with Kate Monro had been all she needed to restore her inner peace. She simply stayed where she was and watched.

Luke looked frantically around the room. 'Well, if we're lining up people for arrest,' he said, 'then take her. Take her over there. She's a whore. A proper whore. A prostitute. She shouldn't be here in a room full of children. Get her taken away as well.'

He was pointing at Laura. Beside her stood her crazy son, looking as though he was about to lose it again.

There was a collective gasp from all the mothers in the room. There they all were, the polite middle classes, shocked to the core.

Silence. Then again Luke said, 'It's true. You shouldn't be after me. She's the criminal. She's the prostitute.' He looked at Laura. 'Aren't you?' he said. 'Aren't you?'

Laura said nothing. She simply stared at the floor.

Kate Monro spoke up. 'That's ridiculous,' she declared. 'Laura is nothing of the sort. She's a respectable woman. She works in a ...' She stopped, and stared at Laura, who was still gazing at the floor. 'Oh, my *God* ...'

Maia wondered if Kate was going to cry now she'd suddenly realised the truth about her friend.

Luke carried on. 'This town ...' he was saying. 'This stupid town and all its stupid people. All your petitions, all your concern for your kids. None of you have a clue what's really going on. None of you know what your kids are up to and how toxic this place is ...'

At that point there was a loud bang on the door. Jo turned from her spot by the window, released the bolts and let the policemen in.

There were two of them, stern-faced and ready to fight.

Jo said, 'Luke, you're wanted.'

He turned around and faced the officers.

One of them said, 'We are arresting you on suspicion of sexual assault. You do not need to say anything, but anything you do say may be given as evidence and it may harm your defence ...'

Maia watched as he walked obediently away with them. He was clever enough to know that arguing wouldn't help.

70

Laura

So that was that. The fair was over. Laura stood in the empty hall and surveyed the damage. The debris from the cake fight was everywhere, half-empty stalls had been abandoned. No one had stayed to clear up. They'd all just left as soon as they could when the police had gone. At the far end of the room, the raffle table still reigned supreme, the raffle undrawn. There was a luxury hamper from Waitrose; a magnum of champagne; crisp white envelopes, still sealed, containing the promise of holidays, weekends away, days at the spa.

The caretaker, still in his Father Christmas costume, slumped into the room and shook his head. 'I've never known a fair like it,' he said.

Laura smiled thinly. 'I don't think anyone has,' she said. 'Would you like some help clearing up?'

She was in no hurry to go home, where she knew she would just be haunted by her memories of the evening. She'd hung back when everyone left, not wanting Max to get caught in the throng clamouring for the doors. She was aware of his rising anxiety and need for space. Staying in the empty hall, even if just for ten minutes, was the quickest and easiest way to give it to him. He wasn't ready yet to face the long slog up the hill in the dark.

The caretaker said, 'Aye, that'd be kind, if you've nothing else on.'

'I've nothing else on,' she said.

She armed herself with a couple of black sacks from the cleaning cupboard and went round all the stalls, tossing everything that was left into them before dismantling the tables.

The awful scene replayed itself in her mind. Luke. The police. The arrest. It made her feel sick.

As soon as the drama had started, Laura placed herself as a shield in front of Max. She didn't want him to witness this, whatever it was going to be. The hall was locked and no one could get out. Most didn't particularly want to, and even those who did couldn't bring themselves to turn away from the promise of a terrible drama. Something massive was about to happen, in a town where nothing ever happened, in a school where the biggest crisis was a week in which overall attendance slipped to 97%.

Laura wanted to get out, though. Laura didn't have a hunger for other people's tragedies.

Then suddenly, the young man turned on her, as if he thought making her the criminal in the room would somehow prevent his arrest.

The bastard.

The bastard.

'Take her over there. She's a whore. A proper whore. A prostitute. She shouldn't be here in a room full of children. Get her taken away as well.'

She heard the gasps from the parents and saw some of them

cover their children's ears. She couldn't fight. She stared at the floor. *Bear it*, she told herself. *Bear it and it will soon be over.*

She didn't even look up when the police came in. She held her breath, and waited for them to come for her.

They didn't, though. They didn't notice her at all.

71

Rachel

The school Christmas fair. It been like an *EastEnders* Christmas special.

The whole school knew. The whole school knew that Jo Fairburn's son had assaulted Rachel Saunders' daughter, and then they all heard that Laura Spence was a sex worker. Such a ripple of shock and excitement ran through the hall at that moment, Rachel wondered if the bars of Burntridge would have enough gin in them to supply the after-party.

She drove home. Tess prattled endlessly about the evening and the police and Luke being caught. Erin sat in silence. Maia did, too, her elbow resting against the window, her head resting in her hand, as if she had a headache. When they got in she took herself straight upstairs. They could hear the sound of her flute, like a balm.

Reuben was out. Rachel let Tess make microwave popcorn and take it to the living room so she could unpick the night's events with Erin, who would hardly even look at her.

Eventually, Rachel said, 'I'm glad they got him.'

Erin nodded. Then in a low voice she said, 'I didn't know you in there.'

Rachel sighed. 'I'm sorry.'

'What did you think you were doing?'

'I was just so angry.'

'But you fought the wrong person, Rachel. You looked like ...'

'I know what I looked like.'

'It's probably a good job Luke showed up when he did. His arrest will hopefully overshadow that bloody cake fight.'

Erin smiled then. Rachel knew she'd been forgiven, and they would be OK. She said, 'And what about Laura? What he said about her?'

Erin sighed, 'It's true,' she said, and she told Rachel the story Maia had shared with her earlier in the evening, when Rachel had been lost in her fury.

'Oh God,' Rachel said.

'She thinks Will knows her.'

'*What?*'

The thought of Will paying for sex was ludicrous. It was laughable. He would never, ever do something like that.

She said, 'That's insane. I know Will. I was married to him for twenty years. He just wouldn't.'

Erin shook her head. 'I don't know. Maybe Maia was mistaken.'

Rachel remembered his fury the morning after Maia babysat. 'It makes some sense that he knew who she was, but I don't believe for one minute that Will has used a sex worker. He just wouldn't. There's a reasonable explanation for this.'

'There probably is,' Erin agreed easily.

'Laura Spence. A sex worker. Everything makes sense now.' Rachel paused, then said, 'What's going to happen next? Do you think someone will report her?'

'They're bound to. This is Burntridge. They can't even handle a pair of lesbians.'

Rachel was silent. She thought of Laura and Kate and their stupid petition, and wondered how Laura squared her strange morality.

'Rachel …'

Rachel looked up. Erin was poised to speak and Rachel knew she was going to tell her, finally. She was going to break the silence that had sat so thickly between them for weeks.

72

Maia

There was no one who didn't know. 'It will all die down, Maia,' her mother promised her. 'A few weeks from now, they'll have found something else to talk about.'

Maia wasn't sure why every time something happened in Burntridge, her family seemed to be at the heart of it. The scandal of her parents' separation and her mother's newfound identity as a lesbian; the LGBTQ protest; and now this. This, of course, was in a whole other league to the usual Burntridge scandal. The headteacher's son had been publicly arrested at a school event for sexually assaulting Rachel Saunders' daughter. It would feed those vultures forever.

School would be breaking up soon for Christmas. She was glad. Maybe in the new year, people wouldn't be so obsessed with it. Clara and her other good friends were sticking by her side, helping to keep the days normal while she waited for the case to reach court. Most people believed her now the police had charged him, even though they'd released him on bail. One of his bail conditions was that he didn't contact Maia, or go anywhere near her. She wasn't sure where he was living now, but it didn't seem to be at Jo's house. Jo had been amazing. Maia wished her mum would talk to her and say thank you.

'I will,' Rachel said. 'I promise you I will.'

But her mother was preoccupied. 'Maia,' she said. 'This thing about your father and Laura …'

'It's nothing. I probably imagined it. I should never have said anything. Dad isn't … He wouldn't …'

She was glad her mother agreed. 'No,' she said. 'He wouldn't.'

'He probably knew her from somewhere else. A dating site, maybe.'

'Maybe.'

'We can never ask him.'

'No.'

'But we both know he wouldn't.'

'So shall we leave it at that?'

'We'll leave it at that.'

73

Rachel

After Erin told her the truth, Rachel thought for a long time about what to do. It was none of their business, except that they were both involved. Max Spence, five years old, alone and half-frozen after spending a November night outside in the woods near his home, and a mother who hadn't reported him missing …

What on earth did it mean?

Erin hadn't been able to get the image of him out of her head. It haunted her, she said, how weak and cold and alone he'd been.

'But she was devastated, Rachel. I've never seen such distress.'

'She should have been frantic. She should have had every police force in the country looking for her child.' Rachel shook her head. 'I wish you'd told me.'

'I promised her I wouldn't. She really loves him.'

'They always do.'

Rachel had seen it so many times. Children, abused and neglected by parents who adored them but had no idea how to behave in any other way.

She said, 'I know she was looking for him, but you found him so close to his home. She can't have been looking very hard.'

'She was beside herself.'

'She's afraid of something.'

'She's afraid of being found out and losing him. She hasn't left him alone since, I'm sure.'

'But did you see the state of him today? The bruises, the sadness. Just looking at that child makes me depressed on his behalf.'

'I know. It's awful.'

'I'd say so,' Rachel agreed. 'Jo says he injures himself when he has those fits of rage Maia witnessed. But even if that's true, something's going on. Laura's so angry herself. And that bruising doesn't sit right with me. And how the hell did he get out of the house? Do you think he ran away?'

'I wouldn't want to speculate ...'

'But if I pinned you down and *forced* you to speculate, which I am about to do if you don't answer me, what would you say?'

'I don't know, Rachel. Stop making me do this.'

'If we assume – and we shouldn't, but if we do – that his mother has outbreaks of violence towards him and that's where the bruising comes from, I'd say it's possible he ran away, quickly got frightened in the dark, and didn't know what to do.'

'It seems possible. But I don't know. I really don't. She loves him ...'

'That doesn't mean anything.' Rachel reached for her e-cigarette on the worktop and inhaled. 'Her son was missing for eight hours on a cold night in November and she didn't call the police. That's major neglect. She's hiding more than just her work, I'd put money on it.'

'So what are you going to do?'

'I'm going to do the only thing I can do and file it with social services. At the very least, she needs help to keep that child safe.'

The homophobic bitch.

74

Laura

Laura reached for the packet of Citalopram on top of the drawers and popped two. They were a high dosage, but not high enough to keep her going. She wished she wasn't like this. She wished she could cope like everyone else. There were plenty of other single parents at the school and they all seemed to get by.

Five days had passed since the Christmas fair, and now it had happened, as she'd known it would. The call from social services that she'd spent seven years waiting for. A woman named Sally wanted to pop round for a chat. She made herself sound friendly and unthreatening, but Laura knew it was just an act. She was coming to take her son.

Laura had to pretend. She had to pretend as if her life depended on it. She was fine, she was managing. There wasn't a lot of food in the house, but that was because it was the end of the week and she was due a trip to the supermarket. Max's new bed would be arriving soon. She'd get him out of that splintered, dangerous thing.

The social worker could see right through her, she was sure of that. Laura had just about managed to drag herself up to tidy the flat before she came. Sweeping the floor took nearly an hour.

Her movements were slow and heavy, as if she were still stuck at the tail end of a Valium stupor. She wasn't. Laura refused sleeping pills, though she took antidepressants. It frightened her to think how bad she'd feel without them.

'It's not easy doing this on your own,' Sally said, after she'd looked around the flat and made her swift judgements.

Laura supposed now that she was just trying to be supportive and understanding, but the comment had upset and angered her at the time, as if she thought Laura had chosen this life, as if she thought she'd been foolish and now had to pay for her mistakes. Also, she couldn't be sure of it, but she thought Sally might have been insinuating that Laura was a failure: a failure as a mother; a financial failure; a failure at getting a man to love her enough to stay with her.

'I'm doing the best I can,' she said. She sounded so prickly.

'Of course you are,' Sally said, and checked her notes.

Laura was waiting for her to ask about the allegation of prostitution, about how she could possibly be a fit mother when she earned her money in such a sordid, immoral trade.

She didn't say that, though. She said, 'We had a report about Max that I just wanted to talk to you about. A child protection issue.'

'OK.'

'Do you have any idea what the issue might be?'

Laura recognised this immediately for what it was. A trap, designed to get her to talk about something and for it to turn out that the real reason Sally was here was completely different, and now she'd have yet another point on her scorecard.

She shook her head. 'I don't know.'

'OK,' Sally said gently. 'I received a report that there was a night when Max had been left alone here, perhaps while you went to work, and that somehow, while he was unsupervised, he'd found his way out of the house. It wasn't until several hours had passed that someone found him, and he was suffering quite badly from hypothermia, and yet you hadn't reported him to the police as missing.'

Rachel Saunders. Rachel bloody Saunders had got her filthy hands on the story and this was what she'd done with it.

'I …' Laura began, and couldn't finish. She didn't want to cry in front of this woman.

'Is it true?'

'Yes. But it's not … I look after my son.'

Sally nodded. 'And I understand he is prone to bruising easily.'

Laura sighed. How many times would she have to explain the reasons for Max's bruising? 'He has tantrums,' she said. 'They cause injury sometimes. You can see how small my flat is. He lies on the floor and flings himself around and he hits the furniture. He barely seems to feel it when it happens.'

Sally appeared to be trying to think of a solution, but everyone knew there wasn't one. When Max was smaller, Laura had been able to move him to the middle of the room and let him flail, but now he was so much heavier and when he was kicking his legs and waving his arms around in that frenzied way he had, she was barely able to grasp him. The only way to keep him safe would be to move to a bigger house, which Laura knew was about as realistic a dream as pushing angels out through her arse.

Sally wanted to know if Max had run away.

'No,' Laura said. 'He has no reason to run away. He was just looking for me, that's all. He woke up and found … he found I wasn't there … and I know I should have been and I won't do it again, I swear I will never do it again … and he went out to try and find me. He was half-asleep and confused, but he didn't run away.'

She could see this woman didn't believe it. Neglect, hypothermia, bruising, running away … Everything was pointing against her. She knew that, later on, this woman would be typing it all up, showing it to her boss, pulling Laura's account to pieces and trying to come up with the truth. But Laura had told them the truth. 'What about his father?' she wanted to say. 'Why doesn't anyone lay into him? I'm doing a better job than he is. I might be a single mother, but isn't that better than an absent father? I'm here, for God's sake. I'm present. He left us.'

But Max was at his happiest with Drew. He was only happy with Drew. Laura was empty. She had nothing left to give him.

Later, Sally talked about how they'd be able to start the ball rolling, to begin the process of enforcing child maintenance payments on Drew. Just for a minute, amidst the anger and humiliation and shame, Laura felt the tiniest stirring of hope. A world began to open up for her, a world where there was enough money not to have to worry about how she could put food on the table for the next week, or where Max's new school shoes would come from, or how she could ever pay for an emergency, like a broken washing machine. But the vision faded before it had even come fully into focus. Nothing like that would ever happen. Things just didn't work that way. Happy endings were for other people.

She picked up her phone and texted Drew.

Do you want Max?

75

Jo

In her whole career, Jo had only ever taken four days off sick. Mainly, this was because she was good at battling on, but also because illness had a habit of only hitting her in the holidays. It was as though the viruses would all lurk in corners waiting for her to finish what needed to be done, and then the moment she relaxed, they'd strike.

Now, she was staying off sick until after Christmas and even when she returned, she planned to keep a low profile. She wouldn't be standing in the yard in the mornings or after school, so anyone who needed to could come and speak to her. She was going to hide away in her office until February half-term had passed, and then she'd return to the schoolyard gradually, and hope they had something new to talk about by then. Someone else to stare at.

She had done what she knew to be the right thing. She'd made sure her son was forced to face the consequences of his crime. There would be people out there who judged her for that, who would believe she should have protected him at all costs. But she wasn't going to. She would attend the court case when it came round and she'd visit him in prison if that was where he ended up – and Jo had always believed vigorously in increasing sentences for sex offenders – but she wasn't going to make any of this easier for him.

After he was charged and bailed, Luke went to live with his father, who agreed to house him until he could find a cheap place to rent in Newcastle. Jo acknowledged that staying with Dave might be a good thing, since Dave was less angry, less heartbroken about his son's criminal tendencies than Jo was, and would be able to talk to him without crying or shouting or hurling furniture.

This was about the worst thing that had happened in Jo's life, worse than the sudden death of a good friend twenty years ago, worse than divorce, worse than growing up with her alcoholic father and all his rages. Her son had betrayed her. All this time he'd pretended to be the boy she'd brought up: clever, hard-working, charming. And yet all this time he'd been hiding a side that was so dark, so sinister, she wanted to believe it wasn't him, it was temporary, it would stop …

She wasn't sure she would ever get over this; somehow this was going to be the event that cut through the timeline of her life. In years to come, when she thought back over the past, it would be split into Before and After. The time Before Luke Became a Sex Offender and the time After Luke Became a Sex Offender.

Once all this was over, Jo would be a different person.

76

Laura

It was the way they'd agreed to do it. The slow transfer of Max from Laura's care to Drew's. She packed extra clothes in his weekend bag so he could stay from Friday till Monday. On Monday morning, Drew would take him to school and Laura would pick him up. Then he'd go again to Drew's on Friday, instead of skipping a weekend and spending it with her. They would continue like this, increasing it steadily – an extra day here and there, the gradual shift of his belongings – until eventually, Max would find that he lived with his dad, while barely even registering the movement.

That was the plan, anyway. They'd devised it together with Sally. There would be no lengthy custody battle, no fighting (Laura had no energy left for fighting), just the recognition by everyone that this was the best thing for her son. He would be happier there, with a man who had energy, whose new relationship with his child seemed to have galvanised something in him, given him some fuel to keep him going, enabling him to hold down a job for longer than two weeks, and to commit to love.

Never again would Laura have to have sex for money so

she could put food on the table for her son. Never again would she have to stand in the schoolyard in front of all those rich, judgemental faces. Never again would she have to set her eyes on Rachel Saunders, the woman who thought she knew everything, but who understood nothing – nothing – about the realities of life for Laura and Max. If she saw that woman on television, banging on about food banks and the closure of libraries, she would take a hammer to the screen and imagine it was Rachel's face.

She thought a lot about Jo Fairburn, and how she'd turned her son in to the police. She admired that kind of strength, that commitment to doing what was right, even though it hurt.

A week after the Christmas fair, she bumped into her. Laura had caught a bus to the Aldi halfway between Burntridge and Newcastle, and it seemed that Jo had done the same. Avoiding people. Placing themselves out of reach.

'Oh, hello Laura,' Jo said when she saw her. They were in the frozen food aisle. Jo was buying ready meals. Laura knew what that meant. No will left to cook.

'Hi.'

'How are you?'

'OK.'

Jo took a deep breath and said, 'I'm so sorry about my son, and what he said about you.'

'It's not your fault.'

'How is Max?'

'Max is going to live with his dad. It's better that way.'

Jo nodded. 'That's hard. A hard decision to have to make.'

'I'm hoping it won't be forever. Just until …' She shrugged, and let Jo fill in the gaps.

Jo said, 'They break our hearts, don't they, these boys?'

'They do,' Laura said.

Jo reached out and embraced her.

77

Jo

It took seven months for the case to reach the Crown Court. Jo resigned from her post at West Burntridge and took on the headship at a tiny school in a village fifteen miles away, where there were only a handful of children in each year, and Jo was a stranger to all of them. It meant a huge drop in salary and a disaster for her pension, but she no longer cared. The mortgage was paid off, her children were gone. She found it soothing to run a school that felt like a large family.

She met up with Luke once a month. She wanted him to plead guilty, not because he'd end up with a lesser punishment, but as a last-ditch attempt to preserve some shred of decency.

'I'm sorry, Mum,' he said.

'Who are you sorry for, Luke? For yourself, or the women you've hurt?'

He stared at her uncomprehendingly.

She said, 'Do you understand what it means to be assaulted? To be helpless while someone else strips your power and takes it for themselves and harms you?'

He looked away from her as she spoke, but she thought she detected a small nod.

She went on, 'I want you to think now, not about yourself and whether you might get away with it if you plead not-guilty, but of Maia. If you admit in court that you did it, and it was wrong, you'll be saving Maia from having to relive that experience and you'll be taking responsibility for what you did, which will also help her to recover.' She looked at him. 'Does that make sense to you, or do you think I'm just talking psychobabble?'

'It makes sense.'

'So will you do it?'

For the full seven months leading up to the court hearing, Luke never said which way he was going to plead and Jo was convinced there would be a lengthy, traumatic trial that would make everyone involved sick to watch.

On the day, he turned up in his suit. Jo and Dave sat in the public gallery, along with Rachel, Erin, Will and a handful of journalists. Now and then, she tried to make eye contact with Rachel, but Rachel would only stare straight ahead, towards the judge.

The judge called him to the stand. Everyone listened as he read the details of his alleged offence against Maia Kernick.

'How do you plead,' the judge asked. 'Guilty, or not guilty?'

For a while, there was silence. Jo held her breath.

He cleared his throat. 'Guilty.'

The room swayed with relief.

78

Erin

A week after the trial, and knowing that Maia was OK, Erin
and Rachel went for a weekend in the Lake District. It would
be their last chance to go away alone together for a long time.
Maia had been offered a place at the prestigious music school
she wanted to go to in Manchester, so in September she'd be
away from home Monday to Friday, and they both wanted to
make sure they were around for her at weekends.

Before they'd left, Maia had said to Erin, 'I want to say
something to Jo. We've all been avoiding her and it feels awful.
She's the one who made this happen. She turned him in to the
police, she called them that night at the fair, and I'm pretty
sure she's the one who talked him into admitting he did it.'

Erin smiled at her. 'I think you're right. Rachel will talk to
her soon, I'm sure, now the trial's out of the way. Why don't
you get her a card or something, and post it through her door?
She'd appreciate that.'

'Thanks. I'll do it today.'

Erin said, 'And how are you feeling, now it's over?'

Maia said, 'I'm glad he pleaded guilty, and I'm glad we can
all move on now.'

'You did the right thing in talking to the police and pressing charges, Maia, even though it would have been easier not to.'

'I know.'

'You should be proud of yourself for doing it. Not everyone has that kind of strength, especially not at sixteen.'

Maia shrugged. It was so unremarkable to be remarkable in her world.

They stayed in a ramshackle cottage far away from anything, overlooking the dark waters of a small lake that Rachel told her was called a tarn. On all sides they were hemmed in by the ferocious beauty of the mountains, the lower slopes purpled with foxgloves and lit by the spear of the sun.

On Saturday, they walked for hours, sometimes talking, sometimes simply in the silence of deep happiness. Their world had been rocked. It wasn't over yet, but they'd survived and they were going to be OK.

Erin said, 'Thank God it's over.'

Rachel paused for a while, then said, 'And thank God for you.'

'Me?'

'You must know we'd all have gone mad without you, Erin. You're the only thing that stopped me from killing that boy.'

Erin laughed. 'You would never have killed him.'

'OK. Well, you're the thing that stopped Maia from killing me.'

'That might be true.'

'And now Maia loves you.'

Erin smiled.

It was late in the afternoon. The day had been warm and

the lake lay mirror-still beneath the mountains. Above it all, the falling sun cast its orange glow over the water.

Rachel let go of her hand and put her arm around her shoulders as they headed back towards the cottage, pulling her towards her. Erin stopped walking, looked up and pressed her lips to hers. They'd done it, she thought. It had taken a crisis none of them wanted, but out of the wreckage, their family was growing.

79

Maia

Her dad had dropped the three of them back at home. Reuben was in his room, Tess was reading and Maia was waiting for Erin and her mother to come back from the Lake District so she could show them the package she'd just received from her music school, with details of the bedroom she'd been allocated. She was sharing with one other girl, from China. Finally, she'd have the chance to meet people who'd grown up somewhere other than Burntridge.

Her mother and Erin had gone away, without trying to drag Maia, Reuben and Tess with them. It was a relief, even though Maia knew perfectly well that it was only because they wanted to have loads of sex without the risk of her walking in on them again. The thought wasn't something she especially wanted to dwell on, but it no longer made her as angry as it used to.

Earlier, she'd written a card to Jo and posted it through her door. It played on her mind to think how Jo must be suffering for what she'd done on Maia's behalf. Maia spent a long time wondering what she should say, but in the end she just wrote *Thank you* and signed her name. She hoped it was enough. She wanted to express sympathy for Jo's situation, but everything she said sounded trite because really, she had no idea what Jo was going through. She couldn't even imagine.

Maia had spent a lot of time recently reading about victims of sex crimes. Her mother was making her see a therapist, too, because even though Maia was all right now, it didn't mean this wasn't going to catch up with her. It happened to lots of women, apparently. They pushed it away, or made use of their anger to propel them forwards, but then something would suddenly trigger them and all the old trauma would resurface, violent and destructive.

It happened to their families, too. Parents, especially. Her mother, Maia thought, would be a prime candidate, bulldozing her way through the world and then suddenly collapsing when she could go no further.

Maia was going to stop that from happening. She was going to face what lay ahead of her – the court case, the gradual fading of shock, her own slow recovery. She wasn't going to enter her forties broken and damaged, longing to travel backwards through time and undo the hurt that destroyed her. She would move quietly forwards, to the world that was waiting to receive her, and knew she'd be upright by the end.

80

Rachel

It was their last walk together before heading home after a weekend of nature, log fires and love. All her life, Rachel had fled to the Lake District when she needed a break. There was something about losing herself among the slate-grey drama of the mountains, hearing nothing but the cold rush of water over rocks, that made everything hurt less.

She knew Erin felt it, too. They followed the waterfall trail that would lead them to the valley. It was a route familiar to Rachel, though unknown to Erin. It took them across streams that tumbled over the rocky edges of the mountains, hurtling down to the river that wound through the woodland below.

They held hands as they walked, and they didn't talk about Maia, but Rachel let her mind drift and she could see her daughter, strong and beautiful, surviving this. Not surviving. Thriving. Maia, she understood now, had what it took to hold catastrophe in her hands and squash it. Luke Fairburn would not ruin her daughter. Her daughter would be OK. She would be OK forever.

She turned to Erin and kissed her. They had no need to speak of love.

ACKNOWLEDGEMENTS

Thank you to my excellent agent, Hattie Grunewald, whose insight and wisdom has helped shape this book into something better than I could do on my own.

Thank you to my editor, Cicely Aspinall, who bought this book so quickly, I didn't have to suffer the torment of being on submission for very long at all.

Thank you to my friend, Dr Beth Griffith, for the discussions about health inequality and for having such an interesting job, I gave it to Rachel.

Thank you to Dr Naomi Thomas, for supplying me with the anecdote about medical students in chapter 53.

Thank you to my friend and colleague, Dr Alice Crossley, who read this from the very first chapter and was enthusiastic enough to keep me going.

Thank you to Maureen Lenehan, who read an early draft and declared it brilliant, when I know she never says a word she doesn't mean.

Thank you to Fi White, for the discussions about schools and for dog walks, childcare and friendship.

Thank you to Jo, Emma, Hannah, Katherine, Anne and Deb for sharing the adventures of mid-life with me.

Finally, thank you to Clay, Bonnie and Sam, for bringing me the world of this book.

Reading Group Questions for *Other Parents*

1. The prologue is a flash-forward and gives clues about events that happen later in the book. How did it effect your reading of the novel?

2. Why do you think Sarah Stovell wrote the story from multiple viewpoints and why do you think she chose all women?

3. Who was your favourite character, who was your least favourite and why? Could you empathise with them even if you didn't agree with their views or actions?

4. Sarah tackles big issues throughout. How does the school setting serve as a setting for exploring these?

5. Erin is a newcomer to the town and to being a parent. How do you think she copes with both, and do you think she is happy with her decision to move to West Burntridge?

6. Prejudice is a key theme in the book. What different forms does it take and how does it cause harm?

7. Jo's son Luke returns home under a dark cloud. What did you think about how Jo deals with that and the later revelations about Maia?

ONE PLACE. MANY STORIES

Bold, innovative and
empowering publishing.

FOLLOW US ON:

@HQStories